A
LETTER
TO THE
LUMINOUS
DEEP

The Sunken Archive: Book One

SYLVIE CATHRALL

orbit

orbitbooks.net

Cover design by Charlotte Stroomer
Cover illustration by Raxenne Maniquiz
Interior illustrations by Raxenne Maniquiz
Author photograph by Roland J. Cathrall

Orbit
Hachette Book Group
1290 Avenue of the Americas
New York, NY 10104
orbitbooks.net

First Edition: April 2024
Simultaneously published in Great Britain by Orbit

Orbit is an imprint of Hachette Book Group.
The Orbit name and logo are registered trademarks of
Little, Brown Book Group Limited.

The publisher is not responsible for websites (or their content) that are not owned by the publisher.

The Hachette Speakers Bureau provides a wide range of authors for speaking events. To find out more, go to hachettespeakersbureau.com or email HachetteSpeakers@hbgusa.com.

Orbit books may be purchased in bulk for business, educational, or promotional use. For information, please contact your local bookseller or the Hachette Book Group Special Markets Department at special.markets@hbgusa.com.

Library of Congress Control Number: 2023949209

ISBNs: 9780316565530 (trade paperback), 9780316565547 (ebook)

Printed in the United States of America

CW

3 5 7 9 10 8 6 4

For J., who wrote back

Chapter 1

LETTER FROM E. CIDNOSIN TO HENEREY CLEL, YEAR 1002

Dear Scholar Clel,

Instead of reading further, I hope you will return this letter to its envelope or, better yet, crumple it into an abstract shape that might look quite at home on a coral reef.

I become exceedingly anxious around strangers, you see, and I dared only write this note after convincing myself that you would never read it. It is only now – when I can picture you disposing of these pages in some appropriately dramatic fashion – that I may continue my message without succumbing to Trepidation.

You do not know me at all, Scholar Clel, but after reading your most recent publication (as well as the four preceding it), I feel as though you have become a dear friend. I only wish a human companion ever brought me as much intellectual bliss as *Your Natural History Companion* does!

Surely you receive letters of this nature from eager readers all the time, though, so I will depart from flattery and approach the more pressing subject that inspired me to risk writing to you in the first place. As a Scholar of Classification, might you assist me from afar with an inquiry of relative import?

A few tides ago, I encountered a species unlike any I have ever seen.

Lacking a name for such creatures, I dubbed them "Elongated Fish". They cannot be Subtle Pipefish, as they do not possess needle-like "noses" and far surpass the approximate measurements you offered in your Appendix. (My Fish are also decidedly Unsubtle.) During my observation of the Fish, I noted the following additional traits: they are remarkably quick in the water, possibly crepuscular or nocturnal, and territorial to a fault.

Allow me to elaborate, if I may.

Yesterday, I sat by my window, watching glimmers of sunset from the surface dye the drop-off waters a stately purple. I do this sometimes when I feel most at odds with my Brain, you see, and find it quite effective. I was all alone – my sister Sophy recently departed on the Ridge expedition – though because you are also a Scholar, I assume you know about that expedition all too well – my apologies – and it was then that I witnessed a most unusual scene starring the Elongated Fish. Their colouring was a kind of magenta speckled with silver, but stretched almost transparent – like strands of hair about to break. Most bizarrely, their bulbous green eyes sat flat on the very tops of their heads rather than protruding in profile. From tip to tail, each measured longer than our house is tall.

O – my apologies again – I hoped to avoid boring you with biography, but I suppose the preceding paragraph might confuse you since you do not know where I live. You may have heard of the late, renowned Architect, Scholar Amiele Cidnosin – she who developed the first underwater dwelling, located a few hundred fathoms off-coast from your own Boundless Campus and colloquially called the "Deep House". Well, she was my mother, and I colloquially call it "home". While I am not a Scholar myself (and pray that you will forgive my boldness in writing to someone of your Academic prestige), perhaps you have encountered my esteemed sister Scholar Sophy Cidnosin (from the School of Observation at Boundless – o, I mentioned her just a few sentences ago, did I not?) or my (rather less) esteemed brother Apprentice Scholar Arvist Cidnosin. (Yes, our mother defied the

2

typical Boundless custom and gave us what she deemed "Scholarly Virtue Names" – which we all promptly despised and altered. "Sophy" is short for Philosophy and "Arvist" (somehow) for Artistry. I dare not tell you *my* given name.)

Now you understand that I am uniquely privileged when it comes to observing marine life in its natural habitat.

I first noticed only one creature: a solitary ribbon lost in looping sojourns around the window. When she (?) first darted past my window I felt my heart vibrate. Her eyes rolled around in perfect circles as she executed repeated stalks – perhaps not quite grasping the presence of the glass that disqualified me as potential prey. (The sharks who frequent the waters just outside my chamber long since learned to ignore me.)

Some amount of time later – I found it hard to keep track of the hour – I marvelled at the moonbeams illuminating the Elongated Fish as she continued watching me. After ages of stillness, she flinched, folding and opening like a concertina. I assumed I startled her with my stirring until I spied an even larger creature pulsing its way around the house. As this second Elongated Fish sped closer, "my" Fish dashed towards the interloper, swirling into a furious helix. They wove around each other, tighter than thread. Tails choked necks and fins found wounds. I watched with rapt horror as they fell into the abyss below the drop-off together. Neither returned.

Now, considering your diverse experiences "in the field", as it were, I suspect you will not find this encounter especially impressive – and I confess that my Elongated Fish can hardly compete with the Exceptional Squid Skirmish my family witnessed at the Deep House in Year 991 – but the novelty of these unfamiliar creatures struck me. I adore how each "Epilogue" of your books invites readers to stop by your Laboratory Anchorage at Boundless Campus to share news of unusual sightings with you, but circumstances prevent me from coming in person. Still, I would be most grateful if you would consider assessing my account of these creatures from afar.

That is, of course, assuming you did not do as I asked by destroying this letter without even reading it.

Sincerely,

E. Cidnosin

P.S. Allow me to apologise for the rudimentary sketch of the Elongated Fish that I enclosed. Please attribute any unforgivable errors to my non-existent professional training.

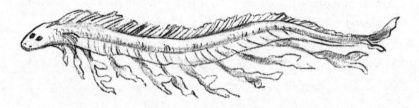

LETTER FROM SOPHY CIDNORGHE TO VYERIN CLEL, YEAR 1003

Dear Captain Clel,

Forgive this unexpected intrusion from your former "acquaintance-through-grief" – otherwise known as me, Sophy Cidnosin (well, Cidnorghe now, technically – as my wife and I are newly wed, we combined our family names in accordance with Boundless Campus custom).

If it helps, I also go by "E.'s sister".

When you and I met for the first (and final) time – just after Henerey and E.'s disappearance – I promised "to keep in touch" in that vague, non-committal way that one so often does. Well, I come at last, a year later, to make that promise less empty. I do not wish to resurrect painful memories for you; rather, I hope that the contents of this package will provide some comfort.

After I lost E., I tasked myself with putting my sister's belongings in order as a distraction. Even after the Deep House's destruction, E.'s safe-box – a funny, waterproof little thing designed by our mother – survived intact, tucked into a crack in the coral bed. When the salvagers presented me with the safe-box just days after the explosion, I wasted no time (nor spared any expense) in hiring a locksmith to open it. I expected to find the box stuffed with drawings, rare books, curious shells, and perhaps a family photograph or two. Imagine my surprise when I discovered that my excessively introverted sister kept a cache of countless letters, the bulk of them dating from the period just before her disappearance – and sent by your brother.

I am a researcher by profession, Captain Clel. When I face a problem, I investigate all evidence and form a hypothesis. But it seems that my logical self vanished when E. did.

I did not ignore the safe-box entirely during those early days. I was not so far gone. I sorted through the box's contents, arranging the letters into neat stacks on my desk for safekeeping. (Oddly enough, it was at this point that I found that daybook of Henerey's I gave you when we met last year. Why, I wonder, would he store it in the safe-box and not take it with him?) Yet every time I thought about opening even a single letter, I felt half-sick.

My guilty conscience tormented me for tides as I resisted the urge to read E.'s personal documents. I considered destroying the papers that serve as her only physical remains – cramming them into a crucible in my wife's laboratory, donating them to my brother in the guise of "mixed-media art supplies", or sailing out to the vast trench in the sea that marks the site where our family home once stood and sending the letters to meet their maker. I suspect my sister may have preferred any of these more destructive options. She was quite a private soul. But, dear Captain Clel, I must confess that tragedy has equipped me with a new propensity for selfishness. I can ignore the lure of the letters no longer, even if that makes me a traitor to my own sister.

A few tides ago, then, I pledged to construct an archive of E.'s existence – which is to say that I have started looking through the letters at last. I realised, however, that my "records" have limitations. I may read only what E. received from others, not her own words (excluding those she sent to myself and our brother Arvist, of course, which I already

5

possess). With the exception of this enclosed draft of her first letter to Henerey (which I intentionally placed before my letter in the package so as to pique your interest with mystery), I do not know anything about what she said to him.

My proposal, then: if you inherited your late brother's personal effects and do not object, would you consider sharing some items of interest with me? Though I imagine the process might be devastatingly difficult, I do hope that together we may make sense of their final days – and feel more connected to them. (I have also included an ambitiously high number of coins in this envelope to cover your potential postal expenses.)

In archival solidarity,

Sophy Cidnorghe

LETTER FROM VYERIN CLEL TO SOPHY CIDNORGHE, YEAR 1003

Dear Scholar Cidnorghe,

I neglected your envelope. As soon as I recognised your name I felt rather overcome. My husband, Reiv, read everything you sent aloud to me. When we finished, he suggested that "sharing with [you] some of [my] feelings about Henerey might prove cathartic", because he is from Intertidal Campus originally and believes that honest emotional expression is an essential act of self-maintenance.

He's right, no doubt.

Your project offers the kind of cleansing that appeals to me. I'm not one for words. That was Henerey's forte. But you are right to presume that I still possess every scrap of paper upon which he ever scribbled and every note he ever received from friend or colleague or stranger or enemy.

Unlike you, I have not touched his letters, nor felt any particular pull to do so. Unexpected deaths produce a museum's worth of detritus. In the early days, a courier seemed to arrive every other hour with another box of Henerey's things from his Anchorage room, his laboratory, his ship-quarters, or his carrel in the library.

I locked every box away without opening them. It seems we respond to grief in different ways. I feared (and still fear) that even the sight of his fashionable shirts or messy handwriting would break me.

But perhaps I need to break. With the support of my husband, I will start looking for things that fit within the timeline you wish to explore. In the meantime, if there is anything else you would like to send me, go ahead. I was intrigued when E. referred to your role on the Ridge expedition. "Ridge expedition" is a phrase you don't hear thrown around much these days. Reiv and I used to read all the expedition missives together. Until they stopped, that is.

I have enclosed the cost of postage to reimburse you.

With gratitude,

Mr. Reiv & especially Mr. Vyerin Clel

P.S. Can't believe E. started this whole thing by sending him a letter out of the blue. He loved that, I'm sure. He also loved her – even surer.

LETTER FROM SOPHY CIDNORGHE TO VYERIN CLEL, YEAR 1003

Dear Vyerin,

Your reply made me feel so radiantly hopeful that I am writing back (as you well can see) just a day later – I trust you won't mind. Many thanks to Reiv for reading you the letters and helping us begin this exciting partnership!

I look forward to seeing anything from E. that you uncover. O, I almost forgot – I also have Henerey's first letter to E. for you, though she reread it so many times that it's nearly falling apart in places. I shall endeavour to make a fair copy for our purposes. Additionally, because you seemed to take particular note of the Ridge expedition and my (unforgettable and regrettable) involvement therein, I shall also make fair copies of some correspondence between E. and myself from around that time period. Perhaps that will be of interest to you. If not, feel free to discard the copies as you see fit.

Enclosed you will find a sum suitable to cover the cost of many letters to come. If you wish, we may also correspond via Automated Post missives so that we can speak with greater speed (when it comes to any shorter questions or clarifications). My A.P. callsign for electronic communication is 2.02.CIDNORGHE.

Does that suit you?

With excitement,

Sophy

AUTOMATED POST MISSIVE FROM VYERIN CLEL TO SOPHY CIDNORGHE, YEAR 1003

Dear Sophy,

Suits me very well. More to follow upon receipt of your package. Though I hate it on principle, I admit that Automated Post is far more efficient than waiting for letters to be delivered. (Still, I would wait any amount of time to get to know my brother a little better.)

Sincerely,

Vyerin

P.S. Reiv had to encourage me to write the above parenthetical. But that doesn't make it any less genuine.

Chapter 2

LETTER FROM E. CIDNOSIN TO SOPHY CIDNOSIN, 1002

Dear Sophy,

If you wrote to me, I know you would open with a summary of your recent activities, outings, and intellectual opinions. Thus:

Activities: None (as I have rarely left my bedchamber since your departure and survived only by devouring a stash of preserves secreted in my closet).

Outings: None (excepting when I realised that said preserves had been secreted in said closet for an unknown amount of time, and might therefore have spoilt, causing me to flee to the library for a full hour to research what potential antidotes I might craft in the event that I fell ill from accidental self-poisoning – but do recall, dear sister, that I spent over eight hours in mortal terror the last time I thought I poisoned myself, so really, this is a wonderful improvement!).

Opinion: One might say that I miss you.

Had you found yourself stepping back through our airlock yesterday morning and striding upstairs to greet me, you would have encountered a familiar sight from our childhood. I spent the entire day (minus that hour in the library, of course) curled up in my porthole, my body almost joining in a perfectly contorted "O".

During this period of – self-reflection, let's say – I spied some rather curious fish. After referring to my dearly beloved copy of Clel's *Your Natural History Companion*, I realised that they were also quite unlike anything currently known to Scholars of Classification. Will you believe what I did next, Sophy? Well, I drafted a letter of inquiry to Scholar Henerey Clel himself! Whether or not I shall send the letter remains to be seen, but goodness, my heart flutters to think that I might have encountered a new species.

Don't worry, dear Sophy – my fish shall not outshine all the unique and undiscovered creatures that you will see. So let me return to you and your adventures! Imagine – my very own sister, one of the first to visit the deepest parts of the ocean! I cannot even begin to picture the Ridge (I say as though I do not keep a fine artistic rendering of the abyssal seascape right here at my desk). Really, I know my eccentric fish will seem quite prosaic compared to the wonders that await you and your colleagues down there.

I strive to keep my thoughts from troubling me too much in this empty house. As always, I wish I could turn back time to our childhood, when we all were safe and comfortable under one roof and countless fathoms of water. At the very least, I'm sure Mother could have identified those mysterious creatures immediately, were she still here! I considered writing to Father again, but, as always, he continues to honour his Vows by ignoring my correspondence entirely.

I hope his reluctance to write does not run in the family and that I will hear from you presently. Please write to me as soon as you can and tell me something about your new life that's taken you by surprise.

With much love,

E.

LETTER FROM HENEREY CLEL TO E. CIDNOSIN, 1002

Dear Scholar* Cidnosin,

I spent the past few days simultaneously wanting to thank you for the letter you sent and to apologise for my own delayed response. Around the time when you wrote to me, I was volunteered (I hope my uncharacteristic use of passive voice will convince you that I had no choice in the matter!) to coordinate a study related to the Ridge expedition: a simulation assessing what might happen if a population of Sustaining Cod were introduced to the abyssal zone as a mechanism for observing long-term adaptation to life in the dark. (The notion of forcibly transplanting species to an unknown environment purely for our intellectual benefit alarms me, of course. And that is to say nothing of the fact that it would take years of experimentation to witness the evolutionary process across generations! But I am convinced that it is indeed a thought experiment, because there is nothing my department enjoys more than keeping me busy with "simulating" things we will never actually do.)

Apologies for my babbling. I suppose I could have simply said that I have been "busy". Yet I mention my troubles only to demonstrate the ways in which your warmly worded letter sustained me during a frustrating time. I would like to imagine that this is some kind of long-distance conversation, and most such discussions (for better or for worse!) often involve informal pleasantries. And I suppose if you and I are to converse, I should formally introduce myself (which seems silly, because you already know who I am, but nonetheless):

Hello there! My name is Henerey Clel, Scholar of Classification at Boundless Campus – though my family (just me and my brother Vy, so a little smaller than yours) hails from the Atoll. I transferred to Boundless two years ago, and the cultural change still overwhelms me. I do not know how much you know of the Atoll, but my home, while driven by Formality and Procedure, feels like a caring community of

11

learners. Boundless, on the other hand, is a place of both Innovation and Intensity, to put it lightly … but I am sure I will grow accustomed to it eventually! (As you may have already gathered from the fact that I read your letter, I am fluent in both Atoll and Boundless short-hand styles.)

Since we are now properly acquainted (or will be, whenever you read these words!), let me admit that your letter not only delighted but utterly perplexed me. As I mention in my book, Subtle Pipefish vary in size (and I know not why I feel compelled to say that again, because your letter demonstrates that you are clearly well acquainted with my writing, but at this point, I'm feeling too abashed to start this letter over so – enjoy this earnest glimpse into my soul!), but I have never seen one larger than half a wavesbreadth at absolute maximum. If I understand the scale of your remarkable drawing correctly (I remain utterly taken by your unusual method of formatting the measurement key on the reverse of the sketch) your specimens were nearly twenty times that, far surpassing even moderately sized Toothed Whales! I do wonder if they might have been particularly robust Fathom Eels, though I have never known one to leave the safety of deeper waters (nor behave in such an aggressively territorial way). Perhaps something agitated them?

Just as your field report tantalised me with odd Eel behaviour, your brief biographical note dazzled me. Forgive me for sounding trite and romantic, but you grew up in the home of my dreams. Though it might seem unusual for a Scholar of Classification to be so fascinated with an architectural marvel, I always envied the inhabitants of the Deep House (by which I mean you) their (by which I mean your) unfettered ability to not only study but live among all the denizens of the open ocean. What a life! Of course I know of your sister (who wouldn't? We can talk of nothing but the Ridge expedition on campus these days, and I do believe I may have met her a few times since moving to Boundless!) and I recognise your brother's name. I never realised, however, that the two of them had another sibling.

I hope this does not make me come across as inappropriately interested in your personal affairs, but please know that if you deem it suitable, I would absolutely adore to hear more about your experience living at the Deep House. To return to the topic of your initial inquiry, let me add that should circumstances arise in which you spot the Elongated Fish/ Fathom Eels again, I would be most grateful if you would send me more sketches (or even verbal descriptions!) so I may continue my studies from afar. I await your reply with incredible interest.

Eagerly,

Schr Henerey Clel

*I pray you will not misinterpret my use of the Scholarly honorific for you as a mockery. You emphasised in your letter that you are not an academic, and I respect that. I have dubbed you Scholar Cidnosin in my mind simply because you possess knowledge that I do not. And while you signed your name to your letter, I know that Boundless folk consider it quite forward to address someone by their first name when they are newly acquainted, so I am erring on the side of caution. This is all to say that I am most truly interested in whatever you have to say. (Though perhaps I should stop saying things now.)

LETTER FROM SOPHY CIDNOSIN TO E. CIDNOSIN, 1002

Dearest E.!

Consider this letter my equivalent of shouting "I made it!" as we dock at last on the Ridge! Our craft's systems informed me that we are now 2190 fathoms below the water's surface and 8060 fathoms from our point of origin at Boundless Campus. (Most importantly, my personal calculations suggest that I am just over 6500 fathoms from you and the Deep House – the furthest I ever travelled from home!)

When I imagined my first deep-sea descent, I assumed that my eyes would never leave the portholes. I pictured myself cheering as the surface light faded from the water and marvelling as I sank through bands of deepening blue, like those in Mother's woodcut illustration of the ocean's layers that mesmerised us as children. Yet, in reality, I spent most of the journey clutching this blank sheet of stationery and staring into its emptiness for comfort – you'll laugh, since you so tout my so-called "bravery", but for whatever reason I seem to fear the abyssal darkness into which only one other person ever journeyed before. It certainly did not help my nerves when the water tossed our vessel about after we intercepted the wake of some anonymous whale, and the currents hardly let up afterwards. But now that my stomach has settled a bit, I shall write to you to distract myself.

It is hard to tell what the rest of the crew thinks about being suspended inside a pressurised sphere. The surprisingly icy winds at the Boundless Campus lagoon froze us into silence before we stepped inside the Depth Capsule (just like a typical depth-craft, but large enough to fit several occupants comfortably). Whether my companions now refrain from introducing themselves due to weariness (you know I am abnormally fond of rising early) or typical Scholarly nervousness, I cannot say!

I also find myself frustrated by my inability to recognise my new colleagues based on their academic portraits (which are always reproduced as such tiny images, to be fair, and our enterprising Expedition Specialist Schr Forghe does not even have a portrait on record). The unpleasantness is heightened by the fact that we all dressed in the most uncomfortably formal clothes, since we had no choice but to pose for an overeager Photographer from Intertidal Campus before we embarked. By the way, E., can you believe that there now exists a true camera – not one of those old-fashioned photo-engraving devices – capable of capturing images underwater? The Expedition Specialist will apparently have access to such a marvel for our field studies. I hope I may have a chance to see it in action.

A group portrait of the scene at this very moment in the Depth Capsule would feature the following figures:

THE FIRST COLLEAGUE: Let us begin with a proper identification, as I believe quite strongly that this Scholar clad in neatly pressed emerald Atoll Campus robes is Schr Ylaret Tamseln. If the kind smile, copper freckles, and cascading brown curls were not enough to bring her portrait to mind, the fact that she is reading a massive astronomical tome makes it undeniable that I sit but a few seats away from the most esteemed Scholar of the Skies living today. Will I sound desperate if I say that there is something about the way in which she hums softly while reading that reminds me of you (and calms me, as a result)?

THE SECOND COLLEAGUE: Another Atoll Scholar, sitting to Scholar Tamseln's left, finds solace in a more recreational activity: playing a one-person round of Columns with bronzed game pieces unlike any I've ever seen before. (Clearly you and I, practising with Father's simple coral blocks as children, were but amateurs!) This unknown colleague's refined crimson robes (stitched with an impressive pod of blue whales) flash against their tan complexion. They are also the tallest among us, and keep scrunching their neck downwards to keep their shoulder-length black hair away from the air vent on the ceiling.

THE THIRD COLLEAGUE: Here we see the only member of our crew not dressed in approved Scholarly robes but rather in what I might describe as a – sleeping gown? – a gossamer cape exclusively for lounging purposes? – featuring a tessellation of geometric patterns in golden thread that seems plucked from the wearer's own yellow beard. No one but an Intertidal Scholar possesses that level of panache. Outside of the striking attire, however, this crew member's pink countenance (tinged almost purple with nausea) and fondness for staring at an idle point on the ceiling suggests that perhaps I am not the only person aboard who distrusts deep-sea travel.

THE FOURTH COLLEAGUE: I have saved the most notable Scholar (I say that from a hypothetical artist's perspective, of course!) in our company for last. Not even the third colleague's fashion can compete with this fourth person's shell-pink robes, sewn with swooping sea stars that iridesce in the dim light of the capsule. (Again – this outfit is so classically Intertidal in its innovation that it almost seems a parody.) A constellation of tiny pearls glistening in a crown of dark braids completes an ensemble that makes my new colleague seem ready for the most elegant underwater gala. Only on three occasions so far has this crew member turned away from the porthole to look back at us, revealing bright eyes surrounded by white filigreed spectacles; deep brown, dimpled cheeks touched with glimmering rose blush; and the charming expression of someone lost in pleasantly complex thoughts. Though I know it is not meant for me, exactly, I find that smile some-what comforting.

Did I succeed in setting the scene for you, sister? I may be the least artistically inclined Cidnosin in the family – but I did try to channel you and Arvist by paying close attention to colour, texture, and com-position! Please be gentle in your critique. (You'll notice that I did not describe myself, as you surely have not forgotten me yet – but I will say that after reviewing everyone's fine robes, I am quite satisfied with the monochrome sleekness of my trousers, blouse, and coat.)

Now I hear the thump of what must either be the docking ramp activating or the sound of our imminent destruction, so I assume we may soon debark. Perhaps I will subject you to another word-picture (a domestic interior this time, rather than a portrait) once I'm settled in! We shall see how soon I escape my duties to pen another update . . .

Hoping that you are taking care of yourself (Elongated Fish and all!),
Sophy

P.S. You did end up sending that letter to Henerey Clel, surely? And surely he must have responded by now? How delightful. I've run into him a few times on campus before – very quiet and charming (in case you wondered).

AUTOMATED POST MISSIVE FROM VYERIN CLEL TO SOPHY CIDNORGHE, 1003

Dear Sophy,

Thank you.

You gave me access to words from my brother that I've never seen. Makes him feel very much alive.

I hope E. will forgive me, as I cannot stop reading this letter over and over and over again. I can imagine him saying every line on the page with a sparkle in his eye.

(That is not to say that the other letters you sent me were not also informative and engaging and of historical import. They certainly were. Especially the last one. Even the simple sight of Henerey's name written in your postscript to E. shook me in the most joyous manner.)

It is very important to me that we continue. I hope you agree.

Gratefully,

Vyerin

P.S. I never realised how many talents Henerey had until he was gone. I did not even read his best-known book until it was too late to congratulate him upon it. These days, I cannot stop paging through it. His rhetorical style is compelling, and his intellectual acumen obvious. But there is, above all, a warmth in his writing that I have never seen in any other Academic publication. To refresh your memory, I am sending you a copy of his *Preface*. I hope you will enjoy.

PREFACE TO HENEREY CLEL'S FIFTH PUBLICATION, 1002

Your Natural History Companion:
The Most Recent Survey of the Marine Species that Frequent the
Boundless Campus Waters and Notes on their Habitats, Breeding,
and Anatomy

By Schr Henerey Clel, Scholar of Classification, Boundless Campus

Dear reader,

I wish I could tell you with conviction that in my childhood I delighted in hearing stories read aloud. Alas, I hold no memories of the tales that my father shared with myself and my brother as we rocked in boat-like cradles towards the horizon of sleep. And yet my father assures me that he most certainly did tell us stories – in great quantities! Please hold my vague adult forgetfulness accountable for any perceived parenting misdeeds.

The first spoken stories I remember, however, reached my ears as a boy of fourteen, a newly appointed Apprentice Scholar. Back then, my days were about as long as they would ever be. My unreliable memory has not relieved me of the ability to reminisce miserably about that busy time! Still, I spent my evenings revelling in luxurious communal dinners hosted by a particular itinerant Scholar of Classification assigned to the grim task of overseeing our messy living quarters.

The final course of our meal would invariably consist of the aforementioned Scholar recounting some notable episode from their illustrious career. Few of my peers lingered for this raconteurial repast – but my hunger for gripping descriptions of my mentor's travels could not be sated. And o, the species they'd seen! Ravenous Seafowl swooping to the waves on spectrum-shaded wings to gulp down swallows of seawater, Wayward Crabs locked in duels to the death with Subsidiary Sharks by the ocean's edge, that spectacle of a million Coruscating Diatoms spawning in an endless circle for one night each year . . .

It was not until I heard these stories that I knew, with every particle of my body, that I must dedicate my life to Classification and Natural History.

Ever since the tragedy of the Dive ushered in our new Society, people who seek to understand the creatures with whom we share this world have published great Treatises to prove themselves as worthy Scholars. In this book, however, you will find no radical theses, no labyrinthine

18

rhetoric, nor any particular attempt at proving my own genius. I am far from convinced of its existence myself.

I simply wish to tell you about some wondrous things I've seen.

May I?

Your friend, I hope,

Henerey Clel

AUTOMATED POST MISSIVE FROM SOPHY CIDNORGHE TO VYERIN CLEL, 1003

Dear Vyerin,

Henerey's brief evocation of the dormitory lifestyle gave me unexpected nostalgia. Considering that I mostly look back on my Scholarly youth with resentment and self-reproach, that speaks volumes about your brother's writing!

Of course we will continue – moving next to the first moment when I started to get acquainted with Henerey in earnest. Naturally, E. chose to write to me about his response long before she had the opportunity to reply to him.

And – by the waves – I was wildly excited to hear that she had a new correspondent.

Onward!

Sophy

Chapter 3

LETTER FROM E. CIDNOSIN TO SOPHY CIDNOSIN, 1002

Dear Sophy,

My initial letter detailed the ways in which my personal health and wellbeing floundered following your departure. I am happy to report that my mood has since improved, and I've made the library my sanctuary of choice rather than my bedroom. Arvist still has not written, by the way. When he did not show up to see you off, I assumed that he simply decided to deny the social construct of the calendrical system for a while, as he often does, and would appear later with no awareness of his tardiness. But no sign of our wayward brother so far.

Yet you may be proud to hear that in your absence I attempted to solicit the companionship of another human being by inviting Seliara for a meal.

(I hope you are not recovering in a pressure chamber after a difficult diving mission while reading this, as I imagine this news will take your breath away. I suspect that when I write to Dr Lyelle about it, she may arrange a festival in my honour.)

Not only did I pretend at possessing the basic interpersonal skills required for an evening of social activity with an old friend, but I also attempted to create the very food that would sustain us throughout our idle chatter. I set my sights on a recipe for spirulina pie I found in one of Father's cookbooks and took perhaps too much joy in shaping the pastry to resemble a Scrolling Sea Fan. (Only thrice did my Brain worry that I might make a culinary mistake that could lead to our deaths.) We devoured the thing in an instant, which rather boosted my opinion of my limited domestic abilities, though I did spy scepticism on Seliara's face when she first laid eyes upon my rudimentary interpretation of baking sculpture!

Do you happen to recall the last time Seliara visited us? I cannot – though I reckon it must have been at least two years ago, since I believe her family's vessel last passed through our waters before you became the Boundless School of Observation's youngest Associate Scholar. Well, at any rate, she is still loud, still gregarious, and still utterly taken in with that "Linguistic Alchemy" nonsense. She asked after you today, of course, and inquired as to whether she might send you a small handmade scroll inscribed with an original Alchemification (?) of her own making – one, she claims, that contains a soothing combination of letters moulded into warm words intended to assist travellers far from home. I let her know that the sensitivity of your mission makes sending parcels difficult, but I did encourage her to write you a short note (contents unknown, but presumably without any Linguistical Alchemical properties).

(On a related note: does the sensitivity of your mission truly make sending parcels difficult? I rather fancied the idea of wrapping up something small for you as a reminder of home. An abalone, perhaps?)

Our feast at an end, we sat in the Crystal Room to talk as we watched the water glisten around us from all sides. I say "we" and "us", but you know that I occupied myself with the glistening water while Seliara took care of the talking.

Were you aware that she recently made Assistant Scholar at Boundless – in the School of Inspiration? I thought she had her heart set on the School of Intuition so she might study to become a Scholar of Society, but apparently she has moved on to Music. She could always carry a tune, I suppose.

Even more shocking was the revelation that she frequently shares meals in the Refectory with none other than our beloved brother. You can picture my shock when I realised that Inspiration's darling Arvist Cidnosin not only discovered the world outside of his lair-away-from-lair but apparently makes a habit of breaking bread with S., with whom you would think he might have little to discuss. According to Seliara, Arvist developed a passion for Composition, an interest he must have nurtured in secret throughout our childhood as he mocked the two of us for enjoying our music lessons so thoroughly! Seliara seems quite pleased to have captured this one-man audience.

As we concluded a thrilling conversation about Arvist's artistic process, Seliara suddenly implored me to show her his studio. She alleged that Arvist gave her full permission – just two days ago, before she left campus to visit her family's ship – to rummage through his things in search of an old sketch gone astray. As she begged and babbled on, I felt twin jolts of dread and delight. You know how much the idea of anyone else visiting Arvist's studio always sent him into a fury – yet I possess an eternal curiosity about what he keeps down there. And she did say he allowed it! How could I lose?

So down we fell into that dark heart of the house, where Seliara gasped – genuinely and audibly, which was a surprise given her typical decorum – at every wrinkled scrap and mysterious prop tucked away in Arvist's workshop. I will not bore you with a detailed description of our brother's domestic chaos, but believe me when I say that I now know what happened to your favourite lamp that mysteriously "disappeared" years ago. Alas, not even your own kidnapped light fixture was functional, so I tugged open the curtains – encased in a thick slime of algae, as though they had never been touched – to see the ocean according to Arvist.

And what a world it is! I think our brother rather cleverly tricked us all: martyring himself by accepting this "sunken closet" as his studio while secretly enjoying one of the best views of the undergarden! His little room juts off the library wall and provides an expansive panorama of the entire reef. More importantly, however, the windows line up with a kind of natural tunnel in the coral that I had never seen from higher up in the house.

It was from this vantage point that we made the discovery.

Sophy, have you ever noticed the moderately sized, beautifully formed, and altogether incomprehensible bowl that guards the perimeter of the undergarden?

Forgive my rhetorical flourish. I assume that if you had noticed it, you would have told me immediately. I also do not know if "bowl" is a decent descriptor. It is wide and cylindrical, made of what appears to be barnacle-encrusted crystal or glass or resin. There's a remarkable transparency to it, you see, which reflects and refracts the sea as it churns about. I could not stop looking at the thing. I should have mentioned that the clear "bowl" part is simply the first "layer", pressed flush against the sand, and on top (like a strange sunken cake!) is a – railing? Some ornament? – of thin metal strings stretched tight across a final ring of the same clear material that holds it all together. It is like a giant pipe (or pipe-shaped coral) has been cut into an enormous bead – o, I cannot describe it. Perhaps I ought to try sketching the thing instead, though I suspect that any skills I may possess when it comes to drawing more natural subjects may not apply to capturing mysterious structures with accuracy.

I will attempt to relay the conversation below for your enjoyment (though please be forewarned that I may have forgotten or misrepresented Seliara's dialogue in particular):

"At last! It is even more impressive than he described!" Seliara gasped.

"Arvist?" I asked. "He knows of this?"

"Knows, dear E.? Why, he made the thing! It is stunning!" She gestured to the window with a dramatic flair that I know she must have picked up from our brother. "I thought that glass was too base a material for Arvist's skilled hands, but I suppose that makes his use of it all the more admirable."

"If you think my brother has the patience to manage glassblowing," I said, "then you do not know him as well as you profess."

(That is a fabrication – I did not say that exactly, though I wish I had.)

Seliara then pressed herself against the window, so close that the tips of her shoes crinkled into the wall, and stared into the sea for what felt like an eternity.

"He called it his Great Project," she said in a solemn voice, enunciating the capitals with obvious reverence. "He told me that once I saw it, I would understand everything about him in an instant. I regret that I do not quite understand, but it does make me ever so much more impressed by his skill."

"That is all very well and good, but how was this project completed? And – more importantly – it is complete, isn't it?" The thought of Arvist continuing to sneak about the house without my knowledge disturbed me even more than the fact that he'd done it in the first place.

"O, I can't say for certain. Is any project truly complete?" asked Seliara with dreamy fervour. "Is not everything we accomplish but one small step in the Greatest Project of our lives – that which we do not complete until we pass from this world?"

"Indeed," I replied distantly, letting her progress into a philosophical monologue while my Brain struggled with this new discovery. To be fair, since Mother died, no one has really spent much time in that part of the undergarden. It is tucked away behind us, and I could not see it from any other part of the house, yet still, Sophy, it frustrates me to no end that Arvist carried out a project here – in secret – and I knew nothing of it. You two always think it unhealthy that I take my role as the unofficial "Steward" of the Deep House so seriously, but here is what bothers me most – if Arvist could create an entire underwater sculpture unbeknownst to all, who knows what more sinister things might take place at the house without my knowledge?

I shall have to check all the airlocks and doors even more thoroughly than usual tonight.

O, but really, Sophy, I do not wish to worry you in any way, and for the most part, I managed to conquer my previous bleakness. In your absence, I have many possible pastimes to which I can affix my attention – natural history, baking, and even my sketching. I have taken a break from reading, however, as it sent me into an existential crisis as usual – there are so many books and so many ideas in the world, and how can I hope to understand, learn, or discover even a fraction of these wonders in my short life?

With all the things I must learn in such a brief time, it seems distasteful for the universe to send me a fresh enigma!

Stay safe and write to me soon,

Your sister

P.S. A few days ago, I received a reply (on official Boundless Campus stationery that initially convinced me the letter could be from Arvist – but again, I should not indulge in such empty fancies!) from none other than the esteemed Schr Henerey Clel himself. Can you believe it? He must receive thousands of letters a day from Scholars far more accomplished than I could ever hope to be. I tremble to have gained his notice at all.

Thrillingly, he seems absolutely befuddled by my Fish (Fathom Eels, he suggests?), and, even more impossibly, expressed interest in hearing more about them (and our home) from me – which is the point at which my excitement turned to nausea.

I do not suppose I will give him an adequate reply at any point, but I shall certainly treasure this letter until the very end of my days. (In personal correspondence, he sounds just as he does in his academic writing – perhaps even slightly kinder, if such a thing is possible? It turns out that he is from Atoll Campus originally, so perhaps his kindness is no surprise!)

P.P.S. What should I do about his letter? Dare I reply? Dare I really ignore it? I so desperately desire your guidance, though given our present circumstances, it is possible that your next letter will arrive long after Scholar Clel has forgotten about me completely (or, even more disturbingly, after I decide in a fit of unprecedented extroversion and scientific curiosity to go ahead and reply to him after all).

LETTER FROM SOPHY CIDNOSIN TO ARVIST CIDNOSIN, 1002

Arvist,

It is I, your sister – you do remember that you have one, and that I am currently at the bottom of the sea, correct?

(While you're recalling my existence, I hope you will also remember to eat, swap your robes every other day at minimum, and bear in mind that most people find it tiresome when someone soliloquises about his own accomplishments apropos of nothing. Enjoy this sisterly wisdom.)

I know that you can barely emerge from your studio long enough to draw a breath, but I hope you will take a moment to heed my words. It may come as a shock, but besides myself, there remains one additional sister in our family whom you should visit once every Abundant Tide at minimum now that I'm not around!

I received a rather frantic letter from her today – something about a surprise sculpture of yours? It has inspired E. to do more of that Compulsive Checking behaviour, so I am troubled. I do wish you had told her about it in advance. You know how these things shake her. I would not wish her to return to those cursed routines that her brain has set for her in the past.

As ever, I do begrudgingly love you. Now, if you don't mind, I shall return to the task of writing E. a letter.

Sophy

AUTOMATED POST MISSIVE FROM VYERIN CLEL TO SOPHY CIDNORGHE, 1003

Dear Sophy,

I now have the pleasure of getting to know you in the past and the present simultaneously. An odd experience, but an enjoyable one. Might I trouble you with some clarifying questions?

When exactly did you and Arvist move out of the Deep House and join Boundless Campus? I'm sure it must have been difficult to leave such an interesting place.

I imagine it was also challenging for you to adapt to life away from the reef, even if you are technically Boundless by birth. Henerey certainly struggled to fit in, as the customs and dress and academic protocol are so different from our home on the Atoll. For example, Henerey used to marvel at how people living at Boundless Campus wear whatever clothes they fancy, on any occasion. Here in the Atoll, everyone, regardless of their personal fashion habits or gender, sports full robes with skirts and petticoats for formal occasions, and trousers and shirts the rest of the time. Without fail!

(More seriously, he struggled with the Boundless Campus' infamous "work ethic", hierarchical structure, and general philosophy that Scholars are only as valuable as their accomplishments. I am sorry if this offends you.)

Finally, I must confess that I enjoy the novelty of these references to Seliara's interest in Linguistic Alchemy. Though I heard of the practice from my brother, I never met a professed acolyte. How very bizarre that such odd superstition could be found among Boundless Scholars, but I suppose they needed some playful respite from the brutality of their Chancellors! (All right, I shall stop lambasting your campus culture now.)

V.

P.S. If I might pry further – who is the Dr Lyelle that E. mentioned?

AUTOMATED POST MISSIVE FROM SOPHY CIDNORGHE TO VYERIN CLEL, 1003

Dear Vyerin,

It touches me, truly, that you have taken the time to read these letters and ask questions, too. I do feel a bit odd sending you so much material – I thought that we might trade documents equally – and I hope what I have sent you will inspire you to share more about Henerey, if you feel comfortable doing so!

Though Arvist is the oldest, I pioneered a life outside of the Deep House years before he learned how to fend for himself. I started studying precociously – I was barely fifteen when I joined the School of Observation – and made Apprentice at sixteen. Rather conversely, Arvist enrolled rather late, at twenty-six – driving us wild for years beforehand as he attempted to use the entire house as his studio. His Presentation took place three years before these letters, but he only moved to the Docked Dormitories full-time about a year before I left on my mission. O, and E. is the middle child, if you can believe that – I am the youngest! And, as you might guess, she made no plans to leave the Deep House.

I'm astounded to hear that it was the fashion and academic culture of Boundless that seemed most surprising to Henerey upon his transition to a new campus! Did he not find it difficult to adjust from the reliable island life of the Atoll to living upon interconnected research stations that drift like ships at the whims of the tide? That proved most difficult for me. The Deep House might be underwater, but the foundations that Mother built ensured that our home is – was – as strong as the healthiest coral colony. While we certainly witnessed the water moving about us, the House never stooped to the indignity of bobbing, you know. Like all young Apprentices, I spent my first night on campus in the Docked Dormitories, which float in the shallower waters off the Boundless lagoon behind the protective embrace of a great wavebreak-wall. Yet even the gentle rocking of those anchored residences made me unbearably ill. As Atoll folk, you and Henerey are fortunate enough to live upon the only known landmass in the world – so he may have felt even more jostled by life at sea, yes?

Answering your queries out of order ... ever since she came of age (around twenty or twenty-one – she was twenty-seven when writing these letters), my sister lived with a Malady of the Mind that made certain things – like leaving the house, interacting with strangers, or not obsessing over the fragility of her own mortality – very difficult. She struggled very much in those early years, but Dr Lyelle, a Physician of the Brain with whom E. began corresponding during her most challenging times, taught my sister ways to get to know her thoughts better. I hope this doesn't sound condescending, or as though I pity E. When she was first diagnosed, I was still a young girl, really, and assumed my sister might be cured in no time. That work was always in process, though, and in the meantime, she adapted her lifestyle so that she would not have to endure a constant onslaught of those things that caused her the most distress. (Before you ask – yes, records of Dr Lyelle's correspondence with my sister exist, but I will not transgress by reading them. Not that Dr Lyelle would share them with me, at any rate. Not that I've tried, of course.)

In anticipation,

Sophy

P.S. I lost myself in discussion of E. and forgot to comment about Linguistic Alchemy! What is truly bizarre – and perhaps Henerey shared this with you? – is that this trend originated as a game played by young Boundless children who made up all manner of complex rules that assigned each letter of the alphabet to a particular feeling. Linear letters like A and V signify aggression, while O and U are soothing, and so forth. Yet as our generation grew up, some decided to pursue this childish pastime with a full-fledged Scholarly devotion. Most people understood it as a bit of an ironic joke, but not Seliara, who at one point briefly refused to use the letter "E" (and stopped when my sister refused to speak with her as a result).

P.P.S. Trust me, nobody finds Boundless Campus more wretched than I, a former Boundless Scholar. Following is a bleak joke my wife shared with me the other day:

A Scholar from the School of Intuition at Boundless runs into their Chancellor's office, tears in their eyes, and announces with a grim face that they cannot teach for the day – due to the sudden and tragic deaths of their entire family in a boating accident just an hour earlier. The Chancellor sighs, rolls their eyes, and answers: "All right, but next time, I would appreciate advance notice."

AUTOMATED POST MISSIVE FROM VYERIN CLEL TO SOPHY CIDNORGHE, 1003

Dear S.,

Understood completely (E.'s story, that is). I briefly saw such a Physician of the Brain several years ago. For a temporary, situational need. But, for what it's worth, if I were to perish or disappear mysteriously, I would prefer that my records remained sealed as well.

Despite our Atoll origins, both Henerey and I took to life on the ocean like – well, I won't embarrass myself by employing the obvious simile. Because he transferred to Boundless after his apprenticeship, Henerey spent no time in your Docked Dormitories, but immediately found both lab and living quarters in an anchored research residence for Scholars of Classification. Then, when his department sought to elevate his position, he moved to an even more elaborate Anchorage, which—

You know, it occurs to me that Henerey can describe this much better than I can.

I will send you a relevant letter shortly.

V.

P.S. Many thanks for the clarification about Linguistic Alchemy. Here on the Atoll Campus, our Scholars only hold one superstitious belief: that after midnight on a full moon, all Boundless Scholars devour books of all kinds. Swallowing down the driest papers with endless jugs of purified water. Helps them absorb the knowledge without wasting time with that peskily human business of reading.

AUTOMATED POST MISSIVE FROM SOPHY CIDNORGHE TO VYERIN CLEL, 1003

V.,

However did you get the impression that was only a superstition?

LETTER FROM HENEREY CLEL TO VYERIN CLEL, 1002

Dear Vy,

My new spaces at the Windward Anchorage are absolutely spacious (thank you for asking!). In fact, I would even say they are objectionably oversized. (I welcome extra room in my laboratories, of course, but I find my personal quarters far too cavernous and desolate for a lonely fellow like myself. Yet such vast rooms would be perfect for hosting a visit from, say, a gruff-yet-charming brother, his gregarious husband, and a precocious niece and infant nephew growing up at an unusually accelerated rate . . .)

I know you dare not get away until the research vessel season ends, but I continue to count down the days until you can! And please tell Avanne that I still work tirelessly to name a species after her as she requested during my last visit. (I remain firm, however, in my conviction that it is not appropriate to name said species "The Usurping Babeling" in "honour" of her new little brother . . . if only because we usually do not use definite articles in taxonomy.)

Naturally, I fear that my "promotion" into this upscale Anchorage must be some kind of consolation prize. You see, I learned recently that the Department condemned my proposal for the Second Ocean habitat assessment project to that cursed state of "administrative hold" (in other words, "placed in some dreaded cabinet to slowly pass from this world"). Chancellor Rawsel continues to push me to join the Ridge study, which I would be happy to try if I didn't consider it an utter waste of time. It's all hypothetical analysis anyway. How can we truly draw any conclusions about the Ridge until we have access to Schr Eliniea Hayve Forghe's field research? Preposterous, I say! Since the Ridge expedition began, Rawsel seems even more committed to keeping us busy with nonsense. I swear he gets stranger and more irascible every day. (But please don't tell Chancellor Rawsel that. (Not that he would survive a conversation with you, I'm sure – you would shame him into silence, or silence him into shame, or something of the sort.))

I strive to focus on the positive aspects of my current existence. These new quarters (regardless of the reason behind my ownership of them) offer absolutely splendid views past the reef – on a clear day, I spy hundreds of (blissfully unanchored) Boundless Campus ships speeding to and from the horizon as though members of a pod of predatory Whales. And when I dare to catch a transport and make the quick journey to the Boundless Campus Library Anchorage, I can even glimpse the great artificial islands of the Intertidal Campus floating like distant, shimmering Turtles. (Though I envy all my Boundless colleagues who serve upon travelling vessels that are not tied to an Anchorage, I am grateful that my transfer was not to Intertidal. While I enjoy their local dress and remarkable theatrical productions, I would feel even more tied down were I fixed like a Limpet to those stationary shores.)

I know not why I spent so many sentences discussing Intertidal, though, because I find myself looking towards the open ocean more often these days. I recently received a most curious letter with a return address of nothing other than the Deep House itself! The sender (one of Scholar Cidnosin's children – did you know she had three? "No, Henerey," I'm sure you'd say, "I was not in fact aware of the precise familial situation of that one particular Architect with whom you have been fascinated since childhood, please forgive me . . .") wanted to share a spellbinding encounter with an exceptionally remarkable pair of Fathom Eels.

Did I spend far too much time drafting out a reply to the aforementioned letter to avoid my other responsibilities? Certainly! Should I regret this ill-advised decision? Probably! Do I? Alas, no, because a wonderful reply just arrived to reward me!

But writing a letter about writing and receiving letters has become too metatextual even for me, so I will close here.

Until soon, brother!

Henerey

AUTOMATED POST MISSIVE FROM SOPHY CIDNORGHE TO VYERIN CLEL, 1003

Dear Vyerin,

How is your brother so effortlessly ebullient in his every word? He is like the sun to E.'s moon.

I'm sure it's no surprise that Henerey's gushing about my sister's correspondence makes me giddy. How privileged we are to see their friendship develop before our very eyes! (Though there is also something a little voyeuristic about it, of course. Alas that the dead may have no privacy in the name of posterity.)

Additional giddiness also erupted when Henerey described your family so succinctly – I cannot imagine a better set of descriptors for you than "gruff-yet-charming". And I suppose your daughter and "usurping babeling" alike must have adored their Uncle Henerey.

With best wishes,

Sophy

AUTOMATED POST MISSIVE FROM VYERIN CLEL TO SOPHY CIDNORGHE, 1003

Dear Sophy,

If your sister is a moon, and my brother is the sun, then which celestial body am I? (Which is the gruffest of the distant Planets?) And which are you?

Yes, Avanne, age twelve, and Orey, now two, loved Henerey and miss him terribly. Both of my children are vivacious, charismatic, and energetic – all traits they share with only one of their fathers, I'm afraid.

    Vyerin

AUTOMATED POST MISSIVE FROM SOPHY CIDNORGHE TO VYERIN CLEL, 1003

V.,

    Clearly I am the Gravity holding this entire system together. (I jest.)

Chapter 4

UNSENT DRAFT OF A LETTER FROM E. CIDNOSIN TO HENEREY CLEL, 1002

Dear Schr Clel,

You cannot imagine how much joy I received from your letter. Yet I must apologise immensely for deceiving you into thinking that I am interesting or accomplished enough to merit your attention

UNSENT DRAFT OF A LETTER FROM E. CIDNOSIN TO HENEREY CLEL, 1002

Dear Schr Clel,

I intended to respond to your letter three days ago – how time speeds by! – but I have had much to do around my house. You see, I noticed something unusual recently, and ever since then, it has become more difficult to silence those intrusive thoughts that suggest a calamity is close at hand. There are so many things that I must check, and one can never be too careful

UNSENT DRAFT OF A LETTER FROM E. CIDNOSIN TO HENEREY CLEL, 1002

Dear Schr Clel,

Please forgive me for neglecting your letter for so long. I can assure you that when I received it, I was most pleased to see that you had taken the time to reply to me. You asked me to describe my life at the Deep House – what an impossible task! But I shall try, for your sake. Imagine, firstly, that you have boarded a small depth-craft to visit us. If you left from the western portion of Boundless Campus (where I believe your Anchorage is located), you would pass first through the most vibrant reef you have ever seen. Should you find yourself growing anxious, with troubling thoughts blossoming in your mind, I would recommend focusing on the intricate details of the Fan Coral – trace each spiny, skeletal sclerite from the root to the tip – and pretending that each bubble you see outside your depth-craft is a pernicious Thought floating out of your head and into the open ocean.

With your thoughts regulated in this way, you might have a spare moment to look up from the coral to the distant depths, where you may glimpse a glimmering sculpture of a Sea Star out of the corner of your eye – a decorative element added by my mother to distract a visitor's eye from the less romantical collection of water-surveying equipment hidden beneath it on the roof of the house. As you neared, you might observe that the house seems to grow right out of the coral. The exterior is painted as gaudily as the life that surrounds it so that the presence of the house will not disturb those creatures who already call this area home. Only indoors will you find elements that speak to our personal decorative tastes and interests (but I would not ever recommend that you come indoors because it would be most impossible

LETTER FROM SOPHY CIDNOSIN TO E. CIDNOSIN, 1002

Dearest E.,

I wish you could send me a thousand shimmering abalones! Sadly, you told Seliara the truth: we are not able to receive personal parcels at present.

I wonder where you will sit to read this? In the library, at Mother's desk? In the dining room, in the fine company of leftover pie and endless sea views? Curled up in your bedroom porthole? In any case, E., settle in, as I have much to tell you!

All the time that you and I spent poring over the schematics of the Spheres together was for naught, it seems (though it was an excellent opportunity to strengthen our Sisterly bond!), because the actual experience of living at the station is nothing like how it looked on paper. First of all, the "Spheres" themselves are truly enormous – I expected cramped quarters like the Depth Capsule (or an Apprentices' Anchorage), not high, curving ceilings. There are eight circular units in total, connected by a series of transparent tunnels. Five are our personal quarters – complete with closet-sized washrooms, massive windows tinted slightly for privacy, and stunningly advanced remote communication stations that we have been assured will be operational shortly! The remaining three spheres contain, respectively, a wet-dock with decontamination and medical facilities, a multi-discipline laboratory, and a simple kitchen/recreational area. Comforts enough to sustain us through our season-long residency!

Yet this place is nothing like the Deep House. Features like organic forms, flowing stairways, and multiple storeys that take advantage of the depth in a way unforeseeable abovewaters are all apparently unique to Mother's architectural style. Here, a surprisingly horizontal complex stretches across the seafloor with little external or internal ornament. Instead, the designers chose to enliven the station with colour – each sphere is illuminated with lights, glass, and shell-shine of its own particular hue. (The colour of my living space, to my delight, is cheerful orange!)

So far, Scholar Forghe – I mean Eliniea, Eliniea, *Eliniea*, I'm working so hard to correct myself – let's try that again!

So far, Eliniea has become my closest acquaintance. If you would like to refer to my previous letter, she turned out to be the elegant Intertidal Scholar in pink, much to my surprise. Schr Eliniea Hayve Forghe is no older than I am, and yet she has already accomplished more than most seasoned Scholars. You'll remember that she was the very first person to survey the Ridge via staffed capsule during the pre-mission assessment. Now she single-handedly runs an expedition before the age of thirty. And here I thought that my presence on this mission made me precocious!

Though she is obviously the only colleague here of my own generation, I felt unsure about whether we could truly become friends – since she is the Expedition Specialist as well as an absolute genius, E. But when I expressed that very sentiment to her during our first morning at the station – when she asked if she might join me for breakfast, as all else were still asleep – she quelled my concerns quickly.

"It will be a lonely mission for me if my position proves such an impediment!" she exclaimed with a confidence belied by the fact that her quivering hand had not yet placed her pink teacup on the table. "The decision is entirely yours to make, of course, and I hope you do not feel as though I am pressuring you to engage with me on a social level! My 'leadership' is simply the product of my familiarity with the Ridge. Like all of you, I hold no special authority and report to Chancellor Rawsel of the School of Observation. But I do not wish to alter your thoughts one way or the other!"

By the time she completed this monologue, I imagine her tea had gone cold in her grasp, but she resolutely kept it at a distance so as not to intrude upon my personal space. I found the entire situation immensely charming.

"I would be delighted if you joined me, Scholar—Eliniea," I said, clearing away the extensive array of cartographic journals I had at the ready to keep me entertained. And join me she did. (She also invited me to call her by the nickname Niea, but there is only so much informality I can stomach!)

In the days since, we've breakfasted every morning together, with our conversations progressing from the Ridge and our expedition to our Scholarly careers and then, at last, our personal lives. She paints, stargazes, and cultivates aquaria in her free time; I realised promptly that my only "hobby" is more studying. Still, I have my own topics to bring to our conversations. I have already spoken at length about you, as expected, and our dear home, and even some especially silly Arvist episodes, which were well received! Her character is, in many ways, at odds with mine – she is graceful where I am brusque, optimistic where I am cynical, and wears such diaphanous and pastel-hued finery that I feel like a barnacle in the company of a pearl.

Still, it has been such a long time since I had a friend (who is not a sister, I should clarify!). I find the experience restorative.

What I find less restorative, unfortunately, is my role in the mission itself! I feel rather abashed to admit this, but I think I envisioned the Ridge as – well, you know, an actual ridge, like the sunken seamounts that surround the Atoll Campus, with rough, jagged cliffs towering far above the ocean floor. Now, it is certainly possible that such topography exists just outside our windows. Unfortunately, because we are surrounded by the eternal darkness of the Abyssal Plains, I cannot tell one way or the other.

Everyone else started their projects days ago. Eliniea, as the presiding Scholar of Life, spends hours observing each shadowy shape or luminescent flash of a creature that approaches our windows. Scholar Irye Rux (the Columns player, and our Scholar of Sound) lets down the hydrophone twice a day. Scholar Ylaret Tamseln has astronomical calculations aplenty to keep her busy at present, and certainly Scholar Vincenebras (he decided long ago to fuse his first and last names into one for efficiency's sake) is able to do ... whatever it is that he does. (I jest. He is a Journalist from the Intertidal School of Intuition and shall record our experiences to share with the public.)

—one hour later—

I considered, for one delicious and delinquent moment, simply continuing the letter and pretending that that Schr Rux had not interrupted me by announcing the arrival of a rare Parochial Squid outside the laboratory viewing window – but why bother to create a fiction for you?

Eliniea promises that as soon as we receive a final shipment of equipment (including the fabled underwater camera!) from "up there", we will embark upon our first mission outside the station – but I've had to occupy myself in the meantime. Perhaps it will delight you to know that I have been sketching ideas of what the invisible landscape around us might look like, simply to keep my mind sharp. I would love to create a true geographical rendering of this place – but instead I grapple with pictorial convention while I wait! O, if Arvist could see me now. (I am rather glad he cannot. He may be frustrating – and he should write to you soon, by the way, I guarantee it – but sink it all, that boy's skill with a brush is incomparable.)

Fortunately, I know that these days of idleness are numbered, and I will soon commence the work of which I have always dreamed. O, how I miss you!

Affectionately,

Sophy

P.S. (written the next morning, moments before I send off this letter) I need say only this – if you do not reply to Scholar Clel's letter I shall be most disappointed.

LETTER FROM E. CIDNOSIN TO SOPHY CIDNOSIN, 1002

To my favourite amateur artist,

I shall supplement this letter with a much longer response at a later date, but at present, I wanted to share some startling news of my own (no new hobbies like painting abyssal seascapes to report, sadly):

Item 1, REGARDING THE STRUCTURE: My discovery during Seliara's visit continues to haunt me. I cannot stop thinking about how Arvist managed to construct this Structure so quietly! I now carry out daily surveys of the undergarden from Arvist's room in an attempt to see the "bowl" more clearly (with unfortunately limited results). Last night, it occurred to me that the tool I needed most to understand it was close at hand – Mother's telescope. I had kept it in her desk in the library as a kind of relic – I will confess to spending a few nights, years ago, clutching it to my eye in the hopes that I would see a fragmented, magnified glimpse of her hair or pores or lashes within it – but it has been a while since I felt the need to touch it. In any case, yesterday I placed the telescope at my eye and pressed the other end to the window. This Structure is truly round, Sophy – perfectly so, as far as I can see. I might put forth the hypothesis that a kind of pattern has been etched into its bowl-like base, but I have also not ruled out the possibility that it was nothing more than dust on my lens.

Item 2, REGARDING MY PROFESSIONAL CORRESPON-DENCE WITH SCHOLAR CLEL: I decided this morning (after my rounds about the house) that I would sit down and respond to him at last. So far, I have walked to my writing desk, sat down, removed a sheet of paper, stood up, and returned to pacing the corridors no fewer than three times. When will it end?

Well, this letter will end with an obligatory—

Item 3, THE MOST IMPORTANT OF ALL: Know that you are most sorely missed, and that I pray your existence under inconceivable amounts of water pressure has not weighed you down.

Please send my best to your new colleagues, especially your new "FRIEND" Eliniea (o Sophy, you are never so subtle as you imagine).

I am grateful you are not alone down there.

E.

THE RIDGE REVEALED, ISSUE 1, RECORDED BY SCHR VINCENEBRAS

Dearest Colleagues,

Do you know how many tides comprise five years? How many sunsets? How many births and deaths and triumphs and failures and seasonal seabird migrations?

Well, no matter how you measure them, the past five years led up to this moment: the first-ever fully staffed deep-sea research investigation, one that will explore the mysteries of the Ridge and the Life that calls it home.

One might even go so far as to include the past hundred years in this journey. When Schr Gavriel Tern first dreamed that people might travel beneath the waves in Year 905, she may never have guessed that her heirs would later use her blueprints to create the first successful Depth-Craft "Capsule", the venerable progenitor of the great chariot that recently bore me and my colleagues to our destination in the depths!

In fact, if you will indulge me by diving still deeper into the misty waters of Time, one might argue that the calamitous Dive of a thousand years ago – that tragedy that shattered the Upward Archipelago and left our ancestors, the greatest Scholars of every Country and Culture known to the mysterious Antepelagic world, bereft of their Islands in the Sky and adrift on an unknown planet – that event ensured that one day we the Survivors would need to get to know our new world.

And so we have. We have grown from a struggling group of survivors to *three* thriving Academic cultures, each with its own values, accomplishments, and philosophies.

O, Boundless Campus – that disparate collection of ships and Anchorages, all adrift yet utterly united! Who but thee could create a *mobile* civilisation upon sea-faring vessels, making fathoms of ocean seem altogether *cosy*? (And who but thee could organise the Ridge Expedition, overseeing the recruitment of Scholars from across the campuses?)

O, Intertidal Campus – *my* Campus, I should note – the most ingenious response to our world's lack of land! Our Intertidal ancestors constructed the great Ring of hand-crafted "islands" to surround the Atoll. Little could they have imagined how much Creativity and Transformation would flourish upon our floating world in the years to come!

O, the Atoll Campus – home to the guardians of the only genuine Landmass known to humanity! While the rest of us innovate upon the water, our Atoll Colleagues preserve ancient practices from the Upward Archipelago on their island home. Agriculture! Terrestrial biology! *Floors that never leak!*

But even with all the combined gifts and accomplishments of Boundless, Intertidal, and Atoll peoples alike at our disposal, one place eluded all of us for a thousand years . . .

The deepest (known) trench in the ocean.

Back to the glorious present! Today, our crew of five will pioneer a new way of life – living in true darkness, as do the species that already call this biome home. Assisting us with her great expertise is Expedition Specialist Schr Eliniea Hayve Forghe, who brings unparalleled wisdom from her famous experimental depth-craft residency on the Ridge that led to this expedition in the first place. Won't you join us as we change the world? Simply detach the enclosed postcard and include the proper payment to experience the Ridge from the comfort of your own chairs.

With abyssal enthusiasm,

Schr Vincenebras, on behalf of the entire Ridge Expedition

AUTOMATED POST MISSIVE FROM VYERIN CLEL TO SOPHY CIDNORGHE, 1003

Dear Sophy,

Have you truly mailed me an extant copy of *The Ridge Revealed*? Do you trust me (and our postal service) so deeply? I cannot believe this. That is a piece of history. Surely you want me to send it back to you immediately!

(Such was my initial reaction. Then I reread Vincenebras' bombastic words and realised that age and circumstance are the only qualities that make this piece of writing so valuable. I particularly appreciate his attempt to "explain" the Dive and the Campuses, as though every single person from the past thousand years does not know every detail about our own origins.)

Thank you for assembling those fragments that E. produced while attempting to draft a reply to Henerey. Your sister was not alone in this practice, of course. Did you know it took my brother fifteen tries, on average, to compose the perfect one-sentence sentiment for a thank-you card? I dread to think how he would have contended with today's advancements in Automated Post technology. He would likely spend hours writing the perfect two-line witticism, only to see a reply arrive mere instants later! Horrifying.

V.

P.S. My husband desperately wants me to mention that he greatly admires Arvist's work. Thinks him a proper genius. I, on the other hand, have no opinion either way, as I have never had much of a head for Art.

AUTOMATED POST MISSIVE FROM SOPHY CIDNORGHE TO VYERIN CLEL, 1003

Dear Vyerin,

Neither has my brother, I'm afraid.

There are many brilliant, remarkable people in the Boundless Campus School of Inspiration, and I never considered Arvist one of them. O, he is talented – immensely so! – and he creates beautiful, meaningful things when he wishes, but he so rarely tries! He also refuses to do anything at which he does not excel naturally, so he never expands his practice like many of his colleagues. He only passed his Scholarly Presentation, I suspect, because one of his three Examiners (the School of Intuition representative) was an Architect who seemed terrified of somehow disappointing the ghost of our mother, or something of the sort.

Sophy

P.S. By the way, of course that *Ridge Revealed* document is yours to keep, if you wish. My wife and I have multiple copies – one of the "benefits" of our time on the expedition. Feel free to sell it if the historical mystique ever wears off for you.

AUTOMATED POST MISSIVE FROM VYERIN CLEL TO SOPHY CIDNORGHE, 1003

Dear Sophy,

O the nepotism of Presentations. I wish I had been so lucky.

Best wishes,

Vyerin

P.S. You are too generous. I shall cherish it always.

AUTOMATED POST MISSIVE FROM SOPHY CIDNORGHE TO VYERIN CLEL, 1003

Dear Vyerin,

I was the lucky one, because I had a prior engagement and could not attend Arvist's Presentation myself . . .

S.

AUTOMATED POST MISSIVE FROM SOPHY CIDNORGHE TO VYERIN CLEL, 1003

O Vyerin – pardon my flippancy in that last note – upon rereading, it occurs to me that perhaps your opinion regarding Presentations and their accuracy was influenced by personal experience of some significance? Many apologies. Sometimes I write too quickly in this format and do not fully understand the emotions at play. Forgive me?

S.

AUTOMATED POST MISSIVE FROM VYERIN CLEL TO SOPHY CIDNORGHE, 1003

How insightful. (I mean that sincerely. Might be hard to tell.) Yes, I once hoped to become a Scholar, but it proved a poor match for my temperament. Every single person in my family tree – going back hundreds of years, they told us (likely back to the Survivors themselves) – was a Scholar, up through Henerey, and I the first to "choose" a different path, as it were. That is all.

V.

AUTOMATED POST MISSIVE FROM SOPHY CIDNORGHE TO VYERIN CLEL, 1003

Yet you have become one of the most talented Navigators working today, so I imagine you made the right choice! (Or so I am told. Pardon me for researching you extensively since you sent that last letter.)

S.

AUTOMATED POST MISSIVE FROM VYERIN CLEL TO SOPHY CIDNORGHE, 1003

I appreciate the compliment, though I do not accept it. It is some comfort that none of this really matters anymore.

Best regards,

Vyerin

P.S. Reread my note and realised it sounds much more morose than intended. I mean all the Scholarly nonsense no longer matters to me as it once did. Navigation certainly does, and always will. Our Society would stop without it. Anyway, it is very late, and I am amazed that you remain awake. (I will soon depart on a chartered vessel run, so this is a typical hour for me.) Rest well this evening and I shall send you a letter from my own records tomorrow (the one that E. finally posted after writing all those fragments) as well as a little surprise. My husband happens to possess the same keen archival senses as you. Over dinner, he suggested that I consult Henerey's infamous daybook you found at the Deep House to see if he preserved or wrote anything of note around this time. I promptly took Reiv's advice and explored this relic from my late brother's "archives", only to discover a pasted-in Academy notice and a few stray notes. I hope you will enjoy them as well.

AUTOMATED POST MISSIVE FROM SOPHY CIDNORGHE TO VYERIN CLEL, 1003

With a postscript like that, dear Vyerin, how could I possibly sleep a wink?

Chapter 5

ACADEMY MISSIVE PASTED IN THE DAYBOOK OF HENEREY CLEL, 1002

The following Announcement is intended for
THE SCHOLARS OF CLASSIFICATION IN THE SCHOOL
OF OBSERVATION, BOUNDLESS CAMPUS
on behalf of HON. CHANCELLOR ORELITH RAWSEL
on this EIGHTH DAY OF THE FIRST SUPERLATIVE TIDE
IN THE SECOND QUARTER OF HIGH WATERS, 1002

Colleagues,

It has come to my attention that an anonymous individual recently wrote to the Campus Mediators to protest the "pressure" allegedly placed upon Scholars in this Department of late.

Let me be perfectly clear. Anyone who cannot handle the intensity of our research responsibilities ought to consider finding another profession. And anyone cowardly enough to sneak away and converse with the Mediators in secret about some perceived offence surely does not respect the values of openness, honesty, and dignity that define the Boundless Campus.

Chancellor Rawsel

NOTE FROM THE DAYBOOK OF HENEREY CLEL, 1002

I once promised myself that I would never write down or otherwise document my darkest days (perhaps because I thought that letting them slip out of my mind with the passage of time would spare me from ever experiencing the pain they caused again). So I will not sully this page with descriptions of what transpired in the Department lately, but I know that if I do not create any evidence of the vile behaviour of those who are supposed to be our leaders, I will wake up tomorrow morning convincing myself that I must "do better" and "prove myself" and "reaffirm my commitment to the Scholars of Classification".

A reminder to the future Henerey who makes these promises to himself:

You (by which I mean I) deserve better.

LETTER FROM E. CIDNOSIN TO HENEREY CLEL, 1002

Dear Schr Clel,

Just as you did, I shall begin by apologising for the time it took me to turn to your letter – isn't it marvellous how much we have in common?

Composing a suitable response to you has been a challenging ordeal, I admit. I say this neither in mock exaggeration to earn your sympathy nor to deter you from sending another letter, but rather because I believe that honesty and openness can go a long way in improving the quality of a conversation.

So let me begin with honesty, then. I felt so flattered that Scholar Henerey Clel, Natural Historian of Great Import, introduced himself to me so kindly. Then I realised that I never properly introduced myself to you, outside of my signature (and that was miracle enough, as I do so frequently forget to sign my own letters). Let me reveal myself formally, then, in all my questionable glory – I am E. (only E., if you please – as I mentioned previously, my full name is quite unfortunate) Cidnosin, and most definitively not a Scholar, despite your kindness to the contrary. I reside within the house of your dreams while living out an existence that is more inescapably mundane, I'm sorry to say, than you could possibly imagine. For example, while you might cite the demands of your Department as an excuse for not writing, I may only say – truthfully – that I was – what? Watching bubbles accumulate outside the airlock door? Checking for leaks everywhere, even in places I've checked already? Waiting for a letter from my sister to arrive, though I know she is preoccupied with exploring a place that few will ever visit in their lifetimes and therefore has but precious little time for correspondence?

Such is my existence at the Deep House. Yes, it does sometimes seem a desecration of my mother's memory that I neglect its wonders so. But your eagerness to hear about my family home tempts me to see it with new eyes. I do feel too shy about my prose to craft an extensive Deep House history unprompted, but if you happen to have any specific questions about my experience, I hope you will ask, and I shall answer as best I can.

The fact that the circumstances of my childhood allegedly "dazzle" you boggles my mind, because as far as I am concerned, nothing in my life could ever compare with your countless adventures. How I yearn to spend as much time with marine life as you do! As you Classify the world around us, you survey rare species in the wild and mourn carcasses swept up on the shores – so I presume from reading your books multiple times and with great enthusiasm (because that assumption about me was most certainly correct) – while I, on the other hand, encounter sea creatures by sheer coincidence through stray glances out the window. I fear that I practise Classification only by virtue of birth and happy accident. As children, my siblings and I felt as comfortable in the sea as we did our own bedrooms. Father nurtured a vast garden outside the watertight confines of our house, where he attempted to

50

cultivate by artificial selection hardier variants of food-grade kelp and seaweed for his culinary exploits. We would don our helmets and slip into the depths with an easy carelessness. One of my fondest memories involves the singular sensation of sitting cross-legged among the coral (not upon it, of course – please don't think that I have such little regard for the reef ecosystem!) and gazing up at the swirling schools as they flashed above me – experiencing a feeling of incredible quietude that I miss enormously.

Looking over what I just wrote, I feel quite embarrassed at how maudlin I've waxed. I sound a bit like a pompous coursebook for Apprentice Scholars – or like Schr Vincenebras from my sister's expedition – but you must understand that I have very little experience speaking with anyone who does not already live underwater and, by this point in the evening, my words often refuse to obey me. I hope you will forgive my boldness, irreverence, and extravagant run-on sentences. Please do not feel obligated to respond, as I'm sure your own occupations and colleagues keep you quite busy. I assure you that I will take no offence. You have been generous enough with your time!

Most sincerely,

E.

P.S. If your path happens to cross with my brother's, would you please give him my best regards and sincerest wishes for his continued health, since he refuses to contact me?

AUTOMATED POST MISSIVE FROM SOPHY CIDNORGHE TO VYERIN CLEL, 1003

Dear Vyerin,

I am awash with emotions – delight, sorrow, and a small degree of guilt – as I read these words from my sister. But the foremost among them is amazement! You would never believe it from this letter to Henerey, but E. was always reticent with strangers – yet she speaks to him of her feelings and our childhood as though he was already an old friend. It dazzles me!

And I also ache for this honest, caring, and vulnerable Henerey of the past, as seen through his daybook. I wish I could have been an ally to him.

I do not know specifically what transpired in his case, but I am familiar with the unchecked power of the Chancellors at Boundless Campus. Far too many of them thrive on control, consider themselves the sole authorities in their fields, and believe that they must denigrate, ridicule, and dismiss those they mentor – if only because the same happened to them when they were but young Scholars. Friends of mine still employed as Scholars at present claim that the situation has improved of late, but I am not hopeful that any policy change or Restructuring of Academy Values can completely eradicate the problem, so long as Boundless culture remains so hierarchical – which is its defining characteristic, of course!

Also, it bears noting that Chancellor Orelith Rawsel in particular is an absolute nightmare, and every day I rage to think that he retains his position. But that is a tale for another time.

I do not know if you felt compelled to investigate me when our correspondence began, but I shall share with you a little bit about my life now. When my wife and I resigned from our respective Campuses, it became Niea's dream to found an independent Institution of Knowledge. (Shocking, I know!) Alas, because I spent much of the last year lost in grief, I could not help her much with this project, but she did it all – she never fails to astonish me – and the Institution will accept its first pupils next year, once we have time to assemble a faculty. She even calls it "The Sunken School", in tribute to the Deep House. The model is designed to be the opposite of Boundless Campus, with all instructors respected as experts in their own subjects, regardless of their tenure. No scholastic system can be perfect, but one equipped with the self-awareness and humility necessary to keep on improving may stand a chance of getting awfully close.

I wish we could count Henerey among our colleagues at the Sunken School. He would thrive with us, and us with him.

Sophy

LETTER FROM SOPHY CIDNOSIN TO E. CIDNOSIN, 1002

Most-missed E.—

You have my sincerest apology for the abbreviated nature of this note. (But you included a similar disclaimer at the beginning of your letter, so I suppose it is no issue!)

I digress out of restless excitement (and the smallest amount of anxiety). The day has come – we shall make our first dives into the deepest ocean! A mail-boat crammed with a wardrobe's worth of long-distance diving suits arrived this afternoon. We had basic suits already, of course, but these new ones have so much life-sustaining equipment attached to them that they are almost like form-fitting depth-crafts. And they were therefore too heavy to carry with us in our initial descent! Initially, I felt rather disappointed when the shipment docked, as I had been in the midst of an enjoyable off-hours painting lesson with Eliniea (her skills are truly remarkable, and you know I need the help!) that I did not wish to conclude, but I could not be more delighted to finally begin what I came here to accomplish.

Certainly you will fret about my safety, but I assure you that the entire operation will be carried out with superlative efficiency and care. We shall venture forth for no more than two hours each day to start, leaving at least one crew member inside the station to communicate with the Chancellors in the event of an emergency (the lot fell to Schr Tamseln this time). Strong backup tethers will attach us to the Spheres if we need them, and we have each been assigned one of the cetacean automata as a companion. I have not had the opportunity to interact with our automated guardians since we arrived – other than spotting, on occasion, the metallic glint of their dorsal fins as they patrol outside of the station – and I am most curious!

My duties call, and my time to write leisurely runs short. In the meantime, please take care of yourself – and I hope you will soon receive a most delightful letter from your new pen-friend Schr Clel! Incidentally, I thought more carefully about my encounters with him on campus, and here is what I can recall:

1. Two years ago: I met Scholar Clel during a mandatory "socialisation" (that is the word you might use for it – they would have called it a "party") for Young Scholars. We were required to dance with and introduce ourselves to a new partner every five minutes (with time kept scrupulously by a self-important Chancellor), and Scholar Clel was my fifth. His hands shook but his smile was kind.

2. A year and a half ago: we happened to present at a symposium during the same scheduling period! (Thus no one who attended my lecture could attend his, and vice versa – apologies if this is patronising or over-explaining, E., I just never remember how much you know about the foibles of the School of Observation!) Under usual circumstances, two rival presenters might compete mercilessly for the largest audience, but Scholar Clel simply wished me the best.

3. A season ago, in the library, after staying awake all night finishing a draft: I believe I overheard several Apprentice Scholars in the carrel behind me (which was not intended for group study, I assure you) discussing quite improperly which up-and-coming Scholars from across the Campuses were most attractive (in terms of personality, erudition, and academic potential, of course, and not physical appearance or sensuality, since I know those matter little to you!). Scholar Clel's name was mentioned with great enthusiasm.

I must away, unfortunately—

Sophy

P.S. And please do not patronise me about my tendency towards love at first sight, sister! I simply cannot help myself!

LETTER FROM E. CIDNOSIN TO SOPHY CIDNOSIN, 1002

Dear Sophy,

By the time you read this, you will be well acquainted with the infinite ocean outside the Spheres. I accept that, functionally, you remain equally underwater (and, therefore, at risk of hypothetical danger) whether you are safely ensconced in your bunk with my letters or making topographical observations while protected only by a diving suit and a tether that keeps you from drifting endlessly through the abyss ... perhaps I should discontinue the progression of this thought before it escalates any further.

I almost dare not write the sentence that follows, as I fear that by the time you read this, the situation will have altered substantially, proving my current optimism foolish. Yet that is a risk I have no choice but to take. For once, I have remarkable news of my own to share.

After so many failures, I finally penned a reply to Scholar Clel's letter!

All right, I shall speak of it no more!

Except to say that I will also ignore your feeble attempt at injecting your letter with praise for him. Though I do agree that he is a truly remarkable man – with whom I would only ever hope to develop a professional friendship!

Your scattered sister,

E.

AUTOMATED POST MISSIVE FROM SOPHY CIDNORGHE TO VYERIN CLEL, 1003

V.,

I hate to be a bother, but I wanted to check that you were all right – I am so used to your near-instantaneous replies! (Perhaps my prior missive did not go through?) Let me know if there is anything with which I can assist you, even from afar.

S.

AUTOMATED POST MISSIVE FROM VYERIN CLEL TO SOPHY CIDNORGHE, 1003

Dear S.,

My apologies for taking so long to respond to your latest communications; it has been quite a tide for me. Since you have shown me that it is acceptable to discuss our personal lives in these letters, I will furnish a brief explanation. Avanne had grown quite fond of one of her fellow classmates. (All very innocently and sweetly, of course – she is only twelve!) Said "courtship" has now reached an untimely end without mutual accord. This being our daughter's first experience with such romantic despair, Reiv and I have busied ourselves with providing her ceaseless access to those essential cures for heartbreak. Emotional support. Helpful advice. Heaps of seabed clay with which she may attempt to sculpt her feelings (Art being her preferred mechanism for "processing" – she is her Intertidal father's daughter through and through).

Word of your burgeoning school reached us out here in the Atoll. In fact, I remember reading about it in a journal even before you wrote to me. Seeing your name brought up all sorts of unfortunate memories, though, so I did not keep up with the press. Pity, really. It sounds like you and your wife will accomplish much together. Henerey would have loved it. I am sure most people ill used by their Schools would. But especially my brother.

V.

P.S. I can assure you that what E. wrote about her childhood memory in the garden captured Henerey's heart in an instant. He likely read that passage out loud to himself. That was his way of "preserving" words that moved him. Do you share this memory with your sister?

AUTOMATED POST MISSIVE FROM SOPHY CIDNORGHE TO VYERIN CLEL, 1003

Dear Vyerin,

Please send my kindest and most uplifting sympathies to Avanne! (And to her fathers, who have been so diligent in her care!) At fifteen, I fell deeply in love with a friend, who promptly rejected me, and I was equally miserable. At the time, adults told me that it would pass, but it felt like death. Then it did pass, and I wish I had believed them. Such is youth!

S.

P.S. Achieving "quietude" was never among my priorities as a child! While E. spent her youthful days observing the sea's majesty, I imagine that I was out pushing my luck by the drop-off: defying my parents' concern for my safety in the hopes of surveying the local topography!

AUTOMATED POST MISSIVE FROM VYERIN CLEL TO SOPHY CIDNORGHE, 1003

S.,

O, yes, I know the sting of young love myself. For me, it was a girl I met in my first Apprenticeship year. We lost touch when I left the Academy and she stayed on. For the better, I think. We would have made a terrible pair – both with hearts full of sleeping fury that awoke at the slightest provocation. We fought constantly. (Every night now, as I fall asleep in Reiv's arms, I thank whatever strange stroke of luck brought a firebrand like me to the most level-headed, peaceful, and empathetic man in the known world.)

Vyerin

AUTOMATED POST MISSIVE FROM SOPHY CIDNORGHE TO VYERIN CLEL, 1003

Dear Vyerin,

What have I done to deserve this emotional honesty? I feel quite flattered that you trust me enough to share a personal anecdote.

In the spirit of shared intimacy (since I am sure you might be surprised to find that we have much more in common than the loss of our siblings):

What you said about your relationship with Reiv (and its comparison to the relationship that preceded it) could not better reflect my own experiences. I won't bore you with further insipid details about "my first love", but let it be known that were it not for the fact that her interests lay elsewhere, we would have also made a poor match in temperament.

My wife, on the other hand, is collected where I am anxious, fluid where I am obstinate, and sceptical where I am gullible. She has taught me – without even realising it! – how I might think more carefully, act more thoughtfully, and love more deeply. Perhaps I should thank her for giving me the mental tools necessary to survive the past year.

I hope you will continue to feel comfortable telling me whatever you like in the future. I truly welcome, enjoy, and learn from every letter you send me. And since you have been so generous, it is my turn to send you a parcel once again! (Keep an eye out for that.)

(Also, please do assure Avanne that she will find happiness one day too! But she might have to make a museum's worth of sculptures first.)

Sophy

P.S. Pardon my boldness, but I would not describe you at present as having a heart full of sleeping fury that wakes at the slightest provocation! (Or will this postscript be just the provocation you need to prove me wrong?)

AUTOMATED POST MISSIVE FROM VYERIN CLEL TO SOPHY CIDNORGHE, 1003

Dear Sophy,

Eloquent as always. I agree with all your closing points.

Perhaps my fury's all spent now – I must have burned through a lifetime's worth during the time after Henerey disappeared. Or perhaps it's what fuels me to keep living.

Just between you and me, I have not had much in the way of friendship (outside of Reiv, who is both Eternal Friend and Lover all at once) in many years. Being open with you is unexpectedly pleasant.

Though from one friend to another, I do feel that it's only fair that YOU share FURTHER "insipid details" of your ill-formed affections. Merely a suggestion. Solely for the purpose of providing additional context to your narrative, of course. For the sake of posterity.

Fondly,

Vyerin

AUTOMATED POST MISSIVE FROM SOPHY CIDNORGHE TO VYERIN CLEL, 1003

For the sake of posterity, I shall consider it.

Also: I hope you will henceforth consider it our narrative.

S.

Chapter 6

LETTER FROM ARVIST CIDNOSIN SENT IN TWO COPIES TO E. AND SOPHY CIDNOSIN, UNDATED (LIKELY 1002)

Dear sisters,

I have not written! O, however shall I atone? I ache, ACHE to see you both. Yesterday the Refectory served spirulina pie. I courageously helped myself to a plateful in the hopes of feeling at home, but I must confess I liked it just as little as I did when Father cooked it.

I absolutely thrill to think of us reuniting at the School of Inspiration's gala on the fourth day of the Second Perishing Tide. I am to be a featured performer! I know you, E., will fret and complain and say you dare not leave the house, but of course you must, and perhaps Sophy might have some difficulty arranging transport from the Ridge, but surely the Chancellors could not say no?

I can't keep it in any longer. Allow me to announce my engagement! We shall be very happy together. Alas – my time runs short. Fondest farewells!

Scholar Artistry "Arvist" Cidnosin

LETTER FROM E. CIDNOSIN TO ARVIST CIDNOSIN, 1002

Dear Arvist,

Is this some new kind of performance art? Please advise.

Your sister,

E. (and also Sophy, most likely, because I imagine her reaction will be much the same as mine!)

P.S. I have, at this point, sent you no fewer than seven letters inquiring about the unusual installation that you (according to Seliara) placed in our undergarden. Have you truly not received my communications? I am anxious for clarification!

LETTER FROM E. CIDNOSIN TO SOPHY CIDNOSIN, 1002

Dear Sophy!

I apologise for writing to you again – there is no pressure for you to respond, I promise! I know you are incredibly busy (and also hope that you are safe and well). And YET—

I assume that by the time you read this, you will have also read that – I would call it a "letter", but I think "pure nonsense captured in pen-and-ink form" might be more apt – well, that announcement, anyway, from our brother. Who in all the seas decided to bind their life to HIM? At this point, absolutely anything seems possible – perhaps the oceans shall dry and leave us surrounded by nothing but immeasurable canyons and dying fish gulping at air! Perhaps you shall become a famous painter! Perhaps I will be betrothed next! (No, let's not stretch the boundaries of possibility that far.)

O how I wish you were here to share in the perplexity and giggle over this whole affair with me. (And in the utterly unlikely event that you were granted shore leave long enough to attend Arvist's ... function, I

61

would brave even the greatest crowds of the Atoll Campus myself just to see you!)

Yours breathlessly,

E.

P.S. I desperately wish that Arvist would respond to my queries about the mysterious "bowl"/Structure/whatever it may be. I cannot stop thinking about it, and the more that I ruminate about the fact that he produced it without my knowledge, the more my thoughts race about other things that I have missed. I have checked the house thoroughly each day ever since, as I might have mentioned, but I continue to feel overwhelmed with worry and feel convinced that because I am apparently so oblivious to what is happening in my own garden I have somehow missed the telltale signs of some other kind of damage to the house and I lose myself in thoughts of how the windows may burst and Mother's beautiful lattice-work coloured-glass designs will be lost forever as I drown, all because I was not paying close enough attention. I have written to Dr Lyelle, but I find myself fretting that she will only receive my letter long after I have already perished due to my own foolish errors.

Other than that, all is well!

LETTER FROM SOPHY CIDNOSIN TO E. CIDNOSIN, 1002

Dear, dear E.!

Firstly! Clearly our brother is engaged to Seliara, is he not? Whom else could it possibly be? Perhaps her love of Linguistic Alchemy softened her resolve to find the perfect partner.

Arvist's asinine display of spectacle makes me wish to contrive a way of stealing the spotlight. O, if only I could announce an engagement! (I mean, I suppose I could if I deigned to encourage the affections of Schr Vincenebras, who greets me with a florid compliment whenever our paths cross.)

Regardless of our brother's flamboyant insensitivity, E., it pains me to see you suffering. I never know exactly what to say – I cannot use logic to argue with that part of your brain that tells you these things, just as you cannot.

But o, an idea has come to me! Since I am not there to help you prove scientifically that there is nothing wrong with the House – and because you seem to be particularly bold these days about writing to scholars! – I might suggest that you reach out to Mother's old Architect friend Schr Alestarre (dear old Jeime – do you remember?). It's been too long since we saw her, anyway!

I know you are also wary of inviting strangers into our home, but she's not truly a stranger, and she had such a gentle demeanour and proved extraordinarily kind to us as children (though I was but very small then – I imagine you might have even more memories of her). At any rate, you could write and say that you would love for her to inspect the premises for damage – because we have lacked a true Architect's opinion since we lost Mother – and perhaps she may relieve your worries. In fact, I might even go so far as to strongly recommend that you invite Jeime over, but that choice remains yours to make.

Perhaps your mood has lifted even more since you responded to Scholar Clel's letter, as I assume you have by now? I can hardly count the number of times I have tried to convince you that occasional conversation with a kindred spirit can cure most ills.

I suspect you will consider what I will write next to be an ill itself, so I am even more eager for you to distract yourself with a budding friendship.

The objectively good news first: our first few dives outside of the station were incredibly successful. I began the arduous process of measuring and surveying the contours of the seafloor that surrounds us, Irye engaged in all manner of sonic experimentation, and even Ylaret (who finally took her turn after kindly sitting out the first dive!) cannot cease her chattering about the relationships between currents and constellations. I thought Eliniea would be especially elated, as she's been swimming after an impressive variety of ferocious fish with great enthusiasm, but I sense that she is troubled.

Perhaps Eliniea worries about the next stage in our investigation, which she presented to the team earlier this morning. She missed our regular breakfast engagement, but I cannot fault her – she had much to prepare! At the behest of Chancellor Rawsel, Eliniea recommended we depart the Spheres for a multi-day "field study" – we will not return to the station until the middle of next tide. The object of such an enterprise, Eliniea told us, is to gain a greater sense of what the Ridge is like in a particular surrounding radius . . . and I must admit that it will help my Wayfinding project immensely!

To enable each of us to research independently, we will not take the capsule: instead, we will simply set off in our diving gear and spend the evenings in what Eliniea refers to as—a "Bubble"? It is rather like a portable depth-craft, if you can imagine such a thing. It can be stored in one's pack and then "assembled" in the manner of a dry-tent when one reaches an intended destination. I remain most anxious to see how it works! We shall swim until we grow weary, set up shelter where we can, and rest in the middle of the abyss until we can travel further.

I cannot say I am especially keen on this journey. The experience of being suspended in these fathomless waters – protected by nothing but the second skin of the diving suit – is like no other. It is silent, save for the crackling of our audio communicators and the pulsing of that all-too fragile equipment that keeps us alive. The abject darkness makes the water feel heavier than usual – or perhaps that is simply the incomprehensible amount of pressure against which our suits fortunately guard us – and I fear that if I were to close my eyes and really think about where I am, I would collapse under the weight of it all. On each of our dives so far, I partnered with Eliniea due to the exceptional brightness of her organism-attracting lamps: they streak the shadows with a rainbow array of coloured light, bringing me some comfort. The creatures that dance into her beams are small, opportunistic ones – little fish with bulging, unseeing eyes, shrimp with dazzling carapaces, and all manner of miniature monsters that no one save Eliniea ever studied before.

It comforts me less to think of the larger specimens that may, one day, swim near us, seduced by those lights just like their smaller prey ...

O, E., do not trouble yourself – I am simply being overdramatic to entertain you, just like Arvist telling eerie stories when Mother and Father were away of an evening! Really, I look forward to our journey – an adventure like no other.

I promise to write to you as soon as I can. In fact, I intend to bring some writing materials with me and will jot down my thoughts on a nightly basis when we are safely ensconced in our "Bubbles", and then send you the whole saga when we return! It saddens me to think of missing letters from you for such a long period of time, and especially when so much is afoot in the Deep House!

Take care of yourself, please remember to sleep, and do not allow thoughts of me or Arvist or anyone else to burden you.

Yours in anticipation,

Sophy

P.S. For your continued entertainment, I have attached a copy of our second public communication. Going forward, I shall strive not to speak overmuch of Schr Vincenebras in my letters, simply because he does more than enough of that for himself in these missives ... (He does lift our spirits, though, in his ridiculous way. I cannot help but feel affection for him. For all my colleagues, really.)

THE RIDGE REVEALED, ISSUE 2, RECORDED BY SCHR VINCENEBRAS

Dear Colleagues,

If my long absence troubled you in any way, take heart! – your Crew has been well and in the highest of spirits (which is rather paradoxical, considering that our depth-position makes us about as practically low as one can get).

In the days since our auspicious arrival, our exceptional team settled in and began the delightful process of surveying the Ridge we now call home.

Let me pause a moment for some SEMANTIC CLARIFICATION:

Coined by our superlative leader Scholar Eliniea Hayve Forghe, "the Ridge" refers to the particular cliff-like expanse of seafloor that borders (what we believe to be) the deepest trench in our Vast Oceans. It stretches countless fathoms in every direction, but we sit on its very edge – overlooking the abyss *within* the abyss that is greater than any one of us may comprehend!

Yet it is such comprehension to which we aspire, naturally. Equipped with Diving Technology that far exceeds even the wildest dreams of Your Humble Writer, we will now survey all aspects of this underwater world in a manner previously thought impossible.

But rather than beg you to take my word for it, I will turn to my colleague, Scholar Irye Rux of Atoll Campus, who will summarise the intriguing aural phenomena of our new home.

INTERVIEW WITH SCHOLAR IRYE RUX

Scholar Vincenebras: Scholar Rux, you have my thanks for joining us today!

Scholar Rux: I was not aware that I could refuse this interview, my
dear fellow, but I appreciate the gratitude nonetheless.

Vincenebras: Naturally, our audience desperately looks forward to
hearing you discuss your most recent discoveries in document-
ing the *sounds* of the Ridge.

Rux: Perhaps. Considering that this interview will be distributed
in print form, however, I somehow highly doubt that anyone
will be able to listen to our conversation.

Vincenebras: Please regale us with tales of the unusual noises you've
been transcribing since our mission began.

Rux: What's unusual is that there is really only one sound of note.

Vincenebras: Then you clearly haven't witnessed Scholar Forghe and Scholar Cidnosin chuckling together at jokes they refuse to share . . .

Rux: I prepared a copy of my most recent Sonic Chart for your enjoyment. *(DEAR READERS, this is the point at which Schr Rux showed me the chart! There were many lines upon it! – Vincenebras)* The variations that you can see are mostly identifiable – like, for example, the occasional distant vocalisations of a Melodious Toothed Whale.

Vincenebras: So you find these whale songs – *note*worthy?

Rux: You misunderstand entirely. There is only one noteworthy sound *besides* the whales, other familiar creatures, and everything anthropogenic, such as the generators for our station.

Vincenebras: For our readers' sakes alone – *I* understand you completely, of course – would you please elaborate?

Rux: I have, on a daily basis, encountered a deep, resonant, rhythmic *Bloorb* that seems to commence and halt at regular intervals.

Vincenebras: A—Bloorb, you say?

Rux: We have only been here for a short while, so my evidence is not yet conclusive. I wonder if there might be multiple sources – whether it is caused by some manner of geological movement in the vent or beneath the seafloor or . . .

Vincenebras: How utterly extraordinary!

Rux: That is one possibility.

Vincenebras: Well, Scholar Rux, on behalf of our dear subscribers, let me thank you for sharing your expertise with us. I am very eager to see how this develops.

Rux: Now we finally have something in common.

Though I'm sure you, our beloved readers, cannot wait to hear more about Schr Rux's discoveries, I must away for now – the glories of Research (and the Bloorb) await!

Yours soundly,

Schr Vincenebras

LETTER FROM E. CIDNOSIN TO SOPHY CIDNOSIN, 1002

My dear Sophy,

Would you believe that I nearly cried when I spied your handwriting on the envelope this time around? I have felt especially bereft of you of late. Though I tried to fill the void caused by your absence through various means – removing a truly impressive amount of aggressive algae from our interior walls and occasionally taking the time to sketch some coral polyps from memory, for example – naught compares to your (distant) company.

I will say nothing else about your upcoming research expedition except for this: you are so brave, sensible, and inspiring, and you have all my love as always.

Speaking of love in its various forms, I suppose you must be correct in your assumption about the victim of Arvist's "engagement". I simply cannot accept that she did not tell me more openly of their love when we last spoke. Then again, it has been a long while since I felt truly close to Seliara – perhaps I am to blame. What do they talk about? I wonder. Are they each other's muses? Will Arvist become an acolyte of Linguistic Alchemy? Given the history involved, I am not surprised that your response to this development was so terse, but please know that I am happy to listen if you ever would like to explore your feelings further.

I appreciate your "recommendation" to contact Schr Alestarre; I

certainly do. I do remember Jeime with fondness. Am I correct in recalling that she took you, me, Seliara, and Arvist on our first depth-craft
ride past the drop-off? I don't suppose any of us were older than ten.
How the great blue darkness terrified Seliara! (How sad that nowadays
I would be the one to cower as my Brain convinced me of the very
many ways in which I might somehow make a fatal error aboard the
depth-craft that would result in the deaths of everyone I care about . . .)
As pleasing as it is to reminisce about happier times with Mother and
Father, I do not know if I dare ask Jeime's advice. The thought of
seeing someone – without you here to calm me and strengthen me as
you always do – makes me feel quite ill. For your dear sake, however, I
will consider it.

O, dear Sophy, please keep your wits about you as you descend
into the abyss! (If one can descend even more than you already have,
of course.) If I go out into the garden and call your name into the
water, might it appear as another unidentifiable sound on Schr Rux's
hydrophone?

Until we write again,

E.

AUTOMATED POST MISSIVE FROM SOPHY CIDNORGHE TO VYERIN CLEL, 1003

Dear Vyerin,

You might notice some indecipherable scribbles – abstract clouds of
ink, really – at the end of E.'s last letter. I can guess at the word "Scholar"
within this self-censored postscript. Perhaps she expressed a fear that
Henerey would not respond to her again, but then grew too embarrassed
to send it to me. She must therefore have been delighted to receive the
following letter (enclosed) soon afterwards . . .

Sophy

AUTOMATED POST MISSIVE FROM VYERIN CLEL TO SOPHY CIDNORGHE, YEAR 1003

Dear Sophy,

I wish I could have reassured E. that Henerey has – as a matter of personal pride – never left a letter unanswered in his life. (This made him a fitting rival for our relatives on my father's side, who behaved similarly. In a particularly notable period of correspondence, I believe Henerey and our uncle exchanged more than three hundred letters – each simply thanking the recipient for his "previous note".)

Vyerin

LETTER FROM HENEREY CLEL TO E. CIDNOSIN, 1002

Dear Schr E.,

I intended to take my time crafting the perfect reply for you – I even drafted a charming introduction in which I attributed my delayed response to your distractingly enchanting description of your family's garden! (That introduction was sincere, I assure you. I could easily lose a great deal of time rereading your words. I suppose, though, that "lose" is the wrong word, as I gained so much from them.)

Yet here I am merely a few days later writing you something altogether hastier and less eloquent. I should probably confess from the start that I am not feeling entirely myself of late and made the ill-judged decision of spending the night in the Library Anchorage (instead of retreating home for much-needed rest, as most self-preserving individuals might!). It does make me feel rather like an overworked Apprentice – perhaps you remember from your siblings' experiences on campus that the library connects to the Docked Dormitories via an underwater tunnel for easy access, so Apprentices can visit the stacks at any hour of the night. I am sure you care little about the everyday melodramas of the Boundless

Campus, so it suffices to say that recent circumstances have made me feel rather less motivated and more disengaged from my colleagues than usual. How can this place be so different from the Atoll School of Observation in which I came of age? I was about to write that these emotions are relatively new to me, but after consulting my daybook, I was surprised to find that I have felt similarly ever since I joined my new Campus. (I hope you do not find it odd that I make a habit of recording my emotions. Sometimes they can get the better of me if I do not watch myself carefully, so it is useful to take notes.)

Fortunately, I happen to have two very delightful pastimes that help me detach from my troubles and enjoy myself thoroughly. The Department plays no role in them! The first (as my presence in the library might suggest!) is my private and thoroughly amateurish fascination with Antepelagic Fantasies. Yes, how funny it is that I, Henerey Clel, a Natural Historian who has spent his life studying tangible, observable, knowable phenomena, passes every free hour reading up on those fictional tales of adventure that imagine the sky-world before the Dive and bring richness to our rigid, Scholarly lives. It is a testament to how sympathetic I find your letters that I dare mention this at all – since I have often been treated with derision for enjoying something so nebulous and illogical.

Regardless of your own interest in fantastic stories from the past, I think you will find the subject of my inquiry intriguing: ever since you mentioned those Elongated Fish, I have found myself drawn to historical accounts of strange sea-life encounters! And when traditional Scholarly literature failed me on this subject, I turned towards my beloved stories. Sadly, progress eludes me thus far. The best match at present is an anecdote recorded over four hundred years ago that accompanies a small woodcut print of massively lengthy Eel (?) circling an unknown landmass.

I swear to you that I shall continue my hunt tonight and into the future and let you know if I discover even the most miniscule clue! As the late Scholar Kenven Darbeni (a personal favourite of mine) once wrote, "even amid an abyssal sea we may still encounter a lonesome phosphorescence", and I feel I can see this metaphorical light reflecting off the walls of the library as I search for a source that can give us some clarity.

Now I must (rather bashfully!) reveal that the second pastime bringing me peace in these trying times is our correspondence. You seem to think your life dull in comparison to mine, yet I would give anything to spend my days gazing out of the Deep House portholes at endless passing creatures, or even counting bubbles and checking for leaks as necessity dictates! (Your maintenance responsibilities must be numerous, and you must therefore be incredibly diligent! I admire that quality greatly.) I must, unfortunately, disavow you of any romantic misconceptions about the life of a Natural Historian. I spend almost no time "in the field" these days: as my Department has quite suddenly and vocally changed its priorities from those that complement my own. ~~A short time ago, Chancellor Orelith Rawsel delivered a most hurtful missive that~~

My apologies: I did say I would try to spare you the melodrama! Please disregard those inexpertly crossed-out words.

Instead, if you will indulge me by reading a little further, I will return your kindness in describing your childhood by telling you a little about mine. Had I been raised as you were, spending all my time underwater, I wonder if it would have amplified my own interests in the marine world or stymied them through over-familiarity.

You see, growing up on the Atoll, I was as far from water as anyone can be! My father is a Scholar of Wayfinding and my parent a Scholar of Life, and both study natural resources of the Atoll. And only the Atoll. Consequently, my family rarely ventured to the coastline.

But, when we did: what specimens I brought back from those trips! My beloured, land-favouring parents quickly found themselves raising two boys fascinated with the sea. As if my budding Scholar of Classification's sensibility was not enough, Vyerin, my brother, developed an interest in coastal Wayfinding and Navigation. Yet since those days, I find that the unadulterated curiosity about the world I possessed in my youth has diminished into a more subdued and socially acceptable "academic interest".

That is, until you sent me your sketch in your first letter – it seemed animated by the vibrant intellectual energy now lost to me as a so-called "Scholar".

So perhaps that is why I feel so compelled to fling word upon word at you as the hour grows later and the overnight library attendant eyes me with unmasked disapproval. Though I dare not say that I wish I were not a Scholar, I have felt of late a desire to escape to—to—well, somewhere else, and at present, I can think of no better elsewhere than the world you inhabit.

Before I embarrass myself further, I should mention that my extensive response should in no way force you to reply with similar verbosity. As you yourself addressed in your last letter, I understand that not responding promptly does not necessarily suggest disinterest. Shall we call a truce, and both pledge that we shall ignore any temporal lapses in our conversation? (Though I do secretly hope they will not be too lengthy.)

Yours with excitement,

Henerey (if I may sign off this way? Surely we have exchanged enough letters now to qualify as "acquainted" by Boundless standards?)
P.S. O! How could I forget to mention that I included a fair copy I made of the aforementioned Eel anecdote! I made a tracing of the image, too. I hope you will forgive its clumsiness. I received artistic training as part of my studies, and can therefore get by due to my experience, but I lack talent! (We are perfect foils for each other artistically, in this sense.)
P.P.S. Regarding the aforementioned fair copy of the aforementioned text—

Perhaps you will think less of me, but I must admit that I take peculiar delight in examining the writing habits of our ancestors. Before the Campuses standardised shorthand orthography, language was a much more creative affair, don't you think?

(I will not be offended if you do not think so.)

H.

EXCERPT FROM "THE GREATE FISHE", 1002

"Many Saye that our Seas host many Hostile Creatures well Vaste. As a Childe heard I once that Greate Fishe Swam the Shallowes just before the Seas Shook. These Fishe stretched more than three Fathoms from Tip to Taile. Some say that these Fishe could be seen by those on Ships passing from Afar – and they thought them Moving Bridges."

AUTOMATED POST MISSIVE FROM VYERIN CLEL TO SOPHY CIDNORGHE, 1003

Dear Sophy,

How funny to read my own biography. We enjoyed a wonderful youth, all things considered. Though I was the eldest, Henerey surpassed me in nearly every skill as soon as he was old enough to speak. Perhaps some would find this infuriating. Not I. I took delight in both learning from him and using my age, height, and considerably superior understanding of social niceties to protect him when I could.

Speaking of sociability – I am sure you will not be surprised to find that my brother struggled to "mingle", or "connect with peers", or "build constructive professional relationships", as you Boundless folk so enjoy doing. With that in mind, it is remarkable how forthcoming, personal, and honest he is in these messages to E. I make a show of mocking my poor husband for his earnest belief in "predestined partners", or the notion that each of us has a perfect match somewhere – but I must confess that I already cannot imagine someone better suited to my brother than your sister. (And, OF COURSE, no one better suited to ME than REIV CLEL – just in case you walk by my desk and glance at the unfinished draft of this letter, my dear fellow!)

Forgive me – this is the first time in ages that I have engaged in so much "reminiscence", or whatever it is called. Such a strange practice. I hope this letter finds you well. As usual, I am very grateful for all that you send me. I feel like a poor collaborator, as I have only a few scraps here and there that can illuminate tiny corners in the vast seascape of history you have assembled. But I shall keep an eye on the dates of your documents and will offer more contributions when the time is right.

Many thanks,

Vyerin

P.S. I thought you might be pleased to know that Avanne is in better spirits lately. Today she crafted a rather lovely and functional vase with her clay instead of her typical output (masks painted with an ocean of teardrop patterns that look wet enough to melt the glaze). In typical Proud Father fashion, Reiv immediately filled the vase with water only to realise that we will need to acquire a kiln if we hope to use Avanne's creations on a daily basis without inviting calamity. Fortunately, the loss of her first vase tormented Avanne less than the loss of her first relationship.

P.P.S. By the by, I wondered how long it would take before Henerey quoted my old nemesis SCHOLAR KENVEN DARBENI to E. How unfortunate. I used to block my ears with my hands and scream gently every time Henerey mentioned that sycophantic Scholar (which was seemingly every other minute). What did my brother find so charming about Darbeni's dull aphorisms?

AUTOMATED POST MISSIVE FROM SOPHY CIDNORGHE TO VYERIN CLEL, 1003

Dear Vyerin,

How many times must I assert that I enjoy reading your letters? (And simply value you, for that matter?) I shall continue doing so until the truth sinks in, you stubborn sailor. It is not as though I have a vast circle of friends and companions eager to assemble and analyse letters written by my missing sister, after all! (Or a vast circle of friends and companions at all, I should say.)

But I will take inspiration from your daughter and try to be more positive.

O! I am neglecting the most important revelation of those past few letters! Dear Vyerin, why did you not tell me that you studied as a Scholar of Wayfinding in your apprenticeship? I suppose you were at Atoll Campus with Henerey before he was transferred, so our paths would not have crossed, but still . . .

With all my best wishes,

Sophy

P.S. I fear you never will, but if you dared to write to Arvist, I'm sure he might have a kiln connection for Avanne to exploit.

P.P.S. Darbeni quotes were beloved in the Cidnosin household, so you'll find no sympathy from me. Do you not appreciate Darbeni's quirkiness, and how he rebelled against Scholarly standards with his oddly formulaic writing? I suppose you will simply have to put up with it – perhaps he will even grow on you. "Even the most rigid rock-face must one day yield to the advances of erosion," you know.

AUTOMATED POST MISSIVE FROM VYERIN CLEL TO SOPHY CIDNORGHE, 1003

S.,

As a captain, I navigate for a living. What else do you think I would have studied (and failed in) if not Wayfinding? Something from the School of Inspiration, perhaps?

I appreciate your postscripted suggestion, but will predictably decline to contact Arvist – I am already far too occupied with the finest of Cidnosin correspondents. If you managed to convince him to discreetly ship a kiln to my location with no questions asked, on the other hand . . .

I shall not even deign to acknowledge your second postscript.

V.

AUTOMATED POST MISSIVE FROM SOPHY CIDNORGHE TO VYERIN CLEL, 1003

Captain Vyerin, I shall accept your mockery without complaint because I am simply so excited to correspond with one who shares my love of Maps! What a glorious discovery!

AUTOMATED POST MISSIVE FROM VYERIN CLEL TO SOPHY CIDNORGHE, 1003

"Even a new-hatched fish knows the seas better than the learned Wayfinder."

Chapter 7

LETTER FROM E. CIDNOSIN TO SELIARA GIDNAN, 1002

Dear Seliara,

Have you been so preoccupied with the thrills of Linguistic Alchemy – pardon me, I mean so preoccupied with research – pardon me again, I truly mean so preoccupied with your surprise betrothal to my brother – that you lost all sense of time since last we met? Or have you simply decided to try out reclusiveness in a competitive attempt to outshine my own antisocial nature?

I jest. I do, however, miss your company, and hope that you might do me a favour by dining with me on any date convenient to you. (I will once again attempt to cook.) In full disclosure, I will confess that Sophy's expedition and recent events have left me feeling somewhat bereft of human company: a feeling I never thought I might experience.

Also, I do wish you had told me about Arvist, but I suppose I am happy for you.

With many pre-emptive thanks,

E.

LETTER FROM JEIME ALESTARRE TO E. CIDNOSIN, 1002

Dear E., if I may,

I hope this letter does not come as an unpleasant surprise. A few tides ago I received a card from your sister. I felt so privileged to hear from her while she's so busy with the Ridge. Her note revealed little, but suggested that you might want to schedule an assessment of the Deep House sometime in the future. I would be honoured.

But first, I do want to apologise for losing touch with you since your mother passed away. (I expressed a similar sentiment in my letter to Sophy.) I felt lost when we lost her. I do not want to make you feel uncomfortable or reawaken your grief, but if you desire my help in any way, please know that I am fully at your disposal. It would be no trouble at all. In fact, I once promised your mother that I would always assist with Cidnosin family matters if called upon, and I do pride myself on keeping my word. I remember all too fondly the days past I spent in (and around) the Deep House with your delightful family (whom I so boldly and so often considered my own).

Your friend,

Jeime (Schr Alestarre)

LETTER FROM SELIARA GIDNAN TO E. CIDNOSIN, 1002

Dear dear dear E.,

Sending you blessings and apologies and asking for forgiveness please! I assumed you had already heard or suspected about Arvist and myself, as clever as you are. He insists we must not fix a wedding date sooner than next year because such an event will require tides and tides of "Dynamic Creative Preparations", which means there will be ample opportunity for everyone to come around to the idea. Let me dine with you in three days' time and hope that we can make amends quite sincerely, for I would be so happy to be as Sisters with you—

With many embraces,

Seliara

LETTER FROM E. CIDNOSIN TO JEIME ALESTARRE, 1002

Dear Jeime,

I must admit that I would not have contacted you had my sister not forced my hand. I am impressed that you remember me, since I was but a girl (and rather less troubled by my Brain as I am now) when we last crossed paths. Sometimes I wonder if the rest of the campuses knows the Cidnosins as a perfect family of four – two Scholars who begat two more Scholars, never mind that "other one" who never leaves the Deep House.

In any case, your letter immediately conjured up the sound of your voice speaking in endless exclamations to Mother as you two gushed over aquadynamics and innovation!

Do not blame yourself for losing touch. She would not wish you to. I am simply happy to renew our acquaintance.

Let me cut straight to the point. If it suits you, I intend to dine with a friend (perhaps you remember Seliara: the girl, now grown, from the research vessel *Alacrity*?) three days from now and wonder if you would care to join us.

Until soon, I hope,

E.

AUTOMATED POST MISSIVE FROM SOPHY CIDNORGHE TO VYERIN CLEL, 1003

Dear Vyerin,

Hello again! What a whirlwind of short letters!

You might wonder how I possess a copy of a letter E. sent to Jeime. I did not know if I could manage it, and did not wish to make any promises that I could not keep, HOWEVER, I am happy to announce the following:

Two days ago, I wrote to Jeime Alestarre to introduce our "project", and asked if she had anything to share – and she did!

Because I mentioned the date that you and I had reached in our discussion, Jeime also sent along a copy of some pages from her personal diary that describe her meeting with E. and Seliara. What a wonderful primary source. I feel so thankful for the coincidental archival fastidiousness of our family friend (and her generosity in giving us something so personal).

Excitedly,

Sophy

AUTOMATED POST MISSIVE FROM VYERIN CLEL TO SOPHY CIDNORGHE, 1003

Dear Sophy,

Your boundless energy for this enterprise is appreciated, as usual. It is oddly convenient that your friend already had such documents assembled.

Vyerin

P.S. Was it uncharacteristic for E. to make social plans with not one but two people at such short notice? She must have been very concerned about getting Jeime to look at the house!

AUTOMATED POST MISSIVE FROM SOPHY CIDNORGHE TO VYERIN CLEL, 1003

Dear V.,

Less convenient is that Jeime does not use Automated Post, and when I followed up to ask if she would be willing to share more journal entries in the future, she did not respond.

I shall have to press further. I am shameless, you see.

S.

P.S. Regarding your question, I suspect this was E.'s attempt at taking care of two problems at once – dealing with the Arvist and Seliara revelation, and re-meeting an old friend – at the urging of Dr Lyelle. From what I heard from E., the good doctor never pushed her to do things that caused her anxiety, but tried to offer solutions that would help her come face-to-face with her fears in a secure fashion. In this case, Seliara's presence would alleviate E.'s fear of entertaining Jeime, while Jeime's presence would spare E. from dealing with Seliara going on and on about her love for Arvist for too long.

(And, by the way, though you would never guess it, E.'s "social stamina" for encounters with those rare people she trusted and appreciated was actually remarkably strong as well – when I spent time with her, I could hardly get a word in edgewise!)

FROM THE DIARY OF JEIME ALESTARRE, 1002

So, I kept my word and joined E. at the Deep House on Second Day of the Second Superlative Tide in the Second Quarter of High Waters, sometime around four bells. When I told Min of my plans, she cheekily suggested I ask Schr Elvo to give me a lift to my evening engagement. (After last week's escapades, no one would deny that Elvo owed me!) Min is better than I deserve.

The Deep House looked exactly as I remembered it. I expected that the sight of the house would make me weep ceaselessly; I did not expect that emotional deluge to occur as soon as I reached the small depth-craft on the water's surface that carries visitors down to Ami's greatest creation. During my descent, I took the opportunity to dry my tears and pull myself together, with mixed results.

Any ground I gained in suppressing my emotions was lost when the airlock door opened and I saw her – E., that is, but also a living portrait of Ami, with the family resemblance clear in every feature. Yet in her eyes I saw and in her speech I heard that same unabashed inquisitiveness and unbridled enthusiasm that I too felt in my younger years. Seeing E. while I suffered from this unexpected influx of motherly feelings makes me wonder what would have happened if—but no, I dare not even write that tragic thought here.

I recognised her companion, Seliara, too. At first part of me resented the other young woman's gregariousness, as E. could barely speak a word in between her friend's bursts of speech. Yet as our evening progressed and I noticed the grins and nods exchanged between them when they thought I looked elsewhere, I realised that E. appreciated Seliara's conversational dominance, since it spared her the burden of sustaining our discussion.

As the end of the meal drew nearer, E. appeared to grow restless and perhaps even troubled. Her hands never stopped moving. She would raise her glass to her lips again and again, even though there was nothing left in it to drink. She stood up to move our forks into the kitchen before bringing them back out again. I did my best to nod along to Seliara's companionable chatter, but I found E.'s frantic activities nearly impossible to ignore. At last, when our conversation reached a pause, E. stood up and gestured towards the door, asking if I might take a turn about the house with her.

The review of the interior went well enough – a few fittings on the south airlock had come loose, and E. was a quick study as I showed her how to screw them back into place. Nothing alarming. Then I begged a spare dive suit, and E. produced a perfectly maintained Scribel Silver

Seas model that was just my size. Based on what I can recall of the Cidnosin siblings' various personalities, I assume it belongs to Sophy. (And one wonders – if Sophy left a Silver Seas suit at home, what did she take with her on her expedition?)

With Seliara hanging back to put the finishing touches on a dessert she had brought along, E. and I dived together into that reef that I used to know so well.

And even now, even here, in my private musings written several hours after my experience – I still do not know how to record what it was I saw. That Structure—

I dare not even ponder it all. How I wish Ami were still here.

AUTOMATED POST MISSIVE FROM VYERIN CLEL TO SOPHY CIDNORGHE, 1003

Dear Sophy,

I find myself very intrigued and cannot wait to read whatever other materials Schr Alestarre shares with you (if she does). To think that even she, a seasoned Scholar, found Arvist's odd installation startling! I do not enjoy mysteries and anomalies – it is only since my life has been changed irrevocably by them that I must contend with the unknown.

Now I must ask you something altogether awkward. Were your mother and Jeime, you know, "involved"? There is a great deal of grief and affection in this letter.

(Also, though it seems unbelievable that someone would censor themselves in their own private journal, I understand why Jeime-of-the-past did not clarify her thoughts about the sculpture – because Henerey would have done the same! He famously refused to write down anything significant in his journals because "you never know what future Scholar might read them".)

I do hope you will let me lighten the mood (so to speak) with a letter from E. to Henerey. At the very least, I will be happy to escape that Structure for a few more pages!

Anxiously,

V.

P.S. I see why you left the Silver Seas suit at home. Got one as a thank-you from a sailing client once. It appears that the amount of money one pays for a high-end diving suit is directly proportional to how uncomfortable it is.

AUTOMATED POST MISSIVE FROM SOPHY CIDNORGHE TO VYERIN CLEL, 1003

Dear Vyerin,

I will admit that Jeime's diary set me rather on edge myself – simply because she is one of the most learned individuals I know, and I cannot imagine something flummoxing her! How I wish to have a proper conversation to see if she can clarify anything about what happened at the Deep House last year. If she does not reply to my letter soon, I may have to send her a second (or a third) . . .

In the meantime, you know I always welcome the opportunity to read a letter from E.

I hope that odd Structure will not end up haunting your nightmares. Will it comfort you to know that it is truly gone from this world – likely blown to a thousand pieces along with the Deep House? Now, if it turns out that a structure can produce a spectre after it is destroyed, I will truly become concerned.

Comfortingly,

Sophy

P.S. Though it makes me a little uncomfortable, I admit that you make a fair point about my mother and Jeime – or at least about Jeime's feelings for my mother. They did study in the same Department as Apprentice Scholars – that's how they met – perhaps they courted each other back then? And, again, that is all the speculation I shall do about my mother's romantic history! (That may also explain why Jeime sent me only this single, puzzling excerpt: did the rest of her diary entry contain more effusive sentiments about my mother that she feared I would find awkward to read?) As far as I know, Jeime is now recently engaged to Scholar Minerin Ili (presumably the "Min" from this journal entry), so I am glad, at least, that she found happiness in the present.

P.P.S. Because you might wonder – and are likely too tactful to ask – our Father still lives, but as you may have seen in a previous letter from E., he has been in "Scholarly Seclusion" ever since Mother died. This might be a uniquely Boundless practice, so I shall explain further. Essentially, a Scholar who is overwhelmed with shame or grief (or, in some rarer cases, boredom) might Vow to spend an indeterminate amount of time on a solitary ship with no navigational capacities (but ample fishing, cooking, and water distillation supplies) that simply drifts wherever the currents carry it. But after he first left us, I employed Current Calculation to determine the approximate radius in which his vessel might float, based on his starting location, so E. and I occasionally sent him letters via commissioned mail-boat. That was more for our benefit than his, of course – he never responded.

I hoped E.'s disappearance might coax him into returning home, but it has only worsened his self-induced exile. Instead of writing to tell him about the quake, I booked a boat and went to find him myself at one point – and when I finally did, news of this second mourning seemed to destroy him. He embraced me, then muttered that he could not stay and picked up an oar he'd fashioned from driftwood that might propel him towards new horizons.

AUTOMATED POST MISSIVE FROM VYERIN CLEL TO SOPHY CIDNORGHE, 1003

Dear Sophy,

Thank you for telling me about your father. I am sorry.

If you ever wish to seek him out again one day, please recall that I know a thing or two about boats.

Vyerin

LETTER FROM E. CIDNOSIN TO HENEREY CLEL, 1002

Dear ~~Schr Cl~~ Henerey (yes, I decided to preserve my mistake instead of starting afresh on new paper so that you may witness how much I struggled to drop your proper honorific! I do it only out of respect for your preferences).

A few days ago, my sister departed the Spheres to embark on a perilous field study that will prevent her from sending me letters with any regularity. I assumed this hiatus from familial correspondence would lead to my despondence. Yet here I am, happily taking up pen and ink to write to you instead while in relatively good spirits. Like you (I'm sorry to say!), I find myself adrift in some challenging times, and decided that the unique nature of the connection you and I share may help me sail through them. I hope you will pardon the intimacy.

In any case, as I mentioned, my sister's most recent letter revealed that she is about to commence her first extended foray outside the (relative) safety of the Spheres down below. This development makes me less inclined to trouble Sophy with my own issues, as they seem rather insignificant in comparison to the taxing experience of surveying the very bottom of the ocean. I appreciate that she takes the time to write to me and share so much about her observations, and the people with whom she spends her days – but I am jealous of them, Henerey! It is pitiful and cruel of me to want to keep my sister to myself, I know. Though she has always been my closest friend and confidante, I will never allow myself to share these feelings with her, out of fear that she would worry for me and return home – which must not happen! (Thanks to your letters, I know that you have a brother, and I wonder if you have ever had a similar experience in your relationship with him?)

Yet with no Sophy to turn to, I feel especially comfortable sharing my puzzling circumstance with you, because you revealed in your last letter that you possess exactly the expertise I might need! Will it surprise you to know that I, too, am fond of Fantasies? Yes – though Mother always purported to find them dull and mentally unstimulating, Father encouraged each of us, in turns, to read one of these imaginings about the early ages of the sky-world every night. Whenever I remember that a thousand years ago, our Society lived in the clouds, on hovering islands bigger than the Atoll, never even daring to sink lower into the atmosphere and see the seas below – well, when I think about that, it fills me with the very essence of Sublimity. (I enjoyed particularly those belief-defying stories of the Star Sailors, and their legendary ascent into the sky beyond the sky in crafts powered by their own thoughts . . .)

Given our shared interests, then, I think you will understand better than anyone that my present situation does not exactly follow the rules of logic.

I will end this dance of delicate suggestion and move onto the point. Several tides ago, I noticed a structure of unusual size and unknown provenance just outside of the carefully cultivated section of the reef under the Deep House that we consider our garden. I assumed that my brother, artist that he is, must have constructed it without my knowledge, and that unsettled me. He refused to respond to any of my correspondence about the matter (or any other matter, for that matter). This would have all been in keeping with my brother's character, but the situation changed dramatically yesterday.

Last evening, Schr Jeime Alestarre (an Architect) stopped by to examine the workings of the Deep House. Schr Alestarre is a family friend, extraordinarily dear to my mother, and even as a child I considered her to be impeccably and unapproachably clever. Yet the "Structure" seemed to make her quake in surprise! When I told her it was but a silly project of my brother's, she locked eyes with me and shook her head – and as the bright water reflected on her helm, I could detect great anxiety on her face. (We were in dive suits at the time – perhaps I should have mentioned that earlier – but then again, it is not as though we would have been out on the reef looking at the Structure in our fine clothes – o dear, I am awful at telling stories, Henerey, especially as I am used to writing only to Sophy – please forgive me!)

When we returned to the house, Jeime apologised for her strange behaviour. All she would say was that the Structure reminded her of something else, and that she was very shocked to hear that my brother had constructed it. I wanted to press her, but I am simply terrible at Conversation. She departed soon after – even before enjoying the dessert that Seliara (my other friend, who – well, I suppose you don't need to know any more than that!) brought for us. Very odd indeed. Though Jeime did ask if she might return to the Deep House sometime in the future with a borrowed depth-craft to examine the undergarden, so perhaps she is not daunted just yet.

The reason why I mention this, Henerey, is because I thought perhaps you might have some resource or reading to which to direct me – you were so generous in sharing "The Greate Fishe", you know! Speaking of which, o, if only I could tell you how much breathless joy I took in poring over the illustration you enclosed. I have never seen historical visual imagery of that nature (though perhaps I might begrudgingly admit that the Cidnosin family library is slightly less extensive than that of the Boundless Campus). All of this is to say that I am awed by every aspect of your letter, including your breathtaking erudition – I can feel Sophy's voice in my mind telling me not to say this as it comes across as sarcastic, but I do genuinely mean that.

In fact, each time I reread your words, I cannot resist the temptation of wondering what "your" library must look like – surely a place that offers such a sanctuary to you in times of need must be remarkable indeed! Is there a particular carrel that you call home, or do you sit in a new nook every time you visit? Do you keep a stack of books that spills over your table as you write, or do you enjoy only a single tome at a time: savouring the quest of seeking out another each time you've finished? (I take the former method myself – I tend to have twelve books in progress at once, and struggle to finish any! My desk in my bedroom is a ship-wreck of a study, with shells and scribbles and pressed seaweed samples scattered all about the place.) Despite our proximity to Boundless, I have never visited that particular Library Anchorage before. As a young girl, however, I once experienced the Atoll Campus library during a cross-campus holiday with my family. You must have fond memories of that one, since you grew up there – how funny to think that we might have seen each other and not known! Things were so much easier for me with Society and my Brain when I was a child, so perhaps if I had met you, we might have become fast friends much sooner.

As lovely as that library was, I do not imagine that I will be able to visit it again anytime soon. For the moment, however, I do like to imagine what it would be like to seek out the answers I desire about this Structure affair in such a place – and, perhaps, to discuss them with you.

Until next time (dare I be so bold?),

E.

P.S. I felt honoured and baffled all at once to learn that my silly sketch moved you so. I assure you that whatever "vibrant intellectual energy" I may possess is merely the product of my childhood circumstances, not a sign of any exceptional talent. You see, my mother was of the firm belief that she ought never to tell us anything outright, because "discovery is the greatest pleasure one can experience". As children, my siblings and I found this philosophy equally freeing (when it permitted us to engage in all sorts of fascinating experiments and adventures that were not entirely advisable) and frustrating (when it prevented our mother from reveal-ing even the simplest information, such as the hour at which luncheon would occur). At the very least, I am grateful that her peculiar parenting style equipped me with an independent spirit and insatiable curiosity.

(And more grateful still that you find such qualities admirable.)

AUTOMATED POST MISSIVE FROM SOPHY CIDNORGHE TO VYERIN CLEL, 1003

Dear Vyerin!

As always, it is a delight to read E.'s words – though I am sorry she felt that her all-too-natural envy of my colleagues at the Ridge was something she needed to hide from me. Perhaps it would comfort her to know that there is a small part of me that envies Henerey and the role that he played during these last few months of her life.

More importantly, however, you were wrong to hope that we'd escape any mention of the Structure! There it is in E.'s letter – prominent and puzzling as always!

But you said nothing about that! Do you truly refrain from reading documents before sending them to me?

With surprise,
Sophy

AUTOMATED POST MISSIVE FROM VYERIN CLEL TO SOPHY CIDNORGHE, 1003

Dear Sophy,

Of course I do not read the letters first. I do not pick them up until I have sent the copies to you. I would like the sense of discovery to be shared, as silly as that may sound.

I too was horrified to see the Structure appear again. And unlike Henerey (and apparently E.), I abhor Fantasies.

V.

AUTOMATED POST MISSIVE FROM SOPHY CIDNORGHE TO VYERIN CLEL, 1003

V.,

Please know that though I lack your immediate archival willpower for the most part, I have only read about half of the documents that I possess from E.'s files. And surely there are more that we have not yet found but may later add to our "project". So perhaps we may "solve" the puzzle of the Structure as a by-product of our other investigations.

Or perhaps we will uncover nothing more than additional mysteries.

S.

Chapter 8

COVER SHEET FOR LETTERS SENT BY ELINIEA HAYVE FORGHE TO E. CIDNOSIN ON BEHALF OF SOPHY CIDNOSIN, 1002

Dear E., Beloved Sister of Sophy,

Perhaps this message – sent by a Stranger! – will alarm you upon receipt. If that is so, allow me to offer you a prefatory apology!

Yet I hope – o, SO earnestly! – that this is not the case – that I am not a stranger, and that Sophy indeed told you a little about me and what life is like down here in the "Deeps". (That, by the way, is highly original researcher slang used to refer to the Ridge – as coined yesterday by Schr Vincenebras. I imagine that soon everyone will use it widely. Welcome to the future!)

Now, I suspect Sophy also told you that our current "field mission" will make it difficult for her to send you regular letters. It is no permanent solution, I'm afraid, but as the Expedition Specialist, I am required to deputise one of our automata to return to the surface bearing updates from the first day of our journey (which happens to be today). Only while we are still close enough to the Spheres to make such a thing practical, of course. I mentioned this to your sister last night, and we hatched a plan together! It is a pleasure to bring you some cheer while we Deep Ones (surely you can work out the etymology there) wander around like eager children playing at hiding and seeking with luminescent sea creatures!

She allowed me to write whatever I wished in this cover letter (I chose nonsense, clearly) if I included the following two phrases:

Are you still writing to HIM?

AND

Please take care of yourself.

Great waves – whatever could it all mean?

While she gave me no further instructions, I assumed that she – and you – would not turn down the inclusion of a silly little sketch of the very cetacean automaton who will carry your letter up to an enterprising mail-boat. (I dubbed this particular creature "Seacilia".)

I look forward to truly meeting you one day, E.!

Niea

LETTER FROM SOPHY CIDNOSIN TO E. CIDNOSIN, 1002

Dear E.,

First of all, I swore to myself that I shall only describe briefly any events in my journey that might bring you anxiety. Even so, if anything in this or a future letter troubles you, please take heart that the very act of writing confirms that I am alive, so you need not fear for me. But you will be pleased to hear that I survived my first full day adrift in the depths!

This morning (was it really that recently?), I proceeded to breakfast only to find Ylaret and Irye already with Eliniea at "our" table, deep in conversation about the upcoming field study. Perhaps this seems out of character, but for a moment, as I watched them chatter – Niea sparkling as usual, smiling demurely at a witticism from Ylaret – I felt a rivulet of nervousness overcome me.

But then Eliniea's eyes met mine and she pulled out the chair right next to hers, and all such anxieties dispersed. Then the "moment" was promptly interrupted by the arrival of a boisterously sleepy Vincenebras, wearing upon his head the elegant blouse he mistook for a hat in his morning weariness.

A necessary few wardrobe changes later, the five of us bid a fond farewell to the Spheres – and to think I had just started to find them relatively homelike! – in favour of the great unknown. My assigned automaton, a sprightly teal-and-steel replica of a Recalcitrant Porpoise, clicked along cheerily as I held tightly to its glimmering back; Ylaret, my dive partner for the day, rode beside me on her stately striped Commonplace Dolphin. Though we did intend to swim much of the journey on our own power, Eliniea decided that it would be prudent to receive an initial "boost" from the automata to help us progress more quickly on the first day.

One of the strangest parts of travelling through the deep ocean is that I find myself incapable of tracking time. Unless I manually count each second under my breath, there are no environmental or human-made signifiers to suggest that the present moment advances at all. I find myself missing that gaudy old baro-clock in its place of pride in the dining room – would you believe that I long to hear its shuddery, off-key chimes to keep me on my temporal course?

It did not help that our first field day was relatively uneventful. An unpredictable current prevented me from descending deeper into the trench, so I had to rely on my portable Wayfinding Device alone for surveying. In this way did I pass my time – waving that sonar wand about like some sunken conductor, monitoring the rose and orange flashes on my Monitor, and attempting to mentally reconstruct the readings to comprehend the contours of the landscape. Relatively banal, with one recent exception.

Some short time ago – perhaps an hour? Perhaps several? – my communicator pulsed, and Eliniea's gentle voice materialised in my helmet. (How sonorous her speech is!)

"Welcome to our lodgings, friends!" she said – or rather, murmured, because there is no need to shout when a microphone amplifies your speech into everyone's ears.

"As we traverse this route for the first time," Eliniea continued, "I thought we might wish to pause here. It is about halfway between the Spheres and the Point of Interest. I hope everyone will have a chance to rest tonight! Please feel free to stop by my Bubble if there is anything you would like to discuss with me." She then gave us a brief introduction to underwater shelter assembly – I cannot believe how portable these "Bubbles" are! – and we all made ourselves comfortable within a companionable distance from one another.

O, but I realise I used some expedition terminology with which you might not be familiar! When Eliniea undertook her first survey of this region – when the station was still being built – she found one area of the Ridge, termed "The Point of Interest", that seemed most fruitful as a centrepoint for our studies. It features impressive biodiversity and the most unique topography, to name a few characteristics that obviously hold no particular meaning to me.

At any rate, though I have no way of judging our distance from the Point of Interest, we do seem to be just out of the range of the Spheres. Before tucking away into the seclusion of our Bubbles, we five floated together to enjoy a rare moment of respite. The station we knew so intimately diminished in the distance, looking more like a necklace of radiant, rainbow pearls than a feat of life-sustaining technology. Yet even thus reduced, the lights illuminated our spirits as they did the water – until the moment when the glow vanished utterly as though it had never existed.

The darkness lasted only for a short while. It frightened me at first – I feared I had overexerted myself and that my vision had begun to falter. I took comfort, however, in the fact that both Eliniea and Irye immediately turned on their communicators to express their shock: clearly I was not alone in witnessing this oddity. In a tone that suggested reassurance for herself just as much as the rest of us, Eliniea noted that one of her Architect colleagues did say that the power system occasionally resets itself when the Station is in "stasis" and unoccupied. Vincenebras scoffed at this, concerned that the existence of such a glitch even in the stasis cycle could easily occur when we were aboard (with potentially deadly consequences). Irye suggested that it might be some abyssal optical illusion – a suggestion that Eliniea, too, found convincing. Only Ylaret stared silently at those reawakened lights, with no commentary to offer.

But as I may have mentioned previously (I find myself too weary to flip back through the pages and confirm), I am now safely ensconced in my temporary quarters for the night. Thanks to the semi-opaque "shields", I can see little beyond the vaguely bright outlines of my colleagues' Bubbles. I am grateful that Eliniea anchored hers adjacent to mine – it calms me to spy her silhouette bent over a book.

Actually, it seems she noticed my shameless spying! And—now my communicator pulses. Farewell!

Sophy

LETTER FROM E. CIDNOSIN TO SOPHY CIDNOSIN AND ELINIEA HAYVE FORGHE, 1002

Dearest Sophy and Niea (if I may), co-conspirators,

Let me express my overwhelming appreciation for your jointly authored scheme to cheer me in your absence. I shall be brief since I know you will not read this for some time.

Yes, I still write to him, and I will do my best to take care of myself.

Please look out for each other and I can't wait to hear news of your field study.

Affectionately,

E.

AUTOMATED POST MISSIVE FROM VYERIN CLEL TO SOPHY CIDNORGHE, 1003

Dear Sophy,

I suppose this is as good a time as any to make an embarrassing confession.

Nothing – and I do mean nothing, short of losing Reiv or my children (or, previously, my brother) – terrifies me more than those deepest and darkest parts of the ocean.

Some people operate under the misguided assumption that a sailor never truly fears the sea. On the contrary, I find that my extensive experience navigating the great waves has taught me too much about the terrors of the endless watery depths. The only reason why I am able to step aboard a ship at all is because I developed an innate ability to "abstract" the sea, if you will. In other words, when I stand on deck and look out at the grey or azure or midnight ripples before me, I pretend they are nothing but creases in a flat carpet, one stretched over the thick floor of the world under which nothing rests, and into which nothing could possibly fall.

I have never admitted this practice to another person, and I fear my attempt to articulate these thoughts will only make me seem rather irrational. But I risk my credibility as a captain to tell you this because I want you to understand how much these letters from your time on the expedition make me want to bury myself in blankets and never leave the house again.

And yet – in an attempt to entertain and connect with your faraway sister, I suspect? – the Sophy of the past is a remarkably fine narrator. Against my better judgement, I must read more. (Though I suspect you will have my husband with whom to reckon if (when?) my deep-sea anxieties disrupt our mutual sleep.)

With anticipation,
Vyerin

AUTOMATED POST MISSIVE FROM SOPHY CIDNORGHE TO VYERIN CLEL, 1003

Dear Vyerin,

I find nothing embarrassing whatsoever about your confession! In my expert opinion (as someone who has spent a record-breaking amount of time continuously underwater), anyone who does not fear the abyss is simply naïve to its perils. There is something philosophically crisis-inducing about the seemingly infinite. This is not to say that the deep ocean is boundless – of course it has a limit, as all things do! – but because we cannot see the seafloor, or really any landmark of consequence that might give us a sense of space, it feels as though it goes on forever.

And that's just the deep ocean on a base level – never mind what we encountered down there.

My apologies in advance to Reiv.

Fortunately, we shall now enjoy a brief respite from my account (I was, indeed, increasingly making my letters more like episodes in a thrilling story, I suppose, to appeal to E.!) because I had no further opportunity to send missives via the unfortunately named automaton "Seacilia" until we returned to the station. Perhaps, in the interim, you might enjoy a letter from Henerey?

Calmingly, I hope,

Sophy

AUTOMATED POST MISSIVE FROM VYERIN CLEL TO SOPHY CIDNORGHE, 1003

Dear Sophy,

O yes, Henerey – the very reason why I sat down to write you an Automated Post in the first place before my ramblings about deep water distracted me. I did so hope you would have another letter that he sent to E. for me to read. I thought it might be useful to precede it (if it will suit you) with a new section from his daybook – including his request log from the library around this time.

V.

NOTE FROM THE DAYBOOK OF HENEREY CLEL, 1002

Moments of delight amid today's frustrations (if I could think of an aquatic metaphor, that would almost be a perfect Darbeni line!):

- A sunrise like no other. Unbelievable colours!
- A dessert well-deserved.
- The Nascent Carp in the Anchorage's Conservatory – how they weave over and under each other in endless tessellations.
- A letter to reread again and again as I try to formulate a reply (and – though it embarrasses me to write this and I know the Scholars of the future will mock it in years to come – imagine what her voice sounds like).

LIBRARY REQUEST RECORD PASTED IN THE DAYBOOK OF HENEREY CLEL, 1002

The following receipt records the Library materials requested by
    SCHR HENEREY CLEL

The following requests have been approved and submitted by the Library Attendant:
    Cloyd, Schr Dovis Elvin. *Size Anomalies of the Second Ocean*. The School of Observation at Intertidal Campus, Year 705.

Darbeni, Schr Kenven. *A Sail, A Sea, A Secret: Further Musings*. The School of Inspiration at Boundless Campus, Year 950.

Parnel, Schr Tyram. *Enigmas of the Abyss (That We May Soon Understand): A Forward-Looking Retrospective*. The School of Intuition at Boundless Campus, Year 1002.

The following request:

Larnard, Schr Jos. *Sunken Splendour Volume the Third: Including Mythes, Tales, and Dreames and Accompanied by Several Mappes and Illustrations By the Author*. The School of Intuition at Boundless Campus, Year 380.

has been denied by the Library Attendant for the following reason:

RESTRICTED CONTENT (COLLECTION OF RARE MANUSCRIPTS)

(Sorry, Henerey, but you know you must come into the Reading Room to look at something that precious. Everyone else does it, and no one has perished yet! – Elaxand)

AUTOMATED POST MISSIVE FROM SOPHY CIDNORGHE TO VYERIN CLEL, 1003

V.,

I assume that note was left by Scholar Elaxand Iyl? I barely saw the fellow, as I often used the Library Anchorage midday when he was not the attendant on duty, but I did know of him. He had a reputation as both a skilled researcher and the most sympathetic of the collections' wardens.

P.S. I, a Scholar of the Future, would like Henerey to know that his desire to imagine my sister's voice is not embarrassing in the least!

AUTOMATED POST MISSIVE FROM VYERIN CLEL TO SOPHY CIDNORGHE, 1003

S.,

Yes, it was Scholar Iyl. My brother considered him a personal friend.

Which meant Henerey's correspondence with E. doubled his "personal friend" count instantly.

LETTER FROM HENEREY CLEL TO E. CIDNOSIN, 1002

Dear E. (if I may? Since you so aptly demonstrated your ability to drop my honorific?)

Once again, your letter arrived precisely when I needed it most – how do you always manage that? It pains me to admit this (and I hope you will not think ill of me), but it seems I can do nothing correctly in the eyes of the Department these days. Another project over which I laboured for many months has been summarily dismissed as "irrelevant" and "backwards" by Chancellor Rawsel, who made it clear that those adjectives also apply to me. For three days I abjured the company of my colleagues, taking meals from our Refectory back to my quarters and spending all my free hours either deep in the stacks of the Library Anchorage, wandering the Conservatory paths in solitude, or collapsed on my bed in a most ungraceful posture. In such a position was I arrayed when the courier passed through my hall a while ago, sliding your neat envelope under the door with a sound loud enough to pierce my malaise.

The sight of your handwriting – and your ever-transporting words – brought about a great calm within me. How marvellous that an unexpected letter introduced me to someone who seems to see the world exactly as I do! All I can do is thank you for your kindness and pray that I will not frighten you away with my melancholic thoughts.

I just reread my previous two paragraphs and am indeed astounded by the melancholia that permeates them. Where are my signature parentheticals and eager exclamations? Let me remedy this henceforth, as the very act of writing to you has already lifted my spirits.

I am gladdened to hear, by the way, that you find the very act of writing to *me* helps you cope with your sister's absence! Everyone at Boundless Campus speaks of nothing but Schr Eliniea Hayve Forghe's "pre-mission update" that she sent via automaton on the first night of their field study. I smiled to myself when I read of the promising initial progress your sister made in mapping the seafloor. How it boggles my mind to remember that "esteemed Scholar of Wayfinding, Philosophy Cidnosin" and "E.'s dear Sophy" are one and the same! It heartens me to know that your sister found kindred spirits among her crew – it is difficult enough to get on with one's Department under the best of circumstances, to say the least of when one is trapped under the sea with them! (I would rather swim with all the predators in the ocean than spend an hour in a depth-craft with Chancellor Rawsel.)

Because you asked, I shall tell you now that I too experience such jealousy with my own brother. If you met Vy, you might think him terse and aloof, or perhaps altogether too intimidating to approach! Yet he remains capable of begrudging conviviality when he wishes. I began my Apprenticeship before he did, and once he joined me at Atoll Campus, he swiftly made more close friends in a week than I did in an entire year of study! For a while, it consumed me – his ability to catalyse a conversation when I siphoned all of its energy, his skill at discussing trivialities in a way that made people feel anything but trivial, the fact that he was tall and well-built and caught the eye of every person imaginable – perhaps I should end this sentence, as it makes it sound as though these thoughts still consume me!

In truth, they do not. I now realise Vyerin and I, though raised by the same parents and possessing similar genetic compositions, are entirely distinct sorts of people. Though I might envy those friends of his who share his personality traits, I take comfort in the fact that there is no one else in Vyerin's life quite as different from him as I am – and the relationship that we share, therefore, is utterly unique. At the same time, this frees me to enjoy spending time with folks with whom I have more in common – including (most prominently!) yourself.

Speaking of our commonalities, I am delighted – but not, as you predicted, surprised – that you too enjoy Fantasies. *The Star Sailors* is a classic, of course. I cannot believe that our telling of it is four hundred years old (and that it describes alleged events from four thousand years prior, long before the Dive) – it feels as though it could have been written yesterday. Which of those noble voyagers did you find most relatable? Hopeless romantic of a child that I was, I found Lady Ei and her dedication to protecting her beloved at all costs admirable beyond belief.

For a moment, I found myself tempted to spill a full squid's worth of ink simply naming stories and asking you for your thoughts about them – but how could I focus on fiction after hearing about the mythical occurrence unfolding in your own garden?

I can hardly put into words how your description of this mysterious Structure makes me feel. I have so many questions for you, and there is nothing I love more than something that piques my curiosity! First and foremost, though – what does it look like? You shared so many other details – your encounter with Scholar Alestarre, your dive in the garden, your hypotheses about your brother's involvement (or lack thereof) – but the Structure itself remains an enigma to me. How large is it? What colours and textures do you see? Do you recognise the materials, or the visual style? Could it be repurposed Antepelagic technology, uncovered over time by the currents as those old machines from before the Dive sometimes are? Is there any chance that it is a coral formation that has coincidentally grown into a shape that our form-seeking eyes identify as "humanmade"? The architectural capabilities of coral colonies are truly exceptional – why, I once saw a cluster of pillar corals that created their very own colonnade!

But you asked for reading recommendations, not endless questions and speculation, so I will try to provide them. Something about your account struck a chord within the resonant recesses of my brain. There was one very old, very rare book I remember from childhood (though it was not particularly intended for children) that offered a brief history of mysterious sunken objects (including Antepelagic machines, but not exclusively). I had hoped to acquire this book from the library and enclose it for you (as my friend Elaxand is most lenient with due dates) as a small token of my gratitude, but unfortunately, the volume is non-circulating. (And I dare not even make a fair copy, because accessing rare volumes requires me to go into the Reading Room – which, despite the title, is more of a social gathering space than a room in which one accesses restricted books. There is only one small viewing table around which everyone must crowd, and you are forced to converse with your fellow readers the entire time. Even though you are supposed to be reading. Alas.) Yet do not despair – I have set some other plans in motion, and I anticipate that I may still be able to share this book with you soon.

Until then, I hope you will remember that you have a friend at Boundless Campus – however far away I might be! – and that he thinks of you with great frequency (but only if that suits you).

Gratefully,

Henerey

P.S. I beg your pardon for adding further length to an already-ample letter, but I realised that I did not answer one of your questions – what "my" library is like!

I am very much the kind of library patron who prefers consistency – so yes, I do have my own dedicated carrell, one that I borrow from a Senior Scholar who finds the space "suffocating". It is a glorified desk on the library's second floor, set before a small porthole window. Naturally, I keep my shelves as crowded as possible. My current "installation" features several Antepelagic fossils excavated from the earth of the Atoll (the gems of my collection – representing three terrestrial species endemic to the Upward Archipelago that went extinct during the Dive), the seventy-five books I currently possess on indefinite loan from the library, three jarred algae plants, a landscape painting of the Ragged Coast to remind me of home, and a small clay figurine ostensibly depicting me and my brother (though you would not be blamed for thinking it was a single porpoise) gifted to me by my precocious niece Avanne in her earlier years.

It is, altogether, a lovely place, and often inspires me to great productivity. I enjoy facing the window, but as I am altogether a jittery fellow, I cannot abide having my back turned towards the rest of the library. (Some particularly uncouth members of my Department seem to take an unfortunate pleasure in "surprising" me from time to time.) Recently, it occurred to me that I might enjoy the best of both worlds by sitting sideways on my chair – so I can turn my head to watch research vessels pulling in and out of the Anchorage on one side or survey the silent bustling of the stacks from the other.

Now that I've furnished you with this preliminary description of where I spend my days, I hope you will do me the honour of returning the favour in whatever way suits you. Where are you as you read this letter? (I promise I ask this primarily because I am curious to know more about the world that surrounds you – not solely out of my continued fascination with the Deep House! Rest assured that I would want to imagine you reading my letters even if you lived in a Boundless Campus dormitory (the "charms" of which, I'm sure, your sister has not praised unduly.)) – H.

AUTOMATED POST MISSIVE FROM VYERIN CLEL TO SOPHY CIDNORGHE, 1003

Dear Sophy,

In a way, these Henerey letters – seemingly sent from beyond the grave – are almost more harrowing than your suspenseful underwater adventures.

It is true that my brother struggled on campus – both when he moved to Boundless and even during his first years of study at home on the Atoll. I wish that I could have been a true older brother to him – helping and guiding him – but I did not fully understand how he suffered. Henerey has always been anxious around strangers. A profound fear of public humiliation coloured his every action as a boy, and the fact that he was the youngest and most accomplished Atoll Apprentice in recent history gave many a desire to embarrass him whenever he showed vulnerability.

Seeing the genuine joy in my brother's words as he finally found someone similar to him comforts me immeasurably. (And thank goodness she enjoyed *The Star Sailors* I found that story unbelievably cloying – I could not bear to hear Henerey go on and on about "dear Lady Ei and Lady Je and their true love". Almost worse than Darbeni.)

In exchange for "your" letter from Henerey, let me offer you a trade in kind – a letter Henerey wrote to me possibly minutes after penning his reply to E.

Your friend,

Vyerin

P.S. I still possess those objects from Henerey's carrell, by the way. Reading this letter inspired me to break open that case and finally put its contents on display. The fossils and painting sit on my own desk as I write to you, and Avanne re-acquired her piece of juvenilia with great pride. Never did a porpoise sculpture give me such emotion.

LETTER FROM HENEREY CLEL TO VYERIN CLEL, 1002

Dear Vy,

Under normal circumstances, the news I shall announce shortly (in my next sentence, in fact!) would do nothing short of utterly delight you. At present, I am plotting a trip homeward! (In the midst of a most demanding time in the Department, nonetheless. What a paragon of familial affection I have become.)

Yet you, Vyerin, know better than anyone that I remain a much finer Scholar than a sibling. I confess that the reason for my visit is all too selfish. I have been charged with a rather unusual research undertaking by a friend of mine, and I find that the answers she seeks just might lie in some of the juvenile Fantasy volumes of our childhood. (Yes, "she" happens to be the very person who wrote to me out of the blue just about a month ago – in the intervening tides, we have enjoyed quite a wondrous correspondence! I cannot understand, frankly, why she would willingly read my miserable ramblings, but I admit that our conversations give me a raft to which to cling as I navigate a difficult time.)

Though I know it will pain you (and Reiv especially), please do not breathe a word of my potential impending journey to Avanne just yet – I want to make sure I may indeed get away, and I would hate to disappoint her! (Surely her righteous fury would match the toxic wrath of a startled Cone Shell.) I shall do my best to offer up a suitable excuse to the ever-demanding Chancellor Rawsel, catch an expedient transport vessel to the Atoll, stay the night, and return in the morning. (I don't suppose anything moderately life-threatening currently ails you or Reiv at the moment? Not that Chancellor Rawsel would consider that a worthy excuse, of course.)

Until we meet again,
Henerey

AUTOMATED POST MISSIVE FROM SOPHY CIDNORGHE TO VYERIN CLEL, 1003

Dear Vyerin,

Your resentment of *The Star Sailors* is understandable. I did not dislike it quite so strongly as you, being rather a romantic myself (with an unfortunate tendency to picture myself and my aforementioned ill-fated childhood sweetheart as the Vowed Ladies), but I did find it dull compared to less poetic, more haunting tales like *The Errors of the Whirlpool*. Yet it seems to have meant so much to our siblings. Perhaps we misjudged it?

Your friend,

Sophy

AUTOMATED POST MISSIVE FROM VYERIN CLEL TO SOPHY CIDNORGHE, 1003

Dear Sophy,

I assume, in these "Star Sailor" imaginings, that you were Lady Ei and Seliara was Lady Je? (Yes, I have deduced the identity of your childhood love quite readily. You only knew one person, after all. Please correct me if I am wrong.)

Unfortunately, I can't say that *The Errors of the Whirlpool* is much better, in my estimation. I suppose you and I are better co-archivists than "book friends".

V.

AUTOMATED POST MISSIVE FROM SOPHY CIDNORGHE TO VYERIN CLEL, 1003

Dear V.,

If you have gained any empathy towards my sister and her situation over the course of our project, prepare to be outraged on her behalf. We are now about to embark on a difficult chapter in the story of the Deep House.

S.

P.S. I begrudgingly admit that you are correct. (About Seliara, that is, and not about the quality of *Whirlpool*.) I am quite sure each of us siblings had a fancy for her at one point or another. (E. most briefly of all. Her standards are – were – quite high.) We shall speak no more of this.

Chapter 9

LETTER FROM JEIME ALESTARRE TO E. CIDNOSIN, 1002

Dear E.,

My apologies for not thanking you for your kind hospitality until now. Were she still with us, your mother surely could not be prouder of the woman you've become – and how skilfully you preserve her Deep House.

I apologise, too, for my odd behaviour during the visit. I did not expect to see that "Structure", as you call it. And I apologise for a third time in advance of writing something especially enigmatic in the paragraph to follow, but I anticipate you shall understand it better soon.

This morning, I happened to encounter Seliara and your brother (whom I immediately recognised – like you, he is the spitting image of your mother – is Sophy the same, or does she take after your father these days?) in the campus Refectory. We discussed the Structure. I anticipate he will soon speak with you and offer some insight about the situation.

That is all for now. I will rather rudely discourage you from writing back, as I may not answer for a while. I have some off-campus projects to complete that may take some time. We shall reconnect when I return.

With kindness,

Jeime

LETTER FROM ARVIST CIDNOSIN TO E. CIDNOSIN, 1002

Beloved E.,

Wonderful news! Tomorrow my betrothed and I shall take up residence in our family home once more! Can you believe that your days of solitude have – at last – reached an end? O let us rejoice!

Until soon,

Scholar Artistry "Arvist" Cidnosin

P.S. Sophy's bedchamber seems far more suitable for a soon-to-be husband and wife than my humble studio. Do you not agree? I know our Sister is as generous as she is intelligent!

LETTER FROM E. CIDNOSIN TO SOPHY CIDNOSIN, 1002

Dear Sophy,

I included the attached note from our brother because I believe one day it will be an artefact of historical significance. Today turned out to be the "tomorrow" of which Arvist wrote. And his letter was only sent yesterday evening, and thus arrived here long after they did. I have confined myself to my bedroom – the one haven left to me – to share my frustration with you. For the first time in my life, I do truly wish I could be anywhere but here!

This morning, at barely six bells (thank goodness I had a restless night and lay fidgeting in my bed instead of fast asleep!) I heard the recognisable creak of the airlock. Worried for a moment that something had gone wrong with the entrance mechanism – I knew that I should have paid more attention during Jeime's visit – I threw on my dressing gown and crept down the hallway, scanning all the while for any visible signs of trouble. I knew not what I expected to find, but my Brain, at least, was quite convinced that my end was upon me!

As soon as I reached the staircase, however, I heard Arvist's and Seliara's voices. You might think that the familiarity would bring me comfort – after all, moments ago, I thought that Death itself awaited me in the airlock! – but their laughter sickened me. I took several minutes to descend each stair, and had I not clung to the railing with all my might, I surely would have tumbled.

Some amount of time later, the pair appeared in the parlour below me. Arvist looked as rumpled and self-satisfied as usual, with a bit of crushed sheet music tucked in a cuff of his jacket.

Between you and me, Sophy, I would have much preferred to welcome Death.

"Good evening, dear E.!" he greeted me. (I assume I already mentioned that it was nowhere near evening.) He touched my shoulder in a modest gesture of affection that must have required exceptional effort. "Why must you play at being surprised? Sophy asked me to come and check on you, you know."

"I certainly did not expect you—" I tried to say.

"And what better way to keep an eye on my sunken sister than to return home at last?" he continued without pause, as though he were an old-fashioned automaton reciting the one dramatic monologue it had been designed to perform.

"I do hope it won't be too much of an intrusion, E.," cut in Seliara. "I did try to warn you, but it seems my letter did not make it in time. I've even brought a hamper for us tonight, with sweets to spare!"

I must confess that I mumbled something rather unbecoming about my appetite spoiling and turned to leave. Arvist, of course, thwarted my escape by leaping inelegantly in front of the door.

"Ah, dear sister," he stuttered, suddenly seeming especially anxious. Did he realise at last how much of a burden he placed upon me?

Alas, no.

"It seems there has been a misunderstanding," Arvist continued, staring at the floor most uncharacteristically, "about that masterpiece in the undergarden."

"How could I misunderstand you, brother, when you refused to respond to any of my letters inquiring about the subject?"

"O, it's all my fault, dear E.," Seliara interrupted once more. "I gave you the impression that Arvist made the piece. I had it backwards – the sculpture he found is informing his newest performance piece, which is why he's returned home!"

Surely this will puzzle you as much as it puzzled me, Sophy!

"If you did not make it, then where in the name of the seas did it come from?"

"O, an ancient wreck, or a storm, or something – who can say?" said Arvist as he stepped out of my way. "At any rate, E., you may retreat now. That is all. Farewell."

Well, I certainly don't like the idea of odd Structures tossed into our garden by unknown forces, but I can barely wrap my head around that. It appears my visitors will be here for an indefinite amount of time, and your room has most certainly been overtaken. While I dare not rebuke Arvist to his face yet, I continue eavesdropping from the landing (in our favourite childhood listening spot!) to obtain more information about their plans. Arvist is under the impression that the Structure will inform his greatest Artistic accomplishment of all time, and he is intent upon developing a Dramatic Intervention (?) in response to it. Apparently, he planned this months ago when he first "discovered" the Structure (and said nothing to us? Nothing to me?), and now he wants to leap into this "interpretation" as soon as possible. When and how he hopes to show-case his performance, I do not know – somehow he gained "research leave" from his Department – but it will decidedly not be during the School of Inspiration's Gala, which has (heartbreakingly, to Arvist) been rescheduled this year.

Interestingly, I also overheard Seliara scolding him: it turns out he had told her that he made the thing himself (posturing to impress her during their courtship, I assume), but she agreed to lie to me and say it was her misunderstanding so he could save face. At the very least, I'm glad that she is brave enough to be cross with him – if only in private!

I don't suppose you have room for an unskilled unScholar in the abyss with you? Please tell your colleagues that I promise to be brave even in the face of great peril – see how I already faced it today? As I sit here at my window once more, I find myself rather hoping that those Elongated Fish will return – they would certainly be preferable company.

I take some comfort in knowing that many days have now passed since you last wrote, and that you should return to the Spheres very soon. I cannot wait to speak to you again! Please travel with all due care.

With endless love (and Trepidation . . .)

E.

AUTOMATED POST MISSIVE FROM VYERIN CLEL TO SOPHY CIDNORGHE, 1003

Dear Sophy,

It occurs to me that we now have a remarkable coincidence on our hands. E. reunited with her brother on the same day that Henerey reunited with his (otherwise known as yours truly). I wonder which pair of us enjoyed the reunions most?

Jests aside, I do feel outraged on E.'s behalf, though as a Recovered Arvist (yes, recall my adolescent popularity) I should say that I do not think such inconsideration is necessarily born out of malice. Just ignorance, and self-centredness, and arrogance. (Which is perhaps equally offensive. I retract my explanation.)

Vyerin

P.S. The sheet music is an amusing detail. Did Arvist try to pick up this skill to impress his future bride?

AUTOMATED POST MISSIVE FROM SOPHY CIDNORGHE TO VYERIN CLEL, 1003

Dear Vyerin,

It baffles and amuses me to think of you as a "Recovered Arvist". I will say that as much as I enjoy mocking him (and especially his past self), my brother has mellowed of late. (I suppose losing a sister well before her time will do that to someone.) He might still indulge himself in egotism, but he is a surprisingly good father, and, on the rare occasions when we meet, a reasonably thoughtful brother.

S.

P.S. Yes. He is still decidedly not musical, though.

GAUDY NOTECARD SENT BY HENEREY CLEL TO E. CIDNOSIN, 1002

Dear E.,

Allow me to apologise in advance for a perplexing second message! O how my circumstances have changed since last we "spoke". I arrived at my brother's home only a few days ago, and already I am set to depart on a new adventure (!) that will keep me away from my Anchorage for the foreseeable future. Do you know that my very first thought was that I must immediately write so you would know my new address? Seized by this desperate mission, I took to my brother's writing desk, where – would you believe it? – I realised that he is completely bereft of proper letterhead.

I hope this will explain why this notecard reads "Happy birthday, cousin."

I feel uncomfortable writing another long letter to you after already sending one so recently, so I will save further explanation of these new developments until a future date. In the meantime, if you would like to write to me again, please send all correspondence to:

Scholar Henerey Clel
Berth 14
Research Vessel *Sagacity*
Boundless Campus Waters

With all usual eagerness,
Henerey

AUTOMATED POST MISSIVE FROM VYERIN CLEL TO SOPHY CIDNORGHE, 1003

My dear Sophy,

I cannot lie to you. I wanted to lie, though. It is undeniable that the next chronologically relevant entry in our "archive" is a letter sent to Henerey the very day he departed for the *Sagacity*.

Sadly, said letter has the misfortune of being written by me, Vyerin Clel, infamous enemy of eloquence.

I hoped it would never come to this. I tried diligently to avoid sending you anything I wrote. Please, have mercy.

Anxiously,
V.

LETTER FROM VYERIN CLEL TO HENEREY CLEL, 1002

Dear Henerey,

I hope this letter will reach you. If it does not, please let me know immediately.

The Clel house echoes with mourning following your untimely departure. Avanne sculpted your bust in memoriam. Reiv sends his best, and I send – well, my mediocre usual. If you tire of the ceaseless whirlwind of activity aboard the *Sagacity* and wish to live a quiet life as a child-minder and occasional gardener in the Atoll, I have an ideal position in mind for you.

I should not encourage your book-hoarding by adding another to your collection. Still, included in this package is that book you hoped to procure during your stay. Are any of us surprised that you left it behind in your haste, though it was the primary reason for your visit?

May you and your new friend benefit from whatever secrets it can share.

Take care.

Your brother Vy

AUTOMATED POST MISSIVE FROM SOPHY CIDNORGHE TO VYERIN CLEL, 1003

Dear Vyerin,

I somehow doubt that an "infamous enemy of eloquence" would use such words to describe himself – nor write such a kindly amusing message to his brother. I am grateful for this honour. (And I do mean that most seriously, Vyerin!)

Now, if you will, may we continue without further self-deprecation?

S.

LETTER FROM E. CIDNOSIN TO HENEREY CLEL, 1002

Dear Henerey,

Many thanks for your birthday wishes. Really, considering that you forgot this special occasion for twenty-seven years, I am truly impressed that you saw fit to send me a card at last!

(I considered inscribing this letter in a whimsical card of my own, but

118

soon realised that I have nothing other than this letterhead upon which to write! This profound lack of excess stationery took me by surprise, as I often enjoyed collecting such items when I was younger. On occasion, when we visited Boundless Campus, I loved stopping by the papercraft marketplace in the Merchants' Anchorage – it has been too long since I visited anywhere! Perhaps both of us could benefit from perusing their wares together one day.)

I must confess that the mysteries of your "new adventure" confound and excite me! Your tone sounded generally positive, so I hope these changes will be welcome. Though you said little of your plans, it is plain to see from your address that you will soon explore the seas as you desire – perhaps the *Sagacity* will even sail by the Deep House one day. How funny it is to think that at any moment, you could be close to my home. ("Funny" is not truly what I mean, but I will leave it at that.)

It also pains me to use the phrase "my home", since any ownership of the Deep House seems irrevocably wrested from my grasp. My brother Arvist and my friend Seliara (newly affianced to the aforementioned brother) took up sudden residence in the Deep House in the most surprising way. Though I prefer quiet and solitude above all, I might have accepted them – if they came here simply because they missed the familiarity of our family home! Yet Arvist can think of nothing but his Structure, so I feel quite confident in attributing his arrival to avarice. Today he donned the too-tight diving gear from his teenage years and set off quite stiffly into the garden. Locked in my room, I did not witness this expedition, but heard all about it from a contrite Seliara later in the afternoon when she brought me a cup of tea and an oyster tart as an apology. She told me that Arvist has now confined himself to his studio to devote himself to "divine creation". With my brother thus occupied, Seliara begged me to leave my quarters and keep her company down below – but I refused, of course, as a matter of principle. I shall not leave my room until I can forgive Arvist for this grim "surprise".

Perhaps my reaction seems overdramatic – I find myself judging my actions more scrupulously after writing them down for you. Yet, dear Henerey, my Brain is such a terrible force – picture it as your awful Chancellor Rawsel, if you will – that I can only keep its anxieties in check when I have precise control over my surroundings. When faced with the unexpected, I flail and lose my way, and find the trifles that once did not trouble me – such as whether I remembered to check the airlock or the details of troublesome conversations I had ten years ago – have suddenly become the most unfortunate calamities.

But in my room all is peaceful, and I know that, in time, I will come to accept (however much it pains me to admit) Arvist's presence. Much like you in your penultimate letter, I discovered that the words of my distant friend bring with them a great sense of stability. How funny that is, considering how unexpected it was that we should "meet" in the first place!

(There I go again, saying "funny" as though it perfectly describes this utterly unique experience.)

To link these updates in my life to the questions in your letter, I must now turn again to the Structure. You see, I recently learned that my brother did not, in fact, create it, but alleges he simply found it in our undergarden a little while ago. I have not questioned him further. (Perhaps I will feel inspired to do so once I finish writing to you.) But I do periodically hear his conversations from the stairwell, and he seems to know absolutely nothing of its origins. Really, if it weren't for the fact that it was located right near his studio window, he may never have discovered it. I desperately wish to view the Structure again, but I dare not go for another dive until I have given up staying in my room out of spite. However, I would be happy to offer some brief recollections from the time when Jeime and I dived around it together.

When I first saw the Structure – a few tide-cycles ago, right after Sophy left – I described it to my sister as a "bowl" or a section of a cylinder abandoned in our undergarden with an odd railing atop it. But I have since produced a more fitting comparison for a Scholar of Classification such as yourself! It is like a Tunicate, Henerey – but

120

instead of a tiny, tube-like invertebrate clustering in colonies of its brethren on the reef, this Structure is enormous and solitary. It has a diameter of about a fathom (which is easy for me to calculate, since Arvist at his full height happens to be about a fathom tall – so I have had a good sense of that unit of measurement ever since he came of age!), and a height of about half that.

That said, I am intrigued beyond belief to hear that my description reminds you of some Fantasy you read in the past. Because Arvist attributed the Structure to wreckage from the Dive calamity, I find myself all too eager to hear more about your ideas. Imagine if it were Antepelagic, as you suggest! That would be most exciting. And, in that case, it would be officially declared an Artefact of Import by the Academy, effectively preventing Arvist from meddling with it. Of course, in order for such a declaration to be made, an endless sea of Scholars of Society would flood the Deep House for seasons to debate the Structure's provenance, and Arvist would insist upon entertaining them all, and they might even suggest that we dare not dwell in the house anymore, given its proximity to something of such great Import, and demand that we abandon the Deep House so it could be used as an Auxiliary Academy and—

Upon reflection, perhaps "most exciting" is not the best phrase with which to describe this possibility.

Let us leave that wave of thoughts behind! Did you manage to find the book you mentioned while visiting Vyerin? I would love to see it. And, more importantly, did you truly enjoy your visit before being swept away to your vessel? (I sincerely hope that you did benefit from some time for rest and relaxation. I can think of no one more deserving.)

Before the "invasion", I might have closed this letter by describing my library to you – since you did such a wonderful job of bringing your carrell to life. (How I envy your fossil collection! I have but one such treasure, featuring an impression of some leafy, primordial specimen that likely never expected to "live on" for ages. It astounds me to imagine the world that prehistoric plant knew – a floating island filled with countless life-forms ignorant of the sea! Haunting. And to think that someone from the Atoll like you might find such precious objects in the very soil upon which you live!) However, considering current events, I shall instead furnish for you a more extensive verbal sketch of my quarters, which will continue to serve as my entire universe until further notice.

Surely your familiarity with the Deep House is such that you already know its basic layout – three proper floors, plus a mechanical level to house our various pumps, engines, and pressure filters on the very lowest storey of the house. The library, kitchen, dining room, parlour, and "crystal room" (our fanciful name for the glass-encased viewing deck) comprise the first floor, off of which Arvist's so-called "studio" emerges. (I hope the spirit of my mother, if she can read this, will know that my vitriol towards this architectural element stems not from her design of the room but from its present inhabitant.) Though Mother and Father kept their bedroom and offices on the third floor, most of the other personal quarters make up the second floor, with mine at the very end of the hallway: the quietest spot in the house, which suits me best.

The decor of my room is also the "quietest", at least when compared to Sophy's fixation with novelty and Modern Living (I don't think there's anything in her chamber, save her books, that is older than a year – she refreshes her belongings so frequently!) and Arvist's ... well, you can very well imagine what his bedroom looks like. I sleep in a simple bunk, store my clothes in an inset armoire, and write my letters to you on a desk that drops down from the wall (with plenty of drawers, containers, and chests neatly folded into it to keep my clutter of belongings intact). Truly, thanks to these convenient amenities, one could tuck all my furnishings away and never know that someone rests, dresses, and writes within these walls! Only through the wallcoverings do I allow myself some degree of permanence and freedom. It is nothing compared to a Campus gallery, but I curate regular installations of exciting illustrations from periodicals – Natural History illustrations, landscapes, speculative portraits – that catch my fancy. I enjoy spinning about my floor and seeing them blend into one mess of an environment.

Does that help you picture me with greater accuracy? Please do write back with any further questions, and I will be sure to elaborate.

For now, I await updates from your new mission aboard the *Sagacity* with great eagerness! How I wish I too could sail away.

E.

P.S. Dear Lady Ei is certainly an aspirational figure from "Sailors". Strangely enough, I found myself fascinated with Lord Neviz. Can you imagine – me, subdued as I am, fond of the boldest and most outgoing of the Sailors? Perhaps it is as that old saying goes about opposing forces drawing together …

P.P.S. After finishing my letter, I realised that I ought to respond to your kind interest in the Structure by simply enclosing a drawing, as I did in my very first letter to you. While the Structure is not nearly as compelling a subject as the Elongated Fish, I hope my humble sketch will offer you some insight into this curious object.

AUTOMATED POST MISSIVE FROM SOPHY CIDNORGHE TO VYERIN CLEL, 1003

Dear Vyerin,

Perhaps you missed it amid the many blatant barbs at my brother, but E. does something truly remarkable in the final line of the second paragraph.

Do you see it? It is subtle and couched in caution, and yet …

"Perhaps both of us could benefit from perusing their wares together one day."

I know my sister, and this is as close to a direct invitation to a stranger as she ever made. It delights me to think of her being so bold, and then getting up from and sitting down at her desk over and over again as she imagined exploring the papercraft market with Henerey.

I always found it nigh unbelievable that Henerey and E. met in person so early in their relationship. Now I begin to see the foreshadowing. And it warms my heart like nothing else.

(So much so that I shall forgive my sister's suggestion that she could "think of no one more deserving" of rest and relaxation than Henerey – it's not as though my mission of a lifetime was exactly a holiday, sister!)

Sophy

P.S. During one of those childhood market visits E. described, I purchased a purple embossed smooth-kelp diary which I intended to use as a travel journal during our stay. I must have been ten, and E. fourteen? At any rate, I still have this diary, and the first entry I wrote reads "E. purchased seventy-two pages of letterhead today and then sat in the corner and admired them for the rest of the afternoon while the rest of us socialised!"

AUTOMATED POST MISSIVE FROM VYERIN CLEL TO SOPHY CIDNORGHE, 1003

Sophy,

It is especially amusing when you consider that it was I, not Henerey, who owned no stationery save the infamous "cousin card" and might therefore more appropriately "benefit" from such a shopping trip.

Shall I be miffed that she did not invite me to come along?

V.

P.S. Call it prying of me, but I simply cannot wait to see how the tone of their letters shifts (or does not!) after they meet in person. It will happen "soon" (relatively speaking, as this is the past we are discussing), I hope?

AUTOMATED POST MISSIVE FROM SOPHY CIDNORGHE TO VYERIN CLEL, 1003

V.,

In recompense for my sister's thoughtless exclusion of you, please know that I would be happy to shop for stationery in your company at any time – just say the word.

In any case, yes, you will soon be rewarded with what you seek.

You simply must survive the deep-sea drama of the enclosed letters first. (Please apologise to your husband on behalf of Sophy, bringer of the nightmares!)

S.

Chapter 10

COVER LETTER FROM SOPHY CIDNOSIN TO E. CIDNOSIN, 1002

Dear sister,

How glorious to write to you knowing that once I finish, I may close the envelope, stroll down to the docking area, deposit it in the next outgoing delivery container, and rest assured that you will hold it in your hands presently. I missed these simple pleasures!

After such a cheerful introduction, however, I must beg your forgiveness. In truth, our expedition ended yesterday evening, but I found myself so weary and confused upon our return that I could not write to you immediately. The summons of sleep proved impossible to ignore.

While yes, in truth, much has occurred since I last wrote, I remain emotionally sound (for the most part), in good health, and eager to process what I discovered. And please know that Eliniea and Irye found no signs of trouble whatsoever in the life-sustaining systems of the Spheres. (It is this discovery that put almost all the crew in a cheerier mood. I say "almost all" because I'm sad to say that Eliniea is distant, of late, and that is particularly disappointing due to—)

Well, you will read the enclosed letters and find out, so I need not reiterate!

Though this package feels like one overextended monologue, please remember that I yearn to hear anything you would like to tell me. Also, would you kindly assist me by informing Arvist that his behaviour officially enrages me? It is a bit grotesque that they claimed my bedroom, but to be honest, E., I find myself willing to part ways with it for now. It's not as though I will come back any time soon.

Please stay strong, dear sister, and feel free to commandeer the library as your home base. He can crawl into his studio through the pipes if he must.

Yours ever so fondly,

Sophy

ENCLOSED LETTER FROM SOPHY CIDNOSIN TO E. CIDNOSIN, 1002

Dear E.,

I begin this letter in the same environment in which I finished the last – afloat in my "Bubble" after a long day and hoping that nothing untoward will glide into my dreams once I finally turn out my lights!

I have discovered much about these Bubbles since writing to you, by the way. For example, if I desire utter privacy, there is a button I may press that will shift the opacity of the shields to encase me in slumber-inducing darkness. (These shields lift on a timer, too, to ensure that my non-existent grasp on the passage of time down here does not impede our mission.) I can also adjust the temperature, which is a boon like no other since I perpetually feel too warm. How curious that is, given that the temperature of the water is near freezing! All these protective layers must be to blame. If Mother were here, she would laugh because I have not yet altered the diving gear into a fashionably cropped style as I did in my youth ...

Most remarkable, however, is that the Bubbles can connect into what is for all intents and purposes a miniature version of a Sphere from the station, allowing our team to converse as a group in relative comfort and protection. I won't bother trying to describe how it works, because

I do not fully understand it myself (though Mother would, certainly), but visually speaking, the Bubbles press together and somehow fuse, creating one larger space. Eliniea demonstrated this feature later last night so we might have a chat (when she caught me spying, you know), and I thought I might return the favour this morning so we could share our breakfast as usual. As soon as I "arrived" in this fashion, Eliniea immediately abandoned her present occupation – which, my inquisitive eyes noticed, happened to be reading a letter signed "With fondness, Tevn" with the most enormous flourish – and gave me a smile fit to illuminate all the abyss.

I wish I could have spent the morning in her fine company, but our breakfast lasted only as long as it took to devour our rations. Time was of the essence – for we were to travel to the Point of Interest, where our research could begin in earnest!

So we broke off into diving pairs and commenced the journey. Irye and Vincenebras joined up again, as seems to be their wont of late. (You would not think from their *Ridge Revealed* interview that these two would make a good match – but somehow Irye's sensibility and Vincenebras' senselessness balance each other out.) I did so very much want to spend more time with Eliniea, but she insisted she must be the "odd one out", as she has the most experience with the region. Plus, I did not want to offend my assigned diving partner, Ylaret, who seemed especially withdrawn.

It took the better part of the so-called morning to reach our destination. I noticed our arrival when my Device immediately revealed the contours of a great canyon, running even deeper than the trench into which we had initially descended. An abyss within an abyss within an abyss! (I say, cheerfully, in an attempt to quell my fears!) At the same moment, Eliniea pulsed all of us on the communicators and asked whether we would prefer to make our first survey of the canyon before or after lunch. (Can you imagine – an expedition leader who cares about the basic human needs of her colleagues? You can tell she is from Intertidal.)

128

I shall not bore you by describing our work for the rest of the day – besides the fact that we swam into the most unreachable place on the planet, you would find our discoveries unremarkable. O, but you would appreciate the series of spectacular illuminated specimen photographs that Niea took with that marvel of a camera. Her artistic skill makes even the most horrific deep-sea beasts seem sensitive and stately. Imagine how much underwater photography will transform your friend Scholar Clel's Natural History practice when these cameras are available more widely!

For your benefit, I will summarise my own cartographical findings in one sentence: "The canyon is very deep." So deep, in fact, that I doubt we will be able to reach its lowest point without a depth-craft – there may be limits, after all, to the pressure our suits can withstand! I will propose to the Department that we invest in a surveying automaton capable of enduring the journey to get a sense of how far down it goes.

Before we separated for the night, I noticed Ylaret gesturing to Eliniea, who joined her in retreating to a metaphorical "corner" (otherwise known as a slightly further-away patch of endless empty water) to talk. One does not eavesdrop on private communicator channels, of course, but I do wonder what they discussed. I hope I have not offended Ylaret in some way! I shall have to make a more concerted effort to socialise with her tomorrow.

Sophy

ENCLOSED LETTER FROM SOPHY CIDNOSIN TO E. CIDNOSIN, 1002

Dear E.,

We "settled in", so to speak, at the Point of Interest, and I promptly neglected to add to this extensive letter! For efficiency's sake, I will now share only the highlights of today – as though they were pearls I've plucked from the seafloor.

Pearl #1: Well, I've picked a poor "pearl" to begin with – I suppose this is more of a grain of sand frustrating the oyster-bed of my mind. I awoke feeling resolute, ready to uncover the secrets of the canyon and my diving partner's taciturn turn. Who could imagine that the former would be easier than the latter?

Upon entering the water, I greeted Ylaret with as much of a smile as one can project through a diving helmet and asked how her research fared. In return, she offered me a few indistinguishable mumbles about stars and seas. Alas – no significant success here. But I did make an effort!

Pearl #2: Around mid-morning, the five of us descended about five fathoms into the canyon, claiming a small outcropping as the temporary centre of our operations. While gathering any number of geological samples from the ridge's wall, Niea spied what looked like a sea of luminescent spheres below us – flashing and fluttering at intervals in purple, blue, yellow, and red, as though a swarm of stars swam beneath our very feet (or fins, I should say!). Niea asked if anyone among us wished to accompany her as she observed the creatures at close range. I responded with great enthusiasm, while everyone else claimed they were far too busy with their own assessments and observations. I imagine that you can hardly believe their reticence – indeed, who could resist the wonder of encountering an unknown species in the company of one of the foremost Scholars of Life? – but I assure you, E., that the average Scholar in the field often becomes so fixated upon their present project that the thought of any "distraction" that does not serve their Thesis seems absolutely repulsive.

We spoke little while swimming closer, as Niea feared that the vibrations of our communicators might alarm the creatures. At one point, we observed that this "school" of unidentified beings was, in fact, drawing nearer to us just as we approached them. Niea flicked her wrist in that most essential Diverspeak gesture, known to novices and experts alike – *Stop here.* I trailed her to the side of the canyon wall, pressing up against it while I treaded water to keep myself in place, and followed her lead as she switched on the smallest and most delicate of lights available on our helmets. The thin beams illuminated just the slightest of cracks in the darkness – but that was light enough for us to see something.

And what we saw was quite the opposite of what I expected.

For even through this fragmented, obfuscated view, I realised that we had not encountered a flock of tiny, glowing creatures, but a single, massive beast, speckled all over with an ethereally precise array of lights. These lights covered tentacles each about as long as our dear Deep House is tall, and the eerie appendages attached to a hulking body unlike any I had ever seen before. Its glowing eye, dear E., possessed a circumference greater than the sum of mine and Niea's heights together.

Suitably convinced that mere shrimp of our size stood no chance of alarming such a behemoth, I dared to flick on my communicator and ask Niea what manner of creature we had encountered. A Colossal Squid, perhaps?

The creature's multi-hued luminescence reflected off Niea's helmet, making the glitter of delight in her brown eyes all the more radiant.

"It is a sort of Nautilus, Sophy! Do you see the chamber?" She gestured towards the bulk at the back of the creature – the protective shell that it carries. (In a way, it rather reminds me of us and our Bubbles!)

"I did not know that a Nautilus could grow larger than a Chancellor's ego," I said, simply because I knew not what else to say. "It is breathtaking."

For a moment, her eyes turned away from the creature – and the viewfinder of her camera – to pause on me.

"Your curiosity and courage astound me, Sophy."

"Do you mean to say," I blustered, struggling as ever to take a compliment, "that we were in danger today? I never would have imagined it!"

As the creature continued its journey through the canyon, Niea began to paddle after it, seemingly half-drunk with Scholarly joy.

"I have never seen anything like it!" Her voice echoed in my ears, warm enough to raise even these extreme water temperatures. "When we came down here for the very first time, I never saw—"

I am quite sure she said "we", by the way, which confused me, because it sounded as though she was talking about her initial solo trip to the Ridge before the Spheres were built – but one never knows the sonic tricks that a Communicator might play. At any rate, Niea's musings were soon cut short by the sudden broadcast of Vincenebras' loudest shriek into our ears.

"By the WAVES, ladies!" he screamed into the communicator. "Why did you send that monster our way? Call it back immediately!"

The Nautilus – fortunately undisturbed by our technology – continued its slow ascent without even casting a colossal eye in Vincenebras' direction. As its luminescence flickered into the distant darkness, I marvelled at how insignificant I am within this vast Ocean.

Pearl #3: You would think that such an encounter would have been the highlight of my day – not so!

When our team reunited at the outcropping and began to make our way out of the canyon (the Nautilus long gone – to Vincenebras' great relief), Niea and I lagged behind.

"So, how does it feel to be the first to see this colossal creature?" I asked her. "Surely the Chancellors will be delighted!"

"Perhaps," she replied, her furrowed brow obvious even through the helmet. "This camera is ineffective."

"But it is the very height of modern innovation!"

"And this Nautilus is beyond modern innovation. The device is intended for capturing images of small creatures at a close range. Nothing of this scale. Certainly, I must obtain some manner of additional proof if I hope to convince the Chancellor of the Nautilus' existence. To make it 'real', you know. Yet I hardly know if it's territorial, or simply wandering through the area, or if others might live nearby."

"What a task it is to prove the existence of something you clearly witnessed with your own eyes," I observed. (How odd for me to say something so – well, anti-Academic!)

"That sounds just like Tev," whispered Niea, so softly that I almost did not know if she had spoken or if the communicator was encountering unexpected static.

"Tev?" I clarified, trying my hardest not to let the wistful nostalgia in her voice lead me into unfounded jealousy.

"O, my former colleague, of course," said Niea. Then she grinned. "Nobody of amorous significance, Scholar Cidnosin. I assure you that he is not my sort."

My breath hitched. Though I live by the rules of decorum, something about hearing Niea say my formal title for the first time, even in jest, was – especially intimate. "And, if I may ask – what is your 'sort', Scholar Forghe?"

She peered down at me with an unexpected confidence that made me feel dizzy.

"Do you really not know?" she murmured, before immediately seeming to short-circuit with anxiety and swimming away from me at high speed.

We have not had a moment alone since, but I caught her glancing at me on several occasions as we dined with our colleagues this evening. Too giddy to write further!

S.

ENCLOSED LETTER FROM SOPHY CIDNOSIN TO E. CIDNOSIN, 1002

Dearest E.,

Tonight, I hope, will be the last time I write to you from a Bubble for the foreseeable future. It has been a strange end to our journey, and I almost do not wish to record it. The frivolous delight of my past letter seems so alien to me today. Perhaps we are all simply too tired.

After yesterday's—exchange—I greatly anticipated a private breakfast with Niea. You can imagine my disappointment when I overslept (can I truly be blamed when there is no sunlight and setting the timer for the shades is so easy to forget?) to find her already with Ylaret. When I pulled my Bubble closer to join them, they stopped talking immediately.

Niea smiled, as though relieved to see me; Ylaret appeared as distant as she has been since we left the Spheres.

"Good morning – well, arbitrarily-determined-start-of-the-day, Sophy!" Niea chirped, though her voice sparkled less than usual. "I was just about to summon you. I shall pulse Irye and Vincenebras so we may all speak together."

When those two arrived – their Bubbles already connected, as they seemed to have been enjoying a spirited morning debate – Niea gazed at us with an undecipherable expression. Was it a smile that hadn't risen high enough on her face, or a frown in disguise?

"First of all, my friends, I would like to commend your excellent work," she said, nodding at each crew member in turn. "Yet I know this unpredictable way of living has been difficult for each of us. You will be relieved, I hope, to learn that we will begin our return journey to the Spheres today."

A mild uproar ensued out of Scholarly politeness – all of us saying *Certainly we can endure another day?* and *O, but there is so much work to be done!* – but we did not protest too much. How comfortable and safe the Spheres seemed after several days drifting in the void!

To my continued disappointment, Niea subsequently announced that she would pair up with Ylaret for the return journey, leaving me as the unwelcome third party to the dynamic duo of Irye and Vincenebras.

"Dear Irye," asked Vincenebras as soon as I paddled over, "as a Scholar of Sound, have you ever quantified that which makes any particular noise most irritating?"

"Not yet, dear Vincenebras, but if you would be kind enough to continue talking, I may be able to complete this groundbreaking work as you speak!"

At the very least, their incessant chatter ensured that I did not ever need to contribute anything more than the occasional "You don't say?"

When we stopped for the night, Niea bowed out of a shared meal, claiming that she had too many reports to prepare in advance of our return. I agonised for hours afterwards, wondering if it would seem inappropriate to speak plainly to her about her sudden change in mood.

I determined that it would seem inappropriate, and yet I did it anyway.

When I pulsed her communicator, she answered with the same forced cheer she had been maintaining all day – which made her voice sound five times higher than its usual pitch.

"It is me," I said, trying to keep my voice at its normal tone. "I wanted to see if there was anything amiss, Eliniea. Did I offend you yesterday? If there is any way in which I might help you, I would be glad to know."

"You are generous as always, Sophy," she said, with a non-negligible amount of her usual warmth. "And I am grateful for you, as I always am. In more ways than you know. Yet I fear it was imprudent of me to speak so informally to you yesterday. But that is little offence compared to dragging you to see that creature, when you did not realise the potential risk involved."

"You said yourself that I am courageous, no?" said I. "I am also a Scholar, equipped with as many years of experience as you. I consider myself capable of assessing risks and acting accordingly. You did nothing wrong!"

"But you cannot even imagine the dangers of this place! And after what happened with ..." She paused, and when she began to speak again, her voice had softened. "My—experience—with you, Sophy, has been like no other. Sometimes it heartens me to dream of how we may become better acquainted once we return to the surface. At the moment, however, I live in fear that all of us may fall into terrible peril. It is imperative that I focus my energy upon preserving our mission and your safety. I apologise, I really do. You know not how—"

Embarrassed by her communicator-distorted sob, I quickly cut in.

"Is there nothing I may do for you, Niea? Nothing at all? Name any task, and I will do my best to make it so."

It took what felt like several long minutes for her to respond.

"If this makes you uncomfortable, you may certainly decline, but I wonder – would you leave your communicator active tonight? Simply so I may hear that someone is there? It is a silly thing, to be sure, but I would appreciate the companionship."

I assented, she bade me good night, and I have lain here for an indeterminate amount of time listening to her breathing echoing in my ears.

It is so painfully clear that Eliniea bears some burden – from her past expedition, that first foray into the depths? – that she dares not reveal to the rest of us. I know she made that initial voyage all alone – and in relative secret, because the Chancellors did not wish the broader campus to know too much about this project until its success was confirmed – and being by one's self down here must have been a challenge like no other. Yet I so wish to help her! And, more shamefully still, there is a part of me that wishes fervently that such help were not necessary – that we had simply met as others do above the surface, in a library or Debate Society presentation or in a crowded refectory – and could enjoy getting to know each other without the perils of the deep sea coming between us.

O, my dear E., how I miss you.

S.

LETTER FROM E. CIDNOSIN TO SOPHY CIDNOSIN, 1002

Long-missed sister,

Hello again! O, it is such a relief to know that you are safely back at your Spheres and no longer wandering the great unknown ...

... but I must admit it surprised me to read how truly tame your mission was! Your Device picked up nothing untoward or mysterious; your encounter with a monster beyond my wildest imaginings ended in flirtation; and the most sinister force at play was some briefly flickering lights at the Spheres!

(Those preceding sentences were my attempt at both bleak humour and reassurance – if I convince myself nothing went amiss during your expedition, then that will become the truth, won't it?)

I am sorry to hear of Niea's woes, and sorry for you – someone who seeks so desperately to help her. The warning Niea gave you – that she did not wish to burden you, or endanger you, or overtax you with her strife – reminds me immensely of what I have said to you on past occasions. I do not fully know of what I speak, but I do know how it feels to be overwhelmed with worry about the safety of those around me.

If I might be so bold as to offer further remarks on the topic of Scholar Forghe, it seems relevant to remember that though she is your peer in practice, her additional experience with the deep ocean might make her feel as though all responsibility falls squarely on her shoulders and no one else's. Consequently, though you think you have not helped her, perhaps the mere reminder that she is not alone assisted her in ways you cannot yet see.

Of course you are better versed in that esoteric vocabulary of human relationships than I. Please disregard everything I wrote!

I will not speak of Arvist and his antics, to spare you further strife, but please know that if I had even an inkling of hope that you would be returning home, I would summon an unprecedented fury from who knows where and eject him from your chamber immediately! Until then, I will remain – unfortunately – my feeble and non-confrontational self, content to let Arvist do whatever he wishes with the Structure while I stay confined to my room for the most part. I reclaimed the dining room, however, and can endure sitting across from him over a meal if necessary. Yesterday he babbled on and on about how the rescheduled School of Inspiration Gala had been cancelled again, and that he must do something, and—I rather ignored the rest, I fear. How tragic for Arvist! And how tragic for me – because at least the accursed gala would have lured him out of the house for an evening!

I hope to find you in better spirits in your next letter. Have I mentioned that I am very relieved you are safe?

Gratefully,

E.

P.S. Because I know this will brighten your day like nothing else – I do continue to write to Schr Clel. In fact, I await his next letter as we speak. (That is quite a significant change from my previous attitude, as I used to assume by default that he would never respond to me again.)

AUTOMATED POST MISSIVE FROM VYERIN CLEL TO SOPHY CIDNORGHE, 1003

Dear Sophy,

I thought that the episode with the Nautilus would have been the cause of the most intense emotional reaction I experienced while reading this set of letters – and yet both Reiv and I have been – I hesitate to admit this – practically weeping over the tense conclusion of your emotional arc with Niea. (Yes, I have taken up the habit of reading particularly engaging passages to my husband from time to time. He sends his regards, by the way. I think he is very happy that I have a "project".)

There is so much more to say, and I can hardly think how to express it adequately. I suspect this was a bit of jesting banter, but in case it was not – would you truly like to meet up, at the papercraft marketplace or otherwise? My only obligation this week is a flexible research cruise and Reiv finds himself with a rare "free day". I would not mind making a short detour to any anchorage of your choice at Boundless!

Tomorrow?

V.

AUTOMATED POST MISSIVE FROM SOPHY CIDNORGHE TO VYERIN CLEL, 1003

Dear Vyerin,

I accept! I do so like thematic relevance, so if it is indeed not too much trouble for you and your husband to come to our part of the world for the market (how lucky we are to have those high-speed vessels these days!), we shall meet you there tomorrow – say, eleven bells in the morning?

Perhaps it will comfort you and Reiv to see Niea alive, well, and happily married to me – our past troubles long passed (for the most part).

When I read your letters, it often occurs to me how little I know of you – what your voice sounds like, the expressions you tend to make, and even what sort of clothes you like to wear! I look forward to making your acquaintance (what a funny thing to say to someone who knows one's life so well).

Until tomorrow,
Sophy

Chapter 11

AUTOMATED POST MISSIVE FROM VYERIN CLEL TO SOPHY CIDNORGHE, 1003

Dear Sophy,

I hardly knew how to put words to page again after we enjoyed our face-to-face conversation. I considered dialling your house Echolator instead. It was kind of you to provide me with the call-number. In the end, I determined the "old-fashioned" format of writing letters (with the convenience of A.P.) still seems best.

I shall not harp on for too long about our meeting, since we both had the good fortune of experiencing it. Reiv did ask me to send his fondest wishes to you and Eliniea. He said you were "both absolutely charming", and "made [him] miss having a social life!" I, for one, was astounded by Niea's admirable extroversion, the remarkable range of the topics we discussed in a few short hours, and most of all, your impressive height!

I expected that we would spend most of our time talking about E. and Henerey, but part of me is happy we did not. Forming this history of our siblings together is a wonderful undertaking, but it can be painful at times, too. I am relieved that we primarily process these emotions through the written word.

On that note – I look forward to continuing to do so.

Your friend,

Vyerin

P.S. I hope the journal you purchased will serve your needs. I thought it fitting to use my new stationery for this letter.

AUTOMATED POST MISSIVE FROM SOPHY CIDNORGHE TO VYERIN CLEL, 1003

Dear Vyerin,

Yes, it is strange indeed! In the past, I never "pictured" you while reading your letters – if someone asked me to imagine the physical appearance of Vyerin Clel, I would imagine a collection of words arranged on a page. But now I know Vyerin the Man as well as Vyerin the Letters, and that makes this all the more enjoyable.

(I can understand why you were so popular back in the day, by the way! You are quite loquacious. I will admit that I mischaracterised you as rather terse to Niea before our meeting, so she was astounded by how you led the conversation. She thought you and Reiv were "perfectly lovely".)

And yes, the journal suits me very well. I intend to carry it with me wherever I go and write down any questions or ideas that may arise relating to our project. (That happens more often than you might think!)

Your friend (and fellow collection of words),

Sophy

LETTER FROM HENEREY CLEL TO E. CIDNOSIN, 1002

Dear E.,

In this new environment, the sight of an envelope adorned with your familiar handwriting made me feel instantly at home! I am so grateful that you received my new address and had the opportunity to write back so quickly – thank you. I regret that I must continue to write to you with subpar materials. The pages upon which these words are inscribed, I hate to say, have been torn from my field journal because I lack anything else. My apologies!

Befitting the ephemeral nature of my stationery, I am sorry to say that I must be brief yet again – as I have few moments to myself these days. The upside of my new expedition is that I no longer have time to sit morosely in my room at the Anchorage while staring at the wall and thinking of nothing; the downside is that my free time to write to you has decreased, and I regret that very much. Two apologies – is that any way to begin a letter?

After writing such a short and suspenseful note last time, however, I feel I owe you further explanation of my new circumstances. When I first received the summons, I wondered if Chancellor Rawsel sought to punish me for general incorrigibility with exile – which I think was his intention – but the joke is on that awful man. This expedition offers what I've been dreaming of doing for months while I frittered away my time with hypotheticals! My task is to focus upon a single issue: anomalies in the patterns of Imposing Ray migrations. Every morning I wake and scan the horizon for the rays. So far, we've seen only two squadrons, but hundreds more should travel through this area over the course of the next few tides. My new Intertidal colleague Scholar Lerin Zuan Vellen (who has spent more than six months aboard the *Sagacity* already!) informed me that the path of the ray migration shifted suddenly over the past two years – as though after centuries of charting the same course, they changed their minds. I hope to track their movements and draw some manner of conclusion about these migrational shifts – perhaps they have found a more pleasant place to spend their winters?

But before I wax too poetic about rays, I wanted to express my extreme displeasure towards your brother and his disregard for your feelings. Am I correct in understanding that it is less his presence that disturbs you, and more the fact that he showed up unannounced, giving you no say in the matter whatsoever? If that is the case, then I under-stand your reaction very well, since I too deal very poorly with sudden changes, visits, or social duties. (As any colleague who has ever invited me to share a meal immediately after a lecture without giving me the opportunity to prepare myself emotionally has discovered!)

How I wish you could join me in watching these rays flapping towards the horizon! Have you ever seen one before? I would imagine not, as the Imposing Ray rarely drops far below the surface. But surely you have All-Embracing Rays at your depth level?

Finally – though I can literally hear Lerin rapping on my door to request my presence on deck – I hope they will grant me but one moment more – your sketch of the "Structure" haunts me. It does indeed resemble a Tunicate! What impressive visual intelligence you possess. What did Arvist say when you asked him about it? I am at the edge of my seat! Please, tell me more and do not take the length of this letter as any indication that I am not interested in continuing our conversation!

I must away, but remain yours,

Henerey

P.S. Now it is time for me to expose myself as a hypocrite. After hearing the new questions that arose in your "Structure Inquiry", I wanted to raise the question of an unexpected social visit of my own. You see, my brother generously sent along the little book I hoped to procure for you during my stay at his home (of course I left it behind by accident) and I considered the possibility of delivering it to you in person – since, as you said yourself, we are now in closer geographical proximity than we have ever been before! I have one blessed day off to use sometime soon, and by that point our trajectory puts the *Sagacity* close enough to the Deep House that I could easily catch a ride from a passenger-boat. I understand, however, that given your current situation at home, you may not be in the frame of mind to meet a stranger, especially when the Deep House is already overrun with people. If that is the case, please let me know, and I will mail you the book and never mention this again!

I only mention the possibility because even I, someone who abjures all human company under most circumstances, find the notion of meeting you incredibly inviting. But I promise I will not be disappointed, upset, or in any way alarmed if you decline. On my honour as a Scholar!

HANDWRITTEN NOTE FROM SELIARA GIDNAN TO E. CIDNOSIN

To my most cherished Future Sister,

O dearest E.! I wish you would give me a chance to speak with you more, as I so wholeheartedly miss our friendship. I never expected that living in the same house would lead to such isolation between us, though truly I will admit that the Deep House in its totality has far surpassed the tiny boundaries of what I remember from when I was a child. I imagine that fifteen souls could live here and never pass each other unless they wanted to. I told Arvist that it was cruel of him to move here without talking to you first and making sure you had time to prepare after living with no one but yourself for so long. There is one other thing he wishes to do and I would like to ask you about that, but time is of the essence because it relates to happenings in the next three days so I pray you will be able to break your seclusion for my sake if not for Arvist's! Will you not come downstairs this morning?

P.S. I have decided to write you a Letter rather than knock. I fear it would feel as though I gave you no chance to say no if I were to come and speak with you in person. And I do want you to feel most comfortable!

INVITATION MAILED BY ARVIST CIDNOSIN TO ONE HUNDRED RECIPIENTS IN THE SCHOOL OF INSPIRATION, BOUNDLESS CAMPUS

Cherished fellows-in-Inspiration,

I find the continued delay of our Gala most disheartening, so I come to deliver you from further misery and propose an alternative gathering. Please join me in the Historical and Singular Deep House (my personal residence) for a performance – and celebration – unlike anything you have ever seen before.

I request your presence at any hour of the evening you so desire in two days' time on the fourth day of the Second Perishing Tide in the Second Quarter of High Waters. Kindly arrange your own transportation, and I invite you to bring your own spirits and sustenance.

Until our paths cross!

Scholar Artistry "Arvist" Cidnosin

LETTER FROM E. CIDNOSIN TO HENEREY CLEL, 1002

Dear Henerey,

Perhaps you did not expect to hear from me so soon. Do your new colleagues suit you? Your mood seems elevated since you last wrote to me from campus, and I delight to think that you found a more suitable "habitat" in which you may prosper!

My own luck with "colleagues" continues to diminish. Today has been a ceaseless onslaught of misfortune, to frame it positively. This morning, I entered my library for the first time since their arrival, hoping to find my well-worn copy of *The Star Sailors* – because our conversation reminded me of how long it's been since I read it last! (I find the second Intertidal translation best of all – perhaps you agree?)

Yet I soon faced a sight even more inexplicable than the Orb that Lady Ei glimpsed circling the planet during the crew's first voyage. My chair, by which I mean, my mother's chair that I inherited – a lovely sand-scrubbed armchair the colour of the evening tide – lay dead upon the floor with one of its legs split in two. Now, I can identify exactly what causes such injuries to Cidnosin family armchairs – it is the infernal act of leaning backwards in them, such that the frontmost legs rise off the floor and all weight is redistributed to the other two. I know this because a fifteen-year-old Arvist once inflicted the very same cruelty upon Father's armchair.

At any rate, I will not bore you with the details of the confrontation that ensued – but I will say that it culminated in something even more frustrating than broken furniture. As if damaging family keepsakes were not enough, Arvist announced that he will host the rescheduled School of Inspiration Gala – in my house! In two days! Recall, if you will, dear Henerey, that climactic moment in which the Star Sailors pass before a dying sun, and Lord Uv calls it "the most wrathful sea [he's] ever seen" – for that is how my heart felt in this moment.

Now I find myself alternately overcome with rage and despair.

Perhaps you will think me ridiculous – after all, Arvist, Sophy, and I are technically co-owners of the Deep House, as my parents wished us always to have the family home as our place of refuge. Arvist himself argues that I am overdramatic and greedy, and that I have no right to be the sole arbiter of what can and cannot happen within these walls. But part of me cannot help feeling as though I should possess such veto powers. Sophy left, Arvist left, and I stayed – does that not make me the closest thing this house has to an "owner"?

Yet I do "love" my brother, as it were, and the gala will happen (solely because the invitations have already been distributed to one hundred recipients without my consent), so I must figure out how to endure it.

On that note, let me proceed to the point, though it terrifies me. Your offer to personally deliver your book (which I cannot wait to read!)

struck me so speechless that I folded up your letter, rose from my chair, and paced the length of my chamber half a dozen times before returning to the desk and reading those words again. Upon further consideration, I must admit that I would very much enjoy the opportunity to converse with you at length.

And, in two days' time, I predict I will be especially grateful for a distraction.

But to be fair to you, I must include a disclaimer first. It has been well over a year since I last spoke to a stranger (one of Arvist's visiting friends, back when he was finishing his Apprenticeship – I said "good day", attempted to flee, knocked over a vase containing what appeared to be one hundred paintbrushes, and then spent the next three days in my room weeping over my great humiliation), and I have not felt comfortable in crowds since before I came of age.

O Henerey, I can tell from your letters and from your academic writing that you have a wonderful imagination, so perhaps you understand how a lively mind can be as much of a burden as it is a gift. Mine tends to fixate on scenarios – memories – difficulties – and then embellish them with such detail that I feel as though calamities have actually happened, and I the cause of them. Even stopping in briefly for a mandatory appearance at the dinner parties our parents used to host when I was a young woman in my early twenties made me sick to my stomach, and I would spend days afterwards replaying and rewriting each word in my head until I was certain that I behaved abominably to everyone I encountered and that they would soon shame my name throughout all of Society. (This ailment is not solely related to social interactions – there are other aspects that I may disclose to you later, if you wish – but that is the most relevant part at this moment.)

Since then, I have worked with a Physician of the Brain to help me, and I can manage it with relative ease these days. My Physician always suggests that one form of treatment for my fixations is to put myself into safe scenarios related to what alarms me, "exposing" myself until I become able to better control the feelings I experience in response. I am cowardly, in some ways, and fear what intensity such an experience might bring.

But I can safely say that there has never been a "stranger" more understanding, trustworthy, and sympathetic than yourself, my friend, and if you are willing – I think I would like to chance this encounter.

I anticipate that you may, after reading all this, decide that a visit to see me might be more challenging than you anticipated. I will hold no grudge if that is the case! Or perhaps you wish to put off this meeting until a future date, when all of the School of Inspiration is not arrayed in my parlour. I understand this, too.

So in order to keep up my courage, I will merely say that I hope to see you soon – whenever that may be.

E.

LETTER FROM HENEREY CLEL TO E. CIDNOSIN, 1002

Dear E.,

I can hardly believe the words I will soon write – I would love nothing more than to attend the gala tomorrow.

I would say "See you in two days!," except, after reading your letter, I certainly do not wish to risk your discomfort in any way, and wanted to give you one last chance to change your mind if you feel this is not the appropriate time for us to meet. Do know that up until the very last hour you can always write me to decline – or paste a sign on a window that simply reads "HENEREY, NO" – and I will happily desist.

Thank you for sharing your experiences with me. I do not share your exact ailment, but I am no stranger to struggles with one's mind. Mine simply take a slightly different form. Perhaps we might discuss this in more detail at a future point. Please do not worry that I will be negatively surprised (perish the thought!) by what I find when we meet. On the contrary, your very existence in my life has been the most wondrous surprise imaginable.

So may I call upon you, and, in doing so, surpass that level of wonder?

Yours,

Henerey

LETTER FROM E. CIDNOSIN TO HENEREY CLEL, 1002

Dear Henerey,

Your card arrived this evening, and I will follow your lead by replying with great haste.

If you are willing to brave a gathering of my brother's questionable compatriots for the sake of one evening in my company, then I suppose I admire your courage.

I say yes.

Until tomorrow,

E.

P.S. But please do not expect to stay too long – I do not mean to offend, but I simply do not want to overestimate my ability to entertain you! This is uncharted territory for me.

P.P.S. You should note that most transport boat captains are often annoyed by the prospect of dropping off passengers at the Deep House – I encourage you to bring a small gift to improve your captain's mood.

P.P.P.S. After we meet, if you would like to stay longer and explore the Deep House on your own, you are certainly welcome to. Of course, I imagine that it would be a much more pleasant experience with a guide, but I do not know if I will be able to accompany you when the house is crowded with strangers. In fact, the more I think about exactly what is to happen tomorrow night, the more I feel as though I should have fibbed to Arvist long ago that the house causes depth-sickness in anyone who has not grown up acclimated to its water pressure and therefore no guests should ever visit!

P.P.P.P.S. I do truly look forward to seeing you tomorrow.

LETTER FROM E. CIDNOSIN TO SOPHY CIDNOSIN, 1002

Dear Sophy,

I apologise for troubling you with a second letter – I know that you have much to do after returning from your expedition. Consider this a long-distance diary entry.

Yesterday marked the apex of my tribulations with Arvist. I went into the library only to find that he had broken Mother's chair, Sophy! Incensed beyond belief, I steamed into the kitchen, where I found Arvist and Seliara conspiring over cake.

"Dear E.!" cried Seliara, standing as soon as I entered. "Did you receive my note? I am so pleased you came to speak with us!"

I ignored this inexplicable plea. (To my regret, I later found her note lost under the rug outside my door. She did try to warn me, I suppose.)

"Arvist," I said, clenching my jaw as soon as the name was out of my mouth, "have you been in the library recently?"

"O, indeed!" He clasped my shoulder. "I forgot to mention this earlier, but your chair has broken."

"Broken? Of its own volition, truly?" I exclaimed. "Has no one been involved in the breaking of it?"

"It can be replaced, of course," Arvist laughed. "There is something far more important I wish to tell you, dear sister."

"There is nothing more important to me at present. Enjoy your cake, dear brother," I said, with an air of petulance that I regret now.

"But there is no time!" he shouted. "I am delighted to announce that I will be hosting the School of Inspiration's Gala in two days' time—"

"Its cancellation has been cancelled, then?" I replied. "Wonderful. I look forward to the peace and quiet."

"E.," began Seliara.

"I will host it here," said Arvist. "I know that may be inconvenient for you, but it is essential for me to demonstrate my creative engagement with the Structure to my most beloved colleagues!"

I began breathing shallowly. I felt as though I needed to take the deepest yawn in the world to clear my chest, but I could not. Words failed me.

"E.," Arvist continued, in a voice suddenly so calm and reasonable that it only infuriated me further, "this is my house just as much as it is yours, and I very much hope we may coexist together. Why, it has only been a year since I moved out, and barely a month since Sophy left! Have you already forgotten what it is like to share the company of others? Here, let me phrase it in a way that will appeal to your Natural-History-loving nature – shall we not find a way to reach symbiosis together?"

I wanted to reply "Never, you parasite," but nothing left my lips. I thought I could hear Seliara asking Arvist if she and I might have a moment alone, though the words felt heavy and unrecognisable. I retreated to my room, sat down at my desk, and wrote to Henerey.

That was a mistake. I should not have communicated with him in such a state of mind, for somehow amid all this, I invited him to visit me during Arvist's accursed party – and Henerey agreed to come.

To keep ahold of my senses, I have convinced myself that he will not appear. Then, if he does, I shall react in the moment; if he does not, I will not be disappointed.

More than ever, I wish you were here.

Your sister,

E.

AUTOMATED POST MISSIVE FROM VYERIN CLEL TO SOPHY CIDNORGHE, 1003

Dear Sophy,

I thought it would amuse you to know that, once again, Henerey wrote to me at the very moment when E. reached out to you.

V.

LETTER FROM HENEREY CLEL TO VYERIN CLEL, 1002

Dear Vy, my anchor:

A thousand thanks for sending me that book!

Be forewarned – I will now break the greatest vow I ever made to myself (namely, never talk to Vyerin about matters of the heart!) and confess that I intend to spend the evening after next at a School of Inspiration party to meet my "correspondent", E., for the very first time. My ship's path will intersect with the midpoint stop of a transport vessel that makes daily rounds through the entire Boundless Campus, and if I catch it and ask very nicely (and offer a small bribe of fine tea, which is always welcomed by navigators, or so a certain Captain told me!), I assume its operator might make an on-demand journey to the Deep House.

What troubles me the most is that my swift departure from campus means that I am utterly bereft of anything suitable to wear! We are clad in waterwear most days on the *Sagacity*; I have but a single frock coat and none of my more dignified robes. Yet I suppose because it is a School of Inspiration event, I might wear suspenders of seaweed and fit in quite well!

I wish you were here so I might ask your opinion as to what hairstyle would suit me best (and accept your choice willingly, though I know that you would have simply picked one option at random, as you always do).

Please send all my best and many apologies to Reiv and Avanne for not staying longer! Perhaps it will amuse them to imagine me attempting to attend a social gathering.

Fondly,

Henerey

AUTOMATED POST MISSIVE FROM SOPHY CIDNORGHE TO VYERIN CLEL, 1003

Dear Vyerin,

O how it charms me to picture Henerey parading in front of you in various get-ups! (For someone who claims disinterest towards fashion, you looked especially elegant when we met – those tan robes were timeless.)

Dare I ask why Henerey feared to ask you for romantic advice?

S.

AUTOMATED POST MISSIVE FROM VYERIN CLEL TO SOPHY CIDNORGHE, 1003

Dear S.,

Thank you for the compliment. Both my husband and I share a distaste for trends and style, as it were, but somehow both our children are exceptionally fashionable. (Orey picked out those robes for me, in fact – by which I mean he thoroughly spilled his breakfast on the ones I wore previously, forcing me to choose an alternative.)

To your question – Henerey has always been a bit of a fool for love. Not in the sense that he was a philanderer – the exact opposite, in fact, because the physical "benefits" of human intimacy that some of us enjoy held very limited appeal to him – but as a young lad, he was prone to indulging in saccharine, dreamy fancies about the nature of romance.

And I, as a young lad, was equally inclined to mock them. We shall leave it at that.

Now, as someone who is not especially sentimental, I find Henerey's and E.'s relationship quite special – certainly living up to Henerey's romantic fantasies. Today, Avanne and I took our luncheon together, and after some resilient prying on her behalf, I deigned to summarise these letters to her, describing the eagerness I felt about experiencing our siblings' first meeting. Then my daughter, ever the pragmatist, stared down at her bowl and observed gently:

"But, Father, that first encounter took place in person, did it not? You will never be able to know what happened when they met!"

And I must admit, Sophy, that after such a grand prelude I find myself rather disappointed that we have no record of what transpired between my brother and E. during this special occasion.

Even though I know that is incredibly invasive of me.

V.

AUTOMATED POST MISSIVE FROM SOPHY CIDNORGHE TO VYERIN CLEL, 1003

V.,

Avanne is absolutely right – it is true that a record of such a moment would be impossible to procure.

Impossible, that is, for anyone but me.

I found this annotated programme (created by Arvist for the night's revels) – creased many times, as though she enjoyed rereading it as much as any other Henerey letter.

I simply cannot wait until you see what has been written on the back of it. (Feel free to share it with your family, since they are so invested!)

With excitement,

Sophy

Chapter 12

PROGRAMME FOR A PERFORMANCE BY
ARVIST CIDNOSIN AT THE DEEP HOUSE, 1002

Scholar Arvist Cidnosin (Soon-to-be *Cidnan*, by the Grace of my
Esteemed Betrothed, Seliara Gidnan)
Presents
"O, MY CRYSTAL HEART LIES BENEATH THE WAVES,
FORLORN AND FORGOTTEN"
A Dramatic Art in Four Parts
Inspired by the "Elusive Cidnosin Structure"
Premiering This Evening
For the Benefit of Those Bereft of the School of Inspiration Gala by
Cruel Misjudgement
At the Deep House, Boundless Campus

WHEN ENTERING THE PERFORMANCE PLACE,
PLEASE PLACE YOUR BODY IN A POSTURE
OF QUIETUDE

HANDWRITTEN ANNOTATIONS ON THE BACK OF THE PROGRAMME, 1002

As it's seemingly impossible to hear anything in this dismal din, shall we try this? I wanted to say that Seliara greeted me & told me where you might be. I promise I was not simply skulking about & hoping I might stumble upon you! – H.

A handy solution! You put your cleverness on full display, Scholar Clel! I am impressed that you recognised me. Did Seliara furnish you with a description of my appearance? I shall have to thank her for guiding you. – E.

She only told me that if you were feeling brave you might be tucked away at the top of the staircase, or else you would be in your room (& I should not intrude!). Very relieved it was the former. She said nothing of your appearance, so that is (if I may) a most wonderful surprise. – H.

You, on the other hand, look exactly like your author portrait – which I'm grateful to have possessed, because it assisted me in imagining quite a clear mental image of my correspondent with every letter you sent. Though I will confess that you are far more vibrant in person. – E. (we needn't keep initialling; I certainly know who you are, Henerey!)

An unfair advantage! Had you sent me a portrait in kind, I assure you that I would have done the same.

I am not in the habit of taking or keeping portraits of myself, seeing as I have no need to share my image with the world, nor any readers to impress with soulful eyes and artistically ruffled hair.

The pose & styling were the publisher's choice.

And the impressively colourful frock coat?

Perhaps I too must shoulder some blame.

I observed that the coat you wore in the portrait was the same cut as the one you have on tonight, though not the same material (and this one is much subtler in pattern, which suits you).

Your careful visual observation skills would make you a finer Scholar of Classification than I am.

I will take that as the highest compliment, coming from you. In truth, I would much rather observe sleeping Shrimp than endure the deluge of human activity invading my home tonight. Present company excluded, of course.

Likewise. I find it extremely surreal to be here. I have achieved a childhood dream by stepping inside the Deep House in the first place (I will not humiliate myself by describing in detail my emotional reaction to entering the airlock this evening), but this "gathering" seems no different than those accursed seasonal balls. From this vantage point, you can hardly even tell that we are underwater.

Shift over a little and sit here next to me (if you dare). If you can catch a glimpse of the baseboard on the westward wall, you might notice a tiny series of portholes. In the daytime with the sunlight filtering through, they rather resemble sunken stars, but at the moment, they look like midnight jewels set into the white plaster.

Phenomenal! I do wish that Schr Bardein were not standing right in the way; the beautiful design struggles to eclipse his ankles. By the way, these are for you.

Two books, not one! Such bounty! Is that the Boundless Campus library crest I spy on this second volume? My, Henerey, what a risk you've taken – I fear I am not worth the potential peril.

If there were any potential peril, I assure you that I'm justified in risking it. Fortunately, I have not stolen from our good Library Stewards, because this book is such a worn copy that my friend in the library, Elaxand, offered it to me on "indefinite loan", & the second is the afore-promised childhood book of Fantasies. I think you will find it enlightening.

O, yes, I had forgotten in my excitement that you did have a reason to visit me! I cannot wait to examine the book in more detail.

Had I not such an excuse, I might have contrived one. Yet I do think this will be a worthwhile volume. What a shame that this stairwell (with the raucous crowd below!) is not the best place to attempt a little reading.

Would you care to see my library? Perhaps I will attempt to talk to you there. We must be quite careful, though, when circumnavigating the anarchy downstairs. If Seliara sees me with you, she will no doubt want to introduce you to Arvist. We shall creep through the back hall, as Sophy and I did so often as children!

Anything to escape this nightmarish revel. I cannot wait to hear your voice. Surely it must be equally enchanting.

O, do be careful, Henerey. Flatter me too much and I will be too shy to speak!

AUTOMATED POST MISSIVE FROM VYERIN CLEL TO SOPHY CIDNORGHE, 1003

Dear Sophy,

You leave me speechless (though I suppose that is a difficult reaction to convey in an epistolary fashion).

Yet as precious as this document is, I am glad it ends so that we may let E. and Henerey enjoy their time in the library without their siblings eavesdropping from the future. I do feel uncomfortable spying on them in this way. It comforts me immensely, though, to know that Henerey found some happiness, if only for a short while.

V.

P.S. I smiled at my brother's derisive mention of the seasonal balls. I always quite enjoyed them, not knowing any better, but then when I left and attended an actual Captains' soiree – with proper dancing and feasting instead of nothing more than Scholarly posturing – I realised what I had been missing.

P.P.S. Though Henerey attempts to employ a few stray ampersands to save time, I appreciate how both he and E. took the time to write these passed notes in full sentences.

AUTOMATED POST MISSIVE FROM SOPHY CIDNORGHE TO VYERIN CLEL, 1003

Dear Vyerin,

It certainly is a treasure, is it not?

Every time I read this "conversation" (I am now on my ninth reread in the past twenty-four hours), I find myself reduced to tears. Not simply because of the emotional satisfaction of seeing my sister enjoy the company of someone for whom she cared so deeply, but also because it makes me miss the Deep House and my family with all my heart. It seems especially cruel to be forever bereft of my sister, my mother, my wayward father, and the only home we ever knew.

But if I lose myself in tears, I shall never be able to finish writing to you, and I did have a question about the book of Fantasies you sent to Henerey. I don't suppose you would know where to find it? I ask because I managed to track down a copy of the other library book he lent her – Dovis Cloyd's *Size Anomalies of the Second Ocean*. I assume he brought this one because it relates to the Elongated Fish! How wonderful to imagine Henerey and E. poring over the first Chapter – I've copied a passage for your reading pleasure.

S.

P.S. I agree wholeheartedly on the subject of Scholarly dances, balls, etc. – everyone stands about and talks over everyone else, insisting that their research is superior in methodology, etc. – and it is supposed to be "enjoyable"!

P.P.S. E. would have purposely taken the time to write those notes without any shorthand techniques to calm her nerves. Perhaps Henerey followed her lead to make her feel comfortable.

EXCERPT FROM *SIZE ANOMALIES OF THE SECOND OCEAN*, CHAPTER 1: ORIGINS AND ANCESTORS

Ask any young person about the existence of beasts of monstrous proportions, and that small child will most likely take great delight in enumerating the many enormous creatures they encounter on a daily basis: including you!

Scale is, of course, all a matter of perspective, and to the Extensive Squid we are but mackerel. Yet it is my aim in this volume to consider size in an objective sense and assess those anomalous members of any given species who happen to surpass their peers in proportion.

What did the seas look like before the Dive? We can only speculate. Our Ancestors, floating above this world in their great Skyships, rarely considered the water-covered planet beneath them. Accounts from various Survivors suggest that the waters of our world used to swarm with the most sizeable of specimens – the majority of which, it appears, perished when the Clouds crashed to the bottom of the sea. (Why the Dive spelled the end for these species remains unknown, but Scholars Elvir and Ute's promising new work on fluctuating water temperatures since the Antepelagic era suggests that the changing chemical makeup of the world might have played a deadly role.) The inscription accompanying the thousand-year-old "Pelagic Circle Map" – one of the oldest authenticated Survivor documents – suggests a few key sources to which we might turn in an attempt to legitimise the oversized monsters that swim through its hand-drawn waters:

"It has been said by Zigor that within the Second Sea were Creatures wider than a ship is long and heavier, besides. As written in Mairvhen, we see also great Knightfish with Horns fit to pierce a hull. Scholars dared not sail outside of the Boundless Meridian for fear of the Knightfish's Interventions."

While it is my opinion that the so-called "Knightfish" is purely fanciful, let us turn to Zigor and the Second Sea. Zigor, the Survivors' celebrated Scholar of Memory, offered the following account (translated from Arcane Scholar shorthand by the author):

"Eventually, one island must sink while another springs from beneath the sea. Likewise, when one creature enters the world, another must leave. I have heard of many folk who witnessed the great beasts begin their departure for a place we cannot reach. One man took his washing down to the tide, and saw the water split by the side of a sunfish large enough to be seen on the horizon. Many children sing rhymes of the dolphins that could carry a vessel upon their backs and the turtles that look to be atolls. I myself have seen one starfish, with arms the size of three men together, moving slowly towards the unknown until it disappeared into the depths."

If only Zigor remained alive today to tell us where exactly we should travel to follow these creatures.

AUTOMATED POST MISSIVE FROM VYERIN CLEL TO SOPHY CIDNORGHE, 1003

Dear Sophy,

O, goodness. Surely I am not the only one of us who gets giddy at the mere mention of the Pelagic Circle Map. I dream of visiting the Wayfinding Museum at the Intertidal Ring to examine it in person. I once carved a Knightfish into the small wooden box in which I held my razors. (I do not know why I employed the past tense here, because it still does hold them.)

At any rate, what an enjoyable aside! I too delight in the image of E. and Henerey reading it together. The book that I sent Henerey was *Sunken Splendour* (plus a much longer subtitle that you might also recall from Henerey's library request) by Scholar Jos Larnard. I believe it was an extensive anthology of Fantasies, written with the intention that the reader would use Scholarly logic to determine how the stories (each of which centred upon a discovery of some miraculous undersea object or place) could be explained with Reason. It was from Boundless Campus, of course, compiled in the hopes of encouraging critical thinking. But Larnard was a lover of Fantasies like Henerey, and though that was less acceptable in her time than ours, I believe she composed the stories with such believable detail that even the shrewdest young sceptic found disproving them an unpleasant task. The book was already rather obscure when we read it as boys. And it is nearly impossible to find a copy these days, unless you are wealthy or a time-traveller (or wish to visit the Reading Room at Boundless Campus, a place I assume is now inaccessible to an ex-Scholar such as yourself).

But I am quite convinced that Henerey left it with E., so if you have not found it in her effects, then I suppose it must be at the bottom of the ocean.

V.

AUTOMATED POST MISSIVE FROM SOPHY CIDNORGHE TO VYERIN CLEL, 1003

Dear V.,

When you go to the Museum at Intertidal (as I'm sure you will one day, even if I must accompany you myself!), keep in mind that there are no fewer than five copies of the Pelagic Circle Map on view that one must pass before reaching the original. These are teaching facsimiles of different structures, colours, and formats, intended to help scholars explore the imagery with students without damaging the extant document itself. Yet I, like a child, assumed that the first tiny copy that I saw when I entered was the real map – and Vyerin, do not laugh at me, but I was so disappointed!

I regret to hear that it's a rare book. I did hope to read it myself. If only there were a great library at the bottom of the sea preserving everything we've lost!

S.

UNSENT DRAFT OF A LETTER FROM E. CIDNOSIN TO HENEREY CLEL, 1002

Dear Henerey,

Though it's been barely a few hours since you departed, I wanted to write to you immediately. After you left, I stood at the airlock, straining for a glimpse of the water's surface – I knew I could not see your vessel, but just the thought of you floating somewhere up there brought me great comfort

UNSENT DRAFT OF A LETTER FROM E. CIDNOSIN TO HENEREY CLEL, 1002

Dear Henerey,

I wish that while you were here I could have had the opportunity to tell you how luminous you are. Sometimes I feel like I am adrift in the abyss like Sophy, but you brought such a light

UNSENT DRAFT OF A LETTER FROM E. CIDNOSIN TO HENEREY CLEL, 1002

Dear Henerey,

I fear it might be best for the both of us if we no longer continue our correspondence. I must confess that you are far superior to me in every way, and surely you do not wish to waste your time with someone who

UNSENT DRAFT OF A LETTER FROM E. CIDNOSIN TO HENEREY CLEL, 1002

Dear Henerey,

Why must I be so terrible at

LETTER FROM E. CIDNOSIN TO HENEREY CLEL, 1002

Dear Henerey,

By the time you read this, you will be safely aboard the *Sagacity*, travelling onward to discover the mysteries of the sea once more – a truly noble cause. Meanwhile, I remain here as always, reviewing in my mind our conversations from this evening (or last night, as it will be by the time you open this letter!).

I hope I did not offend or utterly bore you. I must apologise, because I am often not as – forthcoming – as I was with you. I felt rather out of my depth, as you proved as charming as you appear on the page, and your presence (and mellifluous reading voice!) made every minute of what would have otherwise been a very poor evening rather splendid. From the bottom of my heart: thank you.

If you find that you would like to continue our correspondence, know that I would be most enthusiastic to write to (or even speak with!) you again. Should you decline, however, I will remain forever content to have experienced just one lovely evening in your company.

In anticipation,

E.

LETTER FROM SOPHY CIDNOSIN TO E. CIDNOSIN, 1002

Dearest E.,

I'm writing this so late in the evening that it might as well be tomorrow already, but I hope it will travel speedily to you at the Deep House and reassure you that I am all right! I apologise for my lapse in correspondence, especially at a time when you have need of me. At the very least, I take comfort in the fact that our brother's obliviousness inspired you to see your dear friend Henerey in person! I trust you will not retreat at the last minute and leave him alone in a sea of Inspiration Scholars. I know he will be delighted to meet you.

Since our return, the days seem to blur together. We met with the Chancellors on our first day back in the Spheres, and o, E., this new technology we have at our fingertips is indescribable! Have I mentioned it before? A Vocal Echolator? I do not know how our Mechanists discovered a way to project the human voice through air and water – it is like our communicators, I suppose, but on a much greater scale. And even better – Eliniea says that her colleagues on the surface hope to soon equip us with another device called "Automated Post" that essentially allows one person at a distance to type out words that then appear in that exact sequence on paper for the recipient!

It astounds me to think how much technology has blossomed within the past few years. Our Survivor ancestors could hardly imagine such machines in the aftermath of the Dive, yet even our most sophisticated technology today is probably child's play to an inventor from the Antepelagic era! Irye boasts that one day very soon, everyone will have such Echolators and Automated Post in their private residence. How I wish you had access to them already.

At any rate, this "meeting" was a strange one indeed, because it was the first time I ever interacted with the disembodied voices of my superiors. Somehow this method of communication made Chancellor Rawsel seem all the more forbidding, grim, and disinclined to praise. No matter. I presented the data from my initial survey, and – well, you certainly do not want to hear about that – let us say simply that it was about as well received as an initial presentation of data ever is.

More intriguing news – after spending nearly an entire afternoon in additional consultations with the Chancellors, Niea appeared in our common room (where the rest of us were arrayed, as Irye had challenged me to a game of Columns with Ylaret and Vincenebras as witnesses) and quite abashedly asked us if we might be willing to submit to some tests.

"Do the Chancellors wish to test our senses of taste, per chance?" asked Vincenebras, knocking over the Columns in his eagerness to stand. (It was for the best – Irye was trouncing me thoroughly. Father would be ashamed.) "Then – I volunteer, colleagues! Please ask them to send me seasoned herring, and perhaps a flavoured trifle."

Niea laughed in a way that I can now recognise as her "professional chortle" – it is but a shimmer of her more genuine expressions of mirth.

"Alas, it is your ability to adapt to new technology at great depths, specifically, that they hope I will assess, though I would much prefer your proposed banquet! Perhaps I will suggest it to the Chancellors. At any rate," she continued, "there is some concern that the constant pressure might damage the efficacy of your communicators, so we want to make sure they are all functioning as intended and pose no risks to you."

"Thank you, Scholar Forghe," said Ylaret, rising while avoiding the scattered Columns with practised grace. "I appreciate your constant dedication to our wellbeing during this mission."

Vincenebras, paying no heed to Ylaret's statement, proceeded to pontificate about a full menu of flavours he wished to have sent to us from the surface. Eventually, as we all begged him to stop tantalising us (truly, our preserved rations lack variety), Vincenebras dragged a grumbling Irye off to the galley sphere to attempt some culinary experimentation. Moments later, Niea excused herself to confirm the details of the communicator assessments with the Chancellors, leaving me alone with Ylaret.

"I fear the day when the Chancellors test our basic coordination abilities," I said, eager to cut through the silence, "for I do not wish them to discover that I cannot tell my right hand from my left without relying upon a mnemonic device." (The fact that I willingly revealed this quality to a colleague speaks to my desperation to create conversation with Ylaret. By the way – I do not say this enough, but I am always incredibly grateful to you for teaching me, at such a young age, that the left hand can form a helpful "L" when positioned correctly!)

"Though in all seriousness," I continued, "I wonder why the Chancellors decided to review the communicators now. Do they suspect something untoward?"

As I spoke, Ylaret seemed to stare straight through me.

"Niea wishes to investigate the communicators because I asked her to," she said at last.

"You asked her? But why?"

In response, Ylaret peered out into the "hall", as though to ensure our privacy.

"You've been so kind to me, Sophy," she murmured. "I know I was not a particularly congenial partner on our past dives. I apologise. You see, ever since we began diving outside of the Spheres, I have experienced – how can I describe it? – let us say, 'unexplained auditory feedback of a troubling nature'. I was too ashamed to tell anyone but our Expedition Specialist. And I hope that this test will give me some insight into my difficulties."

Yet I did not have the opportunity to learn more about this "auditory feedback," because Irye, as though on cue, appeared and grabbed us both by the hands.

"If I must endure proximity to Vincenebras' culinary disasters," Irye said, "so shall you."

And endure we did.

Now that I have written all of this for you, E., I wonder what inspired me to share it in the first place! I suppose I should be unsettled by Ylaret's words, but somehow – against all odds – I am not, yet. I keep thinking about our expedition, and the experience that Niea and I shared with that great creature deep in the trench. That is what I hoped to find when I came here – things utterly unknown to me. And if that includes technological oddities, I embrace them wholeheartedly! E., has it ever occurred to you that I chose a dying profession? Ever since the Dive stranded us on this watery planet, Scholars have attempted to sail every inch of our Four Oceans in search of more land that may have survived the Dive: yet as they return empty-mapped, we Scholars of Wayfinding must survey the same seas again and again, decrying our predecessors' scales and keys. But now I – of all people! – have the opportunity to see and experience that which I never encountered before, and attempt to make sense of it.

That is all to say (in far too many words) that you should not worry about me! If you doubt our crew's ability to take care of ourselves, please trust in Niea's skill at doing so on our behalf.

And please send my best regards to Henerey when you see him – when he visits our home!

Yours SAFELY,

Sophy

LETTER FROM E. CIDNOSIN TO SOPHY CIDNOSIN, 1002

Dear Sophy,

Is this the third letter I've sent to you in the past few days? I feel such desperate need of you lately. Currently, it is nearly dawn and I find myself fuelled with that unique blend of anxiety, over-stimulation, and cautious excitement that is not particularly conducive to rest! While the language that follows may seem jumbled due to my weariness, I hope this serves as a useful conclusion to the suspense generated by my previous note.

As I'm sure you will be delighted to know, Henerey did indeed make an appearance at Arvist's gala this evening. Though I will get there in good time!

To start, I will say that as much as the Structure unsettled me at first, I now feel slightly jealous that Arvist claimed it as his own. He acts as though this mysterious thing is all his, and if I try to talk to him about it, he puts me off. I do not know exactly what his "performance" entailed, but Seliara intimated the day before that he intended to "restage its emotions" in various sites around the house. His ultimate goal is to paddle out to it and place a "sculptural response" (upon which he currently toils) next to the Structure as its new companion for all eternity. I must try not to think of it – honestly, a Scholar of the Arts may be better equipped to understand that particular enigma than I am! (I hope more than ever, though, that the Elongated Fish might come back during the installation of his new work to give him a little bit of a fright. How dramatic that would be!)

169

In any case, I estimate that about seventy Scholars found their way to the Deep House last night: can you believe that? I doubt that I have been around so many people in a decade! The sounds that humans create while assembled in great numbers, Sophy, are absolutely abominable. I took up my usual position on the staircase (which made me quite nostalgic for the days when Mother and Father held their dinner parties, and I watched from my fortress on the landing as you and Arvist charmed our guests with your precocious sophistication) and kept an eye out for Henerey. I do not know what action I intended to take if I saw him – the thought of entering that fray made me feel sick with fear – but fortunately for both of us, Seliara directed him my way and before I knew it, I saw a kind-eyed, well-dressed gentleman ascending to the landing in an outfit so perfectly curated that I could imagine him stepping out of a Fashion Plate. Though I had not ever *seen* Henerey outside of his author portrait, I saw the warmth of his words in his gentle smile and sprightly gait. Everything about him looked so comfortingly familiar.

We found a way to initiate communication that suited us both, but after a time, the noise grew unbearable, and we retreated to the library. To my great pleasure, the room was deserted. I showed Henerey in, babbling all the while in what must have been a most unappealing way – about how the shelves are not quite as organised as I would usually like them, since Arvist has been ferreting about as he works on his "Art!", and how I most passionately look forward to having my own space again. Henerey, for his part, seemed desperately happy, which I will attribute to his consummate politeness.

We sat down (since Mother's was broken, I'm embarrassed to admit that we sat in your chair and mine – now I've become no better than Arvist taking over your bedroom!) and enjoyed a moment of silence, interrupted only by Henerey gently tossing one of the books he had brought me from one hand to the other. I studied the way in which the lamplight spun like seafoam around his face.

"As a childhood appreciator of Fantasies," he said, all of a sudden, "are you equally fond of hearing them read aloud?" (I swear that is exactly what he said – I keep repeating it in my head!)

"Naturally," I replied, which was curter than I intended, but what could I do? When we first met, we scribbled notes to each other on the staircase, and I had not heard him speak much until that very moment. Alone in the library, Henerey's voice sounded as expansive and energetic as water rushing over a reef.

"Excellent," he continued, "because I find myself increasingly dazzled and flustered by your presence, and I wondered if perhaps we might both benefit from a reading of this volume as a diversion?"

"That would be most agreeable," I assented.

His voice quavered at first, but as he made his way through the sentences – even strange, verbose ones! – I found myself unable to think of anything but the clear confidence that rang through his every word. To my great shame, I began to daydream about what it must be like to hear him lecture: surely he counts among the most acclaimed Scholars, even to those in the audience who hold no interest in marine life!

While he read, the arms of our chairs just barely touched, and this intimacy gave me a feeling of affection unlike any I have ever experienced.

After spending some time in this enjoyable manner, we said our goodbyes – Henerey seemed quite surprised by how late the hour had become and expressed some anxiety about returning to his research vessel before it continued its pursuit of the migrating rays. He had arranged for his transport to pick him up at half past twelve bells. I pray that his apology was genuine, and that this excuse was not a half-crafted attempted to flee from my company!

I escorted him to the airlock by the back hallway, careful to avoid the carousers in the parlour. As we waited for Henerey's transport ship to arrive, we stood watching the sea shadows through the airlock's portholes.

"I don't suppose we could see the Structure from here?" Henerey asked after a rather comfortable silence.

Arvist staged part of his "staggered performance" in his studio so his visitors might glimpse the Structure itself – thus I had been unable to show it off to Henerey.

I suggested we try the backmost porthole on the south wall – I always forget about that one – and we crept there, standing quite close together in the cramped space. I was just explaining to Henerey that our resident mysterious object would likely be difficult to spot in the darkness when I glanced out the window and saw the Structure glowing.

The circle of crystalline material that makes up the base was illuminated by the most stunning and sparkling tints of pink and pale, watery green. The light did not carry very far – one could not have spotted it from any other part of the house, but I imagine those in the Studio this evening were quite dazzled by it.

"Has it ever done that before?" Henerey asked, looking me straight in the eyes – he has a rather unsettling habit of doing this with great frequency!

"Not to my knowledge," I replied, "though I have only seen it once before in the evening. I suspect I would have remembered the phosphorescence."

Henerey nodded, turning back to the porthole. "A luminous circumference," he said in a half-whisper as he leaned against the wall, twirling his walking stick in one hand as though he were trying to work out some puzzle.

"Are you a poet, too, Scholar Clel? Your talents are seemingly ceaseless."

Goodness knows why I allowed myself to say such a thing!

He looked over his shoulder at me with the greatest warmth in his eyes (which, by the way, are brown, flecked with tan and gold, like the inside of a shell as it catches the sun from above the waves). Have I truly spent so little time around people that I forgot how much can be communicated with a glance?

"Alas, I only recite the words of another. It's from a poem by Darbeni."

"Scholar Darbeni wrote poetry?" I exclaimed. "Surely you jest."

He gasped in mock horror.

"To think you would ever accuse me of jesting about Scholar Kenven Darbeni! No, it was during the very end of his career, and his poems only exist in manuscript form. Very few people know about them. The Boundless Campus holds the manuscripts in the Archives."

"How wonderful," I said. "I wish I could see such things."

A crash from above indicated that Henerey's transport vessel had navigated – inexpertly – into our docking area.

"I shall find the poem and send it to you," he said. "I made a fair copy. The words stayed with me ever since I read them. There is something about it that reminds me of this Structure – I wonder—"

The passenger boat played the captain's personal melody – in this case, four descending notes that were appropriately melancholy – to signify his arrival.

"We will speak more about this," Henerey continued. "But E., I had a remarkable time this evening, and I hope that I shall—"

The cursed melody sounded once more!

"I do not wish you to be late for your boat," I said miserably.

"I will write again soon," he affirmed, taking a single step towards the airlock doors as though he could barely dare to take another. After he left at last, I stood there for quite a long time in a daze – it all felt like a dream!

In fact, in reflecting upon the entire affair, I find myself scrupulously reviewing my every word and action over the course of the evening. Surely he decided to read aloud because he could not bear to converse me any further. Of course he would have been eager to rid himself of someone who kept so brazenly edging her chair in his direction (I do not really remember doing this, but now I wonder if perhaps I did?). And even if there were moments when he tried to express some form of affection for me, how coldly and dismissively I acted! He returned home feeling most drained and disappointed to have met such an uninspiring person, convinced that he must put an end to the correspondence that he must have been previously enjoying (or perhaps even that itself was a façade?).

O Sophy, it occurs to me now that I have – in one brief evening – substantially destroyed whatever friendship might have formed between Henerey and me over the past month. I wish I had never let myself invite him to the house, and that we remained safely in the realm of the written word. In fact, perhaps it would have been better if I never wrote to him at all! Then he would never have had to suffer the disappointment of meeting me.

I will try to sleep now.

E.

P.S. Dear Sophy, one more thought: do you think he could immediately tell how little experience I've had with anyone from outside the family? Do you think he was horrified that I have not left the Deep House in years?

Do you think he is now back on his research vessel laughing about my oddities with some far superior individual with whom he would much rather spend his time?

P.P.S. My worst crime is that I snatched one of your discarded gowns at the very last moment to wear this evening. (It is the old-fashioned garment that you once referred to as "that awful green one", so I hope you will forgive me this trespass. I know you prefer more fashionable and practical frocks or suits!) Before Henerey arrived, I looked in the mirror at myself in my dishevelled white house-dress and cape and thought I looked like a true spectre. I did not wish to give him a fright. I pray you will understand. (I have taken it off now and have laundered it twice just in case I somehow damaged it irreparably with anxious perspiration.)

(Thrice now.)

P.P.P.S. I realise that I did not respond to anything in your letter but I hope you will forgive me. I can barely keep my eyes open—

LETTER FROM HENEREY CLEL TO E. CIDNOSIN, 1002

My dear E.,

I feared that writing to you after the wonder of meeting you in person might feel somewhat diminished. Indeed, I find it frustrating to be faced with the empty page as my only audience – I much prefer your wry glances in response to my bumbling words. Yet there is nothing that can altogether remove the joy I experience when communicating with you in any format.

E., I cannot stop thinking about our time together. As someone who has spent much of his social life getting acquainted with books and specimens, I am often flummoxed by the notion of speaking with a stranger.

Fortunately, you felt nothing like someone I was meeting for the first time.

I write this in great haste (which is probably for the best, as it is extremely late in the evening, I just returned from seeing you, and I fear my prose might otherwise become much more sentimental than might make you comfortable!) because it's – as they say – "all hands on deck" here at present! Our Captain received a letter from the Chancellors informing us of a change in plans: rather than holding our position, we have been instructed to make steady progress southward, with the eventual plan of studying the surface-level marine life at a specific location. What location, you might ask? Why – the very coordinates of the "Point of Interest" famously charted by Schr Eliniea Hayve Forghe, in close proximity to where your sister and her colleagues are currently underwater! Truly, I could not imagine anything more fortunate (excepting, of course, the experience I had at the Deep House earlier this evening). I do continue to wonder how and why Chancellor Rawsel has so entirely redirected nearly all Boundless Campus research efforts to work in service of his Ridge expedition.

Because this has become a more complex mission than any of us anticipated, we will require a day or two to make the necessary preparations. I only brought one suitcase, you know! To my delight and disappointment, the Captain reports that our books, equipment, and personal effects back on campus will be forwarded on to our vessel before we depart – I look forward to having my full wardrobe at my disposal, but I do hope that whoever takes charge of packing my things knows how to fold collars properly!

As soon as I have an opportunity to write more I will continue to discuss the thoughts racing through my head – of which I have too many to count.

Until then, please know that I wish I could have stayed with you longer.

Yours,

Henerey

P.S. I hope you will not mind the intimacy of the salutation with which I opened this letter. I am hypothetically acquainted with the practice of adding "my" before the standard "dear" to imply affection, but when employing it for the first time in practice, I found it may come across as unpleasantly possessive. But now it is too late to write this letter over again, as they need me abovedeck. If my phrasing offends you in any way, please let me know the manner of address that you would prefer, and I will put it to use in future correspondence.

AUTOMATED POST MISSIVE FROM VYERIN CLEL TO SOPHY CIDNORGHE, 1003

Dear Sophy,

There is one more document I would like to share with you – an excerpt from Henerey's daybook (what else?) written to commemorate this occasion.

Enjoy,

Vyerin

P.S. As someone who has been lambasted countless times for my inability to handle my brother's laundry to his satisfaction, I imagine the poor soul assigned to pack his effects back at the Anchorage did not, in fact, know how to fold those collars "properly". Such knowledge was apparently inaccessible to anyone but Henerey.

P.P.S. If you seek an amusing diversion, I dare you to count the number of times my brother uses "remarkable" in his entry.

NOTE FROM THE DAYBOOK OF HENEREY CLEL, 1002

I met her. I met her! How strange to see this stranger stand before me and know that she was ... her! She wore a truly remarkable gown of sea-green weave that was remarkably tailored, with elegant embroidered cuffs adorned with spiralling seaweed stitches and an anemone-bustled skirt. The skirt pooled around her feet along with her floor-skimming red-brown hair. When I looked closely (which I tried to do in the least obvious way possible) I recognised her – her lips drawn tightly in a line, her green eyes raised in such a way that suggested friendliness battling anxiety. Truly remarkable! The candlelight set off her skin, making each freckle flicker across her face as she smiled. There was a radiance in her very laugh that I could not separate from the glimmering language she sent me. A radiance! Remarkable. (Have I said that already? No matter.)

AUTOMATED POST MISSIVE FROM SOPHY CIDNORGHE TO VYERIN CLEL, 1003

Dear Vyerin,

Remarkable! (Truly.)

It is a gift to see E. through Henerey's eyes – certainly she would not have thought of herself as "radiant" under most circumstances. How delightful that Henerey noticed every detail in her dress, including the fact that the gown was not made for her height. It is amusing to think of Henerey's fondness for fashion, since this is a quality that I often associate with those who are more sociable and invested in the opinions of others. But I suspect he did not dress well to fulfil any societal obligation or to make an impression – he simply enjoyed it, did he not?

(And I was, as you will soon see, in no way perturbed that she borrowed my dress. I always detested that awful green one. It suited her much better.)

Radiantly,

Sophy

Chapter 13

LETTER FROM JEIME ALESTARRE TO ARVIST AND E. CIDNOSIN, 1002

Dear Cidnosins,

I arrived home from my errand lucky enough to find mail from you both. I write today in answer to Arvist specifically, though I wanted to include E. as well.

I too am curious about the "Structure", as E. nicknamed it, and now that I am back and we are all quite on the same page about the question of its origins – namely, that it was not produced by Arvist – I am happy to assist with an investigation. E., in case you are not aware, Arvist requested that I bring a depth-craft to your home "the very day after [I] receive this message!" so that we may undertake further research together.

I shall arrive in three days. I hope this will suit you.

Kindly,

Jeime Alestarre

LETTER FROM HENEREY CLEL TO E. CIDNOSIN, 1002

Dear* E.,

*Since I have not yet heard from you, I will do my best to

avoid excessive sentimentality in my salutations until I know it is welcome!

I apologise for sending you a second letter, but an idea came to me shortly after posting the first one that was too appealing not to share! Please forgive my boldness.

My research on this mission will focus on the surface biomes as I track these elusive rays! Consequently, I will spend very little time thinking and learning about creatures who prefer the reefs. My idea is this: as a diversion for us both, I wondered if you might be interested in keeping a field journal for me throughout the rest of my voyage? I have a small notebook perfect for our purposes (emblazoned with a beautiful woodcut print of a Numinous Octopus). Something to keep us connected – and to enable you to explore your talents with Natural History! Sharing this experience with you would be such a gift, if you are willing.

Between meeting you yestereve and the events that transpired today, I can hardly believe that I have not stepped into some Fantasy. I presume in your reading on the subject you might have encountered the tale of "The Scholar of Serendipity"? (Perhaps, as they did, I will soon find myself in charge of the entire Boundless Campus by sheer luck alone! (My first act – using my new position of power to be so kind and sensitive to Chancellor Rawsel that he repents of his cruel ways.))

I must go now – much to be done! (My clothes-trunk arrived from campus this afternoon and – I can hardly write these words – the folding situation is worse than I feared.)

Until soon – I remain yours,

Henerey

P.S. Long overdue, but here is the poem at last – finally had the time to excavate it from my files for you! Desperate to know your thoughts.

#405. "A Luminous Circumference" by Scholar Kenven Darbeni
A Luminous Circumference—
Melodious—to Spy

Anathema to Lecturers
And—Critics! O, I Vie
With Reason when my Shades are Shut—
A Predator—Awaits—
Though I recite my Proofs again—
That Circle Coruscates!

LETTER FROM SOPHY CIDNOSIN TO E. CIDNOSIN, 1002

Dearest E.,

It pains me when I cannot be there to speak with you in your times of need! I know we did not quite embody the stereotype of heart-bound sisters in our childhood – perhaps because we did not share a bedroom and therefore lacked the familiarity forced by proximity in most Boundless families from crowded Anchorages – but reading your letter made me desperately want to sit at the foot of your bed in my nightclothes and converse until morning to make you feel better.

In this imaginary scenario, I would clutch your hands and say this:

Henerey undoubtedly enjoyed his evening with you, and I imagine that he is probably – at this very moment – penning and crossing out and penning again countless sentimental words to send to you (if he has not done so already, of course). I know that you will not believe me, because you are convinced that no individual could possibly revel in your company – but let me see if I can use another approach to convince you.

Henerey is no ordinary individual.

From what I can tell, he is much like you – brilliant, creative, observant, retiring, and altogether uninterested in social mores (with the exception, perhaps, of Fashion). You suspect that he deprives himself of superior company by spending time with you; on the contrary, perhaps

181

last night he felt as though he was truly understood for the first time since he joined Boundless Campus.

I desperately hope (and suspect) that by the time you read this, you will see my predictions – like some sisterly prophecy – come to pass. I also suspect that the dress looked stunning on you, frilly and impractical though it may be. You are welcome, by the way, to any article of clothing currently in my wardrobe, if you can stomach entering "Arvist and Seliara's" suite to retrieve further items. I left behind only those garments that I swore never to wear again. O, how I wish I had been there to help you choose one and style you for the evening, if you desired!

Well, that was a delightful diversion! Let me return to reality. Though that is not to say that my present reality is not delightful – it is simply more complicated than that.

Niea's tests discovered that Ylaret's communicator had been improperly tuned to capture even the faintest of frequencies, which was likely the source of the unusual feedback. You might assume that these promising results brought about the end of this drama. Well, not quite. The evening after the assessments, we all gathered in the galley. To everyone's surprise, Vincenebras and Irye now cook together regularly – quite expertly, if you can believe it – and have been gracing us with the most elaborate meals one could ever create from Cold-Processed rations.

The air – though thin and cold as it always is down here – seemed infused with celebration. Niea, in high spirits, announced that we would undertake a second off-Spheres expedition in just a few days' time. Buoyed by this good news, I also entertained the group with the story of Arvist's gala. I may have mentioned (please forgive me!) that Scholar Clel attended said gala, and that I wished to learn more of his character. O, I know it was indiscreet of me, E., but I did want to hear what my colleagues thought of him – since he is getting so close to you, you know! Well, you can rest easy that their opinions of Henerey are predictably positive. Not that it means anything to you, of course, but

Niea mentioned that she knows "those who find gentlemen attractive" consider him a paragon – a statement Irye was happy to confirm. (After which Vincenebras exclaimed "Irye, do you mean to say that you find gentlemen attractive?", to which Irye responded "If by 'gentlemen', you mean yourself, dear Vincenebras, the answer is a resounding no." And Vincenebras laughed as though it was the merriest thing he ever heard!)

When all assembled had exhausted all possible compliments for your new friend, Ylaret tapped her drinking-shell to draw our attention.

"Will you provide the evening's musical entertainment, Ylaret?" asked Irye drolly.

"Dear Irye, I was about to ask the very same question!" said Vincenebras.

"With much more sincerity, I wager," Irye replied.

Ylaret shook her head.

"I simply wanted to take a moment to thank you all. And I wanted to offer a bit of an explanation. Niea already knows what I will say, and I hinted to Sophy—"

"Really," cut in Niea, "Ylaret, you must feel no obligation to share—"

"But I would very much like to." With that, Ylaret looked around the galley at each one of us with practised skill. (It was in that moment I remembered the acclaim that her lectures receive!)

"Ever since we first entered the water out there," she said, "I have heard the most – well, what I thought was – the most beautiful and unusual music."

"Have I failed so much as a Scholar of Sound that my colleagues will not come to me first when they encounter unexplained aural phenomena?" exclaimed Irye, collapsing on the table in a mock swoon. "How could you tell Niea and Sophy and not me?"

"I should have told you, Irye," Ylaret continued. "Really, I ought to have informed all of you immediately. But I thought I was hallucinating, and that unsettled me. It took me a few days to find the courage to speak with Eliniea, for I knew she would handle this matter in the most calm and reasoned way."

Far better than any of us would, that is for certain. I cannot blame Ylaret for that decision.

"And she did, of course! You cannot imagine the relief I feel in knowing that whatever I heard was simply a quirk of the communicator."

"Well, it was a 'quirk', in a manner of speaking," said Vincenebras, "but the true issue was that your communicator was tuned to a different frequency than ours, correct? So does that not mean that this 'music' was real, but simply impossible for the rest of us to hear?"

"Hypothetically, yes," said Irye. "But the human ear is a marvellous thing. Just as our eyes seek out faces in the most abstract of sandbars, our ears attempt to find melodies in whatever we hear. The fact that Ylaret translated this feedback into songs rather charms and enchants me, if I'm honest. If you consent, Ylaret, I would love to speak with you more about the nature of this 'music'. I don't suppose any part of it sounded anything like – a Bloorb?"

"I would be glad to," answered Ylaret. "I have felt so confused and unhappy over the past few days, and this development gives me a sense of peace. Shall we retire to my chambers and speak further? I would not wish to bore our colleagues."

"O, dear Ylaret, I challenge anyone to bore Vincenebras!" called Vincenebras, following Ylaret and Irye as they departed the galley.

Now that we were on our own, I wished to learn more about Niea's experience with Ylaret's "music", but Niea spoke first.

"So do you approve of your sister and Scholar Clel?" she asked, gracing me with a genuine smile.

I nodded and told her why in as few words as possible. (I promise that she is trustworthy! She found the notion of your correspondence with Henerey very charming.) When I finished, she seemed much more at ease.

"It has been some time since we talked of your family," said Niea. "I wish I could meet E. I do think we would get along quite well!" (I tend to agree!)

"And I would like to meet Aliella, too," I replied (did I mention this

184

previously? Niea has only one sibling, quite close in age to her as you and I are). "How odd to think of a world in which we might call upon our families more regularly. I forget what that is like."

"It is easy to forget while adrift in the depths as we are." Niea chewed on the last remnant of Vincenebras' roasted kelp braids. "That sounds bleak. It is not fully what I mean."

"Perhaps it is easy to adapt while adrift in the depths?" I suggested.

"Adapting! Yes, I prefer that to forgetting. And while I have adjusted to our present situation, there are many reasons why I do wish we could easily visit the surface from time to time. We could have unlimited access to the libraries again, hear the waves – the waves, Sophy, do you remember them? – and you could meet Alie, and I could meet E. ... Wouldn't it be lovely, my friend?"

And, dear E., I do not know if it was the fermentation of the kelp or the sheer intoxication of these dreams about experiencing life on the surface anew with Niea or the way she looked in her pearl-pink dress robes, but E., I said—

"It would be loveliest if you called me by another term than 'friend'."

—which were words that I regretted as soon as I uttered them, and immediately retracted before she could answer—

"That is, I would say such a thing if I were Vincenebras, that old flirt, who still does not comprehend that I have no eyes for him or anyone else, but I will not say this to you, except in jest, because I know you asked that we remain professional in our relationship at present, and I respect—"

And then, gently and cautiously, she took my hand, which silenced me at last!

"Sophy, have you ever visited Stellar Hall?" Niea asked calmly, as though we were simply two friends discussing the popular attractions of Intertidal Campus and she were not holding my hand!

"No," I managed to mumble. "But I have heard it is a place of recreation?"

"I forget," she said between giggles, "that your primary occupation

185

and only pastime is being a Scholar. It is a hall for dancing and social-ising, of course, but one designed for the amateur Scholars of the Skies among us. You see, instead of a ceiling, the top of the building is covered by an enormous lens, the sort you might find in a Telescope. Thus, you can whirl about all evening while the great magnified dome of the cosmos spins above you."

"That does sound like an improvement upon your average hall for dancing and socialising."

"Were we at the surface," whispered Niea, gripping my hand still tighter, "it would give me the greatest pleasure if you were to spend an evening there in my company."

"Any time spent in your company would be marvellous, enormous Telescopes or otherwise," I said. "But Niea, is this not too hasty? Please don't misunderstand. I am not complaining, certainly, though I was under the impression that you did not wish any . . . connection with me."

"Perish the thought, please!" she cried. "As you know, there have been some troubles weighing on me since our expedition began. When Ylaret confessed that she had been experiencing hallucinations, I sus-pected the worst. I thought I doomed you all by subjecting you to an unknown environment with little understanding of the consequences! So this development gives me an opportunity to breathe once more, so to speak. But even if that were not the case, dear Sophy, there is only so long I could pretend to myself that I did not feel strongly about you."

I did not press her to hear more about these troubles, as I felt far more inclined to press my lips to hers.

O dear. Had I anything else to share with you? Had you said any-thing else of import to me? I remember nothing but Niea's embrace. Let us end with that.

Sophy

P.S. O, I do hate to spoil the sentimentality of the moment, but I have also included a copy of Vincenebras' latest missive for you. A delight as always. And it does feature Niea, so we have not really changed subjects altogether, have we?

THE RIDGE REVEALED, ISSUE 3, RECORDED BY SCHR VINCENEBRAS

Dearest Friends and Subscribers,

How we've missed you here in our tiny home amid the great unknown! I apologise profusely for the pause in updates caused by our off-station field study trip. If you know or love a member of our crew, please know that we thought of you constantly throughout our arduous research expedition – even with our ability to correspond restricted.

(And in the event that you do not already know or love one of my colleagues – consider this humble Journalist *available* in every sense of the word.)

I will not bore you with a full recapitulation of our travels just yet, but I can assure you that ever since we enjoyed our first survey of the Ridge, our spirits have been practically luminescent. To brighten the mood even further, I asked one of the most glimmering presences in our Company, Expedition Specialist Schr Eliniea Hayve Forghe of Intertidal Campus, to beguile you with tales – and tails, perchance? – of the beasts we have encountered thus far in this strange environment.

INTERVIEW WITH SCHOLAR ELINIEA HAYVE FORGHE

Scholar Vincenebras: Our most excellent leader! Our subscribers are simply *wild* to hear what you have discovered about the flora and fauna of the Ridge.

Scholar Forghe: Greetings, everyone! It is my sincerest hope that everyone who reads these words will have a wonderful day. Though I'm delighted to be here, I'm sorry to report that I don't have too much to share with you at present.

Vincenebras: Is that because of the tragic dearth of animal life in these parts?

Forghe: Quite the contrary, really! As a Scholar of Life, I do not focus simply on animals and plants like a Scholar of

Classification might, of course. I study the environment as a whole – how species interact and cooperate and prey upon each other – you know, from the smallest Diatom to the greatest Whale. When we complete our mission, I will send my findings to the Scholars of Classification on each Campus, and they will help me catalogue what I have observed so far – by which I mean they will identify these species based on their similarities to creatures from other parts of the ocean. Which does make this interview feel rather premature. But surely you already knew that when you asked me, Vincenebras?

Vincenebras: Dear Eliniea, you know all too well that I know almost nothing about anything!

Forghe: No matter. At present, let me share a few observations about a potential new species, which I call the Abyssal Nautilus.

Vincenebras: Would that be, by chance, that veritable giant you encountered with Scholar Cidnosin?

Forghe: Naturally! I assume that at least some of you reading this missive are well acquainted with the Pervasive Nautilus – that charming reef-dwelling denizen that happens to be the symbol of Boundless Campus.

Vincenebras: Of course. I own seven fine tapestries embroidered with various Nautilus designs.

Forghe: Don't you hail from Intertidal like me, Vincenebras?

Vincenebras: Naturally! I own fourteen fine tapestries embroidered with my beloved Intertidal Campus' Reclusive Crab insignia, dear Eliniea.

Forghe: I wish I could say the same! At any rate, the Pervasive Nautilus – the most widespread nautiloid species – is a fairly small creature, growing no larger than Vincenebras' head on average. In fact, it was only last year that Schr Henerey Clel of Boundless Campus recorded a sighting of an extraordinarily large Nautilus—

Vincenebras: One larger than my Generous and Capacious Heart, perhaps?

Forghe: Yet the creature that Sophy and I observed during our expedition measured on a monumental scale previously thought impossible. Its cirri – those appendages one might confuse with tentacles – extended six fathoms from its shell. I suspect it has few natural predators, as even the deep-diving Hardy Toothed Whales might find it too large to take on.

Vincenebras: I tend to agree with their assessment!

Forghe: I should mention that the most remarkable quality of this creature is its bioluminescence. I have never seen a deep-sea species with such a veritable galaxy of natural illumination at its disposal. Though I still have not managed to capture an image of the Nautilus – and therefore it may not be added to the Universal Compendium of Species at *present* – I took the liberty of sending a verbal description to one of the most celebrated Illustrators working today, Scholar Lerin Zuan Vellen, and hope that with their assistance, everyone may have a chance to look upon the creature's likeness soon.

Vincenebras: Frankly, I would gladly never look upon it again! Before we conclude, Scholar Forghe, is there anything else you would like to share with the world at large?

Forghe: For my sake, dear readers – if you live in a place that experiences even the smallest amount of biodiversity, go outside or get on the water and admire all the different creatures and plants with whom you share your space! And give my best regards to all birds and shore-flowers – I miss them the most in the Abyss.

INTERVIEW CONCLUDES

Isn't Scholar Forghe simply divine? I feel blessed to have experienced our most enjoyable interview yet! Now I must away before some great discovery takes place while I sit here scribbling!

With animalistic fervour,
Vincenebras

AUTOMATED POST MISSIVE FROM VYERIN CLEL TO SOPHY CIDNORGHE, 1003

Dear Sophy,

How long has it been since you sent me this robust of a package? To move from the romance of your long-overdue confession to Niea to the missive from Vincenebras to another letter from my brother – truly, you included everything.

By the way, I'm afraid that "The Scholar of Serendipity", which Henerey mentioned at one point somewhere in all that, was not a shared tale from our childhood. Never heard of it. (O, bring back the Darbeni quotations, Henerey – at least I can recognise those, inane though they are! Yet even I must admit that poem was strikingly different from Darbeni's usual oeuvre . . .)

Have you any more documents from these few days? If not, I do have a letter from E. to Henerey that I assume must have come soon after. Please advise – I am happy to send it over when the time is right.

With care,
Vyerin

AUTOMATED POST MISSIVE FROM SOPHY CIDNORGHE TO VYERIN CLEL, 1003

Dear Vyerin,

O, you needn't worry about explaining that reference to me! "The Scholar of Serendipity" is an exceptionally silly tale that Father read to us only once – we all found it rather too trite to hear again! I will try to make my summary as short and bearable as I can. In this story, a

190

Scholar (of unknown identity, obviously, as are so many protagonists found in Fantasies) who struggles with mediocrity – always the third choice in a competition with two prizewinners or the second finalist for a Senior Scholar role but never receiving the actual position – decides that their best course of action is to focus their studies upon Luck itself. The more they investigate "Serendipity", the more fortunate events transpire. Eventually, by sheer coincidence, they are elevated to the position of Chancellor, and decide to abandon their inquiry into Serendipity in favour of their new duties. Of course, the second their research stops, their luck leaves them. (You have children, Vyerin – do you suspect they would truly enjoy such a fable?)

I will gladly accept your letter from E. to Henerey. However, I must warn you that the part of my archive we must – unfortunately! – read through next may be particularly difficult for me. In fact, I suspect that the document you are about to send me will be closely related to this period. I promise I shall reply, but if it takes longer than usual, please know that I am simply keeping my emotions in check.

Kindly,
Sophy

AUTOMATED POST MISSIVE FROM VYERIN CLEL TO SOPHY CIDNORGHE, 1003

Dear Sophy,

You will find that letter from E. enclosed. I hope your reading experience will be as bearable as possible.

Please never feel any pressure to respond quickly. (This sentiment has a familiar ring – did my brother not write it to E. several times?) I have plenty to do to occupy myself, you know – you need not think I shall hassle you! The touring season has commenced again in full force, and I am fully booked at least half the time. If I do not have our archive upon which to focus, there are always the (often) amusing and (occasionally) frustrating diversions of the Clel family. Perhaps I shall consider (consider!) caving to my husband and children's requests that I join their singing exercises to complete the family quartet – an enterprise I have managed to avoid for the past year.

Until we speak again,

V.

P.S. To answer your question – no, as a father, I cannot imagine either of my offspring would care much for a ridiculous, Scholarship-centric story such as you've described.

They always perfectly enjoyed the Navigational Treatises with which I lulled them to sleep.

Chapter 14

LETTER FROM E. CIDNOSIN TO HENEREY CLEL, 1002

My dear Henerey*,

*After some consideration, I have decided that I do find your fond mode of address (much more than) acceptable. I hope you will feel the same way.

The content (and, equally important, the tone!) of your letters takes my breath away. I ~~simply cannot believe you consider me worthy of~~ am so very happy.

Now, I do regret that I will not see you again anytime soon, given your impending departure. And it may be a good thing you cannot come sooner, for I think I might simply perish from excitement if you did. At least, under the present circumstances, I will have adequate time to prepare for the next visit.

On that note, I would be honoured to complete a field journal with you – though I admit that I am a bit shy about doing so, since I doubt anything I observe would be of interest to a true Natural Historian of your calibre! Yet I cannot wait to see this beautiful octopus tome appear. (I wonder – will the mail-boats that serve you in your new distant location also carry Sophy's letters from the Spheres? Surely there can be only one or two particularly intrepid vessels that trek all the way to those waters!) The idea of sharing a physical object with you gives me a feeling I dare not describe. At any rate, while I await the arrival of our mutual journal, I will take note of anything notable I see – especially this morning, when I suspect I might glimpse a claw-armed mechanical beast co-piloted by an inexpert artist . . .

I write this from the viewing window in the parlour today – the room that we looked down into from the top of the landing when first we met (what lovely words to write). I chose this location because a most unusual happening will soon unfold in our undergarden! Somehow, my most incorrigible sibling wheedled Schr Jeime Alestarre into bringing over a depth-craft. Arvist hopes to use Jeime's vessel to view the Structure up close so he may spend "an hour, or perhaps more or less, as needed" to "respond to" its "physicality". Arvist truly considers the statue his greatest artistic muse: he wants to dedicate his life to "enacting the emotions caged within in its enigmatic crystalline flesh".

I believe he expected her to bring a larger vessel, but Jeime arrived with one equipped to carry only two passengers. Arvist has, predictably, demanded that he must be the one to go; Seliara seems disappointed by this turn of events, but I suppose if I had to choose one of them to keep me company while the other goes off underwater, it might as well be her! (And before you ask: no, I did not have my heart set on joining this journey today. The thought of being trapped in a small depth-craft with my brother horrifies me, as he is prone to mock my discomfort with enclosed spaces. Though I can endure them if I am with someone more sympathetic, like Sophy!)

It is strange – Jeime continues to act as though she knows something about this Structure. Viewing it seems incredibly important to her. She barely spoke a word to me upon her arrival – too busy bustling about. I shall make a point of asking her more openly about her interest in it as soon as the depth-craft returns.

Once the morning's pageantry is complete, I intend to seclude myself with only the company of the books that you left me! Yes, I have not even dared to open them yet. I anticipate, however, that I will soon get over my strange reverence for them and begin promptly. After our experience together, reading alone seems a rather sad prospect.

On second thought, I would like to close this letter by correcting a statement I made while starting it. I suggested, in jest, that I am relieved that your Scholarly obligations will give me time to prepare emotionally for our next meeting. I misspoke. Instead, let me be honest, and share my ardent hope that you, sir, will refrain in the future from making plans to travel into the inaccessible oceans just when I am growing so fond of you! It is incredibly inconvenient.

Yours,

E.

P.S. Thank you very much for sending the Darbeni poem! It is utterly fascinating. The voice hardly sounds like his! But I assume its "meaning", such as it is, describes that deliciously irrational nature of dreams – no matter how much one "recites [one's] Proofs", a dream shall supply you with whatever beautiful and terrible nonsense your Brain can create. And that is all perfectly in keeping with other themes that appear frequently in Darbeni's work. I shouldn't be surprised! Yet it is odd that he so coincidentally encapsulated my experience with the Structure in the phrase "Luminous Circumference" – and the Structure is also rather like a circle prone to "Coruscating"! I don't suppose he might have seen one before? If that were the case, I suppose it lends credence to the hypothesis that it is an Antepelagic artefact! I wonder again what its function is. Would you please tell me more about how you happened upon Darbeni's hidden career as a poet?

P.P.S. O, dear Henerey, there is so much more I wish to say in this letter. But I find it intimidating beyond belief to be vulnerable when I sit across from Seliara (who keeps looking over my shoulder, the fiend!) as my brother bumbles about outside in the depth-craft he guilted from our family friend. Until I have an opportunity to express myself further, I hope you can sense the character of what has gone unwritten.

AUTOMATED POST MISSIVE FROM SOPHY CIDNOSIN TO VYERIN CLEL, 1003

Dear Vyerin,

It is as I expected – and feared. What a surreal letter to read. These words were written in the moments before what was (at the time) one of the most terrifying incidents in the history of the Cidnosin family. (Later eclipsed, of course, by something even worse.)

S.

LETTER FROM ARVIST CIDNOSIN TO SOPHY CIDNOSIN, 1002

Sophy, dear sister,

The unthinkable has happened. Please come as quickly as you can.

Sincerely,

Scholar Artistry "Arvist" Cidnosin

LETTER FROM SELIARA GIDNAN TO SOPHY CIDNOSIN, 1002

Sophy please do not be alarmed but E. has had a bit of a challenging day. She is being treated but we were all very much frightened for her. If there is any way that you are able to leave we would be most grateful.

Seliara

INTAKE REGISTER RECORD FROM THE BOUNDLESS CAMPUS INFIRMARY ANCHORAGE, 1002

PERSONAL AND STATISTICAL PARTICULARS

Full Name: Erudition Cidnosin
Residence (Usual Place of Abode – Vessel or Anchorage): Boundless Campus, "Deep House"
Patient Number: 1432-4
Age: 27 years
Referral Designation(s): "E.," she, her
Single, Partnered, Separated, or Widowed: Single
If partnered, name of spouse: N/A
Department: N/A, see below
*The patient is not a Scholar but the sister of Schr Sophy Cidnosin, who has provided a letter of support in favour of the patient's immediate intake at the on-campus infirmary.

REASON FOR INTAKE

The patient arrived at the Infirmary this afternoon in the care of her brother (Schr Arvist Cidnosin). The brother found the patient floating unconscious after an Unknown Seismic Event impacted their shared residence. Family friend Schr Jeime Alestarre administered artificial respiration to the patient. The patient seems to exhibit symptoms of Extensive Shock and speaks rarely and incomprehensibly. While no administration of medicine seems necessary at this time, the patient will be monitored by the Infirmary until it can be ascertained that she maintains no lingering physical or mental Traumas.

Signed: Scholar Leogroma Marzel, School of Observation

197

LETTER FROM SOPHY CIDNOSIN TO E. AND ARVIST CIDNOSIN, 1002

Dearest dearest E. (and also Arvist):

I anticipate I may arrive at the same time as this letter. Thanks to fortunate coincidence and Niea's quick thinking and generosity, I shall catch a ride on the mail-boat that services our station. I will spend the next day in depressurisation.

Until tomorrow,
Sophy

AUTOMATED POST MISSIVE FROM SOPHY CIDNORGHE TO VYERIN CLEL, 1003

Dear Vyerin,

Thus concludes the blurry period that immediately followed E.'s "accident". Thanks to the – shall we say unhelpful? – communication from my brother and Seliara, I did not quite know what to expect when I arrived at the Infirmary. (In the past, Arvist previously used "the unthinkable" to refer to encounters with faultily made canvases, the sorrow of an unkind review by a colleague, and the experience of going to the icebox thinking that a certain meal might be there and realising that it was not.)

During the journey, I spent nearly twenty hours sealed in the depressurisation chamber in which I had been hauled aboard the mail-boat. Under other circumstances, I might have found the isolation and silence unbearable, but it suited my needs at the time. When I finally stumbled out onto the deck, the sudden rush of air and light and sea spray made me collapse to my knees and shut my eyes in hopes that the comforting gloom would return.

I often think of Adaptation as a process that takes years – generations – aeons – but o, how quickly I adapted to life in the abyss! And even if I did not truly miss the infinite darkness and unquestionably lethal water pressure to which I had become accustomed, I ached for the woman whose presence had become essential to any environment that I might call home. (How sad it is to think that even after the grand romantic moment I shared with Niea, we enjoyed each other's company for only two more days before something tore me away.)

It was out of character for me, but I spent the last few moments of the ride sobbing uncontrollably. Thank the seas for the co-captain, who sat with me abovedeck as we docked, providing me with gentle platitudes in a voice so rhythmic that I confused it with the breeze from time to time.

He even offered to ferry me straight to the Infirmary Anchorage's Urgency Dock in a dinghy, a kindness that I accepted gratefully. I wish I could remember the name of this generous man, because I suspect you might recognise it – surely all kind-hearted captains know one another? Do you perhaps meet over drinks every few months to share stories of the people you have helped? He was an older fellow, far older than my father, and spoke fondly of his partner and their new grandchild, who followed all news of our Spheres expedition in the papers with adorable interest.

And then we arrived, and I bid him a sad farewell, and went in to find E., looking smaller than ever among the colourful tapestries and cushions of her Infirmary bed, and the life that I had led up until that point under the water seemed ages away.

Somehow this letter has transformed into a reminiscence – rather against my wishes, I'm afraid. At any rate, I suppose it is time that I stop reminiscing and send you this package!

My best wishes,
Sophy

AUTOMATED POST MISSIVE FROM VYERIN CLEL TO SOPHY CIDNORGHE, 1003

Dear Sophy,

Of course I know the captain of which you speak. His rhythmic voice, care for his family, and unexpected empathy towards your situation makes it all perfectly clear. That captain was the Vyerin Clel of the future, from twenty or thirty years hence, who somehow discovered the ability to sail through time! How wonderful to have something make sense amid all these mysteries.

(In all seriousness, I wish I could take credit for this man's good nature, or give you his name. Alas, though there are many kind-hearted captains, no one has yet taken the initiative to catalogue them.)

By the way, I appreciated the fact that you granted E. (or should I say Erudition?) entry into the on-campus infirmary, even though she was not a Scholar. (I presume you were able to send me copies of her medical records because you were listed as her Patient Advocate?) Henerey always offered to do so for me. But I'm of the opinion that these new-fangled non-campus Infirmaries are far superior – as actual practising medics, rather than Scholars of the Body, work there. What are your thoughts on the matter?

I write all this to avoid the most pressing topic at hand. What caused this first "accident" that sent E. into such a state of shock? Might I guess that it was the same sort of seaquake that ultimately ended the lives of our siblings? But that seems impossible (or improbable, at the least).

With care (truly, even though I ask so much of you),
Vyerin

AUTOMATED POST MISSIVE FROM SOPHY CIDNORGHE TO VYERIN CLEL, 1003

V.,

I would not be entirely surprised – nor alarmed, quite frankly – if you, of all people, learned how to sail through time. If you do find yourself making such a discovery, would you be so kind as to take me with you? There are some places in the past I would like to visit.

Shockingly, I'm sure, I happen to agree with you on the subject of Infirmaries. Since Niea and I resigned, I have been seeing independent, non-Academic medics for a year now, and they are far more efficient and effective than their Scholarly counterparts – as they prefer the novel method of treating patients rather than debating with their peers while you lie writhing on the table! But the Boundless Infirmary did well enough with my sister, and – as you guessed – they were happy to supply me with the relevant documents when I wrote to them the other day.

Finally: your suspicion about this event and its cause is most accurate.

Will it comfort you to know that your brother – by coincidence – also wanted very much to learn more about this incident?

S.

LETTER FROM HENEREY CLEL TO SOPHY CIDNOSIN, 1002

Dear Schr Cidnosin,

Please forgive my sudden incursion into your family's crisis. I suspect you may already know me – which would be an honour – but in the event that you do not, allow me to contextualise this letter. My name is Henerey Clel and for the past short while, I have enjoyed a correspondence with your sister. At present, I am a Scholar-in-Residence aboard the research vessel *Sagacity*. *Sagacity* recently abandoned its previous relative proximity to the Deep House (which allowed me to enjoy an evening at your lovely home during a fateful party about which I am sure you must have heard) to begin a trek towards the waters above the Spheres, and, in doing so, happened to cross paths with the mail-boat that (I now know) bore you back to shore. As is usual (or so my brother, a sea captain himself, taught me long ago), your ship sent a small automaton-carried bulletin to our captain, informing us that it would be departing from its usual route due to an emergency.

For reasons I could not quite place, this chilled me. The next day, when our supply vessel brought the papers, I read of the Seismic Event at the Deep House — and who was injured — and found I was right to be chilled. As fate would have it, I then promptly received a much-delayed letter from E. describing her brother's exploits in the depth-craft. I suspected it might be best to write to you directly.

Now that my preamble is complete, I will not trouble you further. When time permits, I would be most grateful if you could keep me updated on E.'s condition. (And anything else relevant. What do you suspect may have caused this incident?)

You may find (or, more likely, somehow already can discern) that I care deeply for her.

The relative cheer of this letter is all a façade intended to comfort you, since I imagine you feel an even greater weight of worry!

I await your reply, and give you my sincerest thanks.

Schr Henerey Clel

AUTOMATED POST MISSIVE FROM VYERIN CLEL TO SOPHY CIDNORGHE, 1003

S.,

It feels odd to send you your own words, but here you are — he kept your letter, of course.

V.

LETTER FROM SOPHY CIDNOSIN TO HENEREY CLEL, 1002

Dear Schr Clel,

Circumstances aside, it is wonderful to make your acquaintance – indeed, I have heard much about you. (There is something charming about the fact that you felt the need to introduce yourself nonetheless.)

I am happy to say that the Scholars at the Infirmary say E. should be on the mend soon. Unfortunately, that is all the news I have at the moment. But I have not yet read "the papers" myself, and do not know how much you already gleaned about "the incident", so I will establish some facts as I understand them. Three days ago, E. sat in the parlour while my brother Arvist and Schr Alestarre explored the garden in a depth-craft. (I'm sure E. would like me to assure you that this is not typical of an average day at the Deep House under her watch.) Then something shook the reef horrifically, causing our parlour to collapse. We do occasionally experience seaquakes in this part of the ocean, but never one so strong as this. Our friend Seliara (though part of me sus-pects you know all of us already? I do not know how much E. is prone to gossip!) had just left to fetch some drinks and managed to avoid E.'s fate. I remain so grateful that Schr Alestarre piloted the depth-craft to retrieve E. before . . . the worst could come to pass.

E. still sleeps most of the time and has not yet spoken with us. I fear she is frightened beyond belief. Yet she does not seem to have a single bruise on her – I thank my good luck for small miracles.

Please do try to stay calm. I promise to inform you of any develop-ments. And if you need anything, please do not hesitate to ask me.

Kindly,
Sophy

AUTOMATED POST MISSIVE FROM VYERIN CLEL TO SOPHY CIDNORGHE, 1003

Dear Sophy,

I know I already sent you some documents and a letter, but another thought crossed my mind. Thus, here I am – bothering you once more. (Also, do you find yourself using dashes more frequently now that we've spent so much time reading E.'s letters?)

Reading letters between you and my brother is a most unusual – though not unwelcome – experience. It inspired me to ponder something rather bleak that I dared not even talk through with Reiv. Namely – what would have happened if I had been the one to disappear, and Henerey lived? What if he were writing to you now, trying to piece together the memories you shared of the time before my death? Clearly, this is not a perfect hypothetical – for one, E. never would have been romantically interested in me (there's no accounting for taste) – but it haunts me nonetheless.

Surely the literary quality of the Clel half of the correspondence would increase immensely in this alternate world. Also, I suspect Henerey would have already helped you solve the mystery of what happened to me with phenomenal speed.

That is all.

V.

AUTOMATED POST MISSIVE FROM SOPHY CIDNORGHE TO VYERIN CLEL, 1003

Dear V.,

I also find it odd to look back at my brief exchanges with Henerey and consider how my perspective of him has changed. Back then, he was "E.'s potential partner" and "an esteemed colleague" – now he is still those things, but also your Henerey, and the fact that I had the chance to exchange words with him during his short time in this world seems all the more significant.

There is not much else for me to say to your second paragraph, except that I could not be more grateful for the writing partner I have in this reality.

S.

Chapter 15

LETTER FROM SOPHY CIDNOSIN TO ELINIEA HAYVE FORGHE, 1002

My dearest Niea,

I hate to write to you. How odd that you will not hear my voice. Over the past hour, I have written many versions of this letter, and I hope I may now strike the appropriate tone at last. I know that our connection – whatever it is and may be – is yet nascent, and there is something so solemn and final about addressing you with such intimate terms when it has been but a few days since first we – well, confessed. But as I sit alone in my old quarters in the Boundless Campus Docked Dormitories (can you believe that they kept them unoccupied for my sake while I was away on the expedition? I thought it a certainty that Schr Amble would leap at the chance to upgrade to my sea-facing window!) I find that there is nothing I can do but send words your way in the hopes that they will bring us closer together.

Do you remember when we saw the Nautilus for the first time, and you marvelled at how I did not seem to fear it? (Of course, this is a rhetorical question, as I know you remember it well.) Now, I can say with great conviction that there is nothing under the sea (or above it) that terrifies me in such a way as the thought of any harm befalling my sister. I spent much of my decompression period in great agony as I imagined what I might find when I arrived at the Infirmary. (Knowing you, dear Niea, I am sure you now wonder exactly how successful the decompression process was for me, and whether I suffered any ill effects of note, but I suspect you do not wish to ask me since there are far more pressing issues at hand. I will spare you this internal struggle and tell you plainly. I found it entirely endurable, and I have experienced no significant issues while adjusting to the surface. It is the light that vexes me the most – even now, I have extinguished the ceiling light in my room and write by the glow of a small luminescent algae lamp that I purloined from my old office.)

What an extensive parenthetical. It forced me to glance back up the page to see where I left off. As though I could forget!

I intended to say next that E. appears well, for the most part, though she still has not recovered from her shock. While it lifted my spirits to see my sister in person, she looks so delicate and inscrutable in the infirmary cot. I have not seen her asleep for many years – we did not share a room – yet the peacefulness of her expression brings me some comfort. Her attending Physician suspects that E. may soon feel comfortable enough to speak. (I resisted the urge to respond, in jest, that such a thing would be a medical miracle, as E. is uncomfortable speaking with strangers (to say the least of Scholars) under most circumstances.)

Ought I to explain in more detail what happened before this letter proceeds further? I will tell you all I know in hopes that your brilliant mind may be able to make sense of it. Arvist convinced our mother's friend Jeime to accompany him on some inane survey of the under-garden, so they were outside in a depth-craft when it happened. When "what" happened, you might fairly ask? Well – nobody is quite sure. It has been termed "an anomaly", "a seismic event", and "an unexplained seafloor rupture". In essence, the house began to shake such that the garden-facing windows on the first floor shattered, leaving Seliara and E. watching as the seawater exploded into the parlour. This is the sort of unexpected calamity that gave my mother sleepless nights, I wager. I wonder what she would have made of this. Fortunately, Mother was clever enough to design the Deep House so that the door to each room is equipped with a small emergency airlock that shuts automatically if water breaches the building. Thanks to her ingenious design, everything except the parlour was preserved during this calamity.

In the meantime, there is one person for whom I have no thanks whatsoever. Perhaps it is not fair of me to be infuriated with Arvist – it seems hardly likely that he caused this anomaly, much as I'm sure it would dazzle the artistic world if he could somehow take credit for causing a seismic event – but I cannot help but imagine what might have happened if he had not chosen this particular day to embark upon some ridiculous lark in a depth-craft. Had Arvist stayed indoors, perhaps E. would have remained sequestered and not come down to the parlour to speak with Seliara (how ironic it is for me to say that E. was, for once, justified in her desire to live primarily in her room!), and she would not have suffered the fate she did. The farther reaches of the house at the greatest distance from the undergarden, you see, were spared, and E.'s chambers escaped fully intact.

But then it occurs to me that if for whatever reason E. had been utterly alone – or if Seliara had not popped into the next room just before it happened, which saved her from the brunt of the impact and allowed her to activate the Deep House alarm system – what would have happened then? With that in mind, I have now decided not to dwell upon hypotheticals – but I still may hold my brother at a distance for some time. (Unlike Arvist, Jeime has been wonderfully supportive throughout this entire affair – Mother would not have been surprised in the least.)

O, Niea, it is all so strange and unsettling, especially when I sit by myself in the quarters I once called home that now seem so unfamiliar. I am not the only one put up in the dormitories – Arvist and Seliara are here in an adjoining chamber, which Arvist finds unacceptable. He complains of how "one does not truly live a life unless one is entrenched in the experience of being ensconced in the embrace of a house", and if he ever finds another house in which to live, I hope you will indulge me by supporting my scheme to move in immediately and claim his and Seliara's bedroom as our own!

I feel inappropriate complaining about this when my sister just barely escaped the tidal wave of ill fate, but I miss you, too. How accustomed I grew to our life at the Spheres – to the melodies of the machinery, the glimmer of our automata circling the base, the rippling shadows through the windows. Adapting to this lamplit dormitory, the clatter of Apprentices' boots as they pass in the corridors, and the inescapable sound of my brother's voice – why, it is all most terrifyingly unnatural. Upon writing it all out, I wonder – is this feeling of wrongness, of unsettledness and anxiety – is it how E. will feel when she wakes and realises she is not at home?

Perhaps she and I will have more in common than ever before.

I remain yours (and eager to see what your writing is like!),

Sophy

AUTOMATED POST MISSIVE FROM VYERIN CLEL TO SOPHY CIDNORGHE, 1002

Dear Sophy,

Please thank your wife for her willingness to share the personal correspondence between the two of you! It is most enlightening. For my part, enclosed is one more fine example of your past self's communications with Henerey.

And – something else, too.

I recently discovered that Henerey's daybook takes a rather different turn at this point. You see, following the departure of the *Sagacity* for the open ocean, it would appear that my brother decided to transform his habit of scribbling notes in his planner to proper journaling.

V.

LETTER FROM SOPHY CIDNOSIN TO HENEREY CLEL, 1002

Dear Scholar Clel,

Let the following news reassure you: E. "awakened" today and seems on the mend. (Well, in a manner of speaking – though she now talks, she remains dazed. I do not know the specifics of what troubles her, but I would do nearly anything to spare her from it.)

In any case, if you wish to write to my sister again, please do! When she wishes to listen, I will happily read your letters out loud to her (and would, as a result, encourage you to avoid including anything that you would not want me to read at present – not that I would mind anything sentimental myself, but it might mortify dear E.!)

Take care,

Sophy

EXCERPT FROM THE DAYBOOK OF HENEREY CLEL, 1002

Dear future readers,

Hello! My name is Schr Henerey Clel, and apparently I have an ego sizeable enough to address my personal diary to Scholarly audiences in the centuries to come. Now, before I begin, let me apologise for the cramped format in which you will read these entries (if you decide to continue, of course). This daybook was designed to hold notes of one's appointments, memories, and brief thoughts about particular dates. I certainly never intended to use it as a journal.

Under usual circumstances, I am quite paranoid about writing in my daybook – as I know all too well, as a Scholar, the lives that ephemera can lead after a creator's death – but I shall censor myself no more. I need someplace to explore my own thoughts, and if you, future readers, wish to spend your entire careers footnoting my ramblings – well, don't you think you ought to find a more interesting branch of research?

It has been five days since the *Sagacity* abandoned the familiar waters of the Boundless Campus for the Second Ocean in pursuit of that "Point of Interest" that our colleagues in the Ridge Expedition currently survey. (Well, minus one particularly important colleague at present, but I will discuss that at a later point.) Being a part of the *Sagacity*'s efforts fulfils my life's greatest desire of late – it is a research expedition with a truly important mission, one that might even dictate the direction of the School of Observation in the future. (I did warn you about that ego, did I not?)

As I write, I have made myself reasonably comfortable in what is termed my "berth" – a small cabin equipped with an even smaller porthole that offers the smallest views of the enormous ocean outside. O, it has been over a year since I last spent substantial time on an unanchored vessel, and I am overjoyed to feel the varying rhythm of waves beneath my feet again! Outside of this tiny retreat, I share eating and bathing facilities with two of my colleagues. We have not spoken much – I was surprised to find that many of the other Scholars aboard already knew each other quite well. They seem to be of a slightly older generation than I and have run in the same Scholarly circles for years. When I do feel the rare need for social stimulation, I much prefer the company of our solitary Illustrator, Scholar Lerin Zuan Vellen.

Alas that I may not spend time with the one person whose company I have come to treasure above all.

(O yes, future readers – especially if you happen to be a relative of mine, as yet unborn – I am sure this is the sort of confessions you were hoping to find! "Don't you dare talk about your washroom or who eats luncheon with you, Ancestor Henerey!" you might say. "Please tell us more about your Romantical Inclinations!" Well, descendants, I am happy to oblige.)

Some manner of accident has befallen my dear correspondent E.

Though her sister writes that E.'s condition stabilised at last, I could not have predicted how much this ordeal would – well, devastate me. In my estimation, I am wholly and inescapably in love with a woman whom I have met only once. What a charming surprise!

But it seems that the process of writing this has taken much longer than I originally anticipated. Efficiency beckons! And I suppose I mustn't spill all my secrets in one entry – I ought to give you descendants an impetus for further research!

Signing off,

Schr Henerey Clel

AUTOMATED POST MISSIVE FROM SOPHY CIDNORGHE TO VYERIN CLEL, 1003

Dear Vyerin,

Let us pause for a moment and pretend I did not swoon internally over Henerey's cheerful confession of love for my sister.

Moving on—

Am I to understand that you possessed journal entries from Henerey this entire time and never mentioned it? Have you not read them? What other archival treasures do you keep from me?

With (jesting) outrage,

Sophy

AUTOMATED POST MISSIVE FROM VYERIN CLEL TO SOPHY CIDNORGHE, 1003

Dear Sophy,

I know you jest, but you are right – it is frankly unbelievable that I have not read Henerey's daybook in its entirety. Every time I supplied you with an excerpt thus far, it has been solely because I gave myself permission to open it to that particular date to see what he might have written down.

Why? Old habit, really. Once as a foolish youth I snuck into my brother's desk in the hopes of pawing through his diary and learning his secrets. One entry included fifteen pages waxing rhapsodic about his profound love for Classification as a discipline, and one page doing the same about a girl we knew, which was what I had hoped to discover. When I mocked him with my newfound knowledge of his passions, he went silent and looked at me as though he did not recognise me. Ever since that day, I do not read Henerey's journals unless absolutely necessary.

But somehow reading his letters has felt entirely different. I suppose all rules are off at this point. Brother: forgive me.

Now let us simply enjoy what Henerey has to say (since I presume you possess the letters he ultimately sent to E. after the accident).

Bashfully,

Vyerin

LETTER FROM ELINIEA HAYVE FORGHE TO SOPHY CIDNOSIN, 1002

To my luminescent Sophy,

I chose this moniker because the unexpected pleasure of receiving a letter from you made me glow, truly! You know I did not expect anything of the sort, you lovely one. It takes mail so awfully long to reach us down here – I hope fervently that by the time you read this, E. will have recovered from her shock and that her presence will be a comfort to you. I am ever so reassured to hear that she is otherwise unharmed, of course, and I do wish I could help you shed some light on the mystery of what happened! I know precious little about Seaquakes, but merely say the word and I would be happy to conduct any research that you desire.

Speaking of colleagues, the crew sends their fondest and most sympathetic regards. Ylaret asks for updates every other second and says that if you and your family find yourselves desperate for sustenance beyond that which the Refectory can provide, you must go directly to an anchorage-inn by the name of the "Solvent Seagrass" – apparently the owners owe Ylaret a favour. (She will not give further details.) Without speaking a word, Irye gravely delivered unto me the finest set of Columns pieces I've ever seen (which I have, by grace of the automata, managed to include in this parcel). And Vincenebras keeps threatening to write Imposing and Intimidating Letters of Complaint on your behalf – though he has not specified to whom these complaints might be addressed (the very forces of nature themselves?).

I, of course, wish desperately that I might have gone with you, even if that is an impossibility. I keep thinking of Alie and how I would feel were she involved in such a catastrophe. Under those circumstances, I would need the company of someone whom I could trust above all. And you may certainly trust me, dear Sophy.

Now comes the part of this letter that I dread! I am sure it comes as no surprise that Chancellor Rawsel has been in constant communication with me since your departure and remains most eager to know when you will return. I convinced him that we simply must delay our second field study until such a point at which we are no longer missing an essential member of our crew. The rest of our Spheres colleagues are all in accord. I will do my best to keep the Chancellors satisfied, because it is critical to me that you take as much time with your sister as you need.

With ever so much fondness,
Niea

LETTER FROM HENEREY CLEL TO E. CIDNOSIN, 1002

My dear E.,

To my knowledge, there are few species that can survive underwater without oxygen (or gills) for extensive periods of time. The Intrepid Micro-Gull (which happens to frequent any number of obscure islets in the Second Ocean) requires air to live – yet a significant adaptation allows it to spend colder months in extended hibernation beneath the water's surface. Around its entire body it projects a kind of bubble in which it could conceivably be suspended indefinitely, with its organs shutting down so that its need for sustenance or breath is reduced immensely.

And apparently you too are capable of miraculous survival.

I don't suppose that most people ever write a letter to someone expressing their gratitude that said person is not deceased. (I do not mind being a pioneer in that regard!) While it is true that you have only been part of my life for a short while, the thought of any harm befalling you has rather affected me. (I would say more, but I know your sister has kindly offered to read my letters to you, and I certainly do not wish to embarrass you unnecessarily!) I also do not want to overwhelm you in your fragile state (nor to tax Sophy's readerly generosity overmuch).

Please know that if I had the opportunity and you thought it appropriate (and the *Sagacity* allowed it – I'm quite sure they would not!), I would come to you immediately. My fondness for reading out loud makes me quite a useful companion to someone who is bedridden, or so I suspect, anyway!

Yours with the most amazed gratitude (about you being well, that is!),

Henerey

AUTOMATED POST MISSIVE FROM VYERIN CLEL TO SOPHY CIDNORGHE, 1003

Dear Sophy,

I do not know what you will make of the contents of this envelope. While hunting down what E. sent to Henerey in response to his first post-accident note, I discovered that she wrote him not one but two letters. You might remember the first, but I imagine the second will take you by surprise (to put it lightly).

I will reserve any further commentary until you have had a chance to read.

V.

Chapter 16

LETTER FROM E. CIDNOSIN TO HENEREY CLEL, DICTATED TO SOPHY CIDNOSIN, 1002

Dear Henerey,

It seems like another lifetime when I last wrote to you – and longer still since we met. Far from being some kind of impressively resilient Micro-Gull, I feel completely annihilated, though I suppose I should be grateful that is not literally the case (as it very well could have been).

Today I do feel more like myself. Yet Sophy nevertheless insisted upon writing this letter per my dictation. *(Hello, Henerey! –S.)* I shall stay in the Infirmary only a few days more before I return "home" with Sophy – though the use of that particular word seems especially cruel at present, since I will join her in the dormitories instead of the Deep House.

Even after I leave this place, I imagine I must remain confined to my bed for a long period of time while I recover, so I would be very grateful for whatever you have the time to send me. I hope you will make some wondrous discoveries in your new waters.

You certainly should not come here under any circumstances – you have far more important things to do than worry about me! *(Let the record show that while I disagree with the self-deprecation in this statement, I wrote it anyway to please my sister. –S.)*

Yours,

E.

LETTER FROM E. CIDNOSIN TO HENEREY CLEL, 1002

My dear Henerey,

I apologise for the subdued tone of my first letter. Sophy insisted that I was not yet well enough to write on my own, and while I appreciate her care and concern for me, I have found it just a little stifling at present.

Have you ever been in an Infirmary for an extended period, Henerey? It is a most challenging experience for me. Worst of all is the ceaseless attention – from my siblings, from visitors, from the Scholars of the Body and their Apprentices – constantly, people ask me questions and deliver unto me fast and complex bursts of information, and I feel completely fatigued. There is also a general sense that I am a fragile, delicate creature who will break if she takes up such a strenuous task as writing a letter herself. If I somehow shatter before completing this message to you, I urge you to let Sophy know that she was right all along.

But I hope she will not be.

Henerey, since we last spoke, I have undergone the strangest experience of my entire life. Surely you are curious about what happened to me during the Seismic Event; Sophy and Jeime certainly are. For once in his life, Arvist has become my unlikely ally, because, for whatever reason, he seems to have no desire to learn about anything at the moment (an unusual quality for an artist, and certainly unprecedented for this specific artist).

When I first regained consciousness, I tried to tell them. Sophy, in particular, since she was closest to my bedside. (In the background, Arvist painted, Jeime paced, and Seliara played out some Linguistic Alchemy ritual to help me heal more quickly.) I even whispered a few key words under my breath, trying out how they felt on my tongue.

But then I could imagine with such clarity the conversation that would inevitably follow, were I to confess all.

"It is worse than I feared," Sophy would say, stroking my hair in the most tragic fashion.

And then, turning away from me so I could not hear, Sophy would whisper to the Physician:

"My sister suffers from a Malady of the Mind, and surely this situation makes it even harder for her to determine what is real and what is not."

And if Sophy were to say all that in reality – who could blame her? She is correct about my Brain, which I often feel is out to destroy me!

So I dare not say a word.

At the moment, I furnish any number of excuses to those who interrogate me (however gently) – that I do not remember, that I am too tired to think of such things, that I would prefer not to dwell upon the difficulties and traumas of the past – but I am ashamed to admit that they are all lies.

I remember exactly what occurred. I have replayed this memory of mine hundreds of times (now that is something at which my Brain excels), and it is not like the Ruminations that sometimes torment me. I experienced something new, and if it were not for the fact that I am weighed down by my Malady, anyone might reasonably believe me.

Because unlike the false scenarios and terrifying images that my Brain has crafted for me all through these past ten years, I possess physical proof that this experience happened.

Yet I feel that if there is any living soul with whom I may share this secret, it is you. It is not only because you are so distant geographically and simply cannot trouble me with questions every other second (though I suspect that even if you were here, you would not quite stoop to such levels!) – but because I find myself very close to you in spirit (which is true).

Would you like me to tell you? The choice is yours.

Your E.

P.S. If this will help sway your decision in any way, let it be known that I have a suspicion that this mysterious experience of mine has to do with the Structure. Make of that what you will.

P.P.S. Do you have any recommendations as to where I might find a compilation of Darbeni's poetry? Anywhere but the Reading Room?

AUTOMATED POST MISSIVE FROM SOPHY CIDNORGHE TO VYERIN CLEL, 1003

Dear Vyerin,

Thank you for sending these letters to me, my friend. I apologise for taking so many days to respond to them.

In the early days of our marriage, Niea became the first academic to study the arcane concept of Sophy Temporality – a phenomenon that occurs whenever I become vexed with a particularly unsolvable problem (intellectual or emotional). Under these circumstances, the passage of time seems to come to a standstill as I occupy myself day and night with working out an answer.

On the one hand, I am happy to find myself truly engaging with something again. For the past year, I have felt so numb to curiosity. The grief made me more prone to suppression than solutions.

Here is the puzzle I am now so eager to sort out. If E. had told me this "confession", would I have believed her? Sophy of the Present would, certainly. But then?

When E. got into her states, back when she struggled the most with her Malady, she would spend hours convinced that she had some deathly illness, or that she had somehow injured or killed someone without even knowing it. If she had shared something unusual with me on that day in the infirmary, would I not have perceived it as another one of those pernicious Thoughts that tormented her?

I will be the first to admit that I sometimes thought of E.'s Malady as her defining characteristic. Something that made her vulnerable. Something that made me, whether I liked it or not, into the elder sister instead of the younger, and required me to protect her at all costs. She worked so hard to live with it – she reached the point where her "states" would often only last an hour or two (or even a few moments) before she was able to ground herself – and surely if anyone could tell the difference between reality and a fabricated vision from her mind, it was my sister.

All this matters little, of course, because in the end, E. never told me anything more about this. So I remain uncomfortable and intrigued in equal measure. And to think that cursed Structure is at the core of it! (I am lambasting myself for not looking into it more back then, by the way. I kept forgetting about it – dismissing it as a silly Arvist thing – I should have been more observant!) Though it wounds me to think that she preferred to trust Henerey with this over me, I so desperately want to know what came to pass.

As I'm sure you do, too.

S.

AUTOMATED POST MISSIVE FROM VYERIN CLEL TO SOPHY CIDNORGHE, 1003

Dear S.,

Both of you were operating under challenging circumstances. I suspect, also, that she did not want to worry you – knowing how much you care for her – and might have assumed that Henerey, slightly more removed from the situation, could offer a kind of detachment necessary to help unravel the mystery.

And, as I have said before, I never felt the urge to read through Henerey's correspondence in its entirety, so I will not skip ahead and find out these secrets without you. Perhaps the fact that we will both discover "what happened" together, for the first time, may serve as a comfort. Still, when we read private thoughts that our siblings did not intend to share with us personally, there is always the danger that we might discover something that hurts us.

Kindly,

V.

AUTOMATED POST MISSIVE FROM SOPHY CIDNORGHE TO VYERIN CLEL, 1003

Dear V.,

I see why Henerey called you his "anchor".

S.

NOTE FROM ARVIST CIDNOSIN TO E. AND SOPHY CIDNOSIN, 1002

To my dear sisters two,

Over the past few days, I have been practically ill with grief and guilt – so much so that I nearly asked the Infirmary to book me a bed alongside E.!

After spending many a fraught hour mulling over this matter, I reached the conclusion that it is only due to me that E. experienced what she did and that our home has been taken from us. Had I not been so inspired by the Structure to complete my great works – had I been in the parlour, ready to save E. and my beautiful almost-bride at a moment's notice – who knows what might have come to pass when the Seismic Event occurred?

I must repent for what I have done. I allowed my foolishness to put those about whom I care in danger. I set off now on a quest of Penance and will return to you when I have given up all I have – my possessions, my pride, my finest ideas for art-making (which I will write down upon the tiniest of scrolls and bestow upon random passersby as gifts!) – and may bow before you a changed and humble man.

Your brother,

Scholar Artistry "Arvist" Cidnosin

P.S. Please tell Seliara that I do hope she will wait for me.

RECORD OF INFIRM PATIENT RELEASE FOR ERUDITION CIDNOSIN, 1002

The following record signifies the release of Erudition (E.) Cidnosin from Infirmary care and into the custody of her sister Schr Philosophy Cidnosin for continued rehabilitation from unknown shock symptoms. The patient is instructed to continue resting as much as is reasonably possible, consume a diet rich in sea-minerals, and avoid taking part in situations that might cause excessive anxiety.

Schr Lilé Radnon

LETTER FROM SOPHY CIDNOSIN TO ELINIEA HAYVE FORGHE, 1002

Dear Niea,

I have waited all my life for a lady to call me "luminescent".

Truly, your letter sent me into bittersweet tears. And now that E. and I live together once more, I have no way of hiding them! I forgot how keen her hearing is. (Though, incidentally, Arvist always had the sharpest ears of the three of us – my brother used to allege that he could hear me breathing three rooms over!)

That is all to say that yes, my sister has recovered at last! The Infirmary released her two days ago, and while our House remains indisposed, we have made quite a comfortable home out of some vacant dormitory quarters. (Larger even than mine!) During my time below, I missed nothing so much as simply talking with my sister, and you can be sure that I have told her much of you. And all our colleagues! (But particularly you.)

In the meantime, I hope I may have inadvertently solved a problem of yours – that is, of course, the Chancellor's continued persistence in requesting my return. I do want to come back, as soon as I can, but first I must ensure that E. progresses with her recovery – and I must also attend to the question of the Deep House and our lodgings. I fear if I were to leave, E. would do very poorly on her own in the dormitories.

Right – let us return to my solution! Really, it is unfair of me to claim it as my own, since it was thrust upon me. Today, while trying to coax my recalcitrant sister into a few rounds of Columns (do convey my thanks to Irye for this fine gift), I heard the door-chimes sound – quite unexpectedly, as I gave Seliara and Arvist (against my better judgement) a key, and I did not think any of my other colleagues from campus knew about my new quarters. This surprise made me uncharacteristically cautious.

From the door panel in the hallway, I flipped a switch to activate the "card-claw" – have you ever seen such a wonder, Niea? Perhaps you have always enjoyed more modern dormitories back home at Intertidal, but not I. I am used to the old-fashioned practice of callers slipping their cards under the door to identify themselves prior to a visit. At any rate, this wondrous automatic arm clicks open to catch the visitor's card, somehow flattens and retracts itself through a small hole in the door, and then solemnly presents its catch to the resident. The card deposited onto my palm just moments afterwards was quite refined, all things considered – none of that excessive tracery so in style at present. It read in simple, elegant calligraphy: *Tevn Winiver Mawr. Scholar of Wayfinding, School of Observation (Intertidal Campus).*

O, dear Niea, are you not intrigued now? Of course I remembered the name of your former colleague, about whom I had so pathetically and jealously questioned you on our first field expedition – yet I could not fathom why he had chosen to visit our quarters. I unlocked the door with great haste, though not before shouting to E. that she should keep to her chamber if she did not wish to encounter a stranger in the doorway.

I need not describe Tevn to you, given your acquaintance, but I shall say that standing there in my entryway he appeared both informal and insecure. In a surprising choice for an Intertidal Scholar, he wore plain grey trousers and a loose white blouse – nothing more, nothing less – and spoke slowly and softly. I strained to hear him at times.

"Forgive my intrusion, Scholar Cidnosin," he muttered. "As you might have gleaned, I am Tevn Winiver Mawr. Scholar of Wayfinding, School of Observation, Intertidal Campus. And so forth."

He did not ask if he might come in, and I did not offer (because of E., you understand). It was not a standard meeting by any social standards, but the arrangement seemed to suit us both.

"It is a pleasure to meet you, Scholar Mawr."

"Call me Tev, please," your friend replied. "I am no stickler for Scholarly titles. And I will soon make you a friendly offer, so it would seem fitting for us to be on familiar terms."

"Tev, then. Tell me more about this offer, if you would."

Tevn extended one finger to press against the doorframe. I expected that this clumsy attempt at relaxed sophistication would cause him to fall down, but to my surprise, he appears to be in possession of an excellent sense of balance.

"I wanted to share my regrets about your sister's accident," he said, looking me right in the eyes for the very first time. "I know all about worrying after one's younger sisters. I have seven of them, as a matter of fact."

People do always assume E. is the youngest. But I was too surprised by the size of his family to correct his misinterpretation of the Cidnosin siblings' birth order!

"Yes, seven," Tevn continued, "and a good thing it was that my parents owned their own research vessel. Else I imagine we would be quite cramped in your average Intertidal family apartment." He straightened up, extended his other pointer finger, and leaned onto the doorframe from the opposite direction. "Which is all to say that I am particularly sympathetic to your present situation. And I wish to help."

"I appreciate your sympathy," I said, "and your offer, though I still do not know how you wish to assist us."

Tevn smiled and coughed simultaneously, which I take to be his rendition of a laugh.

"By serving as your substitute. I have already submitted a formal request to the Chancellors. But I wanted your consent before I dared submit myself to the depths."

Now, dear Niea, if it were not for the fact that I recognised Tevn's name from our conversations – and knew that you seemed to hold him in favourable regard – I might have been alarmed by this sudden proclamation from a stranger. But it really all seems quite suitable, does it not?

I told him as much, and he seemed startled – perhaps he did not think I would acquiesce so easily.

"You will not know this, because it was never public knowledge, but I took part in the initial expedition with Niea – Eliniea – Scholar Forghe, you see," he babbled on, as though he had a speech prepared. "But no one knew about it because I grew ill as a result and needed to rehabilitate after we returned to the surface and I was too ashamed for anyone to know. But I have recovered now. So I am equipped to take your place like no other Scholar could. Plus, I am a Scholar of Wayfinding! Though you already know that. I told you, did I not? I think I did. I would join the expedition as soon as the Chancellors deem appropriate and continue your research. Then, as soon as you desire to return – days? Tides? Months? – you need only say the word."

I assured him that these terms satisfied me completely. And indeed, they do! As much as it hurts me to be apart from our mission (and from you, of course), I do not feel that E. is ready for me to leave just yet.

At last, he leaned upwards again, standing tall and proud.

"Thank you, Scholar Cidnosin, for this warm and generous conversation," Tevn said. "When I heard about your sister – well, I told myself that it would be utterly selfish not to return to the field for both of your sakes."

And before I could even thank him, Scholar Tevn Winiver Mawr disappeared down the corridor, leaving his calling card as the only evidence of his visit.

So, Niea, would you not agree that I have found the ideal fix? Chancellor Rawsel will no longer trouble you to trouble me about my return, you and our colleagues can continue work, and you can rely on the trustworthy assistance of an old friend in your hour of research-related need.

Though I must admit that I am intrigued and amazed by his remarkable claim that he accompanied you in secret on that first mission! I mean, stranger things have happened in the world of Boundless Campus experimental missions – did you hear about that one time when three Scholars floated into the atmosphere for three full hours in a flying machine until it collapsed, but the Chancellors thought it unwise to tell the General Campus about the project, so it was not until a captain glimpsed the thing crashing into the Third Ocean that anyone knew humanity had attempted to rediscover Antepelagic Flight?

Returning to my point . . .

It is not at all surprising to me that there were aspects of the first Ridge Expedition that even we did not know, but I am worried about what effect Tevn's "illness" had upon you. We needn't talk about it now or ever. But it occurs to me that if your former expedition partner had been injured to the extent that his very involvement in the expedition was never made public knowledge at his own request, that fully explains why you were extremely anxious about Ylaret and all of us, really. I am always here to speak with you if it would help, you know.

I read back the earlier parts of this letter and now feel foolish. Of course you must already know about this "solution" – for if "Tev" spoke with me and the Chancellors, surely he wrote to you as well?

Above all, please do not think that this means I have no desire to return to you with great haste – o, I wish I could!

Yours always,
Sophy

LETTER FROM HENEREY CLEL TO E. CIDNOSIN, 1002

My dear E.,

I apologise because I will only have time for a quick note this morning – as ten hours of ship repair await me! Would you believe that the *Sagacity* was unfortunate enough to encounter a riotous squall yesterday evening? I dare anyone to describe waves as "raging" until they have experienced a tempest like this one. We are all well, if shaken (quite literally), but the deck suffered immensely, and our investigations of the marine life here in the open ocean must be put on hold as we work together to restore our craft. Thank goodness I happen to be equipped with a not-insignificant smidgen of historical shipbuilding know-how as well as remarkably strong arms (if that sounds as though I am posturing to impress you, please know that only one of those items was written with such an objective in mind – I will leave it to you to guess at which!).

I will respond to your questions efficiently and out of order:

Firstly – yes, in fact I was briefly confined to an Infirmary bed about a year ago. I did not want to mention it earlier, as I feared it might add further stress to an already fraught situation, but I myself once resided in that very Boundless Campus ward where you are, and do not hold altogether fond memories of the place. You see, I injured myself falling off a coastal incline while in pursuit of a particularly winsome hermit crab (I have attempted to become less clumsy in my research expeditions since then, with limited success!). In the days directly following the accident, I revelled in a brief break from the ceaseless demands of my profession: but when it was determined that I would not recover for some time, the novelty wore off and I simply wished to be able to frolic about the seaside once more. Here's hoping that you will be able to do so soon (metaphorically speaking)!

Secondly – I hope that your new quarters, wherever they may be, will at least give you access to a porthole! I never lived in the Boundless Docked Dormitories, but I know they are quite near to a previous

Anchorage of mine. I encourage you to consider continuing your foray into Natural History during your convalescence – I am sure you will see many wondrous creatures (though you might need a very good spyglass if you are on the upper level of the dormitories!). This may well be the furthest thing from your mind at present, but did you ever happen to receive the journal that I sent you? If it is at the Deep House and now lost, do let me know, and I would be happy to write to the Boundless stationery shop to order you a new one.

Thirdly – since I do not yet know if you are reading this letter privately or if Sophy still reads them to you, I will not say overmuch, but I do want to emphasise, above all, that I am always happy to hear anything you would like to share with me.

Anything whatsoever, no matter how unusual.

I will end here by saying that I think of you constantly.

Continually yours,

Henerey

P.S. O, how could I forget! Darbeni! Your questions before the accident that had gone unanswered! Let me see how much I can scribble out before I am torn away. At one point, I intended to cite some of Darbeni's writings in a treatise on the Elevated Diatom and noticed another Scholar's footnote about the poems. Not wishing to step inside the Reading Room if I did not have to, I asked Elaxand if there were any publicly accessible copies of Darbeni's manuscripts, and he directed me to "A Luminous Circumference". It is the perfect poem for me, really. I too value the power of dreams. (And if the "circumference" seems directly taken from your life, then I might say that "A—Predator—Awaits" perfectly describes how I used to feel when I noticed Chancellor Rawsel hovering about me in the Department Office.)

More seriously, though, I do agree that there's a possibility Darbeni might have been inspired by a similar Artefact. If you are interested, ask Sophy to request *A Poetic Hospice: Darbeni's Last Three Years* from the Boundless library – it does not include all the poems in their entirety, but certainly provides some useful contextual information and a few excerpts. That might be a good place to start. I knew there was something untoward about that Structure! But I must flee! Shipbuilding awaits! Fondly, H.

AUTOMATED POST MISSIVE FROM VYERIN CLEL TO SOPHY CIDNORGHE, 1003

Dear S.,

O how this letter sparks my memories. After his cliff accident, Henerey sent me a sheepish postcard from the Infirmary the very next day, reading something along the lines of "injured by crab, please send your best regards," and I was appalled to find that he had unfairly blamed that poor creature for his troubles. (If anything was to blame, it was the cliff.) He hurt himself severely, to be sure, but in doing so gained the excuse to spend a few tides in utter luxury – reading over fifty books – without worrying about his Scholarly obligations. (And also gained the excuse to match highly sculptural walking sticks to his outfits from that point forward.)

Are you ready for another letter from your sister?

V.

P.S. Forgive me if I misremember, but was it not painfully obvious from your earlier letters to E. that you suspected Tevn as a potential romantic rival? Even if Niea had since convinced you otherwise, it seems surprising that you would accept this – slightly suspicious, if I'm frank – offer with such open enthusiasm. (Or am I simply taking advantage of hindsight?)

AUTOMATED POST MISSIVE FROM SOPHY CIDNORGHE TO VYERIN CLEL, 1003

Dear Vyerin,

You have not misremembered in the least. In fact, it was because of my initial – and rather shameful – misinterpretation of Niea and Tevn's history that I felt the need to overcompensate so ridiculously in this letter to my future wife. Of course it was odd beyond belief that this stranger, who clearly left the initial expedition under questionable circumstances, offered so boldly to take my place!

To answer your final question – honestly, no, I am not ready! I dread what E. might write next (even though I am also so intrigued). May I send you some other materials first? They are related to the Ridge expedition, so at least you might find them intriguing. I hope to procrastinate as long as I possibly can! Surely you understand.

S.

AUTOMATED POST MISSIVE FROM VYERIN CLEL TO SOPHY CIDNORGHE, 1003

S.

I will allow such procrastination. Not only because these unknown bits of Ridge history interest me, but because I understand why you seek to avoid these letters from E.

(Remember that we are in this together.)

V.

Chapter 17

LETTER FROM TEVN WINIVER MAWR TO ELINIEA HAYVE FORGHE, 1002

Dear Niea,

Greetings, my friend. I anticipate that this letter might shock you. After all, my calculations suggest that it has been upwards of a year since I effectively disappeared (leaving no word but that most unhelpful farewell letter I sent you in a rush) – and I am sure you might not look upon my name upon this envelope (or, worse, the words contained within it) with the greatest fondness. For that I apologise.

I have rested and recovered, and I would like to work again. And help you, as best that I can. I know that your work is as difficult and thankless as it is inspiring and enlightening. The indisposition of Scholar Cidnosin seemed an ideal reason for me to end my sabbatical. Don't worry – I have made the appropriate arrangements, of course. Even your colleague herself has approved me as her substitute. (And Chancellor R. was most pleased – how droll.) By the time you read this, I will be aboard the Depth Capsule and on my way to the Ridge.

I will say nothing else until we see each other again.

Yours sincerely,

Tev

LETTER FROM ELINIEA HAYVE FORGHE TO SOPHY CIDNOSIN, 1002

Dear Sophy,

Every day, I reread your letter during each moment when I might have otherwise talked to you. Over breakfast – naturally! Before our expedition briefings – when I can! In the quiet hours of the evening that would be much more pleasantly passed in your company with cups of something warm at hand – o, how I delight in your letter's company then.

All of this is to say that I have not been ignoring you these past few days. On the contrary, you were with me constantly! There has been much abuzz in my head, my dear, and I feared I could not explain it properly on paper.

It relieved and troubled me to hear of your encounter with Tevn. Two days after I received your letter, he sent me a note of his own – only to say that he was on his way to the Spheres to take your place! I have not seen or spoken with or written to him in over a year, and now he is here. I had much anxiety about his arrival, I will say, but really, it seems to have lightened the Company's spirits. Not because they do not miss you – in fact, the very first thing Vincenebras uttered to Tevn was "Perish any thought of replacing the irreplaceable Sophy," to which Tevn gravely assented – but because we have all gone so long without seeing anyone else outside of our circle, I wager. Vincenebras spends far too much time interrogating Tevn for gossip about various mutual acquaintances (of whom Tevn has, regretfully, nothing to share), and even Ylaret dared to ask him if some articles she'd been anticipating had yet seen print in their respective journals.

Like you, everyone has questions aplenty about my history with Tevn, but – also like you – many of them seem quite familiar with (if sceptical of) the Boundless Chancellors' tendency towards obscuring elements of the most important missions for the Greater Good, or something of the sort. Being an Intertidalite myself, it is all very strange to me, and this lie I perpetuated about supposedly surveying the Ridge by myself has torn me to pieces ever since our mission began, and it is much more—

Well, there is much more I want to say to you about Tevn and everything, but I find that the quiet nook of the galley I chose as a sanctuary in which to write to you has been invaded at last. They found me! Alas. I miss you so truly. I will write again as soon as I dare.

Niea

P.S. Enclosed you will also find a letter from Ylaret, who insisted upon writing to you! See, you are well missed!

LETTER FROM YLARET TAMSELN TO SOPHY CIDNOSIN, 1002

Dear Sophy,

Will it surprise you to know that I do not enjoy correspondence? I find it unbearably limiting. There is so much "written" in gestures, in gazes, in wrinkles, in the touch of a palm or the flick of an eyebrow. Compared to the rich world of conversation, writing a letter feels like representing a constellation of stars – a collection of enormous Suns! – by drawing simple lines and dots on paper. Serviceable, but leaving no scope for the imagination.

Yet I found myself so frustrated by your absence that I simply had to follow Niea's lead and send you a note. I hope that your sister is well and your spirits have mended. Did you ever visit my colleague at the Solvent Seagrass? (What is the point of people owing one favours if one never has friends who have the sudden need of a free, fine meal?)

We all assumed that Niea keeps you abreast (a word I do mean quite innocently, in case you thought otherwise) of the happenings down here, and thus I hesitate to share too much news to avoid the risk of redundancy. I am sure, however, that you might be interested in hearing more about Scholar Tevn Winiver Mawr. Does it really not offend you that he has arrived here, out of the blue, to take your place? If so, you know that you may tell me.

Though I find myself befuddled by the convenient circumstances under which Scholar Mawr joined us, I have no other complaints about the man himself. I imagine he would have made a perfect candidate for a confidential two-person mission that the Chancellors subsequently pretended was a one-person mission for reasons of "Academic Optics". (You Boundless Scholars are fascinating). Tevn is quiet – which now makes two of us down here – and rather gentle-humoured, except when he expresses his exuberant passion for Wayfinding. He and Niea share a natural rapport – the kind, I recognise, that comes from living under-water together in such close quarters – and it is nice to see how they anticipate each other's every move. (Why, yesterday, when Niea broke a slide for the Microscope while examining some plankton samples, Tevn clipped a new one of the exact grade in place without a second thought – I suppose that sounds less remarkable written out, but believe me, it was a sight to see!) There is some tension between them that I cannot quite explain, however. I have a sense that each has something to say but cannot find the right words to tell it to the other.

And as odd as his arrival may seem, his timing is fortuitous. We dive again in two days. Even with my communicators adjusted, I do fear something might go amiss for me. O, how isolated I felt when that music played for my ears alone! Fortunately, Irye has been a balm on that front – always saying that there is no greater privilege than hearing an unknown sound. Perhaps it is indeed a privilege, not a torment.

There would be no greater privilege, however, than undertaking this mission in the company of the most brilliant Scholar of Wayfinding, whom I have come to consider a friend – and whom I miss very much.

With the kindest regards,
Ylaret Tamseln

AUTOMATED POST MISSIVE FROM VYERIN CLEL TO SOPHY CIDNORGHE, 1003

Dear S.,

Received your letters today. How odd to read about the Ridge mission without you there. And Scholar Mawr still fascinates me. By the waves – I'd feel threatened by him if I were you. Clipping in each other's microscope slides? Scandalous.

May I send E.'s letter now?

V.

AUTOMATED POST MISSIVE FROM SOPHY CIDNORGHE TO VYERIN CLEL, 1003

Dear Vyerin,

Send away, I suppose.

Anxiously,

S.

EXCERPT FROM THE AMATEUR FIELD JOURNAL OF E. CIDNOSIN, 1002

VIEWING LOCATION: dormitory porthole
HABITAT: the surface of the Boundless waters, right before the wavebreak
OBSERVATIONS: It occurs to me as I write from my new quarters that this is the first time in many years that I have seen the ocean from above. With this novelty fuelling my powers of concentration, I noticed several pods of Imperturbable Toothed Whales skipping around the tops of the waves. They seem to enjoy how the Docked Dormitories struggle against the currents. Many creatures make a habit

of jumping up against the walls, as though catching the small crests the bobbing building creates. For the most part, the Toothed Whales tend to rove in groups of ten or more; I did see at least one youngling chattering with the rest of them. I envy their easy comfort in a group environment. (Is this what one does in a field journal? Please advise!) – E. Cidnosin

LETTER FROM E. CIDNOSIN TO HENEREY CLEL, 1002

My dear Henerey,

First of all: many, many thanks for ordering me the replacement journal! I hope you enjoyed my first entry.

I write to you tonight under the cover of darkness and from the comfort of my new quarters! It is certainly no Deep House, but there are two bedrooms, a small dining room and parlour, and a library that fits in a large closet. The family who owns this residence is away on a yearlong research expedition, and I find myself quite intrigued by their decor. On carpets, in paintings, and upon practically every other flat surface, there is a great abundance of unusual iconography – Anemones and Spirals – and Prawns!

I prefer it immensely over the Infirmary (though it comforted me to hear that you too had spent time there – because I entertained myself by wondering what you thought about every particularity, from the unfortunately abstract Octopus wall-hangings to the scratchiness of the sheets!). Yet I still feel – well, I suppose the best word is "exposed". I miss the familiarity and reliability of my Home, and knowing that I am just one tiny person on a massive floating Anchorage filled with countless strangers makes me want to never leave my bed.

Fortunately, never leaving my bed happens to be just what the doctor ordered for my recovery, so I have that to my advantage. Sophy is doting – we have spent hours on jigsaws. Unsurprisingly, my sister is a capable caretaker. She appears in better spirits these days and told me that she will be able to stay as long as I need. Yet my enjoyment of our quiet time together is poisoned by the great falsehood to which I have sworn myself.

But no such falsehood awaits you in the following paragraphs. Before I sat down to pen this letter, I also swore to tell you the truth.

Of course, I write in the past that which you will read in the future. If you are not interested or prepared at this very moment for me to bare my soul, I encourage you to put down the letter. I will think no less of you for doing so!

When it happened, I was sitting in the parlour with Seliara: shortly after Arvist and Jeime departed on their ill-fated "mission". After writing and immediately posting a letter to you, I deigned to chat with Seliara about any number of general topics. Amid a practised debate about the particulars of Linguistic Alchemy, Seliara blurted out that she and Arvist were very keen to have a child sometime soon, which took me by surprise. Shaken and rather out of my depth, I changed the subject by complimenting the pie she baked (as I had not the strength, in the end, to make anything myself), which reminded her that she had brewed some tea to enjoy with it, so she headed off into the kitchen to fetch that. And that was when my home began to tremble.

All at once, the window shattered – it did not even have the decency to crack first, but simply burst into what felt like a thousand droplets of glass – and water spiralled over the carpet. I tried to scream for Seliara, but the ocean moved too quickly. Instead of filling the room, the renegade sea seemed to stay rigid in a ... column, or ... I know not what ... imagine the spray of a whale, perhaps, but greatly magnified? I suppose a Baleen Whale's mouth might be a better comparison, though, because when that twisting water rose, I could not help but be swallowed by it, like the unfortunate Krill. I fell towards what felt like the centre of the world.

Gasping for air, I swam and tumbled through this aqueous tunnel for what must have been no more than a few moments (otherwise how would I have survived without drowning?). When I landed, I did not hit the ground with a sickening crack, but rather slapped down onto a cold, liquid surface, which stung my face and limbs quite bitterly. With seawater blurring my eyes, I tried to make sense of my new surroundings.

I do not know if you ever engaged in casual study of the Physical Sciences (in addition to your aforementioned, impressive, and certainly alluring historical shipbuilding knowledge), but I certainly cannot explain how I ended up on the top of the water's surface after experiencing what felt like falling down for such a long time. All I can do, I suppose, is simply lay out the sensations as I experienced them. Treading water, I looked upwards as my eyes cleared and saw nothing but darkness above me, as though the stars and moon had been painted over with a heavy purple pigment.

Feeling a ripple about me, I used my newly available eyes to detect a dark shadow gliding in my general direction. This mysterious shape inspired my aching limbs to action. I swam forward at a Porpoise's pace, turning my head every which way to seek out some spit of land. At last, I came across what looked like a great island. I paddled towards it with the greatest enthusiasm, as you might imagine! I have never been a particularly accomplished swimmer, but in that moment I thanked my parents for raising us in the sea and demanding that I grasp the basics of long-distance survival strokes.

I should mention that the water felt different from the lovely sea to which I am accustomed. It seemed to ooze around me – warm and slippery, as though it had thickened like a custard. The sensory unpleasantness of the water, however, could not dim its visual splendour. Despite the imposing darkness, the water possessed a kind of luminescence: an odd purple and green and grey glimmer like the last moments of a sunset.

To my cautious relief, the sinister shape that swam behind me kept a careful distance as I made my way to shore. (Normally, I would say that it might have been the shadow of a cloud, or something else of that nature – except I assure you that this "sky" appeared devoid of any discernible forms.) When I first stepped foot on the "island", it felt more like a soft sea sponge than solid ground, but I cared not. I fell onto that beach, panting and exhausted. The water curled around my toes.

After lying on that spongy shore long enough to catch my breath, I collected myself, hitched up my skirts (which were immensely heavy with the water I had absorbed during my swim – I hope it will not embarrass you to know that I abandoned my petticoats quickly thereafter as a matter of self-preservation!), and took it upon myself to discover more about my surroundings.

Perhaps that last sentence will surprise you more than anything else in this narrative. My reaction certainly surprised *me*. How could I – someone so cursed by my Brain that I once believed stepping outside of the house for even a second would result in ineffable doom – feel surprisingly logical and capable when tossed by a column of water into an otherworldly ocean?

Well, I propose that when one spends one's life feeling as though a calamity has happened every other second, perhaps one can better manage a true calamity when it occurs.

Let me pause here to set the scene in more detail so you can fully imagine the depths of ridiculousness – I, a sunken hermit who barely leaves my home and recoils at a simple conversation with a stranger (making the odd exception for a particularly clever and kindly one, of course), stood resolutely on the strangest of shores in what remained of my house-dress (with its sleeves bunched up around my shoulders most unpleasantly after my swim), gazing confidently into the unknown as though I were Lady Ei herself! What *would* you have thought of me, Henerey?

It boosted my resolve to observe that some of the flora native to that "shore" also demonstrated a kind of bioluminescence. Recalling your discussion of this phenomenon in your wonderful book (how long ago it seems that I first read it!), I found the eerie glow quite comforting. A half-fathom from the water, I spied a great strand of kelp twice my height in width – yet on land! – that somehow snaked delicately into the air, giving off a soft blue light.

I nestled myself into a bed of algae beneath the "kelp-tree" and kept a careful eye on the water. Though the island seemed much larger than I assumed at first – I could not even see the end of it stretching into the distance behind me – I did not wish to take myself further into the thick kelp forest. My unexpected bravery could only go so far! How could I know what other predators might lurk within that territory? At the same time, I tried to convince myself that if I stayed out in the open, perhaps a passing boat might sail by and offer me rescue. What manner of phantom vessels haunt waters like those?

Instead of a boat, however, I spied more strange shadows shifting through the waves. I strained to catch sight of their forms beneath the sea's surface. Unfortunately, the luminescence of the island could not penetrate the darkness of the water. I feared that whatever followed me to the island might be amphibious and would soon scrabble up the shore to catch me at last – but my luck seemed to hold out for the duration of my stay.

At last, as suddenly it happened in the Deep House, I felt a horrible shaking of the ground that made my coral-covered island bounce beneath my body. The force must have caused me to hit my head, because I cannot recall how I managed to return to the reef outside the Deep House – what comes next in my memory is the experience of opening my eyes in the Infirmary.

As a result, I have been eager to learn what I can about the following: bioluminescent ecosystems, legendary and unusual methods of transportation that cannot be explained by Science, and ... really, any other previously observed aquatic anomalies.

O, yes, and I did promise you a suspicion about the Structure! I have nothing to go on here, really – except the fact that the unusual phosphorescence of that other world reminded me of the Structure when you and I observed it at night. The light emitting from the surface of the island itself, in fact, included the same shades of glimmering pink and pale green. More significantly, Arvist and Jeime were going out to look at (and perhaps touch?) the Structure when this happened. Perhaps, if it was an Artefact, they activated some ancient, waterlogged technology that soon exploded with age?

Though how that relates to my experience, I cannot say!

And finally – my proof. As I stood upon that impossible island, admiring the monumental kelp, I fished around in the deep side-pocket of my house-dress and discovered, to my great delight, that the short pencil and scrap of paper I carry with me always had survived the flood. (Mother would chide us for using anything other than waterproof paper, you know!) Perhaps artistic documentation should have been the last thing on my mind at the time, but I often find that keeping my hands busy can prevent me from losing control of my Brain in challenging situations.

Henerey, if you can believe this, I made two sketches while I was there, and I found them still tucked in my pocket when I awoke. I can think of no other explanation for their existence. Though I dare not sneak them out under Sophy's watchful eye, I often find myself secretly touching the now-creased papers for reassurance. As the only tangible artefacts of my journey, those sketches remain most precious to me. That said, I would not be opposed to copying them for you in the future, if I had the opportunity . . .

But by this point, I'm sure I must have frightened you – if you were not slightly frightened of me already. I shall stop recounting here, at present. If all of this disturbs you, I hope you will not think unkindly of me – I would be happy to put it behind us and never mention it again, or to claim it is a complex joke I have crafted for your amusement!

(How I wish that were the case.)

Yours in confusion (but most certainly yours, if you wish),

E.

P.S. Thank you for recommending *A Poetic Hospice*. (It occurs to me that, in other circumstances, you and I would probably greatly enjoy reading and conversing about the same books for pleasure – perhaps one day when your sail ends and this nightmare is behind me ... ?) Sophy brought it for me this morning – she was anxious about leaving me here by myself even just so she could go to the library! How silly. I am fine! At any rate, I consumed it in about an hour. I must confess that I hoped for some obvious clue – such as "Near the end of his life, Darbeni was frequently haunted by images of a strange Structure that appeared in his dreams – and eventually, in his underwater garden." No such luck. There was only one passage that seemed vaguely mysterious. I made a copy for you. What do you make of the reference to other "poetry manuscripts"? It is odd that multiple people appeared so fixated on this theme!

EXTRACT FROM *A POETIC HOSPICE: DARBENI'S LAST THREE YEARS*

While Darbeni valued interdisciplinary pursuits throughout his career, the onset of his twilight years inspired him to push Academic boundaries even more aggressively. He began to embark on Antepelagic flights of fancy, spending hours poring over obscure manuscripts in that strange "study" he built in an alcove in his dining room (so he would never be too far away from a hearty meal). His daughter Ulla writes to her betrothed:

"My father used to mock me for even daring to pick up a book not written by an acclaimed Scholar. Yet now he passes his time in the company of the strangest documents I have ever seen! All old, all handwritten, some seemingly even scribbled in scripts that I cannot recognise. And I, a speaker of twelve languages and writer of every Academic Shorthand! Every day, precisely at two bells, he leaves the house to 'research'. Well, you will wag your tongue at me, dearest, but one day I decided to follow him – and what do I find? Father at a public house, with a folio of these precious manuscripts, speaking in hushed whispers with a crew of strangers! (At the very least, I can appreciate that he possesses a far more robust social life than I.)"

Perhaps satisfied with this prosaic reveal, Scholar Ulla Darbeni did not follow her father again. No surviving documentation suggests the identity of this "crew of strangers" – though it has been proposed that they might have been an informal group of amateur poets. By that logic, the mysterious manuscripts Darbeni possessed may be, in this author's opinion, drafts of works by his peers, written in an agreed-upon private shorthand to avoid having their attempts at verse read (and mocked) by their family members.

When I first published my thesis on Darbeni, Scholar Evin Yelt rightly labelled my primary assertion (summarised in the previous sentence) as nothing more than idle speculation. In preparing for the publication of this book, however, I was fortunate enough to spend some time in Darbeni's own home at Scholar Ulla's generous invitation and was given the opportunity to sift through a "forbidden box" (her words, not mine) of the oddest bits of unfiled detritus from her father's study. (Scholar Ulla regretted that she was not able to offer this opportunity to Scholar Evin Yelt when he visited, as alas, she is most particular about who may review those parts of her father's belongings that have not yet already been donated to various Campus Archives.) In it I found what I now believe are the extant manuscripts described in this very letter.

"And how," I can imagine Scholar Yelt asking, "do you know that these manuscripts relate to this mysterious poetry group?"

Because each manuscript has the same title:

"A Luminous Circumference".

The poems, such as I translated them (see my forthcoming volume: *The "Circumference" Circle – Darbeni's Poetical Colleagues*), range in quality. Darbeni's is, frankly, the best of them. Each varies in length and metre and structure, but all address the same theme. Thus I propose that Darbeni was not, as Scholar Yelt might insist, reading historical manuscripts, but actively participating in critical reviews of works created as part of his group's poetry challenge. Though nothing else, at this point, can be discerned about the identities of those within this "poetry circle", we can say with confidence that their presence made Darbeni the most social he had been in years.

And, according to Scholar Ulla, Darbeni continued to think of his poetic colleagues until his very last breath. In a private interview, Scholar Ulla speaks of Darbeni's passing:

"We had no visitors while I waited for Father to leave me. He wished it to be just the two of us, like it had been since the beginning. Yet his 'poetry friends', whomever they may be, seemed to be close to his heart even if he did not wish to see them at his deathbed. He kept repeating fragments of verse, most of it incomprehensible. At one point – and I shall remember this until the end of my days – he seized my hands and whispered 'A predator awaits, Ulla! A predator awaits!' I thought he had spotted a shark through the porthole and opened the curtains to show him that there wasn't a dorsal fin in sight. Later I recognised the line from that odd poem of his. At least he enjoyed a final recitation of those words that meant so much to him. I do wish he would have picked a more sensible poem upon which to focus, like 'A Sonnet to Symmetry'."

(With all due respect to Darbeni, I must agree with his daughter.)

AUTOMATED POST MISSIVE FROM SOPHY CIDNORGHE TO VYERIN CLEL, 1003

Dear Vyerin,

The last time you sent me a letter from my sister that troubled me, I took days to respond. Today, I wanted to write to you instantly.

A new puzzle emerged to torment me – a corollary to the question I pondered last week. If E. had told me this story, would that have somehow changed what happened to her? Am I responsible for my sister's death?

Niea says that is an unproductive thought to pursue. She reminded me that it is fruitless to ponder how each tiny decision might ultimately bring about a greater tragedy or mystery. (By the waves, she and I certainly know enough about that.) Perhaps if Henerey's letter reveals anything at all, it is that he was the person best suited to hear this from E. I suspect it was because he wanted to believe her. He had enough of an open mind to welcome the possibility that what she saw was real.

(Also, the sketches certainly would have helped me believe her, even if I proved reluctant—but—no matter!)

I feel better now. I realise that frustration will get us nowhere. And after talking with my wife, I understand where some of this frustration and anxiety is coming from. There are things I have not told you about myself that might clarify my response to E.'s mysterious account, my friend. I can reveal them if you wish. But before I do, out of curiosity, let me ask another question. Long ago, you said that you were interested in the Ridge expedition, which was why you were curious about reading my letters.

How much do you know about why our mission ended?

AUTOMATED POST MISSIVE FROM VYERIN CLEL TO SOPHY CIDNORGHE, 1003

My dear friend,

I do not know if you intended to end your message without signing off, or whether you simply sent it prematurely. I should feel socially obligated to say, "I understand how difficult this is for you," but, in truth, I cannot fathom how difficult it is.

How can we not experience outbursts and anxieties under these circumstances? This is not a detached academic project that we are completing for the sake of professional glory or historical import. These are the lives of the people dearest to us, and honestly, Sophy – you are the most reasonable of anyone I've met. You certainly deserve to experience emotions from time to time. (Pesky things, aren't they?)

There is a dramatic tone to your final question, so I shall assume that something happened to end the mission other than what we (the Public) understood. I heard that there was a near-fatal accident that many speculated was due to equipment failure because the crew (you!) resigned immediately afterwards, spelling the end of the project. (Though I've heard – as I'm sure you may have heard as well – that some Boundless Scholars now promise to get researchers back in the Spheres within the next five years.)

V.

AUTOMATED POST MISSIVE FROM SOPHY CIDNORGHE TO VYERIN CLEL, 1003

Yes, you understand it about as well as anyone else in the world does. Instead of summarising the truth for you, though, I will let the rest of my letters do the talking.

Something happened to us down there, Vyerin – something that I still struggle to explain – something that I kept shut away in the back of my head just as E. preserved Henerey's letters in her safe-box. The combination of losing E. and the end of our mission removed my logic and curiosity for a time. I have never returned to those thoughts again, as much as Niea would like me to.

I shall seek out and send you more of the letters between myself and Niea. With her blessing, I am happy to finally tell someone else about this.

AUTOMATED POST MISSIVE FROM VYERIN CLEL TO SOPHY CIDNORGHE, 1003

Sophy,

Let me offer an alternative proposal.

I realise at this point that continuing to explore our siblings' letters over correspondence feels – well, somewhat contrived. Think of how much more efficiently we could work were we in the same place. If you consent, I would be very pleased if you would do me the honour of spending a few days in my family's home. We have much to discuss, if you are willing. (Niea is welcome too, of course!)

Fondly,

Vyerin

ANNOTATED CALLING CARD DELIVERED TO VYERIN CLEL, 1003

Sophy Cidnosin – Scholar of Wayfinding, School of Observation (Boundless Campus)

V.,

Apologies for the late reply, and forgive my boldness, but – Niea and I await you on your doorstep. Quite literally, as you can see from this calling card.

See you shortly, I hope? (Our arms are laden with documents! Do hurry, please!)

Sophy

Chapter 18

EXCERPT FROM THE DAYBOOK OF HENEREY CLEL, 1002

Dear future readers,

In retrospect, I am quite pleased with myself for mentioning personal matters in my previous journal entry. I keep many separate scientific diaries for my daily observations, but there is no other venue besides this one in which I may express my heart, if you will.

Today, my heart feels greatly overburdened.

The last time I wrote, I revealed a great epiphany and acknowledged, for the first time, my love for E. Cidnosin. The development of my feelings, of course, has only continued since then. She is the sort of person I never imagined I would be fortunate enough to meet and possesses an outlook on the world that I find simply magnificent and utterly singular.

More singular still is her most recent letter.

When I read it, I am ashamed to say that I feared at first that she suffered a worse trauma than her physicians observed (it would not be the first time that a Scholar of the Body was too occupied with their own research to worry about such trivialities as the health of a patient!). The more I reread her letter, however, the more its details fascinate me. I know E. is a meticulous, keen-eyed, astoundingly astute person, and if she says she experienced something of this nature, then I believe her testimony most thoroughly. (And that is to say nothing of the sketches she mentioned!) I will conclude that I need her account to be real: not only because I want so desperately to support her, but because it piques my curiosity in a way that nothing ever has before.

Our present mission seems dull in comparison, thanks to the taxing repair work that remains our focus for the time being. The labour seems endless. On the bright side, I now hold a great deal of respect for those blessed with natural strength – I might be good at lifting, but my stamina runs thin after a few hours of effort. Truly, I never thought I would build something in my life – in my wildest dreams, I always assumed that my eventual "home" would be a single-room Scholar's Chamber at a homey Boundless Anchorage, perhaps pre-furnished and prepared to suit the needs of a solitary bachelor (or – "perhaps"-ing even more – myself and a partner, though I had never allowed myself to grow too attached to that dream before now. Goodness, dare I?)

Lerin has a family, as I learned today – a wife and four children! Truly remarkable. No single-room Scholar's chamber for them, then, but a rather marvellous two-storey flat in one of the Intertidal Campus's liveliest outer rings of human-built islands. It is because of this family (I also discovered) that Lerin remains aboard the *Sagacity* instead of moving on to greater projects – namely, projects at greater depths in the ocean. It appears that my friend was invited to serve on the first Ridge expedition (for the position which eventually went to Scholar Eliniea Hayve Forghe) but declined due to the riskiness of the operation. (O! But Lerin did have an opportunity to experience some-thing Ridge-related today – producing an illustration of a potentially new Nautilus species, at Scholar Forghe's request! I cannot wait to see the final image.)

I did not confess it during this conversation with Lerin (nor have I told another soul), but my thoughts – when they are not focused on E. – have been moving more and more towards the Spheres. The work that we are doing on the *Sagacity* (construction aside) is well and good, of course. I have learned more about rays in these past few tides than I ever could have in my laboratory, and I must admit that they continue to behave in the most unprecedented ways (as you'll see in my scientific daybooks, dear Scholars of the Future!). But then I remember the esteemed Scholar Forghe and her ability to explore an utterly new eco-system and I become riddled with (good-natured!) jealousy.

—a few hours later—

I cannot stop thinking about E.'s letter. It was remarkable that she said she was surrounded by darkness but could not see the stars during what was apparently the daytime. When I envision her story in my head, I picture something quite similar to those photo-engraved images of the Ridge produced during the first expedition – endless darkness speckled only with the vivid luminescence of the unknown. Where did E. go? How did she get there? Was it a journey of the body (likely not!) or of the mind (but how)? I need to find a map that will give me a sense of what the landscape looks like within a two-hundred-fathom radius of the Deep House. I need to find a map that will lead me to the answers of a puzzle that I cannot comprehend! And I need to understand that Structure! "That Circle Coruscates!"

—sadly, a few hours even later—

Words and images drift through my mind. If I shut my eyes and ignore the night-singings of my jubilant colleagues out on deck, I can create the most vivid brain-picture of truly anything I desire. I must think carefully about each sensory detail – each scent, each sound, the textures of every surface – but I can convince myself, in my head, that it has the appearance of reality. Was E.'s experience only the most glorious dream? Then how can she remember it all with such clarity? O by the seas, Darbeni would delight in this! That reminds me – she asked me a question about Darbeni, didn't she? If only our ship could take a brief detour to the Archives.

ANNOTATION BY VYERIN CLEL, 1003

This entry features all the trappings of a classic Henerey response to a mystery. He receives inexplicable news, immediately segues into another unrelated topic, and then concludes by attempting to write down his thoughts as fast as they fly through his brain. My brother's mind worked like a waterwheel – when something catches the wheel, it will persist in rolling, even if its progress is ultimately impeded by the obstacle.

I miss him ever so much.

THE RIDGE REVEALED, ISSUE 4, RECORDED BY SCHR VINCENEBRAS

Dearest, kindliest Friends and Subscribers,

How gentle you are – how generous, how soft-hearted, how empathetic – to treat me, your Humble Correspondent, with such patience! You may have heard from less eloquent sources about the personal Calamity that recently occurred for one dear member of our Crew. Scholar Cidnosin returned home on a journey of sisterly mercy – and both patient and Sophy are doing well, rest assured! And while we have simply been – Adrift – without her presence, a new Anchor has arrived to provide us with a sense of Scholarly stability. Let me be the first to tell you that Scholar Tevn Winiver Mawr of Intertidal Campus, the secret founding member of the Ridge expedition along with Scholar Forghe – yes, a fact so *thoughtfully* Hidden from the Public Eye by the Chancellors for Reasons As Yet Unknown to Us – I jest, Chancellor Rawsel! – where was I? O, Tevn temporarily joined us to carry on Scholar Cidnosin's work in her absence.

Yes, dear reader, you read that correctly! When Scholar Eliniea Hayve Forghe made her first voyage to the Ridge, she was not alone, but in the company of Scholar Mawr. It is news to us all! Because Scholar

Mawr had to leave the mission early due to a Personal Crisis, he yearned to recover in utter privacy and dear Scholar Forghe was sworn to secrecy. Please pause for a moment to admire the emotional tenacity of our dear Expedition Specialist! How her secret burden – and her devotion to her friend's wishes – must have weighed upon her!

Before you dash off to write up this breaking news in tomorrow's issue of the journal of your choice (which I give you full permission to do, of course – unless your name happens to be SCHOLAR HARDIN EILE OF *THE BOUNDLESS CAMPUS CURRENT*, whom I shall never forgive! And you know why, Scholar Hardin Eile!), I have one more gift to share. An interview with inscrutable Tevn himself. What wonders will we learn of his mysterious past? What caused him to leave the first Ridge expedition – and why is he here *now*?

INTERVIEW WITH SCHOLAR TEVN WINIVER MAWR

Scholar Vincenebras: Dear Tevn, let me be the first to welcome you to the official Interview Chamber, a conduit through which riveting news will eventually travel to the surface in the form of my words!

Scholar Mawr: Apologies, Scholar Vincenebras. "Interview Chamber"? Are we not simply in the Galley? Perhaps I am confused.

Vincenebras: O, you rascal! It is a delight to interview you at last.

Mawr: Are you already recording what I say?

Vincenebras: It is so hard to speak privately with you, dear Tevn, because you are simply inseparable from our beloved Scholar Forghe! Would you tell our readers more about your history? Surely you must enjoy a close relationship after that first mission.

Mawr: Well, yes, Ni—Eliniea—and I were technically the first to survey at this depth. About a year ago.

Vincenebras: And the Chancellors must have known that no pair without a bond as strong as yours could endure such a risky venture, no?

Mawr: No one except young Scholars – equipped with that wonderful beginning-of-career innocence and optimism – would have agreed to this mission. Eliniea and I were not the Chancellors' first choices, nor even their tenth. But when Eliniea's Advisor nominated her, everything changed. Eliniea asked me to join her, and I accepted. It is as simple as that.

Vincenebras: Now, dear Tevn, we would have no story if there were anything "simple" about your life! After you and Eliniea returned from your voyage, she became the rising star of all the Campuses, while you vanished from the public eye. I don't suppose you two had a lovers' spat, did you?

Mawr: Eliniea and I share mutually platonic feelings. If you knew anything about her – or about me, though that seems less likely – you would know that such a thing is highly improbable. I apologise, Scholar Vincenebras, but I tire of this line of questioning. I was under the impression you had asked me here to discuss my present continuation of Scholar Cidnosin's research, not the past.

Vincenebras: O, very well, if you insist! I don't suppose you might be able to – liven that up, could you?

Mawr: I am afraid not. Scholar Cidnosin had been engaged in a survey of the Ridge with the goal of gathering enough data to create a topographical map. Now, my research interests lie more in how these seafloor features were made than what they presently resemble, but I know how to operate a Wayfinding Device. I can supply Scholar Cidnosin with all the information she needs to interpret when she returns.

Vincenebras: Will you survey the Point of Interest in particular?

Mawr: Well, I suppose so. How funny to hear you say that phrase! Did you know that I named it?

Vincenebras: Really, did you? Did not Scholar Forghe discover it?

Mawr: O, of course she discovered it, but I was the one to offer up the name. It was a joke between us. I never would have thought that she would continue using it.

Vincenebras: Finally – something vaguely entertaining!

INTERVIEW CONCLUDES

Well, dear friends, I am sure you will find Scholar Mawr's laconic charm more appealing in due time. To me, his entire Scholarly career seems like one enormous Point of Interest!

With fondness to all (except SCHOLAR HARDIN EILE),

Vincenebras

LETTER FROM SOPHY CIDNOSIN TO ELINIEA HAYVE FORGHE, 1003

Dear Niea,

You never need to offer any explanation (or self-reproach) for taking time to write back to me! Surely the day-to-day responsibilities of single-handedly running the most significant expedition in modern history keep you at least moderately busy. (Have I ever mentioned, by the way, that I find you to be the most remarkable Scholar I have ever encountered – in real life or a library?)

I do hope everyone else is well, of course. Ylaret's letter was delightful – her writing truly sounds just like her voice – but surprised me by revealing that you will embark upon another field journey very soon! (Perhaps my letter might even arrive after you've already left – what an unfortunate thought.) Where will your undersea peregrinations take you this time? I wonder. Back to the Point of Interest? To another Point with some other virtue to its name? I shudder a bit to think that all of you might soon encounter enigmatic wonders that

I may never see. (If you run into the Nautilus again, please give it my best regards.)

Ylaret also mentioned that Tevn has settled in among the crew and works well with you! Glad to hear it. I imagine it is a relief, at least, to have such a trusted friend like Tevn upon whom to rely in these circumstances. (I do hope he is – well, "on the mend" these days? I hardly know what to say about these new developments. Far be it from me to agree with Vincenebras, but he is right on one count – your ability to run this mission while protecting your friend's privacy is astonishing.)

E. and I still spend nearly every hour together – if we are not chattering or reminiscing about one thing or another, we play games, bake, or simply stare out the window and watch the sea. (Now, every so often, she does flee behind closed doors to scribble away to Henerey, emerging hours later with a letter for me to post – which I do with great delight.) Minus Arvist, it almost feels as though we are children again, back in the days when the Deep House was our world.

What I need to keep reminding myself is that the Deep House is still E.'s world. And E., dear E., wants to go back. As soon as possible, really. I do not feel especially favourably about this course of action, but she continues to plead her case. It does not help that Jeime Alestarre – who offered generously to assess and repair our home while I took care of E. – returned to campus yesterday and told me that while the parlour will require extensive (and expensive) work, it was easy enough for her to shut it off from the rest of the house and fix what remained so we can return soon (assuming we don't mind looking out the window and seeing the bones of our front room floating about in the waves).

As you might expect, then, we are all well but a little out of sorts. Though I take such delight in this unexpected time with my sister, I sometimes dream of the Spheres, and wake up disappointed by the brash sunlight slipping in through my chamber's porthole. I yearn to research, to document, to explore. I have never spent this long away from Scholarly work since I was a child, you know! Surely I have surveyed every corner of our quarters a thousand times!

Unsurprisingly, you often make appearances in these Spheres dreams: in both professional and personal contexts.

But I hear E. awakening, so I must dream no more – as I have quite a pleasant reality to distract me in the meantime.

Much affection to you, and well wishes to all our friends – and to Tevn!

Yours,
Sophy

CRUMPLED DRAFT OF A LETTER WRITTEN BY HENEREY CLEL, 1002

My dear E.,

I have thought of nothing else but you and your letter over the past day or so, and I do not intend to start thinking of anything else anytime soon

CRUMPLED DRAFT OF A LETTER WRITTEN BY HENEREY CLEL, 1002

My dear E.,

You might be aware of a particular species of shrimp that moves so quickly (relative to its own body size) that it sometimes does not even realise that it is in motion until it has already caught a current to

LETTER FROM HENEREY CLEL TO E. CIDNOSIN, 1002

My dearest* E.,

*I added on the superlative form in the hopes that it will demonstrate

how my feelings towards you have not at all changed negatively follow-ing your "confession" – as I suspected you might fret about that!

Firstly, and above all else: thank you for trusting me. It means a great deal that you hold such faith in my discretion and understanding, and I shall live up to your expectations!

(While I do not intend to dwell on this outside of a parenthetical, I must admit that my initial thought upon reading the first part of your letter was that I almost feel I am to blame for your woes – if only you had decided to stay in your room that fateful day rather than writing a letter to me in the parlour – but I suppose there is naught to be done about that now.)

My general impression is that you are less troubled by the expe-rience itself (though it certainly sounds harrowing) than by the thought that you have lost your wits or that those whom you care about will not believe what happened. I, however, am not as emotionally con-nected to the occurrence as you**, obviously, so if it does not seem too arrogant, may I attempt to approach it from a scientific perspective and lay out the facts, plain though they may be? A few items of interest to me follow:

Item 1 being that you found yourself in an unfamiliar sea, which means you must have travelled, because otherwise you would have recognised the friendly sight of the ocean around the Deep House (and would not have been surprised by the time of day). There is a possibility, I suppose, that if an extremely fast-moving jet of water burst through the library, it might have projected you somewhere very far away. But then how did you return? No, clearly you did not travel physically in the tra-ditional sense. And if that is the case, you must have either invented this entirely new environment in your brain – in which case, well done! – or you were transported there in a way that we cannot yet fathom. (I find this latter option most intriguing.)

Item 2 being the shadow swimming after you – did you get any sense of its shape? That might help us narrow down what manner of creature it was. I can already think of a few off the top of my head that are sufficiently larger than a human being, and most of them are whales or rays (and thankfully would not have posed much of a threat to you!). Part of me secretly hopes and suspects that it was thin and ribbon-like, as you seem to attract Fathom Eels, but I imagine you would have observed that characteristic!

Item 3 being the one that fascinates me the most – what more can you tell me about the coral-like surface upon which you found yourself beached? This is but a silly, childish fancy, but when I was a boy and first learning about reef colonies, I always wondered if it could be possible for a coral platform to grow to such a height that it simply becomes an island in all but name. Like a complete reversal of how atolls diminish into coral reefs in time!

Item 4 being the Structure itself. Well, as we read in that book I brought (how fondly I think back to that evening, always), people have, from time to time, discovered Antepelagic devices in various parts of the ocean that behaved in unusual ways. Most of them no longer function properly once immersed in water. I suppose it is possible that an old enough machine might short-circuit in a dramatic fashion if damaged.

And how could I forget? Your sketches! Surely you should hold tight to the originals, and I am glad to hear that they bring you comfort. In the event that you feel well enough to trace me some copies, I would love nothing more than to see them.

(Of course, I would much prefer to see *you*, were such things possible.)

As you can tell, I remain incredibly curious about the whole affair – but I do not want to seem callous by discussing your experience in this way, nor do I wish you to think that I am not altogether scarred by the thought of you lost and alone in some unknown place.

It terrifies me.

But perhaps if we think through it together, we can take comfort in each other? If I were a Medic, I would prescribe to you nothing more than careful meditation on your own thoughts with support from those who care about you (including, as I'm sure you may have gathered, this correspondent).

Yours,

Henerey

P.S. Many thanks for your wondrous field journal entry. Imperturbable Toothed Whales can be quite charming, can't they? They were the first cetaceans I ever observed in their natural habitat, and always occupy a fond place in my heart. It is also delightful to think that this is one of the few times you have been "on the surface"! I hope the world above is treating you well.

P.P.S. You know, dear E., I must confess something altogether embarrassing and out of character. That book on Darbeni that I recommended to you – I have not read it entirely. I needed to cite one of the author's translations of a particular primary source for my thesis, but as always, time was short, so I used the index, flipped to the relevant page, obtained my citation, and continued my research. It was shoddy work, really – the kind of thing that suggests I am not reading for my own enrichment but rather so I might choose the right facts to help me make a point to please the Chancellors.

Consequently, I was completely surprised by the passage you produced. I too wonder about that "poetry circle", and what else its participants said about this "Circumference" (and the "predator"!). Sadly, only the Archives know right now! I don't suppose you would be able to go to the Reading Room by yourself, but perhaps you might enlist Sophy? (You needn't reveal your true mission, of course – surely she would understand your desire to surround yourself with "comfort research" about Darbeni.) If she slips through the underwater tunnels to the Library Anchorage between the hours of nine and nine and a half bells in the morning (when the Refectory serves hot beverages) or just before sunrise (when most Scholars are retreating to their beds), there will likely be few people there. My friend Elaxand could help her if necessary.

**In the sense that I was not there, not that I do not care emotionally about what you have experienced! O dear. I suppose I will write more

260

about this in the body of my letter so you do not think me insensitive. (Though I don't know whether you are the sort of person who skips to footnotes immediately after seeing an asterisk or number or if you wait until completing the entire letter before proceeding to such auxiliary material ... perhaps you have already read the body of my letter in its entirety, and still find my sensitivity lacking!)

Chapter 19

LETTER FROM ELINIEA HAYVE FORGHE TO SOPHY CIDNOSIN, 1002

Dear Sophy,

I write to you today from a familiar locale and point in time – a Bubble, on the first night of an expedition! Remember when I sent E. your letter via automaton? Though I would much rather send mail on your behalf than write to you (since the former necessitates you being here with me in person), I enjoy the nostalgia.

I must ask you to forgive me, as I am a little out of sorts today. You know all too well how often an episode of Nerves overtakes me during significant moments of research, and I do not know what turn this expedition will take. My thoughts are so scattered that I can hardly remember what I have and haven't told you already – please pardon any redundancies!

We return to the Point of Interest tomorrow, where I do indeed hope to encounter our Nautilus once again. As the self-appointed Overlord of Scholars of Classification (and All Other Scholars, for that matter), Chancellor Rawsel reminded me that I must obtain photographic, trace, or specimen-grade evidence of the creature for it to be entered into the Universal Compendium of Species, so my task is an imposing one.

Irye and Ylaret packed some more sensitive sound equipment that Irye hopes will help them capture that "music" more clearly. Vincenebras will assist me, since I could use some charming frivolity as a distraction. And Tevn intends to scale the length and breadth of that vast trench, gathering as much information about its contours as he possibly can.

O, Tevn. I apologise, dear Sophy, for seeming so enigmatic about him. As you have gathered from what I told you already, this is a painful and complicated subject for me, and my past actions embarrass me – and I did not wish to share them with you, the one person upon whom I wish most fervently to make a good impression! Because I trust you, and because I want you to know me, even my flaws, I will tell you the tale now. It is "evening", I sit here alone in my Bubble, and I have nothing else to do but express myself to you.

Tevn's "interview" with Vincenebras provides the basic background on our history, but allow me to add some nuance. Tevn and I met while studying for our Presentations as Apprentice Scholars, though people often mistook Tevn for younger (he has managed to catch up to me in height a little more in the years hence – but only a little!). Of course, we were in entirely different Departments, and never saw each other in classes, but our friendship had been prefabricated for us – our parents, though from different regions, knew each other from their Apprentice days. My mother urged me before I departed for the Campus to "seek out Tevn Winiver Mawr". Apparently, his parents told him something similar about me.

Though both of us resented our families' "suggestions" of whom we might befriend, we were delighted to discover that we got along excellently. Tevn liked me, I believe, because he had lots of questions about the world – questions that most Scholars might find too, well, imaginative to dignify with a response – and I was always open to an intellectual challenge. All things unexplained, anomalous, and mysterious fascinated him. I liked him, in turn, because as an academ-ically advanced child, I always found it difficult to make friends who did not resent me – and he never did. In fact, the faster I learned and the better I became at research, the more I could lend context to his inquiries.

I never expected my Advisor to turn down his invitation to join the first Ridge expedition and recommend me and the support Scholar of my choice in his place. Tev could not imagine why someone would say no to such a groundbreaking opportunity. For my part, I could understand it – most Scholars have families or friends or careers on the surface that are too precious to them to risk such an undertaking – but the thought of it still excited me. The potential made the dangers worthwhile.

A year ago, then, Tevn and I squeezed together into the cramped and rustic first iteration of the Depth Capsule and descended into the unknown. There was no station yet, so we spent our time in this tiny depth-craft that was barely the size of a Bubble. For some, living in such close quarters for such an extended period might be excruciating.

Fortunately, Tevn and I were about as comfortable together as brother and sister. We reached the area that we nicknamed "The Point of Interest" (yes, his idea, but I deserve credit for indulging him!) about two tide-cycles – perhaps more, around sixteen days? – into our expedition. By that point, we had played all the mental puzzle games known to humanity (and invented a few of our own, to boot), come up with a full lexicon of phrases to describe different qualities of abyssal darkness, and encountered a charming number of luminescent fish species that taunted me by staying just far enough from the capsule that I could not make out their shapes.

It was at this point that we were instructed to stop, don pressure suits, and commence our first dive. That is when I made my first mistake. I thought we might appreciate a few moments of solitude, and I desperately wanted to pursue some Anglerfish by myself so as not to alarm them (Tevn has always been a notoriously loud swimmer). So, we went our separate ways, planning to meet back at the capsule in two hours (recorded by the timepieces within our suits).

My only consolation, looking back, is that those Anglerfish were truly incredible. I was the first to witness their Conjugal Fusion about which my Advisor had hypothesised for years – really, it was quite horrific! I felt surprisingly comfortable as I swam through the unknown darkness, where, in all likelihood, some massive undiscovered apex predator may have been waiting for the day when Humanity decided to encroach upon its territories. My desire to see something new – something sublime – inoculated me against any terror. Those two hours I spent splashing about in the abyss remain precious to me.

Given my spellbound state, I never expected to be the first to return. We had docked the Capsule on the seafloor and turned off the lights to avoid interrupting the lives of any local species. Take heart – we were tethered, so there was no chance of us slipping away into the darkness forever! When nearly three hours passed and Tevn had not yet appeared, I tugged firmly upon his tether. An hour still later, he appeared at last.

I had never seen my friend so alarmed. In the grim, green illumination of his helmet lights, I noticed that his face was utterly expressionless – such a contrast from his perpetual grin and flushed cheeks.

I asked him what had happened, and he would not – could not? – speak. I feared the worst (or what, at the time, I thought was the worst): that somehow his suit had been damaged, and the slow increase of pressure (or draining of oxygen?) rendered him dramatically ill. Exactly what my Advisor and all those other proposed Candidates for this mission feared might happen to them when imagining worst-case scenarios.

We had a protocol for emergencies, of course, and I followed it to the letter. I tugged Tevn into the capsule, powered it on, began the depressurisation sequence, and set my course for the surface immediately. The research vessel *Alacrity* towed us aboard into the safety of a depressurisation chamber. When we reached Boundless, a team of Medics bore each of us away to separate areas of the Infirmary Anchorage for examination.

And Sophy, would you believe it? I never saw Tevn again.

(Well, until now, that is.)

My stay at the Infirmary was unnecessary. I suffered no ill effects from this experience other than confusion and concern. They let me return to my usual campus quarters on the second day, when Chancellor Rawsel and I met. He regretted to inform me that Scholar Mawr had experienced trauma so great that he would require substantial rehabilitation. Rawsel claimed the medics diagnosed Tev with a "highly Anxious personality" that was "unsuited" to such a journey. Consequently, only I could continue the Ridge mission.

The Chancellor warned me, however, that if word got out about Tevn's experience, people might "mistakenly" assume it was too dangerous to undertake this expedition – when really, Tevn was simply the wrong man for the job because of his Emotional Sensitivities (so Rawsel said). Before Chancellor Rawsel departed, he gave me a small letter – the one I carry with me always – in which Tevn said that he needed time to himself and begged me to say nothing about his involvement in the mission. Tevn feared nothing more – or so he claimed – than the entire Academic world knowing that he was a failure.

Though I wrote to him many, many times, I never received another letter. (I did manage to contact his parents, who told me quite cheerfully that as far as they knew, Tevn was thoroughly enjoying his sabbatical.)

Well, what was I to do? By his own account, Tevn himself had assured me that it was his problem, not a safety issue. Chancellor Rawsel made it quite clear that my refusal of these terms might result in the termination of the project. So, I committed to leading a second Ridge expedition as thoughtfully and carefully as possible. That is why I grew so fearful when I saw Ylaret struggling with something she could not explain, and why I wished above all to avoid putting you in danger during those early days. For what played at the back of my mind was that pernicious thought – if Tevn had not been my friend and had not offered to accompany me on a voyage for which he was not suited, he would not have suffered in this way.

I use the past tense because if you were to see Tevn now (as you have), you would never guess what he experienced. He seems keen and clever as always. Either he has enjoyed the most successful post-traumatic rehabilitation programme imaginable, or it is a front to help him take on the (very brave) task of returning to this mission. That is part of why I tell you this now – because it all seems silly, doesn't it, in retrospect? I thought my friend had experienced something sinister, but he is apparently well, so I needn't worry any more. Is that not so?

I still wonder why he has returned now, of course. I tried on two occasions to speak to him alone, but both times he turned me away. It is difficult to imagine us returning to that Point without it unsettling him in some way.

Goodness, I must have been writing for half the night! I hope this will not take you half a night to read. Now, before I conclude – has E. decided to return to the Deep House? (Or rather: have you decided to let her?) I sympathise with her desire to get home as quickly as possible – and I certainly never found the Boundless Campus dormitories especially hospitable (the ones at Intertidal are so cosy) – but I do hope it will be safe for her. As your Expedition Specialist, I must inform you that the entire crew looks forward to your eventual return.

As someone who grows fonder of you with each passing day, however, I must also inform you that I cannot wait to see you again.

Yours in the depths,

Niea

LETTER FROM SOPHY CIDNOSIN TO ELINIEA HAYVE FORGHE, 1003

Dearest Niea,

I am tempted to open this letter with a gentle admonition along the lines of "I cannot believe you tormented yourself for so long with this 'secret' that has in no way changed my opinion of you whatsoever, whether as a Scholar, a leader, or a – Person of Interest, so to speak" – but o, I myself am prone to cling onto guilt for things entirely out of my control!

So let me be as clear as I can for the moment (knowing that I will likely reiterate these points once I can see your face again): you are not to blame for whatever Tevn experienced. If anyone is the guilty party, it is obviously Chancellor Rawsel, who put you in such a difficult position. I appreciate that you are the most qualified to lead this expedition, but surely it would have been more humane for him to grant you a reprieve while you waited to hear what had become of your friend.

I consider you exceptionally courageous, empathetic, and thoughtful. Now I understand why you were so affected by Ylaret's situation. O, my dear, I have nothing but the utmost respect for you.

(Well, that is not quite true – I also hold the utmost fondness for you.)

I hope Tevn will speak more openly with you. Perhaps he simply does not know how to initiate the conversation. I can sympathise with that, at least, for I have found recently that it is very difficult to talk to my own sister!

I suppose I should have said from the very beginning that we shall indeed return to the Deep House soon. E. insisted, so I agreed – as long as I may come with her for a tide-cycle or two to make sure she is safely settled. As I mentioned previously, Jeime recommended some colleagues who could work on repairing the parlour in the future, but she does say the house is quite liveable otherwise. Outside of that, the only other injury to the House is the destruction caused when Arvist and Seliara took over my bedroom – I imagine I will hardly be able to find my old things among the enormous clay sculptures or whatnot in the closet . . .

The cosy closeness that E. and I enjoyed during her initial convalescence dispersed recently. I can't quite put my finger on it, but she has been odd. Perhaps it's just because I'm so used to writing letters to her and enjoying that kind of endlessly intimate communication. Yesterday morning – about half past nine bells – I was returning from the Refectory with teas in hand when I swear I saw, from my position in the hallway, the door to our dormitory slam shut. Panicked that we might have an intruder – or an unwanted visitor named Arvist Cidnosin – or someone who had gone to the wrong room by accident – I ran ahead, spilling an appalling amount of tea on the carpet. I swung open the door with great fury, only to find nothing more than E. sitting peacefully in the window seat by the porthole, reading a book and smiling at me. I asked if she had opened the door, and she said that she thought she heard me returning and wanted to help with the tea. Perhaps she did. But it was exceptionally peculiar.

Now, I fear that being here troubles E., but dear Niea, she simply won't speak to me about it! She spends much of her time alone in her room. I walk by, sometimes, pausing in the hallway, and hear nothing but the scratching of her pen. She still sends enormous letters to Scholar Clel. I am so happy that they have grown close, and yet there is a part of me that envies that accursedly charming Natural Historian. There has never been a time when E. favoured someone else's company over mine.

That is not to say, of course, that she has been intentionally cruel, or dismissive, or exclusionary of me. We eat most meals together (Seliara occasionally visits, too, though she has returned to her parents' vessel in my brother's absence) and I can often tempt E. into chatter about our childhood antics. But something has changed. I fear that it may soon be time for me to return to the Spheres.

O, how silly of me – of course I do not "fear" that! I would love nothing more than to return to work and you! (In reverse order of desire, naturally.) I simply wish that I could feel more reassured about E.'s condition before then.

I do expect I shall see you sooner rather than later! I will let you know when I make my decision.

Yours fondly,
Sophy

EXCERPT FROM THE AMATEUR FIELD JOURNAL OF E. CIDNOSIN, 1002

VIEWING LOCATION: bedroom porthole
HABITAT: still the surface
OBSERVATIONS: Today the sky has taken on the same sparkling grey tone as the wallpaper that decorates Sophy's former bedroom back at home. Whitecaps dot the water like drowned clouds. The Toothed Whales departed for the day – I wonder where they go when the storms come? After almost an hour without a single sighting, I noticed the gently triangular tip of a ray's wing breaking through the water as the prow of a ship does. I hoped perhaps it might leap from the waves and soar for a moment on the wind, but it decided to be sluggish and not waste any time on needless exhilaration. I feel much the same.

LETTER FROM E. CIDNOSIN TO HENEREY CLEL, 1002

My dearest Henerey,

Let me begin by addressing some of this parcel's contents. As you have likely already seen, I prefaced this letter with my newest "field journal" entry, written just for you, though I do not suppose it will prove quite as interesting as my first foray into the genre!

As I read your letter, your pragmatic approach to my experiences brought me great solace. It comforts me to think that even though I visited "that place" alone, we might reassess the memories together.

Since you have not dismissed my account (for which I am very grateful), I have indeed copied my sketches for you.

But they are not the only notable things enclosed. Not by far!

I went to your library, Henerey! I panicked the entire time – and panic still now – but I did it!

You are probably surprised. I am surprised! Now, this is the point at which Dr Lyelle would kindly say, "It is not that you cannot do things, E.; rather, it's that doing certain things can be much more challenging for you, but if you plan accordingly and prepare yourself for the feelings an experience might cause, you may decide to attempt it anyway." I tried to keep these words in mind as I snuck out of our quarters at quarter to nine bells to visit the Reading Room!

Of course, my Brain decided to torment me all the while. As I crept down the halls, marvelling at how many dormitories there were, it whispered: "You neglected to tell Sophy where you were going. What if another seaquake occurs, but here on campus this time, and you are not there to warn her, and she perishes because you decided to go out jaunting to the library?"

In response, I focused on sensations – the swishing of the thick carpet beneath my feet, the feel of my shoes and stockings wrapping around my ankles, and the salty smell of someone's breakfast wafting from one of the closed doors.

As I descended the staircase and consulted a map of the Campus Tunnels, my Brain cut in once more: "You are not supposed to be here. You are not a Scholar. If they find you here without authorisation, you will be reproached beyond your wildest imaginings and perhaps even Sophy's career will be ruined, thanks to you. Also, someone may kill you, I suspect."

I counted the number of branching tunnelways on the map (seventy-nine) before continuing further.

"Or perhaps someone will accuse you of killing someone else!" continued the chatter in my mind. "You will walk right into the wrong place at the wrong time. And everyone knows you are Mad, and probably thinks you likely to snap at any second, so you will have no defence."

It went on like this for some time. (I jest a little to help make this less of a horrifying affair, but really, Henerey, you wouldn't believe what my Condition leads me to think sometimes. And not just think – believe! In fact, now I am thinking "Perhaps I should not be so open with Henerey about the tricks my Brain plays with me, because then he will think I am unstable and untrustworthy, just like everybody else in this world does" – but I shall try to ignore that!)

Though I had to constantly refocus myself by composing witty retorts aimed at my own mind, I eventually made it all the way to the Library Anchorage. I never would have guessed that those tunnels were underwater, though, because there were no windows! What kind of Architect designed these spaces? I thought about my mother as a young Apprentice at Boundless, wandering these bleak undersea halls without a single porthole, and smiled to imagine her cursing the austerity of the design.

She must have appreciated the library, though.

Once I exited the tunnels and crept onto the lower deck of the Anchorage, the colour and light startled me. An endless line of columns faded in a gradated way from blue to bluer. They drew my eye to that great pointed Library Arch – with the dizzying array of pearl mosaics at which I would have stared for hours were I not already on a mission.

Because you so helpfully informed me about the best time to visit, I was almost alone on the library's first floor. A few lingering Scholars in groups – like pods of Toothed Whales, I thought, trying to calm myself – gathered things from their carrels, but they swiftly made their way to the exit. After spending some time counting the shelves – it is remarkable how high the ceilings are here! Are there truly one hundred shelves per wall? The ladders are extraordinary! – I breathed in, pulled all of the muscles of my body until I could tighten them no more, released them, and walked over to Scholar Elaxand Iyl.

He was the only person at the desk, but still I felt glad to see his helpful nameplate – and gladder still that he spoke first.

"You must be the only other Scholar in all the seas who does not care for hot beverages," he said by way of introduction. "I do find them exceptionally overrated. It is not natural for water that one drinks to be hot, nor flavoured. Don't you agree?"

I regret that I found this friendly introduction deeply intimidating.

"Please, it's Darbeni I'm wanting," I ended up saying, then shook my head, breathed in once more, and tried again, hoping that I had spoken so quietly the first time that he heard nothing. "Good morning, Scholar Iyl," I attempted. "I am here on behalf of Henerey Clel and hope to access the Darbeni archive, if I may. What must I do to enter the Reading Room?"

Scholar Iyl scrutinised me kindly – that is the best way to describe it – until suddenly he hoisted himself out of his chair and opened the gate to his desk, bowing politely before me. I clumsily returned the gesture.

"You're the correspondent, aren't you?" he asked, leading me back through an ornate wrought-iron door. "The one who lives in the Deep House and writes Henerey ever so many letters. He's mentioned you before. Excessively, in fact." (My goodness! Have you really, Henerey?)

"And he deemed you a most excellent friend," I replied. "It is a pleasure to meet you. My name is E. Cidnosin."

"O, I know that, too," Scholar Iyl laughed. "Despite your stated connection to Scholar Clel, I am under strict orders to deny Reading Room access to unauthorised guests – unless Scholars of Repute vouch for them as Campus Visitors. Scholar Philosophy Cidnosin has had you on her visitation list for years." (This took me by surprise! Surely Sophy never thought I would visit here before. Wishful thinking?)

"I also know that you have recently taken ill, and should really be abed, don't you think?" he continued. "I overheard some Scholars discussing your mysterious accident. Worry not – I wasn't reading about it in the morning papers. Too much of a distraction. I prefer to ponder philosophical concepts while drinking my room-temperature, water-flavoured water."

"I can never resist the call of archival research, no matter my personal or physical circumstances," I said with what I hoped was great conviction.

"I believe that well enough." Here Scholar Iyl let me into the Reading Room at last – and o, Henerey, as exciting as it was to think about

273

all the history that surrounded me, I have to admit I was at least as excited by the thought of entering yet another space that you visited in the past!

I settled down on the cushion nearest to the door while Scholar Iyl rummaged about in one of the many numbered vaults. Soon afterwards, he presented me with a beautiful abalone box.

"You are fortunate, E.," he said – not even stumbling over my lack of a Scholarly honorific. "There has been renewed interest in Darbeni of late. In fact, someone even visited us yesterday to access his archives. But today, they are all yours." He gestured towards some supplies under the table for making full-page impression copies – I had innocently assumed that I would have to copy down anything of import all by hand – and left me. Shockingly, I felt rather sorry to see him go.

I imagine that when you visited the Reading Room, you worked quickly to avoid the company of fellow Readers. Thanks to your kind guidance, this was not the case for me. Left to my own devices, I sifted through the box and dissected Darbeni's documents. What a fascinating thing an archive is! To think that a person's entire life could be summed up in the jumbled, incomplete assortment of ephemera they leave behind.

It did not take me long to reach that puzzling folio of shorthand documents. It seems that our favourite Darbeni expert kindly left his translations next to each original so I might read them. I've attached a few for your enjoyment.

But here is what haunts me the most. At the very bottom of the box, I found what appeared to be the "poetry group's" manifest. This particular item was not listed on the catalogue sheet at the beginning of the box – I have not spent much time in Archives, Henerey, but I imagine such an oversight is quite unusual? It was a list of about thirty names, each accompanied by a date, some of which were well past the day of Darbeni's death! It appears that this group's activities continued even without the founding member. But considering these modern additions, how did the manifest end up in Darbeni's archive?

Then I noticed the last among the most recent names – with a membership date of thirty-five years ago. Amiele Nosin. My mother. Naturally.

As you might imagine, I quite elegantly lost all my wits.

Somehow, I managed to stand up, repackage the box, and return it to that odd File Collector mechanism (which whirred quite pleasantly to thank me) before exiting the room. Scholar Iyl gave me a wonderfully warm smile as I emerged.

"Did you enjoy your research? Please send my best regards to Henerey," he said before looking back down at the text he was perusing.

"Are you completely sure that all the documents in that archive are genuine?" I said faintly, hoping he could hear me.

"Certainly," Scholar Iyl replied. "My colleague re-catalogued it two days ago. All accounted for, and all provenances verified."

A thought struck me.

"Who was it, exactly, that requested to view the Darbeni files yesterday?"

Scholar Iyl seemed to search the ceiling for meaning.

"Now that," he said, "is confidential, unfortunately. Unless you are a Department Chair looking to track down an unruly Apprentice."

I realised that the sign-in sheets were simply in a book under his palm. I considered leaning over to steal a glance – then thought better of it.

I didn't need to. I suspected that the person who may have tampered with this archive yesterday could be our mother's friend Jeime Alestarre.

I did not even wait to see how Scholar Iyl might respond to my departure. It was growing late, anyway, and I feared that the Scholars – including Sophy – would soon return from their morning repast. (I was right! As I ascended the spiralling dormitory staircase, I saw Sophy seven flights beneath me – and promptly began to run. I barely made it inside before she did, though I suspect she might have noticed me shutting the door. I still do not want to worry her with this, but I do wonder what she would make of it all!)

This letter has run embarrassingly long as usual. I shall end here and leave my sketches, copies, and notes to continue to speak for themselves. Please take care – how I wish we could simply talk in person. (Certainly I will contact Jeime as soon as I possibly can!)

Yours,

E.

ANNOTATED SKETCH BY E. CIDNOSIN – "THE KELP TREE"

Were I more skilled with scale, I would have sketched a small version of myself standing beside it – but my artistic skills remain far too limited for such an ambitious project. Instead, please imagine the top of my head corresponding roughly with the first quarter of the "tree".

ANNOTATED SKETCH BY E. CIDNOSIN – "THE SHAPE IN THE WATER"

I doubt this will be of any use to you, but while on the island I found it amusing to attempt a scientific illustration of a creature that I barely glimpsed! Certainly I succeeded in capturing the most defining trait: its mysteriousness.

COPIES OF MANUSCRIPT TRANSLATIONS FROM THE SCHOLAR KENVEN DARBENI ARCHIVES

"A Luminous Circumference"
I knew I saw the water glowing.
Turns out there's better things than knowing.

"A Luminous Circumference"
It's born and it burns and it dies
Though never in front of my eyes!
I'm a sceptical sort
Of the things they report—
But remain open to a surprise.

"A Luminous Circumference"
She says it sings visually, looks musical,
feels impossible. Radiant tunnel, elegant symphony, attractive
curiosity?
What does it say about our ancestors? What do they say
about us?
What must I do to see it myself?

277

ANNOTATION ON THE MANUSCRIPTS BY E. CIDNOSIN, 1002

Some Hypotheses (not particularly backed by evidence, but I thought this title seems more convincing than "Some Idle Speculation"):

Firstly, though I read all the poems, I included only a representative sample here. Common threads include mention of a glowing circular shape (20 appearances), synaesthesia (such as a sound you can see, and so forth – 15 appearances), a cycle of birth–life–death (4 appearances), and a mysterious figure referred to as "she" (3 appearances).

All the poems are titled "A Luminous Circumference", but those actual words only appear in Darbeni's original poem. I should note that the manuscript for Darbeni's poem is not officially titled. "A Luminous Circumference" is simply the first line.

It is also worth noting that while none of the poems are signed with full names, many include initialisms or symbols. Darbeni's "A Luminous Circumference" does feature his Scholar's Seal.

In case you were wondering, I did not recognise the handwriting on any document as my mother's. It is possible that the shorthand might have obscured it, but she wrote in quite a characteristic way – always angling all curving letters, making an "o" rather like a little box, for example. I must speak with Jeime!

Chapter 20

LETTER FROM HENEREY CLEL TO E. CIDNOSIN, 1002

Dearest E.,

Reading your letter was an experience like no other. Have you ever considered, E., that someone ought to write a Fantasy about you? You experience something unprecedented, you venture to the library in search of new knowledge, you discover a mysterious familial connection to said knowledge, and then you write all about it to a most peculiar man who does not deserve your attention – surely that is the very stuff of stories! By the way, it warms my heart to think that you've spoken to Elaxand Iyl. He has been very kind to me throughout the years. (And, unfortunately, making an embarrassing comment alluding to depth of his friend's fondness for someone else in that very someone else's presence is not entirely out of character for the fellow . . . but I cannot deny what he alleges!)

At any rate, I did some research of my own while engaging in a rather unique project for the *Sagacity*. My colleagues Lerin, Emte (that is Scholar Emte Manri Yaum, also from Intertidal, and a seabird specialist), and I have finally been "nominated" to participate in that part of the mission that no one ever wishes to complete – the dreaded "Depth-Craft Vigil." In brief, the *Sagacity* possesses a small yet serviceable depth-craft – a model about a decade old, so it's showing its vintage – that we use once a month or so to survey sea life. Now, you might ask me, "Henerey! You are so fascinated with the Deep House, and the concept of life underwater – what makes this depth-craft experience so dreaded?" (Please indulge me – I do wish we could ask each other questions in real time, as it were. I also acknowledge that any question you might ask me would likely be far more eloquent and engaging than anything I can imagine.)

Well, because the depth-craft is rather outdated, it lacks the proper surveying equipment for our purposes, so we must load it up afresh and refuel its spirulina generator before every journey. It was not meant for true depths – it is a transport craft! – and takes so long to prepare for deep dives that after a launch, those unlucky souls chosen to float within it are not able to return to the comforts of the ship until an entire day has passed.

But when our Captain announced that my time had come, I accepted my fate without protest and told myself that I must embrace any opportunity to view the ocean from a new perspective. And of the *Sagacity*'s crew, I find Lerin and Emte the most agreeable – and most dazzlingly wise – so I thought this might provide the perfect chance to ask them for advice. Given the sensitive and unusual nature of our inquiry into the Structure and your experience, I used the utmost tact and discretion.

As soon as the hatch closed, I turned to my companions and asked if they knew any recent accounts of Antepelagic technology.

"That is—oddly specific, Scholar Clel," replied Emte, never taking her eyes off the viewing window. (She wants to witness exactly how the Small-Billed Cormorant manages to prey upon Prolific Squid even though their bills are . . . well, you can imagine . . .)

"Surely you now know me well enough to understand that I am nothing if not oddly specific at all times."

"Actually," said Lerin, "I disagree. I think you're being far too general, Henerey. What inspired your vague interest in the Antepelagic?'

I offered a convincing monologue about how my lifelong interest in

Fantasies led me to take up a new interest in History, especially those unsolved mysteries of the depths—

"Well, you see," I relented in the end, "a friend of mine is researching the subject, and I find myself at a loss to give her any suitable references. So I turned to the two most knowledgeable Scholars aboard this depth-craft."

They both looked at me with great excitement.

"This wouldn't happen to be the 'friend' for whose sake you willingly attended a social gathering, would it?" Lerin asked.

You know, it occurs to me that I should not be transcribing this part for you – let's skip ahead, shall we? It was all irrelevant ribbing from that point onward! It would have served Emte right if a Cormorant swam by at that very moment and she missed it while they both teased me.

"People have salvaged Antepelagic technology for centuries," said Lerin so confidently that I could almost see the footnotes hovering off the words. "For the most part, however, it is useless. Scholars haul massive machines to the surface only to find them so overgrown with algae and rust and so forth that they become nothing more than tragically beautiful, historically significant art pieces."

"Never anything functioning?"

"When I was a child, there was talk of this in the Intertidal Outer Ring," said Emte thoughtfully. "I'd heard that in my father's generation, there was an Architect who found a fully intact piece of machinery that he thought would make his fortune. So he went to Campus and fetched a team to inspect it – only to watch it explode just as their ship arrived."

"That was a Fantasy, I'm sure," said Lerin. "Someone told me a similar story. Except in my case, it was an avaricious Scholar of the Past who learned that one shouldn't pin all their ambitions on one project." This statement was followed by a telling glance at Emte.

"I have many research interests other than the Cormorants, though I appreciate your concern, my friend!" she said. "But I wouldn't be so quick to dismiss these tales as 'Fantasies'."

"I can't argue with you there. We are not exactly living in the most reasonable of times. It takes very little to sow doubt in the most rational human hearts these days when the world is so increasingly incomprehensible."

"Is it?" I asked, wincing at how childlike I sounded. "I mean, Chancellor Rawsel alone is enough to make anyone wish for more reasonable times, but would you really say that the world as a whole has not always been relatively incomprehensible?"

Lerin suddenly became incredibly fascinated by the lack of sea life outside our porthole.

"O, Lerin, you won't be able to shake him now," said Emte. "We are trapped in this vessel for the foreseeable future, after all."

Lerin sighed and turned back towards me.

"I am an Illustrator, not a Natural Historian, but I must study things to sketch them, and I cannot ignore some of the enigmas I've encountered recently. You are from the School of Observation, Henerey. Have you not observed anything especially odd about the rays' migration in your time aboard the *Sagacity*?"

"Everything about them is odd!" I cried, letting my Scholarly exasperation from the past few tides finally emerge in full force. "I understood our objective as a simple one – discovering why the direction of the migration shifted. But it's not just their path that troubles me. Everything about their current actions is absolutely inconsistent with migration behaviours and therefore unclassifiable."

"A Scholar of Classification's worst nightmare, I'm sure," murmured Emte drily.

"Is there any chance that they have supplanted their typical migration activities with actions they usually perform under other circumstances?" asked Lerin. "Breeding, for example. I only guess, of course."

"As a matter of fact," I replied, "that is the very thing I've noticed. Normally, migrating rays form squadrons of ten to twenty and queue up in a triangular pattern, which helps them move more efficiently over long distances. But at present, this squadron alternates their formation as they travel. They shift and swap places, shuffling from shape to shape.

282

Not exactly practical for a marathon swim. It's a short-term diversionary tactic that rays often use when they feel threatened by a predator."

"Which predators tend to set their sights on a squadron of rays?" asked Emte.

"During their migrations, the rays prove almost impossible to catch. A seal might follow behind for a short time, salivating after the stragglers, but none of the rays' usual assailants possess the speed or stamina to pursue them for long."

"Perhaps it is not one of their typical predators, but an odd or opportunistic creature with a cultivated taste for rays," mused Lerin. "An Imposing Toothed Whale? They are awfully fast when they want to be, and enormous to boot."

"I considered that. Yet if some great predator of substantial size and might has been trailing the *Sagacity* all this time, how have we not seen it?"

"Because we are too occupied with pleasant conversation to notice?" Emte concluded.

Though she said it with a laugh, I did feel guilty for distracting everyone, and resolved to remain focused on the porthole henceforth. But as I watched the water, I could not help seeking any signs that might suggest the presence of some unprecedented predator, just out of view . . .

Forgive me; I did not mean to spend so much time blathering on about my rays! I mainly intended to tell you about the earlier conversation, which helped me discover information that I believe complements yours. Based on your most excellent archival research (truly, E., I swoon at the thought of you braving the Reading Room), I now suspect that the Structure's potentially unstable technology may also explain the references to death and destruction in those poems.

What I am trying to piece together is a possible motive for Darbeni. Let us hypothesise that he knew of these Structures, or types of artefacts, and that he – what? Decided to run a social experiment and see if other people would pass on this legend through poetry? Why not communicate this information in a more Scholarly fashion? I assume he must have been the group's leader since, as you mention, all the poems borrowed that first line for their titles. And others (including your mother, apparently?) drew inspiration from Darbeni and carried on this tradition? But to what end?

Please tell me everything that you hear from Jeime! I can hardly wait!

Yours,

Henerey

P.S. Thank you very much for the copies of your sketches! You know, some of the earliest accounts of the Antepelagic Era suggest that great plants flourished on the islands in the sky – "trees" like the palms we have on the Atoll, but much larger and diverse in their forms. I never thought such a tree would take the form of kelp, though. Does kelp even possess the structural integrity to stand upright without water? Astonishing. (Even more astonishing is the fact that you were able to make such detailed drawings in the midst of an unknown world after suffering from a surprise seaquake . . .)

ANNOTATED DOCUMENT FROM ELINIEA HAYVE FORGHE TO SOPHY CIDNOSIN, 1002

Dear Sophy,

Something extraordinary has happened. Please read this extremely confidential missive that the five of us will presently send to the Chancellors. You simply must see it, too. (Don't worry, I am well – just astounded!)

Your Niea

A LETTER TO THE CHANCELLORS, 1002

Dearest Chancellors, fellow explorers of this world through which we sail proudly in the pursuit of knowledge:

Today I write not as Vincenebras, but as the collective voice of all my colleagues. For the first time in my career, I allow others to dictate the words I put to paper. We worked together to determine the structure of this letter – the phrasing, the pacing, parts to leave out and parts to emphasise – and you can imagine how much five such different Scholars as ourselves argued when deciding how to compose such an important missive.

(If I may speak in my own voice for *one* moment, I must censure my colleagues for attempting to remove some of my "bombast" and "pomposity" and "inconsistent reliance upon Adjectives" – I protest, of course, but not too heartily, as I know our mission is far more important than maintaining the integrity of my Writerly Tone!)

When you woke up this morning, I suppose you did not think much of this day – this mere first day of the Second Perishing Tide in the Second Quarter of High Waters of 1002, a moment like any other – but I would advise you to circle this date in your daybook so you may point to it, years hence, and tell your grandspawn "Behold: proof that I was there when the world changed forever."

(Let the record show that a majority of the Scholars present condemned the preceding paragraph as "far too Vincenebras in tone" – but thanks to the kindness of dear Schr Irye Rux, who found it inoffensive, it shall stand as a rhetorical flourish – as long as I promise to stay "on my best behaviour" for the rest of this missive. O, dear Irye, you are truly the most Superlative of Scholars! In days to come, the specifics of our exploits will no doubt be the subject of many fine treatises and literary epics – yet though it truly kills me, I will tamper my raconteurial fervour in favour of providing you, my dearest friends, with the ultimate truth.)

Now we must proceed, though that is easier said than done.

Halfway to the deepest point of the trench, somewhere on an otherwise forgettable, unremarkable ledge, is a crystalline "door" attached to what looks like a ruined entryway. It resembles no known Antepelagic architectural style, but its motifs, surprisingly enough, echo the shape of Protist Plankton known as the Seven-Pointed Diatom (expertly identified in an instant by Scholar Forghe). The door is barely one helmsbreadth by two, outlined with a thin indentation in the rock. It is made from a radiant purple stone, veined with white and flickering with speckles of gold; the only other ornament it features is the aforementioned array of Planktonic forms, overlapping each other at their very tips.

Brevity, yes, brevity! We are breathless at the thought of this mysterious discovery. We also acknowledge that you, our Colleagues and Supporters and Administrators, will require further evidence of this discovery before it may be examined in more detail. In fact, perhaps you now wonder *why* we have not already entered this door, or enclosed documentation of some kind with this missive. The answer is disappointingly mundane: we did not bring the proper tools. We returned to the Spheres to gather the appropriate equipment.

We also wish to share this exciting discovery with the General Public but will await your approval before doing so.

Until then: let us all delight in the knowledge that the mysteries of the Ridge have been ... *revealed* at last. (I, Vincenebras, am being forced by my colleagues to take full responsibility for that final sentence.)

Ever in pursuit of the unknown,

Schr Irye Rux

Schr Ylaret Tamseln

Schr Eliniea Hayve Forghe

Schr Vincenebras

Schr Tevn Winiver Mawr

LETTER FROM SOPHY CIDNOSIN TO ELINIEA HAYVE FORGHE, 1002

Dear Niea,

Though there are many ways in which I do not wish to follow in your friend Tevn's footsteps, I shall mimic him by writing to you while knowing that by the time this letter arrives, I likely will be at the Spheres myself.

With E. back at the Deep House and seemingly safe and well, I may rest easy and continue my work. (In fact, it was E. who suggested that I return to you.)

I will see you – and what else? What else? – very soon.

Yours,

Sophy

LETTER FROM E. CIDNOSIN TO HENEREY CLEL, 1002

Dearest Henerey!

It seems we are not the only two keeping secrets right now! Sophy's colleagues discovered something – I know not what, since Sophy could not betray Niea's trust by telling me (though I think Niea wouldn't mind – she has a sister too, you know!). Of course, I instantly thought – what if it is another Structure? – but it could equally be an exciting new species of Phytoplankton never before seen. Whatever the discovery, it set Sophy all aflutter, and she began (at my urging) her return journey to the Spheres today. Perhaps her transport vessel will pass by the *Sagacity* once again as she heads back to the Ridge. And I am at home at last, to my great delight!

Because Sophy is so concerned about my wellbeing, she insisted, in the end, that I spend this first day of her departure in the company of others. I passed a not unpleasant morning with Seliara, who had much to chatter about – I do feel so awfully for her, because my accursed brother is still "away" – and then past midday, when Seliara departed, my second guest arrived.

Jeime Alestarre did not answer the letters (yes, plural) that I sent her after my trip to the Reading Room. I do know, however, that she most certainly read them, because she came to the Deep House bearing an enormous sea-cloth satchel with what looked like an irregular series of crashing waves embroidered around the letters "AC".

"I never thought you would go to the library," she said by way of greeting. "If anyone ever felt drawn to open the Darbeni archive, I assumed it would be Sophy. Have you told her?"

I informed Jeime that I had not, indeed, shared any of this with Sophy. That feels quite painfully wrong, but she is so very preoccupied with the Ridge expedition.

Jeime swung up the bag onto the table, undoing its clasp with her careful hands.

"Your mother wanted the three of you to have this," she said. "But I suppose she would say that you alone may decide when and if you will share it with your siblings."

"Because I made the discovery on my own, and therefore earned the privilege of learning her secrets?" I asked. "How very like Mother."

"It is not only that." Jeime sat down across from me and laid her hand on the table just in front of mine – not quite touching me in a familial way but suggesting the sentiment. "I'm sure that Ami – I mean, your mother—"

"I know she was your friend," I said. "You can call her by that name, if you prefer."

Jeime smiled at me. "Ami," she continued, "knew that you loved the Deep House like she did."

Well, obviously I do! There is no question of that! But how does that relate to the Structure and the poems? I asked Jeime as much (though I tried to be slightly less smug about my apparent claim to the title of "Most Deep-House-Oriented Sibling").

"Because Ami built this house for a particular reason," answered Jeime. "She hoped that something would manifest here. It never appeared during her lifetime, but it has now, and so I bring this to you."

Then she opened the bag, revealing the following documents:

- A most fascinating map, depicting the entire World-Ocean, with coordinates indicating locations as well as dates (some in the past and others in the future – including hundreds of years hence, Henerey!)

- Yet another copy of Darbeni's "A Luminous Circumference" in manuscript form, written in a different handwriting that I did not recognise, without Darbeni's seal
- A letter, signed by Jeime herself, which she pressed into my hand.

"Now I leave you to read," said Jeime, standing up. "I will keep in touch, E. If this is an Entry, as your mother suspected, and it just experienced its first cycle, then we have approximately two months until it vanishes. You are safe at present. But soon we must hatch plans and make decisions."

"Do you mean to say that you are not available to 'talk more' with me now?" I asked, rather more fiercely than I intended. "I cannot even begin to understand anything you just said!" (Though I do now, of course – more on that in a minute.)

"It is all in the letter," she said, dismissively. Then she took my hand. "My apologies. I am weak when it comes to emotions, you know. I would rather let you read it, ponder it, read it again, and then we shall speak. That approach seems more in line with your mother's philosophy, don't you think? Besides, I know you would likely prefer to be by yourself."

Now, in reality, I had to walk Jeime back to the airlock and run the departure sequence before she could leave. But let us pretend, for drama's sake, that the conversation ended there!

In short (because this letter is anything but), I shall enclose a copy of the letter from Jeime for you to peruse. I know it will interest you. I'm sure you will be particularly excited to see that your conversation with Lerin and Emte bore some fruit – you were on the right path. (Though where this path leads, I know not.) So why don't you skip ahead, read that letter, and then return here to see my final thoughts below?

You've done that now, I presume? Wonderful!

Here is what I propose. Sometime – sometime soon, since I worry about when this next "burst" may come, even if Jeime says we have two months – I will swim out and inspect the Structure myself. I am not the most skilful diver. O! And as soon as I have a chance to observe it myself and think more carefully (and have enough proof to convince even my accursed Brain that all this is real), I will go straight to Sophy at last and tell her everything! That thought makes me feel much better.

I will, of course, keep you fully informed. (Do you remember when we were writing to each other about our lives and everyday occurrences and favourite Fantasies? I wouldn't say that I prefer this genre of communication over the other – as entranced as I am by the Structure, I look forward to the days when we can return to slightly more mundane topics of conversation.)

Yours,

E.

LETTER FROM JEIME ALESTARRE TO E. CIDNOSIN, 1002

Dear E.,

Let it be known that I do not personally believe in or support any of the ideas that I am about to relay to you.

Or, I suppose, I did not. I am no longer sure.

I have also never had to write an extensive letter detailing "family secrets" that I could not reveal unless it became "necessary", so I apologise if the format or tone of this letter seems unusual. I write to you now to fulfil a pledge I made to your mother – may she rest soundly in the waves – shortly before she was taken from us. Well, I fear she would have preferred if I continued providing you with mysterious scraps of information instead of offering a fully explanatory note, but even a sickbed promise cannot convince me to do so when the matter is so urgent.

I met your mother almost forty years ago when we were Apprentices at the Academy, assigned to the same dormitory hall. We once climbed up the parapets of the Intertidal Campus Central Tower, sat up there in the sea-salted air, and read poetry to each other for hours until it grew so dark that we could not figure out how to get down. We began courting officially two years after our friendship began, but if I were to trace the genesis of our relationship, I would say that it commenced the very first day we laid eyes on each other. And all was dizzyingly, impossibly wonderful – that is to say, I'm sure it wasn't, and I'm sure we had many mundane days and silly arguments and poor Assessments, but in my memory, it glitters.

Until she found the Fleet. (Or they found her, as the case would be.)

It was the last year of our Apprenticeship, and we were on the cusp of becoming full Scholars. Ami expressed her remarkable creativity through a rapid-fire series of ambitious Architecture projects, all of which proposed innovative ways of living with the sea rather than simply floating above it. But even though she excelled at and delighted in her work, she loved words more than anything else, and became quite renowned around Campus as an amateur poet. (She even dragged me to a recitation club on a few occasions, which required us to sneak into the misty pockets of the Water Gardens in the dead of night – but I suppose I haven't time to get into that.)

As her reputation grew, it became very likely that an Arcane Society – those organisations on campus that delight in a somewhat self-parodic secrecy – might take interest in her. But when a most unusual circular envelope arrived in our dormitory, emblazoned with Ami's name in a colourful gouache that seemed to glow, neither of us knew what to make of it.

And I never would, because the meetings of this Society quickly became the one place to which I dared not follow Ami. They always asked her to go alone – at a different hour and to a different place each time – and when she came home, she constantly wrote or read things that she would not show me. Her assignments suffered, though I tried to help her when I could. Even her Advisor grew concerned. Then, one day, after stumbling in late to a critical presentation, Ami gave the most eloquent and innovative proposal for an underwater habitation module integrated directly into a coral reef. She even identified a specific location and demonstrated how her design would draw upon the water pressure, depth, and light penetration at those exact coordinates. She stunned everyone present. Unanimous Chancellor decree granted Ami funding to produce further designs for what she had deemed the "Deep House". Ami was only twenty.

After that meeting, I did not storm after her, or beg her to tell me how she had produced so much work in such a short time, or even ask for an explanation about her involvement in this mysterious society. She came to me. She bore me away to her room, papered the walls with the enormous blueprints she'd carried with her to our session, and sat me down beside her.

"I designed this house for us," she said with delicious secrecy. "There is something very important I must do with my life, Jeime. Though I thought it my calling alone, it occurs to me that I am simply incapable of doing anything without you. So I must tell you the secret of the Fleet."

I was swept away by the notion that my beloved wanted to share an underwater house with me – we never spoke openly of a future together – and let her continue.

"A hundred years ago," your future mother said, leaning back into her chair and staring at the ceiling as though letting a well-practised speech wash over her, "a poet had a vision of the world to come. She recorded her vision in a poem and knew she must share it as widely as possible. She wrote more and more. Everyone she knew discouraged and betrayed her. In the end, she decided to lock the poems away – all except those she had already sent out to friends and confidantes. The only reliable one among them was Scholar Kenven Darbeni, and it was he who founded the Fleet – a society of Writers who became Soothsayers and Saviours committed to uncovering the truth that our Poet wrote so long ago."

That was not at all the explanation I expected. It only went downhill from there.

Ami raved about how this "poet" – and her trusting followers – perceived our floundering society as the remnant of a robust Antepelagic world that vanished a thousand years ago when it fell from its home in the atmosphere but now flourishes somewhere else entirely beyond the bottom of the sea.

If you are even half as fond of historical literature now as you were in your youth, dear E., I imagine you immediately identified the discrepancy in your mother's version of the past. Surely you are still haunted by first-hand accounts of the Dive and recall how the old poets described the great cities in the clouds raining into the ocean moments after the Survivors fled. Statues shattering. Libraries flooding. Words and art and instruments and engineering becoming nothing more than shipwrecks somewhere in the depths.

Through my conversation with Ami, I learned the Fleet's core belief. The Antepelagic civilisation was not lost but lives on, and it is up to *us* to reach it. According to this interpretation, the Dive was no unpredictable calamity, but rather a carefully orchestrated move by the great minds of the Antepelagic world that was intended to protect humanity from something.

Yet our ancestors – the Survivors – were a small group of arrogant Academics who did not believe in whatever danger the rest of their society foresaw. As the Dive occurred, the Survivors split from their people, starting their lives afresh and forsaking the rest of their world.

But the rest of their world did not forsake them.

What remains of the Antepelagic society, Ami claimed, knows that something still threatens us, the descendants of the Survivors who stayed in the seas. To rescue our civilisation, the Antepelagic folk send both "Entries" and "Envoys" to help us find the way back to them. (I paid little attention to her descriptions of these two unknown nouns back then, I must admit, but I now believe that your vexing Structure is an example of a so-called "Entry".)

She also told me that the Fleet grew quite paranoid in their old age.

Most of the members, back then, were far older than Ami. Apparently a young member betrayed the Fleet or something like that – using Fleet research to work against their purposes and destroy the Entries, etc. – so the group stopped recruiting altogether (making one exception for Ami, because of her exceptional talent). Thus it was up to her and her heirs alone to carry on their legacy. (O, and a note about the name – "Fleet" is wordplay, apparently, because not only did they imagine themselves to be as numerous as a great crowd of ships, they aspired to be quick enough to interpret these poems before it was too late and the Danger struck.)

Ami finished her monologue with great excitement, smiling at me so beautifully as she – my wonderful, lovely, logical partner – told me that humanity on this planet only has a chance at a future if we pursue these Entries and Envoys and gain access to the world beyond our world.

It went over about as well as you might expect. I reacted poorly to this revelation. And that's how your father ended up being your parent and not me.

Not that I hold any resentment. After we ended our relationship – and after Ami married Bron Cidne and I found Min, to whom I hope I may introduce you one day soon – Ami and I rekindled a tentative friendship, just before you were born. She had, funnily enough, neglected to tell her new spouse about her secret society – "I wouldn't dare scare him off," she once said to me with a nervous laugh – which put me in the unique position of being the only person outside of her Fleet who knew of all this nonsense.

So I was also the only person she could call upon to preserve her legacy for you.

You were here, you know, on the day when I made my promise to Ami. You did not come out of your quarters to greet me, but I could hear your quiet movements even from your parents' bedroom as I spoke with your mother. How dark and distant her mood seemed as she shifted the subject to the Fleet once more, mourning that she would never be able to complete the work she believed was her responsibility – unless I helped her.

"You want me to tell your children a secret that you won't even share with your own husband?" I asked. "Why not speak with them yourself?"

"I do not wish for anyone to simply *tell* them anything," your mother replied. "I fear they will not believe a word of it unless they figure matters out for themselves."

"Have you lost your confidence in the Fleet after all these years?"

"No," she murmured. "I merely know that the truth can be hard to accept. You helped me understand that."

I told Ami that I suspected I would not have accepted the Fleet even if she had sent me on a treasure-hunt of independent discovery to seek out my own evidence. That, at least, earned me a smile.

"At any rate, we could not possibly tell them now, because it is likely that some very tangible proof may emerge in the years to come," Ami continued. "If an Entry—well, I won't trouble you with that. But Jeime, won't you please promise me that if I am gone, you will keep the Fleet to yourself until my children come to you first? The last thing I want is for them to learn about it in the wrong way – and, perhaps, think less of me."

She was very kind not to say, *As you did, when I told you.*

E., please know that I would not have made such a commitment to Ami if I truly believed that I would ever be called upon to fulfil this pledge. She was so ill, and I had loved her once, and I still didn't think that anything would ever come of this nonsense. So I swore to keep your mother's secrets and figured I would carry around this valise of documents forever in the event that I outlived her.

How greatly it grieves me still that I did. If it had been in a depth-craft accident, or a shipwreck, or anything vaguely linked to her interest in this conspiracy, I would have fully cursed the Fleet (or the Fleet's enemies, or both) for being complicit in her death. I still yearn to blame them for her illness. Alas, I suspect the Fleet are long dead themselves – considering most of them were eighty or older back then.

I hope this explains a bit about the personal connection you have to this situation, dear E. How I ached to tell you everything when I first saw the Structure. How I wished that Ami could tell you – but I knew that she never would, even if she were alive. She would want you to gather evidence, ask questions, and draw your own conclusions, all of which I believe you have now done to her satisfaction. So I shall let the other documents from the Society – just a few things that Ami probably purloined from the Darbeni archives – speak for themselves. Let us speak again soon, especially before two months pass. It is extremely urgent that we keep an eye on that Entry.

Yours fondly,

Jeime Alestarre

MISSIVE FROM KENVEN DARBENI TO THE FLEET

Dear New Member,

By the time you read this, I have most certainly perished. But before I fell from this world – just as a singular Mussel, beaten too long by the waves, might one day lose its Grip and slip into the ocean – I wanted to write a letter that would live on long after I stopped doing so.

Five years ago, a woman who preferred to be kept anonymous sent me a most Peculiar Poem, exhorting me above all to believe it.

How does one believe a poem? So I asked myself at the time. But I found it so striking, so unusual, that I had to speak with her further. And when I did, she begged me to spread her word and to encourage others to muse on these visions, to study them, and to write their own poems as we seek the Better World – one to which we must flee if we hope to survive the perils that are to come.

Here are our axioms. You are welcome among our numbers.

We Perfect the Poems.

We Anticipate the Entries.

We Listen for the Envoys and the Ones to Come.

And Fleetly we accomplish what must be Done.

Sincerely,

The likely late Scholar Kenven Darbeni

THE FLEET'S ENTRY TIMELINE, PAGE 4

Year 899 – Entry budded at 15, 3, 23 in the Second Ocean at a depth of 8 fathoms, burst first on the Fifth Day of the First Quarter of High Waters (with Songs detected two days prior), and vanished in its second explosion on the Sixth Day of the Third Quarter of High Waters.

Year 911 – Entry budded at 7, 1, 62 in the Third Ocean at a depth of 6 fathoms, burst on the Third Day of the Second Quarter of Low Waters, and vanished in its second explosion on the First Day of the First Quarter of Mid-Waters. Witnesses also noticed unusual behaviour in local marine life populations in the days after the bud but before the burst. Two Primordial Sharks – not seen at these depths for centuries – engaged in a vicious territorial battle before disappearing as quickly as they'd come.

Year 920 – Entry budded at 5, 3, 2 in the Second Ocean at a depth of 8 fathoms, burst first on the Second Day of the First Quarter of Mid-Waters and vanished in its second explosion on the Second Day of the Third Quarter of Mid-Waters. An unsuspecting Scholar of Sound conducting a dive in the area right after the first burst claims to have experienced a "hallucination" of an island (though none of his colleagues believed him).

Based on rough calculations about the geographical and temporal arrangements of these Entries, we predict that Entries will appear at the following locations:

Year 990 – Entry predicted to bud at 20, 1, 1 at a depth of 6 fathoms

Year 991 – Entry predicted to bud at 7, 33, 1 at a depth of 8 fathoms

Year 1002 – Entry predicted to bud at 22, 3, 2 at a depth of 14 fathoms

Year 1003 – Entry predicted to bud at 1, 34, 2 at a depth of 20 fathoms
Year 1004 – Entry predicted to bud at 6, 2, 22 at a depth of 10 fathoms

ANNOTATION FROM E. CIDNOSIN TO HENEREY CLEL

I don't suppose you and I ever discussed "vicious territorial battles" between creatures behaving abnormally, have we, dear Henerey? Nor has a strange correspondent ever shared with you her mysterious trip to an island and a shadowy sea?

(I can't say I have heard any odd music lately, but at the very least, that explains "Melodious—To Spy—" . . .)

Most importantly, in case you haven't guessed, that listing for this very year includes the coordinates for the Deep House!

Mother must have been counting down the days ever since she built it. To think that she lived for this and yet the sickness took her before she could accomplish her goal.

Well, I feel determined to accomplish it for her – no matter what that requires.

E.

LETTER FROM SOPHY CIDNORGHE TO JEIME ALESTARRE, 1003

Dear Jeime,

Since you abjure Automatic Post and neglected to reply to any of the seven letters I sent over the past few tides, I shall not expect a timely response. However, I do hope you will consider calling upon myself and Niea at the Atoll Campus home of our kind hosts, the Clel family, at your earliest convenience.

There is no need to confirm or send a note beforehand. Simply stop by when you can. I assure you that we will all be eager to discuss how my sister's disappearance relates to the so-called "Fleet" at any hour of the day (or night) that suits you.

You can rest assured that I have, by this point, completed more hands-on research into this subject than even my mother would have demanded.

Until we meet,

Sophy

Chapter 21

LETTER FROM SOPHY CIDNOSIN TO E. CIDNOSIN, 1002

Dear E.,

Are you still well? Please be as careful and cautious as you can back at the Deep House. It comforts me that you are in the place most comfortable to you. And do remember to use that Vocal Echolator if you need to summon someone quickly – it cannot call me directly but will put you in touch with the nearest Emergency Services transport ship for a speedy rescue.

Compared with my long and tense journey to find you in the Infirmary, my capsule trip to the Spheres was swift and pleasant. And what a welcome I received upon my return! I exited the airlock to find everyone assembled in the entry vestibule (a space intended for perhaps two people at maximum), greeting me with a semi-musical cheer of my name conducted by Irye. I'm sure I even spotted some of my colleagues dancing in a festive way, but I have no evidence to confirm – as I only had eyes for Niea, lovely Niea in a soft coral-pink set of dress robes, looking even more radiant than I remembered.

There were questions, of course – polite inquiries about you and the Deep House and various personages at Boundless whom we might have possibly encountered during our stay on campus. I gave limited answers as quickly as I could, after which I could take it no more and cried:

"By the tides, my friends, will you not tell me what in the world you discovered at the Point of Interest?"

"See!" crowed Ylaret. "Vincenebras, I told you she wouldn't want to waste her time with small talk!"

"Forgive me for inquiring about our colleague's wellbeing after she returned from her family emergency," drawled Vincenebras. His uncharacteristic compassion shocked me and I told him so, which set everyone to laughing again.

Tevn spoke last. In fact, I noticed that he had not joined in the laughter – once I arrived, he pushed himself towards the edge of the vestibule, nodding and smiling at the appropriate junctures. I could not blame the fellow at all for that. In fact, he rather reminded me of you.

"It is unbelievable," he said. "But it is now our task to make it believable. I am grateful that you joined us again, Scholar Cidnosin. No doubt your insight will prove immensely beneficial to this mission."

I did not like "joined *us*", nor "prove", to be sure, but at the very least he tried to be complimentary – I believe!

"That is precisely what I wish to know more about," I replied. "The mission, that is. What do you intend to do next?"

"That is all you have to say?" asked Ylaret.

"You certainly accepted the validity of an inexplicable occurrence at the bottom of the sea much more quickly than I," said Irye.

"To be fair, I was in a capsule by myself for several hours and had ample time to open my mind to new possibilities," I replied. "Will you not tell me what you saw?"

"It was Scholar Mawr who discovered it!" announced Vincenebras, clapping Tevn on the shoulder in a gesture of friendship that made its recipient wince. "What luck you've brought us, Tevn! Perhaps we should have had you with us from the beginning, eh? No offence, dear Sophy."

"None taken," I said slowly, my eyes never leaving Tevn. "Scholar Mawr, then, would you please tell me more about your discovery?"

Now E., I am afraid I must be quite careful about what I tell you

301

next, because as I mentioned, the Chancellors forbade us from sharing anything with the world until we document this "discovery" thoroughly. Will you promise not to breathe a word about it to … say, Henerey, for example? I know you trust him, but I can hardly risk Niea getting into trouble.

Do you promise?

All right, I accept your promise pre-emptively. And I shall be appropriately vague. Beneath the ocean, my colleagues discovered a humanmade bit of architecture, likely a very far-flung piece of a ruin from the Dive.

Now I think I might have been overly vague. To be clear, it is a DOOR, E., or at least it was a door when it graced the entryway of some sky-bound building millennia ago.

Clearly Niea did not befriend Tevn on the merit of his storytelling abilities. He relayed their experience with the door in a lacklustre, anxious account that matched, beat-for-beat, the narrative put forth in the jointly authored mission statement.

He concluded by remarking that in two days we will depart once more, burdened with documentary equipment – more advanced recording machinery, a dazzling array of lanterns, and the whole host of automata, who might prove useful companions as we return to those mysterious depths. The Chancellors, you see, require much more context – "evidence", as Tevn said with a frown – to further understand the scope of our discovery.

Then the conversation naturally devolved into Irye extemporising about a colleague who once composed an entire symphony about "the Insignificance of Evidence". Finally – after what felt like hours, truly – my social obligations ended, the crew disappeared into their respective quarters to prepare for the long day ahead, and Niea and I had a moment to ourselves. Or so I thought! A few moments after our moment to ourselves, a metallic knock rang out on Niea's door.

"Niea," said Tevn, just outside the chamber, opening the door even while asking for permission to do so, "may I come in? I wanted to—"

He stopped when he saw me, chastely wrapped in an embroidered blanket.

"Scholar Cidnosin? I apologise; were you two already discussing something? How odd to see you here. I did not expect to find—"

"Tev," said Niea, standing up and putting a hand on his shoulder with an expression of gravitas, "Sophy and I are courting."

Of course, neither of us had ever announced such a thing aloud before, so you can imagine that I was delighted to hear it, Tevn or not! Imagine me courting someone!

"O," squeaked Tevn, his face reddening at its edges. "O. My apologies. I understand now."

"I should have mentioned—" I began.

"It is none of my business, really," he cut in, flustered. "I just wanted to ask you a few questions about, o dear, our field equipment? For the mission? But that can wait. I hope your nascent relationship is ... pleasant?"

With that, he fled, and Niea smiled to herself.

"Poor Tev," she said. "He might have benefitted from advance notice."

"Will he detest me now, I wonder?" I asked, far more sadly than I intended.

Niea grasped my hand and looked into my eyes with such care that it took my breath away.

"Are you quite all right, Sophy?"

"How long has Tevn borne feelings for you? Truly?"

Niea grasped my hand still tighter.

"Goodness, Sophy, you are as bad as Vincenebras! How many times must I profess that Tevn and I have a strictly collegial relationship?"

"It is not your interpretation of the relationship that concerns me," I responded. "It is his. Niea, did you not see how he blushed? How my presence made him quiver?"

"That was because you are wearing only a blanket. In addition, he finds romance and passion and all that overwhelming and uninteresting, for the most part," said Niea. (In which case, dear E., he is rather like

303

you, though I know you are not immune to the charms of Romance, at least!)

Then I felt simply awful about my jealousy! I thanked her for the reassurance and resolved to handle all this a little more gracefully in the future. Perhaps it is because I had unrequited passion for my dear "friend" Seliara as a child that I projected that experience onto Tevn and Niea. Have I ever had a platonic friend, I wonder? At any rate, I told Niea that because she trusts and respects Tevn, I shall try to do the same.

"I would trust him with my life," she said gravely. "Though I will say that he is most certainly keeping something from me. And I wish above all to find out what it is."

What an auspicious way to begin our return to this mysterious door, no?

Until soon (or as soon as I can manage – we depart presently, so you might not hear from me until long after I've discovered something wonderful!),

Sophy

ANNOTATION BY SOPHY CIDNOSIN, 1003

Let the record show that I am now very lucky to have found my first platonic friend and archival partner, Vyerin Clel.

ANNOTATION BY VYERIN CLEL, 1003

What a relief. I desperately worried that you'd fall in love with me.

LETTER FROM E. CIDNOSIN TO SOPHY CIDNORGHE, 1002

Dear Sophy,

I know it may be many days before you read this letter, so I will try to keep it short. It was lovely to hear of your warm welcome back at the Spheres, and I am relieved that you and Scholar Mawr reached an unsteady peace. It impresses me that you so readily accepted the existence of this "Door", and I look forward to discussing it further.

When you return, I don't suppose there's any way that I could communicate with you via the Echolator? Even for just a few moments? There is much that I would like to say to you – it is no emergency, you needn't float back to the surface instantly – but I would enjoy a brief conversation. (In the meantime, please do not worry about me – I have the written company of Scholar Clel, and Jeime and I have been in close contact.)

Stay safe – I do love you,

E.

LETTER FROM HENEREY CLEL TO E. CIDNOSIN, 1002

My dearest E.,

Normally, I read your letters and find myself energised and delighted. Today, if I may be so frank, I am consumed with nothing but longing.

(Upon reflection, perhaps I—could have phrased that better. That is the sort of unwitting statement I might have made in the past and been roundly mocked by my peers for it. You of all people know what I truly mean, I suspect! But alas, paper is still at a premium here, so I will attempt to explain myself better rather than starting over.)

I wanted to write *You figured it out, E.*, but in truth you have done something far greater – you summoned new questions and produced new context that I never could have imagined. I get the sense that this is far greater than we know even now – greater than Eels, greater than a mysterious Structure, greater than your mysterious journey, greater even than a strange Fleet society of which your mother was the last surviving member. (The word "greater" looks rather strange on paper when you write it over and over, doesn't it?)

And I long to be there with you instead of on this ship. This morning I slumped out to the main deck. I thought that there was no way for me to leave the vessel without abandoning my mission – and it would take days for a transport ship to reach you at the Deep House from our present location (that is, assuming you would even like me to come!). I might beg for some "shore leave", but I do not want to risk being replaced and sent back to work on campus with Chancellor Rawsel again – perish the thought!

So there I sat, boldly dangling my legs over the edge of the ship (though the lovely cool water was tragically far out of reach), pondering everything you had written and not progressing particularly far in my assessment of what I should do. Moments later, I heard someone settling in beside me, and turned to see – to my relief – Lerin, bearing two cups of tea, one of which quickly found its way into my hands.

"We will not have another 'Depth-Craft Vigil' for a few days," Lerin said conversationally. "The old thing will be stored belowdecks, and no one will think anything of it until five days' time, when we will need it again."

"That is interesting," I replied.

"I thought it would interest you, but your voice suggests otherwise."

"My apologies. Surprisingly, my thoughts fly far away today – far past the reaches of this ship."

Lerin laid a friendly hand on my shoulder.

"I know. And I assumed that might be because you would like to visit the Deep House sometime soon. So perhaps I should have begun with this – were you aware that the depth-craft, when launched at full speed and used as intended, could reach that particular part of the ocean before the evening tide?"

Well, that certainly caught my attention!

The venture is not without its risks. Lerin volunteered to cover for me, but I still suspect the Chancellors would not be pleased if they ever discover that I commandeered a depth-craft for personal (research) purposes. Still, E., I feel very much as though we could work through this together if not constrained by medium of correspondence. I hope this will not come across as inappropriately overprotective, but it would bring me great comfort to know that you will not be alone when you venture out to see the Structure – or should I say "Entry"? – again. (And also, this means that we would be able to investigate it from the comfort of a depth-craft. It might surprise you, but I am not over-fond of diving. The options for aesthetically pleasing patterns in wetsuit fashion are so restricted, you know.)

Finally, I must admit I would still yearn to see you even if we were without the excuse of attempting to solve a historical riddle.

As before, however, I leave the decision entirely in your hands. Please let me know your thoughts, and I will begin to set my plans in motion.

Yours, as ever,

Henerey

ANNOTATION BY VYERIN CLEL, 1003

It seems relevant to mention that I turned to my archives in search of more information about Henerey's colleague Lerin. Again employing the assistance of my **EVER GENEROUS** (thank you, Reiv, for that additional annotation) husband, I managed to uncover an unopened letter sent to me a year ago. In fact, it was among many condolences bestowed upon me by Henerey's colleagues – I simply could not bear to read endless streams of words that did nothing but reiterate that he was gone. But I feel that this one might have brought me some comfort, had I been in the correct emotional state to peel back its seal.

It seems silly to write this down when we have already discussed it at length, but by the seas – E. and Henerey had a depth-craft during the seaquake! That gives them slightly more of a fighting chance, doesn't it? But where did it – and they – go?

LETTER FROM LERIN ZUAN VELLEN TO VYERIN CLEL, 1002

Dear Capt. Clel,

Pardon me. I stole your address from a "Notice of Loss" posted at Boundless' School of Observation. ("Stole" is not an extreme exaggeration, as I did literally tear the paper to take your contact details away with me. I am always somehow without a pencil.)

Let me proceed to the point. I miss Henerey very much. I never quite know how to write in response to death, but if it might cheer you to learn that your lost loved one was indeed well loved by everyone who had the chance to strike up a firm friendship with him, then – well, please know that was very much the case.

Henerey spoke constantly of E. Cidnosin, and I can only imagine that, if given a second chance to decide whether to visit that house on that fateful day, he would not have changed his plans. That, at least, comforts me.

Now it's time for something quite sentimental that I doubt any other well-wisher will be capable of sharing with you. During our brief acquaintance aboard the *Sagacity*, I often teased Henerey about his fondness for creatures that some might find rather unsettling. The Winged Nudibranchs, for example, which flutter like flying fish in the First Ocean waters (and which we discovered together), seemed perfectly charming to him. (I found them horrific but awe-invoking – truly Sublime.) At any rate, I have proposed to the Department of Classification that we call this particular species "Clel's Winged Nudibranch". I will think of your brother each time I look upon those

eerie creatures (which, unfortunately, is more often that I would like) –
and I hope that might bring you some pleasure.

With fondest regards,

Schr Lerin Zuan Vellen

P.S. You may wish to avoid reading this postscript until years hence,
because I have a more practical question for you. Have you any idea
what became of Henerey's scientific journals from his time aboard
the *Sagacity*? He shared with me some remarkable hypotheses about
the behaviour of our infamous rays, and I think they are worthy of
further investigation by his colleagues. I attempted to raise this in
the Department (when suggesting the aforementioned memorial
Nudibranch renaming), but they ignored me entirely. If his writings on
the subject still exist, I would encourage you to seek publication for them.

Even via alternative channels, if necessary.

LETTER FROM E. CIDNOSIN TO HENEREY CLEL, 1002

Dearest Henerey,

It is well past three in the morning, but giddiness kept me from my
bedtime. Your – "plans", as I shall euphemistically term them – leave
me breathlessly anxious, but I accept them. So long as you're sure that
your journey in the depth-craft will go safely, I would love nothing more
than to see you. Of course, I shall certainly spend the next few hours
fixating on all the possible ways in which our plans could go awry, but
I pulled out my sketching materials and now scribble to keep my mind
busy. (This activity often helps me resist the urge to "check" things when
I feel anxious.)

Please do not be troubled! I do not anticipate that our meeting will
involve anything other than the indescribable delights of enjoying your
presence while simultaneously assessing the nature of the Entry from a
depth-craft. If we happen to make a slight detour into that luminescent

world – well, then, I will consider myself lucky to do so in your company. (Was that too bold? I am far too weary to care.)

Yours with love,

E.

LETTER FROM HENEREY CLEL TO E. CIDNOSIN, 1002

Dearest E.,

I must be brief. The plans I set in motion are moving indeed. Somehow, impossibly, barring an error in navigation, I will be at the Deep House in a mere three hours. Perhaps I shall even beat this letter there! In which case, I presume you will open this letter after I've already left. I hope we enjoyed our time together in the future!

~~There is much more that I wish to say to you~~

~~I assume you chose the words with which to sign off your letter after an exhausting evening of research and perhaps you did not intend to express the exact sentiment that you expressed but I very much happen to agree but I do not wish to echo it back to you until I have confirmed that you are comfortable~~

O, never mind all that – I will see you soon!

Yours with love and haste,

Henerey

EXCERPT FROM THE DAYBOOK OF HENEREY CLEL, 1002

Dear future readers,

I write this while tucked away in the very belly of that funny little depth-craft my colleagues were all so eager to avoid, riding off on a secret journey to visit my dear correspondent E. and investigate a mysterious Structure! I feel like a boy again (which is a funny statement indeed, as I am quite sure that I never defied social expectations and professional responsibilities in the name of Love and Discovery like this when I was younger).

It turns out that I am quite a deft hand at captaining! Which is to say that even this old thing possesses automatic navigation. Hence I may journal while I slide through the water at an alarming speed. And can you guess what else? Up above me, far away on the surface, I spy a distinctive silhouette that I recognise as a mail-boat! Yes, it is that sleek, conical vessel in its recognisable blue and gold. Thanks to a fine engine, it moves just about as fast as my depth-craft. Perhaps I should have stowed away on one of those instead and avoided this whole affair. At any rate, it delights me that I may now cruise in the mail-boat's wake and enjoy the same journey undertaken by many of our letters carried to and from the Deep House!

I am not entirely alone inside the depth-craft – to my surprise, I see a small sandfly buzzing about the control panels. I must confess that I know very little of insects (my studies have focused so entirely on marine animals that those who fly and skim their way across the water make me feel completely out of my depth!). I marvel that this otherwise unremarkable representative of the species has become a pioneer – the first of its kind, perhaps, to travel so far and so fast beneath the waves. (Or perhaps every day a new fly becomes trapped by accident in a depth-craft and perishes, never telling its peers what lies beyond their world. Goodness, what a morose thought. How unlike me!)

In any case, I appreciate the insect's companionship, because I am slightly anxious about what might await me when I return – what a lovely word to use – to the Deep House. What E. and I shared over the past few months seems too unbelievable to be true. As much as I cling to that one glimmering evening we spent in each other's company, there is a part of me that fears she will face disappointment once she meets me again. (I must have changed the visual narrative of my outfit

311

four times this morning in preparation. I hope I look my best in the final option – attempting an elegant yet adventurous appearance, with a flexible floor-length Research Robe that would prove suitable both for quiet conversation in a cosy corner of a library or sloshing through waist-deep algae for a field investigation.) Yet I force myself to turn to the letters and reread them again and again in these moments of doubt, letting her words face off with my fears. O, E., she is like no other. Now I gaze off into these sunset-hued clouds that I can spy – filtered through the water – with the rosiest and most sentimental of emotions.

I find the journey increasingly turbulent as we draw closer to the reefs. Unfortunately, even with its convenient speed, this depth-craft does not offer such useful, modern features as safety restraints – so I fear that I must abandon my pen and cling as tightly as possible to the wall in the hopes that I will not be too irreparably jostled!

I shall sign off here, at last. Since I've now reached the last page, I hope I might be able to drop off this daybook at E.'s home before we head out on our mission. I do so hate having too many things in my bag when I do not need them. I will carry my usual scientific journal with me, of course, to record any observations that cannot wait until we return to the Deep House and enjoy a cup of tea.

Sincerely,

Schr Henerey Clel

ANNOTATION BY VYERIN CLEL, 1003

So there you have it. The last thing my brother ever wrote, as far as I know. Optimistic, earnest, vulnerable.

I never thought that we would find such an intentional finale of a document. It felt tragic enough to think that my brother and his mysterious love interest planned a romantic tryst that ended in disaster.

All we have read and seen thus far, however, suggests that our siblings were better prepared for this calamity than we expected. I know we hoped that compiling this narrative would help us better understand what happened in the past. Yet it seems that we may only succeed in that mission by bringing this mystery into the present and employing all that is at our disposal to solve it.

(I am in accord, of course. —S.)

Chapter 22

TRANSCRIPT OF A CONVERSATION BETWEEN JEIME ALESTARRE, VYERIN CLEL, AND SOPHY AND NIEA CIDNORGHE, 1003

(Transcribed at the insistence of Clel and Cidnorghe through the kind generosity of Mr. Reiv Clel: Husband, Stenographer, and Unofficial Archival Assistant)

SOPHY CIDNORGHE: Thank you for meeting with us, Jeime.
> Yes, I know it's contrived, but I did want to greet you officially
> so we could record it in our transcript.

(Duly noted! –R.)

JEIME ALESTARRE: The pleasure is mine. Of course, I had no
> choice. I knew this day would come.
SOPHY CIDNORGHE: Then why didn't you say anything to me?
> Anything at all?
VYERIN: Sophy's—
SOPHY: Do you object, Vy?
VYERIN: I was about to say that Sophy's questions are fair, Jeime.
> You could have spared us this entire archival adventure.

JEIME: What would you two have me say? Would you have believed me if I told you what I knew? Your own sister could not even tell you! She told me she worried that you—

SOPHY: That was a different time. You have no idea what I've seen, and what I've experienced, and what I believe. Now, at any rate.

JEIME: I am sorry. *(To be fair, she does look rather contrite. No one involved here is in the wrong, in this humble Stenographer's opinion. –R.)* But you must understand. I already feared I had broken my promise to your mother by giving E. so much information – information that, as far as I knew, sent your sister to an uncertain fate! While I did not encourage E. to go out to the Structure with Scholar Clel, and would have warned her against it if she'd told me, I felt responsible all the same. So, as your mother would have done, I chose to wait instead of approaching you with this confession. I hoped that once you read all your sister's letters, you would come to me, and I could own up to my actions and provide answers. Which I am happy to do now.

SOPHY: I am sure Mother would have been immensely pleased that you inspired E., of all people, to literally dive into the unknown in her search for the truth. And I understand, Jeime, that it is not your fault that she did. But how did you know that E.'s letters contained any of this information?

JEIME: A fortunate guess. I knew from E. that she wrote to her correspondent about the Structure. Also, speaking of which, seeing the Captain here is a surprise. I did not even know Scholar Clel had a brother.

VYERIN: Nor did I, until now.

(My dearest, while I am awed by your active participation in this conversation – what does that statement even mean? –R.)

SOPHY: You said you would provide us with answers, so let

315

us proceed to some more difficult questions, if you would be so kind.

VYERIN: We know about the, er, lifecycles of the Structures. I mean, the Entries. Whatever you wish to call them. We've learned a little, anyway. You said the Entry at the Deep House would explode or what have you in two months' time. Why did it happen earlier than predicted?

JEIME: I thought perhaps you would have figured this out already.

SOPHY: More's the pity. I second Vyerin's question.

JEIME: The Entries emerge from—wherever. That's the first stage. The following "burst", as I understand, charges them, as though they were a Battery. The second and more powerful "burst", on the other hand, is their dying breath – the end of the Entry when it does not complete its mission.

VYERIN: What mission?

JEIME: As far as I understand it from what Ami told me – their mission is transportation. Or, more fittingly, evacuation.

REIV CLEL: To where and from what, respectively?

(Behold! I too may pose questions. –R.)

JEIME: I do not know the specifics, but the gist is: away. To another world. To a better place.

NIEA: Is this an examination question with multiple answers from which to choose? In that case, I select "Away".

VYERIN: I, on the other hand, am personally partial to "a better place".

SOPHY: As far as I understand, then, the Fleet were one's garden-variety misguided idealists, yes? They dreamed up a fantastic "better place" to replace – what? Academic ennui? Unfortunate social situations? The Campuses struggle with many issues, to be sure. Scholars like Rawsel – thoughtless, even cruel people – they live among us, of course. But, if you'll

316

forgive the rational pessimism, people like that would exist in *any* civilisation, regardless of how mystical or mysterious its origins. Do you not agree?

JEIME: Perhaps I have mischaracterised their desire. If you will recall what I wrote to E.: yes, the Fleet might seem like just another silly Society of daydreamers. Yet their motivation was not idealism, but fear. If what Ami believed is true, the Entries would bear us to safety. To our very last hope, in fact.

SOPHY: Yet it did the opposite for E. and Henerey.

JEIME: It seems the Fleet calculated exactly how long an Entry could last before our world destroyed it. Perhaps there is something in seawater that is not compatible with Antepelagic technology. I cannot say. But the Deep House Entry did not follow the pattern. And as I said, Sophy, if I thought—if I had suspected that E. was in danger—

SOPHY: I know. I know, Jeime.

JEIME: Here is what I propose. We all know, by now, that E. and Henerey did not disappear during a simple courtship call. Henerey came to the Deep House in a depth-craft to take E. out to investigate the Structure. The explosion that occurred on that fateful day was not the destruction of the Entry. It was the Entry fulfilling its mission because two people in a depth-craft had entered it.

(We all sit in silence. Suddenly, Vyerin starts guffawing out of nowhere, which he has only done before on precisely one occasion. Dear Vy, are you quite all right? –R.)

VYERIN: I knew it. I knew Henerey was too clever and too kind – that slippery seaborn, he's escaped death!

SOPHY: But escaped to where? To that peculiar island that E. visited in her vision?

JEIME: Your sister had a vision of an island? She did not mention that to me.

VYERIN: O, she did far more than see it.

SOPHY: "Vision" is not quite the right term, but I am not sure how to describe it. She told Henerey that it felt as though she travelled to an ineffable elsewhere. A world lit by luminescence instead of sunlight. E. even brought back sketches, if you can believe that!

JEIME: I can indeed. Because I believe I saw the place myself when I was with Arvist in the depth-craft that day.

SOPHY: You—so you and E. were both—

JEIME: No, I did not encounter her. In fact, unlike her, I would not say that I "travelled" anywhere. It was only the briefest glimpse – dark skies, glowing water, the hint of land in the distance – that crossed my sight for a moment before I returned to the task of piloting us away from the explosion. I assumed it was some strange hallucination caused by shock. Perhaps E. and I both witnessed yet another mysterious function of the Structure's technology.

SOPHY: But what manner of technology could transport E. there in such a perplexing fashion? And to what end?

JEIME: I cannot say. This is beyond even the knowledge Ami entrusted to me – o, Sophy, don't look so cross. I can't even begin to hypothesise, I'm afraid.

SOPHY: Cross? Is that what you think?

(Now SOPHY guffaws. Niea pats her arm comfortingly. –R.)

SOPHY: I am—terribly sorry—

NIEA: She hardly knows how to—

SOPHY: I hardly know how to respond to any of this. If this is true, if I can let myself believe that this is true, that E. might be—if this is true, how do we pursue them? I apologise for

318

my outburst. The facts, yes. Must we wait for these "Entries" to appear again?

JEIME: Yes. We require an "Entry" or an "Envoy" to lead us to one. Though from what Ami told me, we know even less of the Envoys than we do the Entries.

VYERIN: And I know even less of the Envoys than you do. Would you care to elaborate?

JEIME: According to the Fleet, the "Envoys" are like – well, they are really like nothing else known to Science. Darbeni proposed that they were akin to automata, created by our Antepelagic ancestors, but other members of the Fleet disagreed and suggested they were a different order of beings with forms unlike our own. All Fleet Scholars seemed to concur that these Envoys travel to various points around the world to guide us to Entries. But no one has ever seen them. I think that anonymous poet that Darbeni revered wrote a poem about them once.

NIEA: Surely not. Sophy, surely not.

JEIME: No, she most certainly did write a poem, otherwise how would we know about this?

SOPHY: No, that is, I—o, blast, Niea, could that really be—

VYERIN: Please tell us, my friend. Is this about the Ridge mission?

(Niea looks at Sophy and nods. –R.)

SOPHY: There is something I simply must show you. The last letter I ever wrote to my sister – she never saw it, as far as I know.

NIEA: And don't forget Tevn's letter.

SOPHY: I think—o, seas, I think it might help us understand this even further.

(We stopped talking here so that Sophy may produce the letters. O, I do hope this is not a fool's hope. –R.)

319

LETTER FROM SOPHY CIDNOSIN TO E. CIDNOSIN, 1002

Dearest E.,

~~I hope this letter will not trouble you~~
~~I have gone back and forth in my attempts to~~
~~Today was unlike any other~~

As you can see, I hardly know how to begin.

Ever since your accident, dear E., I never know what to say to you. Before I left, I noticed this stiffness between us, some strange spell that I did not know how to disenchant, and I sorrowed to think that I might have said or done something during your convalescence that offended you. But it occurs to me now that my interpretation of your behaviour has been rather limited and self-centred. For I imagine that whatever experience you had in the water made it hard for you to understand how to return to "normalcy" – if such a thing exists. I understand this now because I too experienced something unexpected and I do not know how to proceed.

So, in my confusion, I turn to you. And I hope that if there was anything about your accident that you did not wish to share, that you did not know how to process or understand – I hope you will understand my position, in this moment, and perhaps feel comfortable telling me about your experience in the future.

Yesterday, we travelled directly from the Spheres to the Point of Interest without stopping along the way, without speaking often, and with much buzzing in our minds. We could not have made it without the automata, which carried us quite cheerfully. Their clicks brought solace to us – or to me, at any rate. I think the repetitive noise certainly annoyed Scholar Mawr, and possibly even Vincenebras.

Once we arrived, we assembled our Bubbles, enjoyed a brief meal – accompanied by an appetiser of more nervous chattering. Thus sated, we descended into that canyon once more. I found myself strangely nostalgic for the great Nautilus – at least it brought some light to the depths!

I was not nostalgic, however, for those days when the connection between myself and Niea was more tenuous. This time, she squeezed my hand as we swam downwards, and even through my diving glove I felt her fondness and warmth!

For some time, I almost thought that we would never reach this door – that my colleagues shared a hallucination, that it had been a waking dream, that some great creature would steal the door away before I would have the chance to lay my eyes upon such a spectacle. But sure enough, Irye's lantern soon cast eerie beams on something glimmering in the depths, and we floated downwards to the inexplicable.

Due to the isolated circumstances of our upbringing, dear E., I can remember with near-perfect clarity most of the doors I have encountered in my short life. The airlock portal, of course. Mother and Father's elegantly carved white-coral door, always open. Yours and Arvist's – both always closed. The grey door of my dormitory, the windowed door of the lecture hall where I spent much of my time as an Apprentice, the tall cast-bronze door inlaid with reliefs of great Cartographical Accomplishments that swung open with such cacophony every time I dared to enter the Department of Wayfinding—

Compared to all of those, I would not deem this door particularly exceptional in form alone. It was finely wrought, to be sure, but so are the tracery doors that lead to the School of Inspiration studios, or even the way in which Father carefully finished Mother's handiwork at the airlock by adding in a wreath of sea-floral forms for the tympanum. What was so unusual about this door was the location and the history. Was it last opened on a floating island in the heavens, a thousand years ago, by people who never thought their world would one day be destroyed? What Antepelagic history might we find inside?

Vincenebras and Irye set to pressing a kind of clay onto the door to take an impression, while Niea glided to the front of our group, took several photographs, and then placed her gloved hand tenderly on the door-ring. Ylaret offered her a crowbar, but Niea shook her head.

"I will open it if it gives," Niea said, softly. "But if it does not, we will proceed with caution. I do not wish to damage it unduly."

We nodded in agreement. I thought perhaps Vincenebras would have objected, but he – for once – said nothing. As soon as Niea gave the ring the slightest of tugs, the door floated open, revealing a tunnel of water lit by bioluminescent algae.

Tevn was the first to speak. He played it so casually – slipping into that passageway as though it were the door to his dormitory and turning around to face us with a look of careful confusion.

"Who can make sense of this?" Tevn's question crackled through my communicator, and I find myself pondering it still. Did he choose those words with intent? He did not say "What is this?" or "I think I've found something" – he asked us for interpretation.

"Perhaps we will find it more sensical once we enter," replied Vincenebras. "If you agree, Niea?"

Niea nodded her assent. "So long as one of us stays here and goes for help if we—do not return," she said. "I am happy to take this role myself if necessary."

"Nonsense!" exclaimed Irye. "Surely you, of all assembled, should go if you wish. I will remain and content myself with listening to you if the communicators stay in range. I shall keep an ear out for other strange sounds, too!"

The tunnel – or hallway – or whatever you would like to call it – behind the door took us all by surprise. There was nothing to suggest it was wrought by human hands – it resembled a lava-carved passageway, or perhaps those sheaths in which the Tube-Worms sleep. Unsurprisingly, Niea turned to me moments after we entered, her eyes alight.

"If a great Tube-Worm made this tunnel, dear Sophy, I shall simply perish of excitement!"

I do believe I love her.

Though the tunnel was filled with water – not an air pocket in sight, disappointingly – I could tell that it did not flow in and out regularly. The ceiling stood about a fathom above my head, and both top and bottom of this "cave" featured the most extraordinary seagrasses the height of my waist, growing in such great quantities that it felt as though we walked through a sea of clouds. Once I thought I felt something far more mobile than seagrass slip across my leg – but I did not glance down quickly enough to identify it. Perhaps that was for the best.

The tunnel proceeded horizontally for a time before reaching a wall beneath which stood another descending hole. And into that inexplicable pit swirled the topmost steps of a spiralling staircase. I cannot tell you what colour the stairs were or of what material they were crafted, for each step's surface was encrusted with a millennium's worth of deep red algae.

Because of the water, of course, it was difficult to walk down the stairs as we would at home – and you know I certainly thought back to the dear old Deep House staircase, remembering how you mastered the art of stepping just so to keep the stairs from creaking and prevent anyone from hearing you from up above. At any rate, we had no need to worry about that, since we swam our way down instead. We did not speak – at least not that I can recall, anyway. The only sound was the occasional clicking of Niea's camera.

At the bottom: another door, in the same style as the one guarding the mysterious place, though this one seemed smaller, lither, and certainly less worn by the constant efforts of the ocean. Its iridescence was unsurpassed. If I half-closed my eyes (which I did frequently enough, if only to recalibrate my vision to ensure that I might truly see everything before me) I could imagine that the door consisted of constellations reflecting on the water.

"Would someone else prefer the honours this time?" said Niea. Even her ebullient voice was hushed. None of us accepted her offer, but I did swim forward and take her hand in mine once more. Before she could reach with her opposite arm to pull on this door, it glided open of its own volition.

And our ears began to pick up something unexpected.

"Irye!" shouted Ylaret. "Can you hear this?"

Though Irye's communicator was nearly out of range, I heard their voice crackle faintly.

"Hear what, dear Ylaret?"

"No matter. I shall describe it to you," she replied, switching to a private broadcast. I saw her lips moving silently under her helmet.

Indeed, at the back of my mind, I sensed some unknown melody – extremely faint and barely pushing through the static of my communicator, but present nonetheless. A sound lush and complex and made with no instrument I could recognise – perhaps in the string family? – with what felt like a thousand tempos layering over and over each other. I did indeed wish, in the moment, that Irye could hear it!

But that music quickly became the least important sound. Because interwoven into it – I swear, E., though we had no way of recording it, and likely we shall never be believed after what else came to pass – was a voice. No. It was more like the music became a voice, a voice that rang through our communicators and vibrated through the water like an ocean of choirs.

"You return," the voice sang. "It worried me. I spent nights thinking you perished and enumerated all the ways in which that might have come to pass. But you are here at last! Why do you not enter?"

Formal words. Odd words. Strangely enough, I remember the precise thoughts that flooded my mind as soon as I heard this speech – namely, that the voice spoke in crisp Academic Vernacular rather than a regional language, and that the unknown entity talked – not quite with an accent, but it was rather as though the mediocre sounds of our speech were impossible for the mellifluous being to recreate. Later, Niea compared it to the experience of hearing a trained soprano drone in a drab monotone.

Such thoughts, however, halted when this mysterious announcement received an unexpected reply.

"My apologies," said Tevn. "I did not intend to leave you for so long. I was prevented from returning. May my friends enter with me?"

How did the figure hear these words? I wonder. Tevn spoke into the communicator with his helmet still on. Yet as if in response, the water rippled about our bodies, pushing us – well, I can hardly say pushing, as that sounds far more aggressive than I intend – perhaps I mean propelling us through the hall into the chamber until we reached what appeared to be a cosy, well-equipped conservatory that just happened to be at the bottom of the ocean.

It appeared to be made entirely of glass, and the sunlight dazzled in—

Well, it occurs to me now that of course there is no sunlight under the water in the abyssal zone. Perhaps, in retrospect, I should say that there was – o, how would I even describe it – some form of carefully cultivated phosphorescence that produced the illusion of light shining through these windows?

At any rate, I can say with confidence that there were plants, hence the conservatory analogy, but instead of being pinned back in pots, they were wrapped around large, metallic sculptures – the forms of which were all soft, biomorphic shapes – so that the overall appearance of the place suggested it had been built by a mythical Scholar of Life who also happened to affiliate with the School of Inspiration. O, and in case you somehow forgot, let me remind you that this entire "room" was still filled with water – from floor to ceiling – but it felt warmer, and softer, and clearer than any water we encountered previously, such that I nearly forgot we were completely immersed!

In the centre of the room, sitting on a throne made of what looked like the pulsing, breathing appendages of some massive unknown Nudibranch, was a finned figure. She was tall, perhaps a few fathoms in height, but utterly transparent – which is not to say that I saw her internal organs on display (thank goodness). She was more like a phantom: I could discern the outlines of her face, her rippling hair, and the gown-like wrapping that covered her torso but did not obscure the great tail beneath. (Niea pointed out, afterwards, that the tail was not that of a fish but cetacean in nature. Covered in barnacles. Not scaled, but soft like a dolphin's skin.)

"O, curious one, comical one," she sang, "I missed you! You are so delicate that I was certain some ill had befallen you. But you brought me the greatest gift that you could! So many wise ones, so many scholars, though I asked only for one more!"

"Please wait – I have not yet told them," Tevn said, quickly, as he swam across the strange little room to this sunken singer.

"Tevn," whispered Niea. "This was what you saw."

Tevn nodded slowly, tipping his helmet over as though its weight might sink his head to the very floor.

"But what is this?" asked Ylaret – only to me, I think, as nobody else seemed to react.

What was it indeed, E.? As I gazed around the room, I searched for recognisable signs of Antepelagic architecture or technology – images of rainbows, clouds, and other Upward Archipelago iconography, you know – anything that might look vaguely and comfortingly familiar. But it was all incomprehensibly new. The panels that made up the radiant glass room were not joined together. It was as though a sleek cube dropped fully formed from the surface to land here. Even Mother could not mask her glass seams so well! And while I initially thought the glass lacked any ornament, upon closer inspection I could detect tessellating geometric forms.

The sea-woman swam slightly closer to us, maintaining a safe distance. Her eyes – transparent domes, as ethereal as the rest of her – swept over our company.

"Your lives are the greatest treasures to me, the most precious – is it morsels?" she hummed inquisitively, inching nearer so she could wrap her transparent fingers around Tevn's hand.

"Let's hope not!" uttered Vincenebras in a tone so far from his usual joviality that it made my heart skip.

"The word you want is 'jewels', my friend," replied Tevn, daintily holding her hand like an adult might hold fondly on to a toddler. "Let me speak with them."

Niea gripped my hand like an adult might desperately hold on to a toddler who has tumbled too close to the side of a ship.

"Please do, Tev," Niea said.

Tevn shrugged as the song continued. He did not look scared, but rather – bashful?

"Where do I even begin? Do I begin a year ago, when I left you during our dive and first discovered this place? Do I begin when—"

"Is it true?" called the sea-woman, suddenly dropping Tevn's hand. "Is it true what I see?"

"Yes," said Tevn patiently, "they really are here, and now I need to explain—"

"No, not here," she said, cocking her head as though gazing at someone in the far distance. (I turned around and saw nothing.) "Two have found an Entry. Two are curious. Two will escape. At long last, a chance emerges!"

Suddenly, the sea-woman patted Tevn on the shoulder – affectionately, I might even say, as Father might have done to us! With unexpected force, she propelled herself down to the "floor", where I noticed – for the first time – how the tiles glistened. For just a moment I saw a ring of light form around her – like how one might see the sky flash green after the sun sets – and then, right before our eyes, she began to glimmer away, becoming fainter and fainter. As she faded, a great tremor suddenly shook the room.

"My vigil ends at last," she called, singing out one last time in that voice to which I had not quite grown accustomed. "You must leave. This is not your path!"

"No!" shouted Tevn, his cry reverberating painfully through my ears – since he had not thought to silence his communicator before screaming.

The room shuddered violently again, sending one of the sculpted plant "vessels" spiralling to the floor. Right after it shattered, object and plant alike vanished completely. Like the sea-woman, they seemed to dissolve, but, o, E., I hardly know how to explain this – it was as though they dissolved into sound. Three pulsing notes, again and again, seemed to project from that very spot on the floor where the vase had fallen.

Then the windows cracked, and a sea of sound poured in, erasing the walls in broad strokes, consuming the plants and the carvings and producing different harmonies and tempos for each object, and horrific though it all was I thought for a moment what a wonder it would be to become a part of that melodious multitude—

Until another sound – Niea's voice – brought me back to myself.

"To the door!" she shouted as the ever-hungry music multiplied.

"You needn't tell me twice!" cried Ylaret before slipping back into the hallway, Vincenebras hot on her fins. By instinct, I pulled Niea towards me, but she wrested free of my grasp.

"I will collect Tev and bring up the rear," she said in the most cursedly reasonable voice, pressing her helmet towards mine in a diver's kiss. Indeed, Tevn stayed stalled in the centre of the room, paddling aimlessly. A thousand new harmonies emerged around us.

"You had better," I said with far more force than I intended.

The vibrant colours blurred my vision, but I kept my eye on the darkness of the tunnel beyond the door. Ylaret and Vincenebras made good time – I could barely see them in front of me – and they'd left not a moment too soon, as the walls of the tunnel itself began to shake and sound. I lagged a little, as I kept glancing behind me, and eventually spotted Niea tugging Tevn. The music rolled in a great circle around them, consuming the tunnel walls just after Niea cleared them. And her pace kept slowing.

So I turned back.

I never thought of myself as a particularly strong swimmer – you and Arvist could easily overtake me – but the circumstances gave me a speed I did not know I possessed. I glided to them, seized Tevn, grabbed Niea by the hand, and pulled them both along. My legs burned beneath me as I kicked through the seagrass. Moments later, we emerged, shooting out of the tunnel just as it collapsed behind us.

Even the door was gone – not broken or damaged, but vanished. The wall of the canyon remained intact. As it was meant to be.

And the music stopped.

Perhaps we should have taken some more photographs or measurements. Surely all of our Scholarly instincts would have urged us to. Instead, we returned to our Bubbles, breathing heavily, crowded together in one fused space, and ate a simple meal.

Well, I say together, but there was one of our number missing. Tevn seemed utterly spent when we returned. Ylaret gently assessed his injuries, though shock appeared to be his foremost symptom. Quietly and dazedly, he begged to return to his own Bubble and spend some time by himself. Perhaps he feared we might interrogate him. There was such a pallor to his face that Niea agreed, urging him to sleep and recover.

The rest of us, I expect, will not rest for some time. It has been hours and we are still awake, talking among ourselves, replaying and reciting everything that we can remember about the experience. Irye, our brave lookout, proved the most reassuring of us all, and promised to personally validate and support our "story".

Why do I invalidate it by putting it in quotation marks? Do I doubt what I saw with my own eyes? Certainly I fear others will not believe it. At some point – when we feel we are ready – we will begin the difficult task of preparing a statement to share with the Chancellors. To think that this marvel occurred for us and we cannot understand it – and that we have no proof, no evidence, no data to analyse! (There are the photographs, of course, though they need to be developed. Niea fears that our perilous escape may have damaged the device's delicate machinery.)

And yet there is no one in this world, I believe, who may understand this feeling so well as you, my dear sister. I do so very much love you.

More to come,

Sophy

P.S. It is morning now, and I decided to write you a few more lines. Tevn is gone! I know not how. He left Niea a note, which she reads right now as I write. I find it difficult to believe I am not dreaming. When I first awakened, I forgot everything – it felt like a normal day on the expedition – and then it rushed back to me.

E., do you believe me? What do you advise? I hope I will be able to speak with you soon. I find myself completely adrift and in need of my elder sister. I am desperate to talk about this and anything else that you would like. I shall end this letter here for now. I cannot wait to see you again.

LETTER FROM TEVN WINIVER MAWR TO ELINIEA HAYVE FORGHE, 1002

My friend:

I hate to disappear once more. Truly. But this time I will not do so without an explanation (of sorts). I do apologise for my silence last night. Too much happened too quickly. I cannot abide with Chancellor Rawsel etc. any longer. So I must take the time to put my thoughts in order as though they were a conservatory of underwater plants tended by a mysterious guardian from another world (see, at the very least, I can still jest about what has happened).

I suspected I could not deceive you for long. In fact, you know that I am incapable of deceiving anyone, so perhaps it is surprising that my various ruses vaguely succeeded at all. But you may still have many questions, so please enjoy what follows as I attempt to fill any gaps in your knowledge.

I encountered her – the sea-woman, the spirit, whatever you wish to call her (her name, she told me, was a particular melody that I could never write down, not even with Irye's composition paper to hand) – during our mission a year ago. When we left the capsule that day and you suggested that we explore by ourselves, I agreed with a haste that surprised me. I did not feel entirely myself. As I swam away from you and dived deep into the trench, I could barely control my strokes. Heavy music enticed me closer to a destination I could not name. Though you will hardly believe it, I have the distinct, dreamlike memory of unfastening my tether to swim further, even while my rational mind lambasted me for such life-threatening foolishness.

Freed from my one connection to you and our depth-craft, I reached the ledge. I noticed the architecture, opened that glistening door accented with algae – and found myself in the unnatural light of the chamber for the very first time.

You know that I always dreamed of the day when I would discover something truly inexplicable, something magical, something that no one else had ever seen before.

But then as soon as I did, it shattered me. I did not feel remarkable. I did not feel clever or curious or awed by the mysteries of the sea. I became ill. My hands shook. My head ached. I could not grasp the fact that she was real. I could not believe my own senses. And that shock weakened me in ways I did not expect – as you discovered when you pulled me back to the depth-craft that day. (Impossibly, I have no memory of finding and reattaching my tether. Yet some inexplicable providence intended for me to return to the surface.)

Thanks to your quick thinking, I made it safely back to campus. Though I stayed quiet throughout our return journey, I began indiscreetly babbling about my experience to the medics who received me at the infirmary. Clearly they were alarmed, given the importance of our expedition, and promptly reported their observations to Chancellor Rawsel. One very polite and sinister private interrogation later, and the Chancellor announced his verdict: he wanted so very much to believe me, but I had nothing – no proof, no corroboration by my partner, nothing other than my relatively un-besmirched reputation as a young scholar of moderate promise – to confirm my account.

This I expected. Ever since you and I joined the Expedition and started dealing with Rawsel and Boundless Campus, I learned early on that there is no room for anything that does not fit into the neat categories into which the Boundless Scholars organise their little World.

But I did not expect him to make me a bargain.

Because my account was "so remarkable" and my description "so lucid" and the Ridge expedition "of such monumental importance", the Chancellors would allow me another opportunity to prove what I had seen.

Provided I, strictly speaking, was not the one to prove it.

In Rawsel's mind I was biased – and possibly traumatised – and in no mental state, he told me, to return to such a high-stakes mission. It was all for my own wellbeing, of course, that I would take a brief sabbatical in a medical rehabilitation apartment – off-campus, in the complex by Sapient Bay – so I could restore myself. And to ensure that the rest of the new team – for now Rawsel would form a team to return to the Ridge, to guarantee as many corroborators as possible – was not in any way influenced by my opinion.

Most of all, I was not, under any circumstances, to contact you until the mission was complete.

Why did I agree to these ridiculous terms, you might ask? Well, Niea, you understand my weaknesses better than anyone. Somehow, Chancellor Rawsel appealed to my greatest ambition in life – to change the world by discovering something anomalous. If what I saw was real, then our entire perception of the deep ocean would change forever. And to think I would be the one – along with you and your colleagues – to usher it in! I could not resist.

The Chancellor was not pleased with the speed of your progress, I'm sorry to say. You see, in his attempt to formulate this contrived and relatively nonsensical plan, he neglected one thing – only I had been to the door in the trench. You attempting to find it on your own would be like searching for an oyster in the open ocean. (Unless the music were to lure you as it did me, but how could we count on that?)

So when Sophy left unexpectedly, I decided to strike a deal of my own. I proposed that I would rejoin the mission and "help" you find the door. Unobtrusively, needless to say. And Rawsel accepted my new terms.

Now, you might think to yourself – *Tevn, that makes no sense. Did Rawsel not set up this entire complicated operation* because *he was concerned about you "influencing" the mission?*

Well, I tend to agree. It is all contradictory and confusing. Here is the best that I can understand it – Chancellor Rawsel, for reasons unknown to me, wanted desperately to find that door. Needed to find it. Quickly. And when his complex first attempt did not produce satisfactory results, he decided to try something else.

Perhaps I would have been more suspicious if it weren't for the fact that I had another reason to find the door again.

You may have predicted all I've written so far. But I would be most impressed if you had deduced this: that the sea-woman and I became ... friends?

We did not exchange a word during my first encounter. At least, not in any language that I could understand. She did sing, of course, and somehow that song followed me out of the sea.

It was during my first week of rehabilitation that I heard her again. I would not say that the voice was "in my mind": I could hear it reverberate around the walls of my flat, and it grew louder under particular circumstances (in the evenings, when the rain fell, when I lay prone, and, fittingly, whenever I held a seashell to my ear in that childlike way). Somehow, she spoke Archaic Scholar and quickly picked up Academic Vernacular – she told me at one point that she had "requested every book" (?) on the subject of our language as soon as she met me – and while she found my metaphors incomprehensible and my slang laughable, we connected. (Dare I say she reminded me of you?) She told me such things, Niea, things you would never believe – talk of a Society in some incomprehensible Elsewhere, where great Scholars and Artists and Mechanists and Leaders wait for us – for our return – no, it's more than that – for our rescue – and more than anything I wanted to go there with her, and she said I might, and I could even bring someone with me to that other world, and—

And now she is gone. And I will never see all that of which she spoke.

But I intend to sneak out before you wake and my time for this exposition runs short. I shall have to tell the rest in the future. Whatever happens, I hope you will remember how much I respect and care about you. You would think that a man with seven sisters would not have need of an eighth – but I am fortunate beyond words to have found you.

With love,

Tevn

P.S. I reread my letter and found it far too predictably sentimental for my tastes. Let me make you a promise, which I hope shall speak louder than words. If you ever find yourself face-to-face with a thrilling anomaly or unexplained event – let me know if I can help. I don't suppose I will be particularly useful with my Anxious Personality and all that, but I offer my assistance nevertheless. It is the least I can do. To that end, my parents will be happy to provide you with my current whereabouts in the future should you need them. (Yes, this time I have told them where I am going.)

ANNOTATION BY SOPHY CIDNORGHE, 1003

The story must be finished, so I shall now write down what I can remember. After Tevn left, we returned to the station. (Now, I don't fully understand how Tevn managed to "leave", but I imagine he simply got a head start back to the Spheres on his automaton, used the station communicator to contact some trusted contact (his mother?), and borrowed the emergency capsule to make his escape. Though I understand his desire to depart dramatically, I do think it must have been an awful lot of extra work.)

When we arrived, Niea crammed us all into that funny little communication room so that we could "call" Chancellor Rawsel as a unified body. Our plan was to briefly summarise our experience of the day prior and to argue the following – that this "experiment" to verify Tevn's account was unethical and that it was under no circumstances appropriate for us to continue our work until Rawsel came clean with us about his interests in this expedition.

It failed. Spectacularly. Now, we did not tell him everything – we said little of the music or the conservatory or really anything other than that the door and all behind it had been destroyed. And, at any rate, Chancellor Rawsel seemed to hear nothing. All he would say – over and over again, as though they were the only words he knew – was this:

"And what has become of the envoy?"

(Well, now I recognise that the last word should have been capitalised.)

I might have folded there, I must admit. Even Niea seemed shaken by Chancellor Rawsel's odd behaviour. But then Ylaret pushed in front of us and waved at the communicator (as though the Chancellor could see her – understandable, since it is so very strange to just hear a voice coming out of nowhere!).

"It's Scholar Ylaret Tamseln here, Chancellor Rawsel. I do not know what has gotten you into such a state, but please believe me – whatever was down there is gone. Still, we would very much like to know what it was, and Scholar Mawr suggested that you might have some answers for us. We desperately want to understand, you know. If you do not offer us some explanation, I am afraid we might have to enlist the assistance of our Colleagues to puzzle out this strange occurrence. We did take photographs. Surely you would not mind if we took this story to the papers to see what the public makes of it?"

Vincenebras grinned, applauded, and parted his lips as though he were about to cheer – which likely would not have helped our position. Irye, thinking quickly, placed their hands over Vincenebras' mouth and pulled him into an awkward embrace.

Static played over the communicator for a few minutes before Rawsel spoke again.

"I need not provide you with any answers. I am satisfied with your account that nothing down there could have survived the destruction, Scholar Tamseln. At this point, I happily declare this mission complete, and I will tell the other Chancellors and the presses that I pulled you out of the Ridge due to a recently confirmed study that suggests extended exposure to deep-water pressures can cause hallucinations and Maladies of the Mind. You will all be given a sabbatical to recover, and once a few years have passed, we will discuss your return to Scholarly work."

"That won't be necessary," said Niea. "Please send my best regards – and my resignation – to the Scholars of Life."

Now it was my turn to open my mouth, though I needed no Irye to silence me. It occurred to me just then that everything I had worked for – my career, my research, all I had hoped to discover and learn – might vanish in an instant. I had heard rumours of Scholarly "exiles", those given extended "sabbaticals" due to antisocial behaviour that eventually turned into self-induced Scholarly Seclusion like my father's, and how even those who decided to leave the Academy of their own accord would never be able to—

Then – for the first time in my life – I silenced that Scholarly part of myself.

"And mine to the Scholars of Wayfinding," I said.

I suspect there was some assorted chatter afterwards – perhaps more quiet fury from Rawsel, perhaps Vincenebras cutting in to say, "I too resign!" or something of the sort – really, it's been a year, and a traumatic one at that, and it's remarkable that I remember any of this with clarity.

But I do remember how Rawsel bid us farewell. It was, with unbelievable cruelty, through these words that haunt me:

"As you have all decided to end your relationships with the Academic world, perhaps your research skills might be better put to use in investigating the Deep House – since I hear rumours that there has been a second seaquake."

I won't continue, as you know how this part of the story ends.

But here is the part that embarrasses me the most – no, "shames" is perhaps a more appropriate term. Niea and I do not speak about what we experienced in that "conservatory". (O, yes, she would like me to clarify that she has tried to raise the subject before, but I did not wish to discuss it.) Our crew managed to move on with our lives, for the most part – Niea with her work on the Sunken School, for example. Irye, I believe, continues research with the Scholars of Sound since that particular department is far too chaotic to even notice that one of their members has been excommunicated by the Chancellors – and occasionally advises Ylaret and Vincenebras in their joint business venture (shocking, I know), which involves offering "writing workshops inspired by the cosmos" to participants for a small fee.

To be fair, when we all ascended to the surface for the last time in the capsule, we came to a general agreement that it was probably for the best that we forget our experience. First of all, what we saw was gone – permanently – and though some clues might remain in the wreckage, we did not feel particularly inclined to pursue them. Perhaps this was because we all realised, in an instant, that though we are Scholars, there are some parts of the universe that we just cannot understand – and should not, moreover.

I suspect it was also some kind of self-denial: if we did not research this further, it would be all the easier to catalogue the experience away in our brains as something strange that happened in the past from which we have moved on. What we saw down there terrified us – and more than that – threatened to completely restructure our understanding of the world, defying everything we had ever known.

And in my case personally, I had too much else on my mind to worry about the sea-woman – because my sister had disappeared. In a grimly convenient way, my thoughts were far more occupied with her whereabouts than other mysteries under the sea.

Now, however, it is abundantly clear that these two mysteries must be intertwined. At least, I hypothesise that they may be. And I intend, as you might imagine, to go after them.

ANNOTATION BY VYERIN CLEL, 1003

Let the record show that *we* intend to go after them.

337

Chapter 23

HANDWRITTEN NOTE FROM SOPHY CIDNORGHE TO VYERIN CLEL, 1003

Dear, dear Vy:

My apologies in advance for sneaking out, unnoticed, before sunrise – it was very kind of you to offer to see me off, but since you all seem so happily fast asleep I will leave a written farewell instead! (I also did not have a piece of stationery at hand, so I appropriated this opera invitation (Reiv's?) from the waste-bin to scribble on its empty verso – I hope you will forgive me, as I rather suspect he did not know that "Someone" disposed of it . . .)

I could waste an indefinite amount of ink praising your charming family and your generous hospitality, but we both know there are far more pressing matters afoot. I am so pleased with the progress made in just one short visit. (Can you believe it has only been seven days since my wife and I arrived at your lovely home bearing documents and questions? How much we have discovered since then!)

I considered intentionally sleeping in and missing our scheduled transport vessel so we might enjoy more time with you, but I have far too much to do. Now I must journey to the Boundless Navigational Expedition Office. Based on the description we crafted yesterday, I will submit a summons – "Courageous and creatively thinking crew members sought for an expedition unlike no other to a place as yet undisclosed. Some degree of peril can be expected. Endless possibilities for discovery guaranteed. Send experience, references, and any inquires to S.C." I hope that we will receive good responses, and I look forward to reviewing the candidates. (Of course, if my wildest dreams come true and Irye, Vincenebras, and Ylaret respond positively to the invitations I will soon send them, it is possible we may not need to recruit many new crew members after all. And Niea is off to visit Tevn's parents!)

Jeime, meanwhile, promised to go to her fiancée and obtain her aid in securing a depth-craft of appropriate size that we can carry aboard your ship. You know, as frustrated as I felt with Jeime's "scheme" of making me believe in this (unfortunately real) nonsense before revealing it all, I admit I am grateful to have her on our side. She will also peruse both official and less official Boundless Campus archives for any other information about the Fleet and their fears. (I do find that our new understanding of my mother and her "circle" has given me a lovely new sense of dread. "A Predator Awaits" ... o, before I forget, would you write to Lerin about those rays and see if they still seem to be migrating so fearfully? And if they have noticed any other species behaving in such unusual ways? How I wish we had Henerey's scientific journals.)

Based on the Fleet's prediction of where an Entry may appear in the year 1003 and beyond, I shall begin to draw up a map for us when I complete my other tasks. (Who knows what we shall find out on the seas as we seek the Entries – perhaps we'll even run into Father!)

It reassures me to know that we did not concoct this plan in secret, and that your family is in accord. I know that Reiv is anxious – as he ought to be – and I know the two of you have much to discuss, just as I do with Niea. (I almost wish I could convince her to stay behind like Reiv and your children – just so I could know she is safe! But I know I would never let her voyage into the unknown without me, so it is hypocritical to ask anything otherwise.)

Yet, Vyerin, I am convinced that together we will plan this mission in a way that minimises risk and maximises the potential of success. Technology has progressed so fantastically in the past year – perhaps, if we recruit the proper Mechanist, we may be able to communicate remotely from this "other place" if we reach it! (The Envoy seemed to suggest that each Entry seeks out a pair to enter it: if that is the case, and only two of us may "travel", some manner of correspondence will be absolutely necessary. What a wonderful opportunity to experiment with the capabilities of Automated Post.)

All remains to be seen. But I, for one, cannot wait.

Your friend,

Sophy

P.S. As much as I appreciate our dedication to creating a paper trail for posterity, perhaps you might be SO bold as to use your Vocal Echolator to get in touch with me in the future? There is too much at stake for us to wait even for Automated Posts!

UNSIGNED LETTER TO SOPHY CIDNORGHE, 1003

Dear Sophy,

My sincerest apologies for not replying to your kind card for my past Birthday.

And the one before that.

And – o, it's not as though you don't know how awful I am at staying in touch. I assume (gratefully) that Seliara wrote to thank you for the gifts you and Niea sent for baby Erudition. (Though the name seemed a necessary tribute at the time, I suspect our lost sister would be relieved to know that our daughter prefers the nickname "Eri" these days.) My wife has always been much better at human interaction than I. You would not believe how much Eri has grown – I fear one day soon she will reach that age when a child realises how utterly inept and deplorable her father is.

I know you will roll your eyes at my glibness. It's possible you may not even read the rest of this letter and will tear it to pieces presently. Don't worry – I pre-creased the stationery in advance to make such cathartic shredding easier for you. I do not wish to trouble you, Sophy, but I heard from a contact that you plan to hire a crew for "an expedition unlike no other to a place as yet undisclosed", or so my contact told me.

(All right, I confess – the "contact" also goes by the name of "me browsing through the papers and seeing your announcement".)

I must beg you not to go on this mission, Sophy. There are much more important things for you to do right now. You see, old girl, though it pains me, I am about to tell you something that I have never revealed to any other soul. But I deserve these pains, for in experiencing them I am doing penance for a transgression that can never be absolved. All that has come to pass with our family in the past year – it is, directly and otherwise, my fault.

(Might I suggest, then, that you avoid destroying this letter until you've at least read it all?)

I will set out my crimes for you one by one. It began when I, a young lad, finally abandoned the family home to follow in the footsteps of my younger – yet somehow undoubtedly superior – sister by joining Boundless Campus. For all my young life, I had wanted nothing else but to be—not a Scholar of the School of Inspiration, as I would have been labelled at the time, but a true artist. I did not want to study art – I wanted to live it, to . . .

I suspect you think this autobiographising is merely an attempt to postpone my actual confession. But I assure you that it is all most relevant. (See, sister, how I have grown?)

I was a lad of twelve when I learned about the Phosphorescent Place. At that age – caught in the twilight of childhood, not yet reaching the resplendent dawn of adulthood – I often experienced vivid dreams that troubled my sleep. Though, as the eldest, I did not wish to ever admit to being scared, I found them more and more terrifying. (I have since learned that my habit of consuming excessive kelp before bed to sate my ever-present adolescent hunger was likely to blame for this experience, but that is neither here nor there.)

One night, I awoke sometime around two bells in the morning in a state of absolute horror. I ran from my room in a panic, still half drowsy, while you slept dutifully and E. read surreptitiously in her chambers. I rapped upon the door to our parents' quarters until it swung open in protest, revealing Father conducting one of his snoring symphonies. Seeing as he would not be disturbed, and Mother was nowhere to be found, I dashed downstairs to the library, where I discovered her sketching something with her face turned towards the great windows.

So intent was she upon her work that Mother did not notice me approach. Over her shoulder, I spied a graceful drawing – not one of her blueprints, mind, you, but true art – done in the most exquisite hand I had ever seen. The sketch depicted what I could only perceive as some kind of kinetic sculpture, with a lattice of string-like forms that stretched across a perfect bubble of a base. Who among us could not squeal when faced with such splendour?

"Mother!" I exclaimed. "You are a superb draughtswoman! Why did you never say so? O, Mother, I would be most honoured to be your apprentice."

Upon hearing my voice, our mother immediately arose, causing her chair to fall to the floor with a clatter (as she had been leaning back on it, with the first two legs in the air – the only way to sit, dear Sophy!).

"Arvist, dear," she said, putting the drawing down. "You should be long asleep. Another nightmare?"

I had not uttered a word to her about my bad dreams – o those wondrous instincts that all parents (except, perhaps, yours truly) possess!

"All has been dispelled by your Art," I sang. "Might I please have another look? Are you designing something?"

Of course, Mother responded neither affirmatively nor negatively to any of my queries. In her typical fashion, she revealed nothing, and merely stepped out of the way so I could view her creation more closely.

"What does it look like to you?" she asked, neutral as ever in her phrasing.

"Is it a musical instrument? Or a moving statue? Or, perhaps, a funny little underwater home very different from the Deep House?"

When Mother simply smiled at me, I continued examining the

drawing to please her. Then I noticed, in the corner of the paper, a smaller sketch done in coloured pencils – a seascape with an island, illuminated in pale green and pink tones that transfixed me.

"But you've made two sketches! Is that the place where the sculpture comes from?"

Is it because of hindsight that I now remember how she froze, just for a moment, before her placid expression returned?

"Perhaps you will find out yourself one day," she said. "That seascape relates to an old story. If I share that tale with you, will you return to bed?"

I nodded eagerly and arrayed myself inelegantly upon the floor.

"Imagine a place like a living spectrum. A place that glows and grows in every colour and texture you know, and perhaps even a few that you do not. I call it 'The Phosphorescent Place'. This place, Arvist, is the dream of every artist like us."

I forgot my childish nightmares in an instant as I fell into this beautiful dream. To think that our mother, who detested Fantasies, would tell a story for only me to hear! Even as she continued, spinning tales about a fantastical realm of pure inspiration, nothing charmed me more than that sense of unity – of a shared secret with our mother, one that neither of you two sisters could claim. *Every artist like us.* And with that kind of motivation, how could I have denied her when she told me not to mention the drawing to you?

"Can't I ever tell E. and Sophy?" I asked, solely because I did, just a little, wish to brag about the fact that Mother and I had enjoyed a philosophical conversation long past bedtime.

"Perhaps one day they will come upon this drawing themselves, as you have," she said. "I shall strike you a bargain. If you ever see something like the object or landscape that I drew here, you may tell your sisters and discover its secrets together."

"Is that place real, then? When will we see it?"

"We may never see it, I fear. But in the meantime, the place is simply ours to dream in, is it not?"

And dream in it I did. In fact, though I knew it was just a fanciful tale, I could not help imagining the Phosphorescent Place even as I grew into a man. I tried every artistic medium to find something that would help me recreate what I remembered about that sketched structure and the glowing world our mother described – and from stagecraft to sculpture, every format failed to capture what I saw in my head. Eventually, I resolved to abandon this odd artistic fixation of mine, joined Boundless Campus, and fell Rapturously in Love with Seliara.

Then the Structure appeared in the undergarden.

Appropriately, I noticed it shortly after Mother's death, while I sat in the studio in a heap of grief and grime. It started out as just a grid-like form that I spotted below the sand, but as each day passed (as I sat there without bathing), it grew taller and more recognisable. The Structure blossomed out of the seafloor, rising inch by inch to reveal an exact three-dimensional copy of what Mother had sketched so long ago. I remembered her "story" as though she'd whispered it to me in the library just moments ago. So too did I remember her saying that I might share this information with you two if I ever saw something of that nature.

But I wanted to be sure, Sophy, so I said nothing! And, be honest: would you or E. have believed me, back then, if I told you that the strange thing outside our house was some kind of device related to an enchanted world of art that Mother discussed with no one but me? Would my claims not seem as ridiculous to you as the rest of my Artistic ventures so often did?

Thus, I decided to do what I do best: act like an egotistical, lofty-minded artist seeking to use the Structure for my own Great Accomplishments. It's not as though I had to work very hard to convince you. But I'm afraid that nothing turned out how I expected.

Let us begin with the best-known of my offences. Though none held it against me at the time, it was clear that my initial meddling with the Structure was responsible for E.'s first experience. I do not simply refer to the accident. This might surprise you, Sophy, but something else happened to E. that sent her into such a state. How do I know this? Well, I was in the room when she whispered about it at the Infirmary – just a few scattered words under her breath, like "island" and "ocean" and "luminescence". She was only practising a difficult conversation in advance as she was wont to do, but it was all my keen ears needed to hear. I was painting to calm myself, naturally, but I was there! I do not know if you ignored her intentionally, or if you simply did not catch her words, but you are far less at fault than I.

Because I said nothing, nothing to support her, even considering that I too experienced a vision I could not explain!

"What vision, dear brother?" you might ask me with great shock. Well, dear sister, I hope you are sitting down, because I have much to tell you.

I will try to use my simple words to paint a brief landscape of my experience for you. When that first seaquake hit, my brain went on a journey for but a short while. In what felt like a great painful snapping of reality, I found myself transported from the sterile comfort of the depth-craft to icy and fathomless waters trying to swallow me whole. All around me were colours and confusion. My eyes blurred the lovely sunset phosphorescence of my dreams into the blinding hues of a nightmare. I only had just enough time to glimpse the foreboding silhouette of some distant island before my vision cut short and the water carried me back. I want to say "it felt like death itself", except I do not literally mean that – I imagine death is quieter and less overstimulating than this experience. But at the same time – what rapture, what awe, what sheer sublimity to see that which no one else (except our sister, it seems) had seen before!

When I "returned" in the depth-craft I processed my disorientation through a most embarrassing and unpleasant gastrointestinal form of self-expression. Yet I yearned for that place from this inexplicable vision, even though it terrified me. I do not remember how Jeime reacted, and if she saw what I did. But I was thoroughly beyond reason, so it is she whom we must thank for piloting us back to the Deep House to rescue E.

After a cursory examination at the Infirmary and some rest, I found myself capable of carrying on as usual. Or at least putting on an appearance of doing so. That Phosphorescent Place I saw for the briefest of moments consumed my every thought. I could not close my eyes without seeing that glowing world – so different from my childhood imaginings – and it did not exactly spare me in my waking hours, either. When my ability to feign normalcy with my siblings and betrothed reached its natural end, I did what every self-respecting thoughtless, melancholic, and overdramatic young person might do – I threw myself into exile.

(When I chose to leave rather than face an emotionally difficult situation, did you think of Father? I certainly did. I heard his voice in my mind crowing "A true Artist does what he must to preserve his sanity, son!" Imaginary praise from him unsettled me.)

Justifying my departure as some nonsensical "mission of penance", I begged a depth-craft off a munificent colleague who excelled at discretion. Then I returned to our undergarden, where I spent several days – full tide-cycles? – in a stupor, hoping that exposure to the statue would help me slowly immunise myself to the effects of the Journey. It did not.

When I navigated through the wreckage of the parlour for the first time and saw the recognisable features of my childhood displaced and damaged – here a favourite book tossed in an anemone with its pages nibbled upon by the tiniest of scavengers, there a column from the staircase emerging from the coral like the mast of a long-sunken vessel – I felt utterly destroyed. And among the carnage, perfectly intact and peaceful, was that sinister Structure, its serenity increasing in direct proportion to my frustration and confusion. It injured my Home, it ignited in me this eternal Longing for a place that was most likely not Real – o, how I raged!

I am embarrassed to admit that my very first course of action was to gear my depth-craft into its fastest speed, equip its rock-breaking front arms, and smash into my silent nemesis while screaming incoherently.

Which, of course, caused severe cosmetic damage to my depth-craft.

But as soon as the craft touched the Structure, I found myself struck by the vision again.

Again – the agony! The delight!

I spent the night without sleeping, focusing on recreating my Place – did I write "my Place"? I meant "the Place", but I suppose it's all the same – in my head. The colours! The vivacity! Surely what Mother said was true – this was the realm of Art – or, more simply – surely this place was Art in its truest form! And I, cast away from it like a stone into the sea?

After a few hours of emotional catharsis in my solitude, however, my mood changed, and over the course of the unknown number of days or tides I spent down there, I began to take—dare I even say it? You may mock me, I will not mind – a SCIENTIST'S approach to this mystery. I would make contact with the Structure several times each evening, recording (in appropriately embellished prose, obviously – if I must research, I shall do it in style!) my observations. For the most part, they were overwhelmingly consistent. I would press the depth-craft's most prehensile arm to the statue, prepare for that fleeting encounter with the unknown oceans to overwhelm me, and then return to reality.

In all my Journeys, I never found myself anywhere but in that perilous sea. I was never afforded the privilege of "staying" long enough to swim about, either. My notes suggest that only once more did I spot strange shores in the distance, and even then, they were well out of reach. And sometimes, after I returned, the depth-craft's hydrophone would pick up the most unusual sounds – dare I call them melodies? – in the distant waters. (Because I know you'll ask this next – no, they certainly weren't Whalesongs.)

Though this will sound unforgivably naïve, given what is to come, I must admit that I enjoyed myself during this period. Survival proved easy enough. When my provisions dwindled, I used the depth-craft's specimen-gathering appendages to prey upon unwary reef fish that I inexpertly roasted over the internal engine. (I do not recommend this experimental culinary technique under usual circumstances, but it will suffice in a pinch.) Because I feared you or E. or Jeime might return to the Deep House at some point, I spent much of the daylight hours hiding near the drop-off. Each time I approached the Structure at night, I gathered some stray sea urchins and kelp strands and used them to camouflage my depth-craft (quite artfully, if I may say so myself). With my basic human needs attended to thusly, I had ample opportunity for new discoveries.

I always thought I had a keen eye for detail – what artist does not? – but these stretches of self-reflection taught me to see the smallest changes unfolding in the world before me. It reminded me of when I was a boy, with my bed pushed against one of the portholes in my chamber so I could spend the last moments before I fell asleep and the first blinkings of the morning getting to know the denizens of the reef outside my window. I grew to recognise the vibrant nudibranchs and sea-cylinders as they pulsed their way along the floor and knew exactly when a prying octopus might creep out of its coral dwellings. All enchanting to my ignorant eyes.

It was all most fascinating, and while I was an apt student of these newfound observations, I did not have the capacity to draw any conclusions based on them. So I continued my "experiments", until one night I was interrupted.

I am drawing closer to my darkest confession, Sophy (and E., to whom I am really writing in spirit though she cannot read this) – I am so close, nearly there – and I hope you will forgive me as I hide myself in extraneous language and contextualisation.

I should have pointed out one important discovery paragraphs ago: I determined that the experience I termed "the Journey" seemed, generally, to be separate from that of "the explosion". Each time I touched the Structure on my own, I travelled to the Realm of Art, but nothing else out of the ordinary took place. This correlated with the fact that during the first incident with Jeime, I touched the Structure, made the Journey, and then several minutes after – I do not remember how many, being rather out of my head – something set the Deep House waters a-trembling. By the time the fateful night in question rolled around, I had become convinced that the first quake happened through utter coincidence – perhaps truly caused by shifting tectonic plates, as Scholars suggested – and marvelled at the ill humour of the universe.

That evening, finishing my nightly rounds, I approached the Structure head-on, turning the back of the depth-craft towards the Deep House. I pressed into the Structure's side (which glowed as it always did in the evenings), witnessed the intoxicating darkness of that other world, returned to my senses, recorded a few notes in my log, and was about to feast on some unfortunate fish when my depth-craft indicated the presence of another vessel.

Why was my first instinct to flee the scene as fast as I possibly could? I do not know. Perhaps, in that moment, I related to E. more than ever – having been bereft of human company for so long, I found it difficult to imagine interacting with anyone else.

After jetting into the distance with some speed and secreting myself behind a coral archway, I finally felt brave enough to turn my depth-craft around and take a peek at the intruder. It was an old depth-craft of the same make as mine, dull in the vintage grey and ivory colouring of the Boundless Campus. Sitting inside the protection of its great glass window, hand in hand – if you can believe, this, Sophy! – were our sister and a most handsome fellow who I can only assume was Scholar Henerey Clel. I used the periscope to view them more closely, and I could see E. gesticulating in her nervously invigorated way, and Scholar Clel smiling thoughtfully, nodding at intervals, but never interrupting her.

And before I could consider the prospect of approaching them – still burdened by the shame of causing her injuries in the first place – the most unexpected thing happened.

They piloted their craft towards the Structure, carefully rose above it, and docked, as if they were a ship coming home to harbour. Right in the centre of that circular form!

And then the world shook again.

Sophy, I saw the reef rip before my eyes, with chunks of coral swirling

349

through the water as a vicious maelstrom emerged from nowhere. Perhaps fuelled by some involuntary instinct of preservation, I sped as far away as I could while watching our home disappear into the anarchy.

Shaking ceaselessly, I piloted my depth-craft well past the darkness of the drop-off. When I dared to return hours – who knows how long, really – later, the entire reef I knew was replaced with a chasm of unfathomable depth and inscrutable darkness.

And E. and Henerey were gone forever, courtesy of my ineptitude.

I headed into the open ocean with no particular destination in mind. Gone were the blissful days of my "research". Instead, I starved myself, lived in my own filth, and did not even shave. I might have perished there, had not something tailed me into my far, abandoned corner of the ocean – a depth-craft captained by my wife.

Seliara thought I suffered from a Malady of the Mind, and she begged me to come home so that she might get me the assistance I required. Her generosity and tenacity humbled me. I did not deserve happiness, that was for certain – but making more people I love suffer unduly would certainly not compensate for my mistakes.

So I came home. When I returned, you – having somehow already surveyed the Deep House's wreckage – had the grim task of informing me of E.'s disappearance and presumed death. I wanted to tell you what I had seen – you, my dear, strong, capable sister – but I could not. Not for the life of me. So I wept true tears for a loss I already mourned.

At the same time, I became a real husband, and more recently, a father. I tried to do my best with each new profession. I wouldn't say that I've succeeded – I'm middling, at best. But now, I want to take up a new profession – adventurer slash decent brother.

I don't know what you are planning with this mission, Sophy, but now that courage has found me, I beg you to CANCEL it and consider undertaking a new mission with me to find our sister, if she still lives. How? I do not know.

Although I'm sure I will be more of a bother than a brother, I know we can do this together. And if in the end I descend into this

350

Phosphorescent Place only to find her gone forever – well then, I will not rest until I can seek out whatever remains of that Structure in the depths, and ask it what dark vendetta it had against our family to tear us apart in this way?

LETTER FROM SOPHY CIDNORGHE TO ARVIST CIDNAN, 1003

Dear Arvist,

You know that you could simply call me rather than rely on "the papers" for information about my activities?

Incidentally, I am already planning to find E.

I refuse to respond to the bulk of your confession in this written form. Please come visit me. There is much we need to talk about.

You are a foolish man, and I do foolishly love you.

Until soon,

Sophy

LETTER FROM ARVIST CIDNAN TO SOPHY CIDNORGHE, 1003

Dear Sophy,

Marvellous! I shall visit you presently. By which I mean in just a few minutes, though I sent this letter ahead because the transport vessel I was going to catch to come and see you has been grievously delayed—

No. No! I have become a Better Man, and I shall lie no longer! The truth is that I missed my intended vessel departure because I was so busy arguing with the sweet-shell vendor at the docks about the quality of the breakfast I purchased.

See you presently,

Arvist

P.S. An idea just occurred to me. Perhaps before we set out to look for E., we might sift through whatever remains of her private correspondence to find out more about what became of her? Perhaps we shall survey E.'s letters as a pair? A daring archival duo? And then perhaps we might publish a book with all the letters we've organised together! Just imagine! Perhaps we can start the book with this very letter I've written to you just now – you never know who might find it compelling.

The story continues in...

Book TWO of the Sunken Archive

Acknowledgements

Dear readers,

I'm grateful to everyone who took the time to pry into this archive with me! I do have some specific people to thank, however, so I hope you'll indulge me by reading further.

I must begin by acknowledging my superlative agent Natasha Mihell, who worked incredible magic by getting my manuscript exactly where it needed to go and supporting me throughout the journey that followed! Thank you for truly understanding my story in a way that no one else had before, and for your endless enthusiasm, compassionate advice, and exemplary taste in music.

Speaking of "exactly where it needed to go", I was fortunate enough to work with truly fantastic Orbit editors – Nadia Saward, Priyanka Krishnan, and Angelica Chong – who approached this epistolary adventure with eagerness and good humour. I would also like to express my appreciation for everyone else on the Orbit US and UK teams who helped bring this book into existence.

I want to recognise the authors who kindly read and blurbed my book: Freya Marske, H. G. Parry, Louisa Morgan, Lyra Selene, Mary McMyne, and Megan Bannen. And as someone who unashamedly does judge books by their covers on occasion, I must applaud Raxenne Maniquiz and Charlotte Stroomer for illustrating and designing the most fittingly enchanted underwater scene . . . and Raxenne for bringing E.'s sketches to life!

Before I address anyone I know personally, I ought to mention that there is another, historical "E." of some renown who relied on letter-writing during the reclusive years of her life. The fictional poem "A Luminous Circumference" is a tribute to her love for that particular geometric term. At any rate, while this book is not exactly about that other E. (despite many inside jokes and references relating to her family), I did draw inspiration from the story of how her correspondence was preserved posthumously by her sister.

Let's turn to my own family at last – my sister and my parents, who helped my imagination thrive and are privy to the details of many ambitiously embarrassing childhood novel attempts. There's also my newest family member, The Baby, who is younger than this manuscript and perhaps may consider it a kind of literary sibling one day!

Now I need to celebrate my oldest friend and fellow writer, who was the first to read this draft – you know who you are! Though my sixteen-year-old self might be shocked that I did end up publishing a book, the fact that I'm thanking you in it is no surprise at all.

Thus far, I've resisted the temptation to use phrases like "this book would not exist without", but the truth is that it would *not* exist without my own pen-pal-turned-partner, J. You are, if I may, the most remarkable person I ever met. From the moment I decided on some strange whim to email you one of my short stories, you have sustained me creatively and emotionally, in art and in life. Diolch yn fawr for reviewing all of my writings that require a second opinion (including text messages, the bane of my existence), chatting about fictional worlds on our long walks, and being Tevn Mawr's #1 fan from Cefn Mawr. Plus, you know I am only able to write romances so authentically thanks to you. (What have you wrought?)

Finally, I don't want to thank my OCD, but I will acknowledge it, and express how empowering it was to take one of the most challenging aspects of my life and use it to create this story.

extras

orbit

meet the author

Roland J. Cathrall

Sylvie Cathrall writes stories of hope and healing with healthy doses of wonder and whimsy. She holds a graduate degree in odd Victorian art and has handled more than a few nineteenth-century letters (with great care). Sylvie married her former pen pal and lives in the mountains, where she dresses impractically and dreams of the sea.

Find out more about Sylvie Cathrall and other Orbit authors by registering for the free monthly newsletter at orbitbooks.net.

if you enjoyed
A LETTER TO THE LUMINOUS DEEP

look out for

THE HONEY WITCH

by

Sydney J. Shields

Marigold Claude has always preferred the company of meadow spirits to the suitors who've tried to woo her. So when her grandmother whisks her away to the family cottage on the tiny isle of Innisfree with an offer to train her as the next Honey Witch, she accepts immediately. But her newfound magic and independence come with a price: No one can fall in love with the Honey Witch.

Then Lottie Burke, a notoriously grumpy skeptic, shows up on her doorstep, and Marigold can't resist the challenge to prove to her that magic is real. But soon, Marigold begins to

*care for Lottie in unexpected ways. And when darker magic
awakens and threatens to destroy all she loves, she must
fight for much more than her new home—at the risk of
losing her magic and her heart.*

CHAPTER ONE

Saying no—even thirteen times—is not enough to avoid
tonight's ball. On this unfortunately hot spring day, Marigold
Claude is trapped between her mother and younger sister, Aster,
in a too-tight dress, in a too-small carriage. It's her sister's dress
from last season, for Marigold refuses to go to the modiste to get
fitted for a new one; an afternoon of being measured and pulled
and poked is an absolute nightmare. Her blond hair is pulled up
tightly so that her brows can barely move and her eyes look wide
with surprise. Her father and her younger brother, Frankie, sit
across from them, likely feeling quite lucky to have the luxury
of wearing trousers instead of endlessly ruffled dresses. A bead
of sweat snakes down the back of her neck, prompting her to
open her fan. It's as if the more she moves, the larger the dress
becomes. With every flap of her fan, the ruffles expand into a
fluffy lavender haze. She is almost sure that she is suffocating,
though death by silk might be preferable to the evening ahead.

This ball is the first event since her twenty-first birthday, so
now she has a few months to marry before she is deemed an
old and insufferable hag. The ride is far too short for her liking,
as with any ride to another Bardshire estate. The opulent vil-
lage was a gift from the prince regent himself; it is the home of
favored artists from all over the world, including painters like

Marigold's father. Sir Kentworth, a notable composer, is hosting tonight's event as an opportunity to share his latest works. Though the occasion is more of a way to hold people hostage for the duration of the music, and force them to pretend to enjoy it.

The carriage door flies open upon arrival, the wind stinging Marigold's eyes, and she is the last to exit. Under different circumstances, she would have feigned illness so she did not have to attend, but her younger siblings are an integral part of the program this evening, and Frankie requires her support to manage his nerves before his performance. He's been practicing for weeks, but the melodies of Sir Kentworth's music are so odd that even Frankie—a gifted violinist who has been playing since his hands were big enough to hold the instrument—can hardly manage the tune. Aster will sing Sir Kentworth's latest aria, even though the notes scrape the very top of her range. Since their last rehearsal, Aster has been placed on vocal rest and openly hated every minute, her dramatic body language expressing her frustration in lieu of words. That rehearsal was the first time Marigold saw the twins struggle to use their talents, making her feel slightly better about having none of her own. She's spent her entire life simply waiting for some hidden talent to make itself known. So far, nothing has manifested, meaning she has only the potential to be a wife, and even that is slipping by her with every passing day. Her back is still pressed firmly against the carriage bench. If she remains perfectly still, her family may somehow forget to usher her inside, allowing her to escape the event altogether.

There are countless things she would rather be doing. On a night like this, when the blue moon is full and bursting with light like summer fruit, she wants nothing more than to bathe in the moon water that now floods the riverbanks. She wants to sing poorly with no judgment, wearing nothing but the night sky. And like all nights that are graced by a full moon, she has a secret meeting planned for midnight.

"Marigold, dear, come along," her mother, Lady Claude, calls.

Dammit, she thinks. *Escape attempt number one has failed.*

She huffs as she slides out of the carriage, declining the proffered hand of the footman at her side. Her feet hit the ground with an impressive thud.

"Do try to find someone's company at least mildly enjoyable tonight," Lady Claude pleads. "You're not getting any younger, you know."

She adjusts her corset as much as she can without breaking a rib and says, "I do not want any company other than my own, and I do not intend on staying a moment longer than required."

Her mother has long tried (and failed) to turn Marigold into a proper Bardshire lady. The woman has introduced her to nearly every person even remotely close to her in age, hoping that someone will convince her that love is a worthy pursuit. So far, they've all been bores. Well, all except one—George Tennyson—but Marigold will not speak of him. He will most certainly be here tonight, and like always, they will avoid each other like the plague. Their courtship was a nightmare, but there is great wisdom to be found in heartbreak. Call it intuition, call it hope, or delusion, but Marigold knows she is not meant to live a life like that of her mother.

Rain whispers in the twilight, waiting for the perfect moment to fall. Dark clouds swirl in the distance, reaching for the maroon sun. This oppressive heat and the black-tinged sky remind her of a summer, almost fifteen years ago now. The summer they'd stopped visiting the only place in the world where she felt normal—her grandmother's cottage.

She'd always loved visiting Innisfree as a child. It was like a postcard, with fields of thick, soft clover to run through, gnarled trees to climb, and wild honeybees to watch tumble lazily over the wildflowers. And best of all, there was her grandmother. Althea was a strange woman, speaking in riddles and rhymes and sharing folktales that made little sense, but it didn't matter. Marigold didn't need the right words to understand that she and her grandmother were the same in whatever they were. She closes her eyes tightly, trying to remember the last summer she'd visited, but it's fuzzy with age.

She had made a friend—a boy her age who was dangerously curious and ferociously bright. He would come in the morning with his mother, and as the ladies sipped their tea, he and Marigold would run among the wildflowers together. She thinks of him often, dreaming of their mud-stained hands intertwined, though she does not remember his name. After what happened that day, she doesn't know if he survived.

She remembers the cottage window—always open, always sunny. Most of the time it could have been a painting, the world behind the glass as vivid as soft pastels. That day, she and her friend were told to stay inside. They snacked on honeycomb and pressed their sticky cheeks to the window, searching for faces in the clouds until the storm consumed the sky and turned the world gray. Her grandmother had run outside and disappeared into the heart of the storm, and the boy tried to grab her hand before he disappeared from her side. She remembers her mother's cold fingers pulling on her wrist, but everything else is blurry and dark.

For years, she has been asking her mother what happened. What was the gray that swallowed the sky? And what happened to the boy who tried to hold on to her hand? Her questions have gone unanswered, and they have never returned to her grandmother's cottage. She still questions if any of these memories are real. But her mother's hand bears the beginnings of a white scar peeking out from a lace glove. The truth is there, hidden in that old wound.

The other attendees spill out of their carriages in all their regalia. They stand tall and taut like they are being carried along by invisible string. Just before they walk inside, her father pulls her into an embrace and whispers in her ear, "Come home before the sun rises, and do not tell a soul about where you are running off to."

He winks, and Marigold smiles. Her father has always been kind enough to aid in her escape by distracting her mother at the right moment.

"I never do," she assures him. It's already too easy for people to make fun of a talentless lady trapped in Bardshire. She and everyone else know that she is not a normal woman. She sometimes wonders if she is even human, often feeling a stronger kinship with mud and rain and roots. Every day, she does her absolute best to play a part—a loving daughter, a supportive sister, a lady of marital quality. But in her heart, she is a creature hidden beneath soft skin and pretty ribbons, and she knows that her grandmother is, too. These are the wild women who run barefoot through the meadow, who teach new songs to the birds, who howl at the moon together. Wild women are their own kind of magic.

She is standing in between her twin siblings when Aster, stunning with her deep blue dress against her pale white skin, is immediately approached by handsome gentlemen. Aster was not meant to come out to society until Marigold, as the oldest, was married. After a time—really, after George—Marigold abandoned all interest in marriage, and the sisters convinced their parents to allow Aster to make her debut early. It was a most unconventional decision, one followed by cruel whispers throughout Bardshire at Marigold's expense, but she has lost the energy for bitterness. She tried love, once. It didn't work, and it is not worth the risk of trying again with someone new. Now Aster is the jewel of the Claude family, and Marigold is simply resigned.

Frankie clings to her side, his hands clammy with preperformance nerves. She flares her fan and waves it in front of his face, calming the redness in his cheeks.

"Thank you, Mari," he says with a shaky voice. She hands him a handkerchief to dry off his sweaty palms.

"You're going to be fine, Frankie. You always are."

He scoffs. "This music is nearly impossible. It was not written for human hands."

"Well, we'll get back at him next time when you have fewer eyes on you," she says with a wink. She and Frankie have always found some way to playfully disrupt events. Snapping a violin string so Frankie won't have to play. Pretending to see a snake in the middle of the dance floor. Stealing an entire tray of cake and eating it in the garden. Anything to escape the self-aggrandizing conversations. She leads Frankie through the crowd while noting the tables lined with sweets and expertly calculates how much she'll be able to eat without any snide remarks. She can probably get away with three—the rest, she'll have to sneak between songs.

The dance floor has been freshly decorated with chalk drawings of new spring flora. The art perfectly matches the floral arrangements throughout the ballroom. Decor of such elaborate design is not common, but Sir Kentworth is known for his flair, and he is exceptionally detail-oriented. His signature style shows in his music as well, though his latest works are growing increasingly baroque, as are his decorations. As they stroll toward the banquet table, Marigold catches the eye of her mother, who is leading a handsome young man toward her. She tries to increase her pace, but the crowd around her is impene-trable. In a matter of seconds, she's trapped in the presence of her mother and the young man while Frankie leaves her alone, set on taking all the good desserts.

Lovely. My freedom is thwarted, once again.

As she turns away from her brother, she flashes a vulgar ges-ture at him behind her back. Her mother places a hand on each of their shoulders.

"Marigold, this is Thomas Notley," her mother says. She knows this name—Sir Notley was the architect who designed the remodels of the Bardshire estates after they were purchased from the landed gentry. The man in front of her is the famed architect's grandson. They have seen each other many times, across many rooms, but this is their first proper introduction.

Her mother looks up at Mr. Notley. "And this is my beauti-ful daughter, Marigold Claude."

"It is an honor to be introduced to you, Miss Claude." His smile is bright and earnest as he takes her hand and kisses it. His cropped hair allows the sharpness of his facial features to be fully admired, while his warm brown skin glows in the yellow light of the ballroom. He is extremely handsome, but like Marigold, he is plagued with a very poor reputation as a dancer. It is likely that not many people will be fighting to add his name to their dance card, despite his good looks.

"The pleasure is mine," she replies with a clenched jaw. It is embarrassing enough to be her age with no prospects or talents, but her mother makes it so much worse with these desperate matchmaking attempts.

"Well, I'll leave you two to dance," her mother says as she pushes them slightly closer together and disappears into the crowd. Marigold glares in the direction that her mother left. Normally, she at least gets one bite of something before she takes to the ballroom floor. "Mr. Notley," she says, "I know not what my mother said to you, but please do not feel obligated to dance with me. I should warn you I have no rhythm."

"Nor do I. My talents are better suited for sitting behind a desk and drawing architectural plans," he says with a smile.

"Then who knows what disaster will take place if we take to the floor together? It may become dangerous for all others involved."

"I disagree, Miss Claude. I believe we'll make a perfect pair."

She often has trouble filling up her dance card, and she must get out of this place as quickly as possible, so she devises a plan to make this work in her favor. Softening her demeanor, she looks up at him through her thick lashes. "All right then, Mr. Notley. Would it be too bold of me to request that you have all my dances tonight?"

He looks stunned, but then a pleased smile inches across his face. This proposition is perfect—she doesn't have to wait for anyone else to ask for a dance or feign interest in multiple stuffy artists all night long. If she can hurry through the obligations of the evening with this gentleman, she'll be able to leave with plenty of time for her own nightly plans. Now, if she can simply pretend to have a good time long enough to get through her dance card...

"I would be honored. Shall we make our way to the floor?"

She pauses, for she absolutely requires a scone while they are still warm and fresh.

"Might we get refreshments first? We have a lot of dancing ahead of us," she says sweetly, and he obliges as he leads them to the table. The luxurious scents of ginger, cinnamon, and cardamom grow stronger as they approach.

"I am guessing you are a fan of sweets?" he says with a bewildered laugh.

She nods as the excitement falls from her face, replaced by embarrassment. "Eating sweets is perhaps my only talent."

"I was not teasing. Please forgive me if it felt as if I were. I am known to have a sweet tooth as well. Shall we select our favorites and share them with each other?" he says politely, and his idea is delightful—less dancing, more eating. The pair find themselves stuffing each other's faces with scones and marmalades and other small nameless cakes that are too tempting to ignore. She removes her glove with her teeth and picks up a small square of honey cake. The white icing is covered in a thick layer of warm honey that drips onto its sides, so it must be eaten quickly.

"Open," she commands, and he almost cannot stop smiling long enough to allow her to feed him, but he does, and she drops the cake into his mouth before taking her fingers to her lips and sucking off the dripping honey.

"That is fantastic," he says with a full mouth, and she laughs as she nods in agreement.

"People always overlook the honey cake because it's messy and impossible to eat with gloves. But that never stops me. I refuse to walk past a tray of honey cakes without tasting them. They have always been my favorite, and the only part of these events that I actually enjoy," she says as she takes another and pops it into her mouth, savoring the sweet golden liquid that coats her lips.

"Miss Claude, you have a little…" he says, gesturing to the corner of her mouth. She tries to wipe where instructed but continuously misses the mark. He finally removes his own glove and wipes away the small bead of honey from her lip. He licks it off of his thumb and smiles.

"There. All better," he says, and she blushes. They maintain eye contact, the heat of his fingers lingering where he touched her face. The two of them are currently breaking a number of etiquette rules, but she doesn't care.

"Well, I recant my earlier statement. It turns out that I am not exceptionally talented at eating sweets either, or I would be able to do so without making a mess of myself," she says, wiping around her mouth to ensure there aren't any lingering crumbs.

They share a genuine laugh, and at this moment, she thinks that maybe marriage wouldn't be the worst fate in the world. Mr. Notley is extremely handsome, comes from an exceptional family, and seems very agreeable, which is an important trait of any person who is going to attempt to fall in love with her.

But something still does not feel right. It would be like painting the walls of her life beige. It would be a safe choice, a comfortable choice that no one could fault her for, but it does mean that every day she would have to sit in her room and look at her beige walls and wonder what could have been if she had painted them bright yellow or pink. What if she had forgone paint entirely? Or better yet, what if there were no walls at all? Only sky, sunlight, salty water, fresh rain, and spring flowers and no one else around to comment on the paint color of the walls. That would be perfect, and that is why it is only a dream.

"What is that?" Marigold asks as she points over Mr. Notley's shoulder at nothing in particular. When he turns, she quickly takes a honey cake and wraps it in a piece of cloth before carefully hiding it in the small reticule purse that hangs from her wrist.

It's not for her, though. It's for her midnight meeting, so she must be sneaky. Mr. Notley turns back around and says, "What? I'm afraid I don't see anything."

She shrugs. "Ah, must have been my imagination. Shall we attempt to dance?"

He smiles as he follows her lead. She takes him in front of the band, where Frankie, Aster, and the other musicians are positioned like statues behind Sir Kentworth as he raises his sparkling conducting baton. Aster's voice fills the room, and though the melody is strange, it seems the vocal rest worked— she sounds undeniably angelic.

"Your brother and sister are extraordinary," Mr. Notley says. "I hear that often," Marigold says quietly.

She turns her head and pushes through the dance. Mr. Notley is slightly better than she is, and they keep with the beat as best as they can. Focusing on her steps helps her forget the rest of the world for a small moment. The music is demanding—heavy, punctuated beats dictate a complicated dance. The command of the strings and the swift obedience of the dancers fill her with ferocious envy. How unfair that she may always desire but never earn that much control over a room.

A brief intermission follows so that the musicians may rest their overworked hands. People are still filing into the room like ants back from foraging, eager to show off their finds—an artifact that should not be in this country, a new wife wearing the late wife's dress. And then, as if he was waiting for Marigold's eyes to land on the door so that she would have no choice but to witness him, enters George Tennyson: a poet, a prodigy, and the most beautiful monster she has ever known. She has not spoken to him—beyond obligatory pleasantries—in two years, not that he would have given her the chance if she wanted to. He has not even looked at her for more than a few seconds since she was ten and seven and he left her on her knees outside of a ball just like the one they are attending tonight. Bardshire is a small world, so his occasional presence is unavoidable, but she always pretends that he is a ghost when she sees him. A hollow, transparent creature of only the past. Tonight, though, he is too close. She can feel the warmth of him from here. He is so undeniably and mercilessly alive.

He looks at her, intentionally so, surveying her body and settling on her hand intertwined with Mr. Notley's. His cheeks flush red and a devilish grin stretches across his face. His eyes find hers, and she cannot withstand the memories conjured by his gaze. Flashes of promenades and poetry and promises that proved to be empty. He starts walking toward her, and she wishes the floor would open up and swallow her whole. He's smiling, and she surprises herself when she smiles back. Hers is a cautious smile—what if he grants her the closure she has always wanted but never sought? Will he take back the worst of his words? Or could she, with one sharp sentence, ruin him? Words sit heavy on her tongue behind her saccharine smile. He's right in front of her, so happy and so handsome that she almost forgets what made her hate him so. Were they that bad? Could they be good again? His hand is reaching toward her. She takes a breath, moves to reach back, and then realizes too late that his hand is not reaching for her. He sidesteps her. From over her shoulder, she hears, "There you are, my love."

She turns slowly, against her better judgment, to see him kissing Priya Gill's white-gloved hand. The pair moves as one through the crowd and stops in the center. George calls for the attention of the room, and oh God, she knows it before it happens, hears it before he says it, the nightmare is both almost over and only just begun—he proposes to Priya Gill. He does so loudly and with such flair that there are no dry eyes in the room. Everyone else sees a beautiful couple, a grand wedding, another romance for the poets to wax on and on about in their leather-bound journals that apparently everyone takes as law. It's sick, all of it. His gaze locks onto Marigold for one brutal moment, as if to say, "*This could never be you.*"

His hand is wrapped around Priya's, but it's soft. It's not a death grip where he's pulling her back in line or squeezing her knuckles when she says something out of place. There is something prideful about the way he holds on to Priya, and it's maddening. He never loved Marigold like that. It was never soft, never gentle. George is a decade older than her, and during their courtship, he often cited his age as if it meant that he could never be wrong. He was too wise, too well-versed in the nature of people to make an improper judgment. No—George always had to be right, and it killed him every time he was bested by her: a young girl who was only meant to be a muse.

The hold George once had on her was punishing, like he was trying to mold her into a different shape, make it so she took up less space in every room. She blamed his father, high society, social pressures, and the like. Maybe things could have gotten better if they weren't trapped in Bardshire with all eyes on them all the time, if they simply gave up on everything except each other and ran away. She begged for that as he left her. She prayed at his feet like he was a god who might listen if her suffering was compelling enough. He never wanted her, though—not in any true way. He only wanted a bride who would succumb to his violent pursuit of civility.

Congratulations to dear old George. He has all that he wanted and did nothing to deserve it. The men will shake his hand and the women will watch Priya slowly realize that she is trapped, and they will teach her how to pretend that she is not breaking. Marigold, decidedly, will never be broken by him, or anyone, ever again.

The music resumes, and Mr. Notley sweeps her away into a new dance, twirling her until George and his betrothed are out of sight. But she cannot escape the whispers that snake through the room.

"Priya is a much better choice."

"Remember when he was with the Claude girl? What a lark."

"It's too late for her. She will never, ever marry."

She scrunches her nose in a way that makes her look like a lapdog, so says her mother. A bitch, Aster once said before she knew exactly what that word meant. Marigold laughed then—what is so wrong about being a bitch? It is the closest a girl can be to a wolf.

Mr. Notley studies Marigold's face for a moment. "Miss Claude, will you allow me one prying question?"

She squeezes his shoulder as they turn in time with the music. "It seems I am trapped. How can I refuse?"

"How is it that you are not married?"

Marigold flinches. "What makes you think that I should be?"

"You are beautiful and full of life, like springtime," Mr. Notley says.

"And why should those qualities merit promising myself to another? Perhaps there is a reason you cannot marry the spring."

"But I could marry *you*."

"You speak as if that decision belongs to you alone." Marigold steps on his toes and does not pretend that it is an accident. "I am not married because I have yet to find someone who makes me feel seen."

He steadies himself on his throbbing toes. "You don't believe that I could see you?"

"No. You see only springtime. What happens when I am winter? I will tell you, Mr. Notley. When winter comes"—she leans in close so their noses are almost touching—"you will freeze."

Heat lingers on her lips, and surprisingly, Mr. Notley smiles.

They dance through six songs, enough to fill an entire dance card. Aster makes eye contact with Marigold, her eyes full of apology as they flit between her and George. Marigold bites the inside of her cheek and shakes her head as she makes her final curtsy to Mr. Notley. She begins to walk away from the floor, fighting against an ocean of tears behind her eyes. It gets easier with every step, and so it is decided—she will walk through the whole night if she must, for she will not shed one more tear for that man. He is not worth the energy, and neither is anyone else. As soon as she reaches the door, her elbow is caught, and Mr. Notley pulls her around to face him.

He looks at her as if he thought his hand might pass through her, as if she were only a wish. "Are you leaving, Miss Claude?"

She swallows the last of her sadness. "Yes, I'm afraid all that dancing has left me feeling quite faint. I must rest," she says breathlessly, hoping to make her story more believable.

"Might I help you to your carriage, then?"

Her eyes widen, for there is no carriage waiting. She intends on escaping on foot, through the gardens.

"That will not be necessary. I feel that the fresh air is just what I need," she says as she attempts to turn back toward the door.

"Have I done something wrong? I must admit I thought we were having a lovely time," he says. His words are kind enough, but nothing he says can change the fact that there is somewhere else she would rather be. Her skin starts to burn underneath his unwavering grip.

"My haste has nothing to do with you. I simply have somewhere I must be. Have another honey cake for me," she says as she yanks her arm away and then shakes his hand firmly in the same manner that she has seen her father do many times to end a meeting with a patron that has dragged on for too long. He holds her hand there, still seeming somewhat dazed and confused at her rush.

"Is there someone else, Miss Claude? Another man waiting for you out there?"

She cannot help but laugh wildly. Since George, Mr. Notley is the only man in Bardshire she has been able to stand speaking to for more than five minutes, so the idea of having two men who she would want to spend an evening with is a hilarious joke that seems to be entirely lost on him.

"There is no other man. I can assure you."

"Then why must you leave me so suddenly? I will not let you go before I understand."

She lets out a sigh of frustration. "Mr. Notley, I intend to run out to the meadow barefoot and soak up the blue moonlight. I intend to sing loudly, to dance freely, maybe even scream if I wish. I intend to ruin this dress with the mud and the rain. And if I don't go now, then I will miss the brightest hour of the blue moon, which only happens once a year. Now, if you will excuse me," she says. She looks back at him as he stares at her with absolute bewilderment.

"You are a wild creature, Miss Claude. I hope to see you again," he calls after her. She waves goodbye and then takes off in a run, knowing that she will not allow herself to be tamed.

if you enjoyed
A LETTER TO THE LUMINOUS DEEP

look out for

THE UNDERTAKING OF HART AND MERCY

by

Megan Bannen

Hart Ralston is a marshal, tasked with patrolling the strange and magical wilds of Tanria. It's an unforgiving job, and he's got nothing but time to ponder his loneliness.

Mercy Birdsall never has a moment to herself. She's been single-handedly keeping Birdsall & Son, Undertakers, afloat in defiance of sullen jerks like Hart-ache Hart, the man with a knack for showing up right when her patience is thinnest.

extras

After yet another run-in with Merciless Mercy, Hart finds himself penning a letter addressed simply to "a friend." Much to his surprise, he receives an anonymous letter in return, and a tentative friendship is born.

If only Hart knew he's been baring his soul to the person who infuriates him most—Mercy. As the dangers from Tanria grow closer, so do the unlikely correspondents. But can their blossoming romance survive the fated discovery that their pen pals are their worst nightmares—each other?

CHAPTER ONE

It was always a gamble, dropping off a body at Birdsall & Son, Undertakers, but this morning, the Bride of Fortune favored Hart Ralston.

Out of habit, he ducked his head as he stepped into the lobby so that he wouldn't smack his forehead on the doorframe. Bold-colored paintings of the death gods—the Salt Sea, the Warden, and Grandfather Bones—decorated the walls in gold frames. Two green velvet armchairs sat in front of a walnut coffee table, their whimsical lines imbuing the room with an upbeat charm. Vintage coffee bean tins served as homes for pens and candy on a counter that was polished to a sheen. This was not the somber, staid lobby of a respectable place like Cunningham's Funeral Services. This was the appalling warmth of an undertaker who welcomed other people's deaths with open arms.

It was also blessedly empty, save for the dog draped over one of the chairs. The mutt was scratching so furiously at his ribs he didn't notice that his favorite Tanrian Marshal had walked through the front door. Hart watched in delight as the mongrel's back paw sent a cyclone of dog hair whirling through a shaft of sunlight before the bristly fur settled on the velvet upholstery.

"Good boy, Leonard," said Hart, knowing full well that Mercy Birdsall did not want her dog wallowing on the furniture.

At the sound of his name, Leonard perked up and wagged his nubbin tail. He leaped off the chair and hurled himself at Hart, who petted him with equal enthusiasm.

Leonard was an ugly beast—half boxer, half the gods knew what, brindle coated, eyes bugging and veined, jowls hanging loose. In any other case, this would be a face only his owner could love, but there was a reason Hart continued to patronize his least favorite undertaker in all the border towns that clung to the hem of the Tanrian Marshals' West Station like beggar children. After a thorough round of petting and a game of fetch with the tennis ball Leonard unearthed from underneath his chair, Hart pulled his watch out of his vest pocket and, seeing that it was already late in the afternoon, resigned himself to getting on with his job.

He took a moment to doff his hat and brush back his overgrown blond hair with his fingers. Not that he cared how he looked. Not at Birdsall & Son, at any rate. As a matter of fact, if he had been a praying man, he would have begged the Mother of Sorrows to have mercy on him, no pun intended. But he was not entirely a man—not by half—much less one of the praying variety, so he left religion to the dog.

"Pray for me, Leonard," he said before he pinged the counter bell.

"Pop, can you get that?" Mercy's voice called from somewhere in the bowels of Birdsall & Son, loudly enough so that her father should be able to hear her but softly enough that she wouldn't sound like a hoyden shouting across the building.

Hart waited.

And waited.

"I swear," he muttered as he rang the bell again.

This time, Mercy threw caution to the wind and hollered, "Pop! The bell!" But silence met this request, and Hart remained standing at the counter, his impatience expanding by the second. He shook his head at the dog. "Salt fucking Sea, how does your owner manage to stay in business?"

Leonard's nubbin started up again, and Hart bent down to pet the ever-loving snot out of the boxer mix.

"I'm so sorry," Mercy said, winded, as she rushed from the back to take her place behind the counter. "Welcome to Birdsall & Son. How can I help you?"

Hart stood up—and up and up—towering over Mercy as her stomach (hopefully) sank down and down.

"Oh. It's you," she said, the words and the unenthusiastic tone that went with them dropping off her tongue like a lead weight. Hart resisted the urge to grind his molars into a fine powder.

"Most people start with *hello*."

"Hello, Hart-ache," she sighed.

"Hello, Merciless." He gave her a thin, venomous smile as he took in her oddly disheveled appearance. Whatever else he might say about her, she was usually neat as a pin, her bright-colored dresses flattering her tall, buxom frame, and her equally bright lipstick meticulously applied to her full lips. Today, however, she wore overalls, and her olive skin was dewy with sweat, making her red horn-rimmed glasses slide down her nose. A couple of dark curls had come loose from the floral scarf that bound up her hair, as if she'd stuck her head out the window while driving full speed across a waterway.

"I guess you're still alive, then," she said flatly.

"I am. Try to contain your joy."

Leonard, who could not contain his joy, jumped up to paw Hart's stomach, and Hart couldn't help but squeeze those sweet jowls in his hands. What a shame that such a great dog belonged to the worst of all undertaking office managers.

"Are you here to pet my dog, or do you actually have a body to drop off?"

A shot of cold humiliation zinged through Hart's veins, but he'd never let her see it. He held up his hands as if Mercy were leveling a pistol crossbow at his head, and declared with mock innocence, "I stopped by for a cup of tea. Is this a bad time?"

Bereft of adoration, Leonard leaped up higher, mauling Hart's ribs.

"Leonard, get down." Mercy nabbed her dog by the collar to drag him upstairs to her apartment. Hart could hear him scratching at the door and whining piteously behind the wood. It was monstrous of Mercy to deprive both Hart and her dog of each other's company. Typical.

"Now then, where were we?" she said when she returned, propping her fists on her hips, which made the bib of her overalls stretch over the swell of her breasts. The square of denim seemed to scream, *Hey, look at these! Aren't they fucking magnificent?* It was so unfair of Mercy to have magnificent breasts.

"You're dropping off a body, I assume?" she asked.

"Yep. No key."

"Another one? This is our third indigent this week."

"More bodies mean more money for you. I'd think you'd be jumping for joy."

"I'm not going to dignify that with a response. I'll meet you at the dock. You do know there's a bell back there, right?"

"I prefer the formality of checking in at the front desk."

"Sure you do." She rolled her eyes, and Hart wished they'd roll right out of her unforgivably pretty face.

"Does no one else work here? Why can't your father do it?"

Like a gift from the Bride of Fortune, one of Roy Birdsall's legendary snores galloped through the lobby from behind the thin wall separating it from the office. Hart smirked at Mercy, whose face darkened in embarrassment.

"I'll meet you at the dock," she repeated through gritted teeth.

Hart's smirk came with him as he put on his hat, sauntered out to his autoduck, and backed it up to the dock.

"Are you sure you're up for this?" he asked Mercy as he swung open the door of his duck's cargo hold, knowing full well that she would find the question unbearably condescending.

As if to prove that she didn't need anyone's help, least of all his, she snatched the dolly from its pegs on the wall, strode past him into the hold, and strapped the sailcloth-wrapped body to the rods with the practiced moves of an expert. Unfortunately, this particular corpse was extremely leaky, even through the thick canvas. Despite the fact that he had kept it on ice, the liquid rot wasn't completely frozen over, and Mercy wound up smearing it all over her hands and arms and the front of her overalls. Relishing her horror as it registered on her face, Hart sidled up to her, his tongue poking into the corner of his cheek. "I don't want to say I told you so, but—"

She wheeled the corpse past him, forcing him to step out of the autoduck to make room for her. "Hart-ache, if you don't want my help, maybe you should finally find yourself a partner."

The insinuation lit his Mercy Fuse, which was admittedly short. As if he would have any trouble finding a partner if he wanted one. Which he didn't.

"I didn't ask for your help," he shot back. "And look who's talking, by the way."

She halted the dolly and pulled out the kickstand with the toe of her sneaker. "What's that supposed to mean?"

"It means I don't see anyone helping you either." He fished inside his black vest for the paperwork she would need to complete in order to receive her government stipend for processing the body, and he held it out to her. He had long since learned to have his end all filled out ahead of time so that he didn't have to spend a second longer in her presence than was necessary.

She wiped one hand on the clean fabric over her ass before snatching the papers out of his hand. Without the consent of his reason, Hart's own hands itched with curiosity, wondering exactly how the round curves of her backside would feel in his grasp. His brain was trying to shove aside the unwanted lust when Mercy stepped into him and stood on her tiptoes. Most women couldn't get anywhere near Hart's head without the assistance of a ladder, but Mercy was tall enough to put her into kissing range when she stood on the tips of her red canvas shoes. Her big brown eyes blazed behind the lenses of her glasses, and the unexpected proximity of her whole body felt bizarrely intimate as she fired the next words into his face.

"Do you know what I think, Hart-ache?"

He swallowed his unease and kept his voice cool. "Do tell, Merciless."

"You must be a pathetically friendless loser to be this much of a jerk." On the word *jerk*, she poked him in the chest with the emphatic pointer finger of her filthy hand, dotting his vest with brown rot and making him stumble onto the edge of the dock. Then she pulled down the gate before he could utter another word, letting it slam shut between them with a resounding *clang*.

Hart stood teetering on the lip of the dock in stunned silence. Slowly, insidiously, as he regained his balance, her words seeped beneath his skin and slithered into his veins.

I will never come here again unless I absolutely have to, he promised himself for the hundredth time. Birdsall & Son was not the only official drop-off site for bodies recovered in Tanria without ID tags. From now on, he would take his keyless cadavers to Cunningham's. But as he thought the words, he knew they constituted a lie. Every time he slayed an indigent drudge in Tanria, he brought the corpse to Birdsall & Son, Undertakers.

For a dog.

Because he was a pathetically friendless loser.

He already knew this about himself, but the fact that Mercy knew it, too, made his spine bunch up. He got into his auto-duck and drove to the station, his hands white-knuckling the wheel as he berated himself for letting Mercy get to him.

Mercy, with her snotty *Oh. It's you.* As if a dumpster rat had waltzed into her lobby instead of Hart.

Mercy, whose every word was a thumbtack spat in his face, pointy end first.

The first time he'd met her, four years ago, she had walked into the lobby, wearing a bright yellow dress, like a jolt of sunlight bursting through glowering clouds on a gloomy day. The large brown eyes behind her glasses had met his and widened, and he could see the word form in her mind as she took in the color of his irises, as pale and colorlessly gray as the morning sky on a cloudy day.

Demigod.

Now he found himself wondering which was worse: a pretty young woman seeing him as nothing more than the offspring of a divine parent, or Merciless Mercy loathing him for the man he was.

Any hope he'd cherished of skulking back to his post in Sector W-38 unremarked vanished when he heard Chief Maguire's voice call to him from the front door of the West Station, as if she had been standing at the blinds in her office, waiting to pounce.

"Marshal Ralston."

His whole body wanted to sag at the sound of Alma's voice, but he forced himself to keep his shoulders straight as he took his pack out of the passenger seat and shut the door with a metallic *clunk*. "Hey, Chief."

"Where you been?"

"Eternity. I took out a drudge in Sector W-38, but it didn't have a key. Decomp was so bad, I decided to bring him in early. Poor pitiful bastard."

Alma scrutinized him over the steaming rim of her ever-present coffee mug, her aquamarine demigod eyes glinting in her wide brown face.

Hart's lips thinned. "Are you implying that *I'm* a poor pitiful bastard?"

"It's not so much an implication as a stone-cold statement of fact."

"Hardly."

"You have no social life. You work all the time. You don't even have a place to hang your hat. You might put up in a hotel for a few nights, but then you come right back here." She jerked her thumb toward the Mist, the cocoon of churning fog that formed the border of Tanria beyond the West Station. "This shithole is your home. How sad is that?"

Hart shrugged. "It's not so bad."

"Says you. I assume you took the body to Cunningham's?"

"No."

She raised an *I take no bullshit from you* eyebrow at him

before leaning on the hood of his duck, and Hart frowned when she spilled a few drops of coffee onto the chipped blue paint. It was rusty enough as it was; she didn't need to go making it worse.

"Look, Ralston, we rely on the undertakers. We need them to do their jobs so that we can do ours."

Great. A lecture from his boss. Who used to be his partner and his friend. Who called him Ralston now.

"I know."

"You are aware of the fact that Roy Birdsall almost died a few months ago, right?"

Hart shifted his weight, the soles of his boots grinding into the gravel of the parking lot. "No."

"Well, he did. Heart attack or something. In theory, he's running the office, but Mercy's the one taking care of everything at Birdsall & Son—boatmaking, body prep, all of it."

"So?" His tone was petulant, but the memory of a disheveled Mercy with corpse rot smeared over her front made a frond of guilt unfurl in his gut.

"So if you're going to patronize Birdsall's, cut Mercy some slack and play nice. If you can't do that, go to Cunningham's. All right?"

"Yep, fine. Can I go now?" He adjusted his hat on his head, a clear signal that he was preparing to exit the conversation and get on with his job, but Alma held up her free hand.

"Hold on. I've been meaning to talk to you about something."

Hart grunted. He knew what was coming.

"Don't give me that. You've gone through three partners in four years, and you've been working solo for months. It's too dangerous to keep going it alone. For any of us." She added that last bit as if this conversation were about marshals in general rather than him specifically, but Hart knew better.

"I don't need a partner."

She gave him a look of pure exasperation, and for a fraction of a second, Hart could see the old Alma, the friend who'd been there for him when his mentor, Bill, died. She dismissed him with a jerk of her head. "Go on. But this conversation isn't finished."

He'd walked a few paces toward the stables when Alma called after him, "Come over for dinner one of these days, will you? Diane misses you."

This peace offering was almost certainly Diane's doing, and he could tell that it was as hard for Alma to deliver her wife's invitation as it was for Hart to hear it.

"Yep," he answered and continued on his way to the stables, but they both knew he wouldn't be standing on Alma and Diane's doorstep anytime soon. Although he and Alma had long since made peace on the surface of things, the old grudge hung in the air, as if Bill's ghost had taken up permanent residence in the space between them. Hart had no idea how to get past it, or if he wanted to, but it was painfully awkward to miss a friend when she was standing right behind him. It was worse to miss Diane. He almost never saw her anymore.

The stables were dark compared to the brutal sunlight of Bushong, and blessedly cooler, too. He went to the stalls to see which mounts were available. He knew it would be slim pickings at this time of day, but he was unprepared for how bad the pickings were: a gelding so young, Hart didn't trust it not to bolt at the first whiff of a drudge; an older mare he'd taken in a few times and found too slow and plodding for his liking; and Saltlicker.

Saltlicker was one of those equimares that bolted for water every chance he got and maintained a constant, embittered opposition to anyone who dared to ride him. Some marshals liked him for his high-spiritedness; Hart loathed the beast, but of the three options, Saltlicker was, sadly, the best choice.

"Wonderful," Hart griped at him.

Saltlicker snorted, shook out his kelp-like mane, and dipped lower in his trough, blowing sulky bubbles in the water, as if to say, *The feeling's mutual, dickhead.*

All at once, an oppressive sadness overtook Hart. It was one thing to dislike an equimaris; it was another to have the equimaris hate him back. And honestly, who did genuinely like Hart these days? Mercy's barbed insult, which had followed him all the way from Eternity, surfaced in his mind once more.

You must be a pathetically friendless loser to be this much of a jerk.

She had a point. Only a pathetically friendless loser would face his nemesis time and again to pet her dog for five minutes.

Maybe I should suck it up and get another dog, he thought, but the second he entertained the idea, he knew he could never replace Gracie. And that left him with nothing but the occasional visit to Leonard.

Hart knew that he needed to get to his post, but he wound up sitting against the stable wall, shrouded in shadows. As if it had a mind of its own—call it ancient muscle memory—his hand snaked into his pack and pulled out his old notebook and a pen.

When he had first joined the Tanrian Marshals after his mother died, he used to write letters to her and slide them into nimkilim boxes whenever he and his mentor, Bill, made their way to the station or to a town. Then, after Bill was killed, Hart wrote to him, too, mostly letters full of remorse. But he hadn't written to either of them in years, because at the end of the day, it wasn't like they could write back. And that was what he wanted, wasn't it? For someone—anyone—to answer?

Poor pitiful bastard, the blank page splayed across his thighs seemed to say to him now. He clicked open the pen and wrote *Dear*, hesitated, and then added the word *friend*.

He had no idea how much time passed before he tore out the page, folded it into fourths, and got to his feet, relieving his aching knees. There was a similar relief in his aching chest, as if he'd managed to pour some of that loneliness from his heart onto the paper. Glancing about him to make sure he was unobserved as he crossed the stable yard, he walked to the station's nimkilim box and slid the note inside, even though he was certain that a letter addressed to no one would never be delivered to anyone.